The Prince
of
Las Vegas

A Novel

by

Brian Malanaphy

For Karen and James

"That money get funny." – Peter Tosh

CHAPTER 1

July 1, 1973

Deputy Ed Hensley thought he heard something and blinked his eyes open. The sparkling Milky Way stretched across the dark and moonless desert sky. He watched a spider crawl overhead, across his patrol car windshield, looking like it was traversing the shimmering sky. He sat up and rubbed his eyes. A cool breeze drifted in through the slightly opened window.

BOOM! In the distance, there it was again. He turned to look. What was it? Machinery? Heavy machinery, diesel trucks? He glanced at his watch. 1:15. What the hell could be going on out there at this hour?

Hensley stepped from the patrol car and stood with his hands on his hips, looking in the distance, listening. Rumbling diesel engines broke the serenity and stillness of the cool night. Scanning the faint horizon, he saw a glowing orange dust cloud rising in the distance. It must be coming from one of the farms, or ranches. What the hell was it; somebody burying their cow in the middle of the night? Working this late wasn't unheard of, but it *was* unusual. Hensley decided to take a closer look.

He turned his patrol car off Highway 170 and onto a dirt farm road that led through the fields towards the glowing dust cloud. In the distance, he could see a backhoe clawing at the ground, its overhead lights shining brightly, and what looked like an eighteen-wheeled belly-dump truck.

He drove his patrol car into the field, following in the bumpy tire tracks already lain toward the worksite. A fastback Buick Riviera was parked there too. It was black with a white vinyl roof, and its headlights were on, facing the worksite, further illuminating the rising dust. Three men were carrying something that glimmered in the bright lights. Shiny bricks? Hensley wasn't sure. He brought the cruiser to a stop. The men stopped and stared at him. He reached for the dashboard switch to turn on the flashing lights, but hesitated. Should he call the chief and wake him up? Yes, call the chief. Follow protocol. He reached for his radio.

"Sally," he said into the microphone. "SALLY!"

"Yes sir," she finally answered. "Sorry, just trying to stay awake."

"Call Wade and have him meet me out here by the ranch road, mile marker 41. I got something going on here."

Sally hesitated. "You sure you want me to wake him at this hour?"

"Yes, wake him up! Something weird is going on out here and I may need backup."

"Something weird, like a flying saucer?"

"Just get him, there's guys working out here burying something."

"Roger that . . ."

Hensley flipped on the patrol car's whirling lights and stepped out with flashlight in hand.

The men dropped their loads to the ground. They stood frozen in place looking at Hensley. There was a large hole—a trench, maybe fifteen feet wide by thirty feet long. Instead of hardhats and work clothes, the three men appeared to be wearing slacks and button down shirts, with sleeves rolled up. The backhoe shovel came to a stop. One of the three men stepped over to Hensley.

"Hi sir, are you with Sheriff Wade?" the man asked, an excited grin on his face.

"I'm his deputy," Hensley said.

The man hesitated. He was nervous.

"Well that's great," the man said. "Sheriff Wade said it'd be OK for us to finish this job tonight. Hope we're not disturbing anyone."

"Ain't nobody out here to disturb," Hensley said. "What job you workin' on?"

"The water. It's an emergency."

Hensley raised an eyebrow and stepped closer.

The man continued. "We're digging up this here well." He motioned toward the pit. "It's gotta get done tonight."

"I see," Hensley said, his eyes fixed on the man. Why would they be digging up a well in the middle of the night and dressed like they just left a disco? It didn't make sense. The hairs on the back of his neck stood.

The man smiled at Hensley. He was an older man, obviously the one in charge. The two other men were young and brawny, maybe in their twenties. They weren't laborers, but their slacks and button down shirts were covered in dirt and they were soaked in sweat.

"Well." Hensley glanced over to the trench. "Let's take a look at the situation."

Keeping an eye on the men, Hensley carefully stepped over to the edge of the trench half-expecting and even hoping to see a muddy hole with a well head sticking out. He pointed his flashlight down into the hole and instead saw maybe a half-dozen pallets stacked high with gleaming silver bars and another half-dozen stacked with canvas money bags, fat with coins.

Hensley already had his revolver out and pointed at the men. Their attention on the gun, they raised their hands in a half-hearted gesture of surrender.

"Hey, take it easy," one of the young men said.

The boss-man stepped forward and smiled.

"Look deputy," he said. "I can explain."

"Keep your hands up where I can see them," Hensley said.

The boss-man turned to his men. "Yes, boys, keep your hands up, we don't want any trouble here. We don't need any heroes, got it?"

They nodded.

The boss-man turned back to Hensley.

"See," he said, "this is Jack Romano's silver. Before he died, he told me if anything ever happened to him I should get the silver out of here ASAP to safeguard it for his family. You know he died, right?"

"Yeah, I heard that last month."

"It was a damn shame, such a great guy." The man lowered his arms. "But that's how come we're digging it up. It's for Jack's family. He didn't want us to attract attention, so we're doing it now — in the middle of the night."

"Keep your hands up," Hensley said. "And tell that guy to come down out of the backhoe."

The backhoe operator climbed out. He was the only one who looked appropriately dressed. He was a short Mexican man and wore a cowboy hat, overalls and heavy boots. Fear gripped his face.

"I haven't done anything wrong," he pleaded.

"Shut up," the boss-man said.

All four men now stood in front of Hensley with their hands raised. Hensley glanced at the belly-dump truck and could see it nearly buckling under the weight of its load, its tires sinking into the soft earth.

The boss-man shifted his eyes from the truck to Hensley.

"What's in the truck?" Hensley asked.

"Nothin'" the boss-man said.

"Nothin'?"

"Dirt."

"Well," Hensley said, "let's take a look at that. After you."

He motioned the flashlight toward the truck, and held the gun on the men.

"Sure," the boss-man said.

The two younger men and the Mexican led the way while Hensley followed behind the boss-man.

A straight ladder rested against the truck, leading up to its sidewall. Hensley ordered the men to back away before climbing up the ladder. In the bed of the truck were piles of glistening silver bars, perhaps hundreds, just thrown in and strewn over the whole twenty foot length of the truck. Where had it all come from? There must be tons.

Hensley looked back down toward the men, but one was in flight already, lunging at the base of the ladder. Hensley went flying and hit the ground, his gun firing with a blistering crack as it flew from his hand and tumbled across the dirt, landing a few yards away.

He scrambled on all fours for the gun, but one of the men kicked it away. Another landed on top of him, rolling and tumbling with him in the dirt. Hensley tried to fight back, but his arms got pinned under the man's knees. The man, now on top of him, punched at his head repeatedly. Blood splattered across the man's shirt and Hensley went limp, his face falling sideways into the dirt.

"Tie him up and throw him in the hole," the boss-man said.

"What about his car?" one of the other guys said.

"Let's bury that in the hole too," the boss-man said. "After we're done grabbing all the loot."

CHAPTER 2

Seven Weeks Earlier

No one said a word. Nicholas Romano sat facing backwards on the fold-down jump-seat in the back of the frigid limo, his knees up, his fine black trousers stretched against his legs. It was like sitting in a child's chair. He gazed through the tinted window at the monotony of cinderblock walls, cement driveways, cacti and rock gardens gliding by. It was all grey and lifeless, dried out and baked by the desert heat.

The late afternoon sun cast his silhouetted reflection on the glass—his gold-rimmed aviator sunglasses sparkling within the misshapen blob of his curly hair. The reflection floated over the rushing sidewalk, flickering with the light. It was weird that his dad was gone now. Dead, just like that. Here and then not here.

Nick pushed his fingers under his glasses and rubbed his eyes. Things happened so quickly. His dad was only 63. There had been so much he had wanted to tell him, but now he couldn't.

He straightened his cramped legs, brushing them accidentally against his mom's, who sat across from him. He glanced up at her.

Frances Romano held her head low. Lost in her own thoughts, her hazel eyes listless, strands of her golden blond hair hanging across her face.

His gaze shifted over to Claudio DeVito, who sat sunken into the limo's cushy leather seat next to Frances, a smug expression on his fat face. Nick glared at him—at his fine Italian suit with its wide lapel, at his gold cufflinks, at his fine white Egyptian cotton shirt and fashionable silk blue tie, and especially at his arm snuggly wrapped around his mom's.

As if Claudio even cared about his mom. All he cared about were fancy suits, watches, gold jewelry, and power. Money and power, plain and simple, that's what it boiled down to.

Nick smirked and looked back out the window. His sister Anne Marie, sat across from him on the other jump seat incessantly cracking and popping a piece of chewing gum, oblivious to how annoying it was. When were they going to get to the house?

His mom's leg suddenly jerked. Claudio had leaned over and placed his hand on his mom's thigh, pushing her black dress up over her knee. Frances casually removed his hand and glanced at Nick. He straightened up on the jump-seat.

"Can you have some friggin' decency?" Nick said.

"What?" Claudio sneered.

"*What?*"

"Nick." Frances raised her voice just enough to grab his attention.

Nick leaned back in his corner and glared at Claudio from behind his sunglasses.

"What's your problem?" Claudio asked. "I just wanna know."

Nick shook his head.

"Tell me," Claudio said. "What do you got a problem

with?"

Nick took a deep breath and clenched his jaw.

"Look," he said, "you've been sticking your nose into everything, and none of it's your business."

"What's not my business?"

"That's enough, Nick," Frances interjected. "Have some respect — it's your father's funeral."

"Me?" Nick shot back. "Me, have some respect?"

"Wait." Claudio raised his hand. "I want to hear this. What's not my business?"

Nick looked at him. "My dad would be rolling in his grave if he saw you sitting in this limo, next to my mom, touching her like that. And in front of me and Anne Marie too."

"Don't worry about it."

"Don't worry?" Nick echoed.

"What would you suggest?" Claudio asked. "I'm the one that's been working with your dad at the casino, helping him. Do you have any idea of what goes on there while you're away partying at college? Somebody's got to do it, *and* be there for your mom too, to help her . . . get through this."

Nick turned away in disgust, biting his lip. The parched suburban landscape rushed by.

After a moment of calm, Anne Marie said, "Mom, did you order enough food?"

"I don't know dear, I hope we did," Frances said.

"We ordered plenty," Claudio said. "Don't you ladies worry. And if it runs out, there's always plenty of booze."

"I could go for a drink right now," Anne Marie said. "Pops would want us to have a drink for him. Hey, there must be some booze in this limo?"

A small bar with wine glasses clipped upside down sat between Anne Marie and Nick. There was a small fridge under the bar. Claudio pushed himself forward and stretched to reach it.

"Ahhh, here we are." He pulled a bottle from the fridge and held it up. "Dom Pérignon, let's pop the champagne! That's all we got."

"Better than nothing." Anne Marie shrugged.

Nick kept quiet. They were going to drink champagne, as if there were something to celebrate. It was too depressing. He stared at Claudio huffing over the champagne cork.

"Nicky boy," Claudio said. "Have a glass with us."

Nick held up his hand. "No thanks."

Claudio smirked. "Come on, let's do a toast, a toast to Jack."

"No thanks," Nick repeated.

"Nick, please," Frances said. "At least *do* the toast."

"Yes," Claudio said. "A special toast to your late great dad."

Nick glared at Claudio again. "I don't think we need a toast . . . *from you*," he said.

"Well . . . I," Claudio stammered. "Shit, you do the toast then."

He shoved the bottle and glass at Nick.

His mom glared back at him. Reluctantly, he took the glass but not the bottle.

"No," he said. "You go ahead and do it, it's your toast."

"All right, Nicky boy." Claudio poured the champagne as each held out their glass, then turned to Frances.

"Let me think a moment," he said.

He stared at Frances, as if for some insight as to what to say. Then he suddenly raised his glass. Frances and Anne Marie raised theirs, too. Nick sighed and slowly lifted his.

"Well, let's get on with it Claudio," Anne Marie said.

Claudio smiled. "To Jack. Welcome to your new location!"

"Shit." Nick rolled his eyes.

"Yes." Anne Marie raised her glass. "Welcome to your new location, Daddy!"

"No." Nick lifted his glass higher. "I'll do the toast." He paused. "Dad, we love you, and we're going to miss you. We're really going to miss you."

His eyes became watery and his lips began to quiver. He took a small, tentative sip of the champagne, the sweet liquid fizzing on his tongue. Tears welled up in his eyes. He turned away toward the window

"Cheers!" Claudio said.

"To Jack." Frances took a sip.

Anne Marie drank her champagne in one quick gulp, then pushed her glass towards Claudio.

"Another," she said.

CHAPTER 3

The limo pulled around the circular driveway, and Nick could see Roman Lorenzo abruptly cut short his conversation with his cousin Albert. Roman took a quick last drag from his cigarette, then pushed it into the sand of the granite pedestal ashtray at the foot of the walkway to the house. He stepped quickly toward the limo to open its door. Nick got out first, the jump-seat springing up with a thud.

"Thanks," he said, unsteady on his feet.

"No problem," Roman said.

A weak breeze blew past the walls of his family's sprawling split-level ranch house. Coconut palms swayed gently overhead, their leaves glistening in the sun. Heat waves rippled off the driveway.

The chauffeur unloaded Nick's suitcase from the trunk and set it next to him.

"Thanks," Nick said.

Having flown in that morning, he had gone right to the funeral from the airport. Now, he was back home.

Frances came out next, careful to place her platform shoe solidly on the sidewalk. His mother wasn't very tall and wore the shoes to give herself a couple of extra inches. She smiled as Roman took her hand.

"He's at peace now. He's at peace," Roman said.

"I know." Frances pressed her thin lips together. "He looked good. They did a nice job making him up."

"Yes, I'm sure they did," Roman said.

Claudio maneuvered his way across the seat and with a heave of effort emerged from the limo.

Roman laid a hand on Claudio's shoulder. "Take it easy Boss," he said. "What can I get you? Scotch on the rocks?"

Claudio took a breath and adjusted his pants. "You know what?" he said. "I think Jack's got a bottle of Johnnie Walker Black in his den. We need to have a special drink, in his honor."

Claudio half-winked at Roman.

"You got it, sir," Roman said and hurried off to the house, apparently forgetting that Anne Marie hadn't exited the limo yet.

Nick stood watching them from the sidewalk. Frances and Albert waited on the path for Claudio, his mother adjusting her veil.

"Everything will be fine," Albert said.

"It's just so stressful," Frances replied.

"Don't be stressed. You've got Claudio watching your back. He's a good man. Believe me. I've known him all my life."

Claudio hurried past Nick without saying a word. Nick watched him take his mother's arm and walk up the pathway toward the house, whispering something in her ear, and chuckling. Albert lead the way and held the door for them as they entered the house.

Nick turned to see Anne Marie getting out of the limo. She stepped over to him.

"Nice of them to wait for me, huh?" she said. "Let's go in and have a drink. Wait till you see the house, you'll feel like you never left. It's sad though because all Dad's stuff is still there."

"You go ahead," Nick said. "I just wanna wait here a second before going in."

Anne Marie shrugged her shoulders. "Sure, suit yourself." She headed for the house.

Nick stretched his neck left and right, his curly, black hair brushing lightly against his opened shirt collar. Women somehow found him handsome, although he didn't understand why. His face was oval and slightly elongated with high cheekbones, and he often tilted his head just slightly to the left, as if perplexed. His lips were a bit asymmetric too, and even a little crooked. But he had a distinctive jawline and deep-set, intense blue eyes.

His eyes were barely visible though behind his gold-rimmed aviator sunglasses—their amber color fading from top to bottom. He wore these glasses because they cooled the brightness of the sky without affecting the color of the foreground.

At almost six feet tall, he stood motionless. He wore his favorite jacket, a black leather Pierre Cardin, over a black cotton dress shirt with a flared collar and two buttons opened at the top, revealing a thick gold chain and a touch of chest hair. His trousers were black, as well as his fine Italian leather shoes. Overall, his clothes were well tailored, and he exuded a neat, crisp appearance. A heavy gold ID bracelet hung loosely around his right wrist and read *"Nick"*. A black-faced Rolex Submariner watch adorned his left wrist.

He rubbed his hands together, trying to warm them after the frigid, overly air conditioned limo ride. The hot afternoon sun felt good on his skin. He closed his eyes and lifted his face toward it.

He should have come home a week earlier, when he

had first heard of his dad's death. Instead, he stayed at school to finish the semester. Couldn't he have just gotten a waiver to finish his junior project later? And, he should have come home during Christmas break. Why didn't he? It was almost a year since he had last seen his dad and now, he wouldn't be seeing him *ever* again.

Sweat beaded up on his forehead. Bright orange from the sunlight swirled and danced under his eyelids. What if he stood here in the roasting sun forever, how long before he might melt away?

"Stupid idiot," he mumbled.

He opened his eyes and turned toward the house.

In the vestibule, he put his suitcase down. The place was empty, and except for the sound of kitchen activity down the hall, it was quiet too. Maybe the guests that had already arrived were out back? Memories began to well up. He had forgotten the smell of the house's air conditioning, with its tinge of mustiness, and the sound of the front door sealing the room when it closed behind. It was all coming back to him. Even the old black and white photograph on the wall by the door, how could he have forgotten about that? He must have seen it a thousand times — his family just about to eat, all sitting around the picnic table at their Montana ranch. His dad with a big grin on his face, holding a hot dog, and everyone else, horsing around, and smiling too. He was just a little kid then, sitting next to his dad, and Anne Marie sitting across, and mom, at the head of the table, she was so young and pretty, *and so vibrant!*

The polished, white marble tiled floor and the beige and gold paisley patterned wallpaper — this was home and it felt good. But it also felt awkward, like a regression, like someplace he had grown out of.

A small table stood against the wall near the door. On it a bouquet of flowers in a green vase, a lit candle, and a picture of Jack wearing his white Stetson hat and khaki shirt, a broad smile spread across his face. Below the picture an embossed card read:

Jack Nicholas Romano
Beloved Father and Businessman
Always in Our Loving Memory
February 14, 1910 – May 7, 1973

On either side of the card were a few $1 and $5 Cornetto Club Casino chips, each with his dad's smiling face and signature tall Stetson. Two decks of cards were next to the chips, a red Ace of hearts and a black Ace of spades propped up against the decks. Poker, Nick smiled. He looked back at the card. 1910. 1973. He was only 63 — just 63!

Nick pulled his eyes away, picked up his bag and stepped into the living room. On the wall, the old ornate Bavarian cuckoo clock hung, with its wooden pinecones dangling on chains halfway to the floor. Next to it, a large painting of Freemont Street at night, with its glowing neon lights. Two copper peacock wall hangings hung above the Marantz stereo receiver with its polished aluminum knobs and switches. And those Bose speakers on their thin pedestal stands, they looked like they were from the future. His dad loved Frank Sinatra, Jackie Gleason and Dean Martin and would sometimes sit in his easy chair with a glass of scotch and a cigar, listening to their records.

Everything reminded him of his father. Even the

bookcase, still crowded with the same sculptures — two bronzes of wild horses running in the wind, a longhorn bull standing at attention, and a Spanish fighting bull with shorter horns that curved upward, in a fierce stance, digging its hoofs in, getting ready to charge. Nick always liked that one. And there were still the same family photographs scattered among the shelves too.

And, prominently displayed on the living room wall, his favorite photograph. A portrait of his dad wearing the white Stetson standing proudly next to his Caddy with huge bull horns mounted right on the front of its custom silver grill. It was taken right in the middle of the Freemont Street in front of the Cornetto Club Casino — it's brightly lit sign glowing in the background with what must have been a thousand light bulbs. The photograph was black and white and taken from a low angle. It made Jack appear much taller than he actually was. The photograph was sharp, the chrome of the Caddy's front bumper looked like it was right there in miniature. He always wondered how the photographer could have taken such a great picture. It was so crisp and realistic — he had never seen a better photograph in his life. And his dad, as usual, looked so happy and proud. Nick smiled, then saw something he had never noticed before. His dad was wearing a bolo tie, and it looked familiar. Was it the one his dad had given him years earlier, when he was still in high school?

Nick moved closer, squinting at it, from just a few inches away. It definitely looked like the same bolo tie — the one with the silver dollar. How could he have forgotten about it?

It was on his 15th birthday. His dad had taken him to the casino and given him a grand tour. Afterward he sat him down in his office and said, "Son, how would you like to someday be running all this here?"

"Me? Run it?" Nick was more than surprised.

"Well, of course you can't do it now," Jack said. "But soon, after high school, you can start working here and getting to know what goes on."

Nick remembered the conversation clearly, and telling his dad he wanted to go to college, *"and get a regular job."*

His dad chuckled, "Son, this is a regular job. And I can teach you the ropes better than any college. They don't deal with the real world. This is the real world here, the people are real and the money is real. Shit, it's those corporations and government guys that are the crooks. They just paint it over to make it look legit. I've been dealing with those bloodsuckers my whole life. Remember, I lived through the depression, son. How do you think that happened? The banks. The government. Your so-called legit friends!"

Nick shrugged. "I don't know."

"Look," Jack said. "It ain't all that complicated. You just gotta learn how to deal with people. And I'm talkin' about the problem people. They're the ones that trip you up. Boozers, hoodlums, bums, cheats, con men—and the politicians, especially the politicians and government people. You gotta watch out for them. They're a slippery breed. Other than that, it's an easy game."

"I'm not sure, Dad."

"Look," Jack continued. "We don't always do everything by the book, but sometimes when you want things to happen, that's the only way to operate." Jack got up and walked around the desk. He put his hand on his son's shoulder.

"You see how loyal my employees are? Why is that? Is it because of some contract I signed with them? Of course not. It's because they trust me. Because I keep my word. Stay close to those people that keep their word, son. Those are the people that you can trust. And watch out for those people waving contracts and rules and regulations in your face. They're backstabbing devils."

Nick nodded and shifted uncomfortably in his chair.

Jack shook his finger at him. "Looky here boy, somebody's going to need to take over this place when I die, retire or get fired. Now who's that gonna be?"

Nick wasn't ready for this and shrugged his shoulders.

"It's gonna be you, boy," Jack said. "And the quicker you start getting familiar with things, the better."

"Well you're not going to retire for a while, right?"

"No, not if I can help it. But what if I got hit by a truck tomorrow?"

Nick looked at his dad.

"Sorry son, but things happen, and you gotta be prepared. Now look, I got something for you."

Jack opened his side desk drawer and dug around. Then he pulled out a small white box.

"Aahhh, here it is," he said.

"What is it, Pops?"

Jack handed him the box, "It's for you. Open it."

Nick examined the box, shaking it and feeling its weight in his hand.

His dad leaned back in his chair, watching him.

Nick carefully opened it. He peeled away a layer of tissue paper. It was some kind of jewelry. A leather braid with a shiny, large, silver coin set in a clasp. It was a silver-dangled bolo tie, and it pretty looked cool.

His dad smiled, "You know, that's always been my favorite bolo. But now, I want you to have it."

"Really?" Nick said.

"Yes, and that's a double strike uncirculated 1884 Carson City Morgan Silver Dollar. It's a very rare and special coin. I'm giving it to you boy, to remind you that someday this whole casino will be yours, and someday you'll be responsible for it all. You'll be responsible for everything that I built, that I worked, sweated and struggled for, and . . ." his dad took a breath, "you'll be responsible for Mom, and our family too."

Jack leaned forward across the desk.

"And I expect you to always keep this in the family."

He waved his hand indicating the whole Cornetto Club Casino. Nick looked around the room.

"Vegas will keep growing, and we're gonna grow with it. And someday, it'll all be up to you. So, this bolo, my favorite bolo, is for you, to remind you."

Nick stood up. "Thanks Dad, it's really cool."

"Keep that safe, and don't lose it."

"I won't lose it."

His dad stood and gave him a pat on the back, then a big bear hug.

Nick meant to wear it later that day, but forgot. Maybe it was because he mostly wore T-shirts back then—he wasn't sure what happened.

He examined the bolo around his dad's collar in the photograph. Now he felt guilty and stupid. Somehow, he had actually forgotten all about it. And, he didn't even know where it was now! Was it still in his drawer, in his room? *Had he ever worn it?* He couldn't remember.

Maybe he had put it in his metal security box? The one that he'd hand-painted in mod Peter Max letters, *"Nick's Box"*. Growing up, he had always kept his prized possessions in that box. And the last he knew, the box should still be in his room, in his desk drawer, where he had always kept it.

Nick grabbed his suitcase. Roman walked briskly in with a bottle of liquor in his hand, smiling.

"How ya doin'?" he said to Nick as he passed.

Before Nick could answer Roman was gone, out toward the game room.

Nick headed upstairs to his room. The hallway somehow seemed smaller. His room looked almost as he had left it months before, except now it was clean. His mom must have done that while he was at school. He threw his suitcase on the bead and noticed the day-glow stars on the ceiling. He had forgotten about them too. He'd put them up there so long ago, seems they'd been up there forever. There was a poster on the wall of an astronaut walking on the moon. He loved space. Also, a movie poster above his desk, for "The Harder They Come" with Jimmy Cliff holding a pistol in each hand. Such a cool poster, he thought, and yes, the harder they fall, too.

Nick glanced at his desk and grabbed the left-hand drawer, pulling it so firmly that he almost yanked it right out and onto the floor. The familiar gray metal box was still there, with the words *'Nick's Box'* painted boldly on top – and *'KEEP OUT!'* in smaller marking pen letters underneath. He stared at it for a moment. What was in it? He could hardly wait to see. He placed it on the desk and sat down in his chair. He unlatched it and took a deep breath. Under some papers and other trinkets, the small white box with the bolo was still there, slightly discolored, but probably exactly as he had left it years earlier.

He opened the box and unfolded the tissue paper. And there it was, the double strike uncirculated 1884 Carson City Morgan Silver Dollar bolo tie. He held it up, examining it closely. It was struck twice, so there was a bit of a shadow image of Miss Liberty. It was still in nice shape, not even tarnished, and on the back, under the eagle and the wreath, the small CC mint mark was clear. The bolo's braided leather strap was still supple too. Without taking his jacket off, he placed the bolo over his head and around his upturned shirt collar.

He stood at the mirror and adjusted the silver dollar to just the right height. But it clashed with his thick gold chain, so he took the chain off and threw it in the draw. He pulled his shirt collar down and tugged his sleeve cuffs. He looked at himself and patted down his curly hair in a few places. Turning left and right, he studied how the bolo looked. The silver dollar stood out nicely against the black shirt.

"Perfect Dad," he said out loud and smiled. "It's freakin' perfect."

He grabbed the box to put the cover back on, but a small card fell out onto the desk. He opened the card and immediately recognized his dad's handwriting. He took a deep breath and sat down.

Nick,

This is my favorite coin and favorite bolo. I've worn it for many, many years. Now it's your turn to wear and treasure. I believe in you, I love you and I always will.

Your dear old dad,
*   –   Jack*

Nick rubbed his thumb over the ink of his dad's script. Tears began to well up in his eyes. He put the card down and closed his eyes. A tear dropped off his cheek and fell onto the card, spattering the word *will*, and dispersing its blue ink like a watercolor painting.

CHAPTER 4

Nick took a deep breath, hesitated a moment, and stepped off the bottom stair into the living room. Thankfully most of the guests had not yet arrived. A few people he didn't recognize talked by the front door as they examined the photograph and tribute to Jack.

He walked to the main hallway, which led to the kitchen. It was lined with more photographs—all of his dad standing with different celebrities, politicians, and other dignitaries. But these pictures never really interested Nick because the people in them were just props and not real friends of his dad's. They just happened to be at the casino on a particular day, and so became an opportunity for his dad to promote and portray a legitimate, straight up image. But his dad had become a local celebrity himself, so maybe they wanted their picture taken with him? Maybe to promote their own bad-boy image?

He gazed at the photo of his dad shaking hands with Frank Sinatra.

"Hmmm, the man himself," Nick said quietly.

He turned away from the photograph and practically walked right into his Aunt Stephanie.

"Nick!" she exclaimed. "How are you!"

She reached up and kissed his cheek, smearing it with red lipstick.

"I'm OK," he said.

Always well-meaning, Aunt Stephanie smiled and squeezed his hands, her strong perfume filling the air. Her wide smile revealed her smoke-stained teeth. She looked at him with her deep-set eyes.

"You're all grown up now. Seems like it was just yesterday you were such a cute little boy. How's college?"

"Oh fine," Nick said. "Hard work, but fine."

"That's good," she said. "Better to be at college than to be here. You're the only smart one, you know that?"

She looked at him with sad eyes, "So sorry about Jack. How are you doing?"

"OK, I'm OK." He avoided her glance. "It's tough you know, but I'm OK."

"That's good," she said. "What can you do? It was a shock to hear what happened. Your uncle Frank didn't take it too well."

"How is he?" Nick said.

"He's good, he's sitting in the back. Go say hello. And get yourself something to eat." She smiled. "Don't they feed you at that school?"

"Yeah." Nick laughed. "Well, let me go find him and say hello."

He pulled his handkerchief out and walked toward the kitchen as he wiped the lipstick off his cheek. Amid the sizzling sounds of cooking, he could smell the sweet aroma of roasting garlic and butter wafting up the hallway. It was the smell of home, and it felt good.

In the kitchen, with its quaint yellow wallpaper and country flower motif, a bustle of cooking staff frantically prepared the food. Large bowls of spaghetti, meatballs and sauce, trays and pans full of eggplant parmesan, chicken marsala, lasagna, ravioli, piles of Italian bread, garlic bread, a large bowl of green salad, and a tray of antipasto, were all positioned and spread out across three folding tables. In the corner along the wall sat a lavish multi-level assortment of Italian pastries including; cannoli, napoleons, pignoli, macaroons, amaretti and more.

There was enough food for a feast, which meant there would probably be lots of guests and plenty of booze. Nick rubbed his thumb on the silver dollar pendant of his bolo tie and smiled. Somehow, he was content and happy. But why did he suddenly seem to feel good? Was it the warmth and smell of the food? The excitement about seeing family and old friends? Was it because he finished his semester? He slid opened the sliding glass door to the back yard.

A bar was setup on the spacious patio under the shade of a long awning that hung down from the house. Dozens of bottles of liquor, wines and mixers where carefully laid out. Two bartenders were making drinks, and Anne Marie had just stepped away from the bar, a glass of white wine in her hand. Nick was about to go talk to her when somebody grabbed his shoulders, spun him around and hugged him.

"Nick baby!" Mario Baldacci shouted.

"Ahhh, Mario!" Nick said.

Mario released his hold and stepped back. "Oh man, it's great to see you."

It *was* good to be back home.

"Sorry to hear about your dad. What a drag," Mario said.

"Yeah . . . it's a real bummer," Nick sighed.

"And sorry I couldn't make the funeral."

"No problem, man," Nick said. "But you're looking good, sporting a mustache now, huh? Looks like you lost some weight too. How the hell are you?"

Mario wore a heavy gold chain around his neck. He was shorter than Nick, but solidly built like a bull, his blow-dried hair carefully combed back, his thick black eyebrows set prominently above his dark eyes.

"Good, good. Yeah, man. I'm good."

"So, what's going on? What are you doing with yourself?" Nick said.

"What am I doin'?" Mario laughed. "Nothing. I was bartending at the Hilton, but that didn't last. I'm looking for another gig now."

"What happened?"

"Nothing, they just didn't like . . ." Mario smiled. "Sharing."

"Sharing?" Nick chuckled. "What'd you do?"

"It was just a few cases of wine, you know."

"You gotta be careful, man," Nick said.

"Yeah I know." Mario nodded, then said, "Hey, nice bolo!"

"Thanks, it was my dad's. He gave it to me."

"Wow, cool." Mario nodded again. "Hey, listen," he said and placed his arm around Nick's shoulder, then leaned in close. "I gotta talk to you, *now*."

Nick was surprised at Mario's sudden turn of demeanor.

"OK, sure, man. Is everything OK?"

"Let's go to your room."

"No problem, man. What's up?"

Mario raised his eyebrows and put a finger to his lips. They began walking back towards Nick's room.

"So, how's school?" Mario said, making conversation.

"Not bad, lots of reading." Nick was confused.

"They teach you anything good over there?"

"Sure, man. Lots of good stuff."

"Like what?" Mario said.

"Well," Nick said. "Like Alice in Wonderland."

"Huh? Ain't that a kid's story."

"Yeah, don't laugh."

"At college?" Mario smirked. "What kind of lessons are they teaching you?"

"The kind of lessons that lessen and lessen!"

They both laughed.

"That's from Alice in Wonderland. Ain't that cool? Lewis Carroll wrote that. He smoked Opium, man. That's how he came up with such a flipped out story. He was high!"

"Really?" Mario looked at him.

"No shit, that's what I learn at college. Alice goes down the rabbit hole and takes magic mushrooms. It's not really a kid's story!"

"OK," Mario was impressed. "That's cool."

They headed up the stairs.

"Hey, I also took a Shakespeare class too. That dude was cool. He wrote some great shit; you wouldn't believe it."

"Shakespeare?" Mario gave Nick a puzzled look.

"Yeah, like Macbeth — this greedy motherfucker and his wife decide to kill the King, so that he can become King. And she encourages him, and even helps him, so that she can be the Queen. But once they kill the guy and get blood on their hands — they fucking go crazy, killing one rival after another — killing anyone who threatens their plans. It's like a freakin' bloody Hollywood horror movie, except they did it like three hundred years ago, in a theater."

Mario stopped and poked Nick in the chest. "Cool, so,

you got a girlfriend up there?"

"I got girlfriends." Nick smiled. "You wouldn't believe it, so many cool college chicks, it's crazy."

Nick pushed the door open to his room and Mario followed.

"Yeah, well." Mario patted him on the shoulder. "That's great. I broke up with Barbara."

"Really?"

"Yeah, she's too much of a hippy freak for me. And a total Deadhead, too. I don't know what's so great about the Dead. Except for Truckin', that's a good one."

"Sugar Magnolia's good too," Nick said. "And a Deadhead is not so bad, but I know what you mean. All that tie-dye and flowery shit."

"Yeah, well, look." Mario sat at the edge of the bed.

Nick sat in his swiveling desk chair and spun around to face Mario.

"Shoot," he said. "What's up, man? You got some new deal going, or something?"

"Na man. Look, this is serious." Mario leaned forward. "Here's the thing."

He hesitated and seemed to be gathering his thoughts.

"Yeah?" Nick prodded.

"Well, see, the night your dad died . . ."

"Yeah?"

"You know he was in his office at the casino, right?"

"Right, I guess so."

"Well, I was at the casino too that night and believe it or not, I was on my way at that moment to go talk to him."

"You were *there*?"

"Yeah, and I was on my way to his office, walking

past the craps tables, when all of a sudden, here comes Claudio flying around the corner from Jack's office. And he's huffing and sweating and slams right into me—almost knocked me on my ass. And he's all fucking nervous and jumpy. I'm thinking, *Fuck man, what the hell is he on?* I mean he was freakin' wired. And he's like in shock to see me. He freakin' grabs my shoulders and yells, MARIO!"

Mario opened his eyes wide and contorted his face, mimicking Claudio's expression.

Nick sat up straight, "And . . ." he said.

"And so, he stands there and he's right in my face like this, and he's sweating and slobbering, and he fucking stinks man. Goddamn it, I swear, he stinks like alcohol and sweat. And then for just a second, there's this look in his eyes . . . like, like I don't know how to describe it. It was spooky and it freaked me out. I'm thinking, *What the hell is going on?* I step back and throw his hands off me and say, 'Yo, man, take it easy Claudio. What the fuck's going on?'"

"'Nothin', he stammers, 'Just gotta go. I'm late.'"

"Then he looks at me, like scrutinizing me, and says, 'What are you doing?'"

"'I'm just going to see Jack,' I said."

"'Oh, he's . . .' but then Claudio stops, like he's stuck and can't think of what the hell to say. And then he says, 'Oh, he's gone. Door's locked.' Like I should have known that. Next thing I know, he pushes past me and hurries off.

"I'm like, 'OK', thinking it was weird that Jack left early. I even knocked on his door, but no answer. So I left and went back home to my place."

"You just left?"

"Yeah, shit, I didn't know anything was going on."

Mario stood up.

"Look," he continued. "I don't have a good feeling about this. I know Claudio was up to no good. He was coming from your dad's office, on the night your dad died. Maybe he even killed him. That guy's a snake, I'm telling you. Claudio's a snake."

"What?" Nick stood up. "You really think he might have killed my dad?"

"Shit, Nick, don't you see, he's practically appointed himself 'Czar of the Cornetto Club Casino'. It's totally fucked up. Something ain't right."

"I don't know, man." Nick's skin felt prickly. "They said my dad died naturally, of a heart attack."

"Yeah, I know that's what they said. But I don't believe it. Look, your dad was young, what, in his early 60s?"

"Sixty-three," Nick said.

"See, that's young, man." Mario was getting excited. "Maybe Claudio set it up, and made it look like a heart attack. Or, maybe the police covered it up for him. Shit, I know he would've fucking done it if he could. It was that look of shock he had on his face when he saw me—like he was scared, and guilty as shit. I know it. And it was the very night your dad died."

"Shit," Nick said. "Could that really be?"

There was a rapid knock on his bedroom door and it pushed open. Frances popped her head in.

"Is everything OK?" she asked. "What's going on?"

"Nothing, Mom. Mario and I were just catching up."

"Hi Mario," Frances said. "Haven't seen you in a while. How are you?"

"Good, Mrs. Romano," Mario said. "Sorry to hear

about Jack."

"Yes," she said.

"But it's good to see Nick," Mario said.

"Yes, well." Frances looked at Nick. "The guests are arriving and Lawrence is here. He's asking about you, come downstairs and say hello."

"OK, in a minute," Nick said.

She closed the door.

"Shit," Mario said. "You think she was out there listening to us?"

"No." Nick walked over to his bedroom window and looked down at the backyard. Guests were milling around the gazebo and pool. There must have been thirty or forty people down there.

He turned to Mario, "You think he really did it?"

"It wouldn't surprise me, man," Mario said. "Not one bit."

Neither spoke for a moment as they considered the implications.

Then Mario said, "Look, I'm sorry, man."

"Shit, it's OK," Nick turned back toward the window.

Raucous laughter suddenly seeped up from the air vent on the floor just below the window.

Nick raised his hand.

"Did you hear that?" he whispered and looked down.

"What? What are you looking at?"

"The vent, man. That sounds like Claudio."

Nick knelt down and tilted his ear toward the vent.

"No shit?" Mario said and crouched down next to him. More laughter could clearly be heard from inside the depths of the vent.

"Sounds like that scumbag and his crew," Mario said.

"Shoosh . . ." Nick cupped his ear and put it right up to the vent. "They must be in the game room," he whispered. "Go lock the door!"

CHAPTER 5

Claudio and his crew gathered in the game room, located directly below Nick's room. It was an expansive room, with white faux wood panels covering the walls. On one side, above a fancy Magnavox console TV hung a large painting of Jack—a head and shoulders portrait of him in his white cowboy hat and western style jacket and shirt. In the background of the portrait, a colorful collage of Vegas icons surrounded him—a roulette wheel, a craps table, dice, a pair of aces, a row of show girls in their feathered headdresses kicking up their heels, the *Welcome to Fabulous Las Vegas* sign, and of course the bright phosphorescent red neon sign of the *Cornetto Club Casino*.

An impressive array of high-end audio equipment sat stacked on custom shelving—a Marantz stereo receiver, a preamp, an amplifier, a Pioneer turntable—all sleek with brushed aluminum knobs and switches. Large AR speakers, with walnut finishes and tan fabric grills, sat on the floor on either side of the TV. A modern orange couch with plastic slip covers sat in front of the stereo, TV, and portrait of Jack, along with a plush lazy-boy lounge chair to its left.

Across the room along the opposite wall sat a Drop-A-Card pinball machine and next to it a dart board hung on the wall, and to the right, a slot machine. In the middle of the room stood a pool table and next to it a full-sized craps table. And at the far end of the room, a poker table, and next to it, in the corner, a well-stocked wet bar.

Claudio sat at the poker table in the dealer's seat with

the bottle of Johnnie Walker Black in front of him. In one hand he held a Padron cigar and in the other his torch lighter, firing the flame at the cigar's tip, waiting for it to light.

Roman Lorenzo, who was a slight, nervous man, brought over glasses and a bucket of ice. Roman's cousin Albert Lorenzo, who's physique resembled Claudio's except that he was shorter, pudgier and a bit older, took his seat next to Claudio. Albert shifted his weight left and right in the chair, before carefully pulling his shirt cuffs out from under his suit jacket sleeves. He calmly folded his hands on the table, thereby signaling he was ready for whatever business was at hand.

Picking up on that cue, Claudio said. "Ahhh, it's good to sit and relax a moment, before everyone gets here, huh?"

Roman stood, clinking ice into the glasses. He looked at Claudio and said, "Yeah, there were a lot of people at the funeral. Shit, the Mayor was even there. How'd Jack get so many friends?"

"And enemies," Claudio said. "He was no saint, that's for sure. Shit, do you know he killed a man down there in Texas and only went to prison for two years? I heard he cut some kind of deal."

Claudio puffed on his cigar, blew the smoke, then tapped its tip in the heavy cut-glass ashtray which sat on the poker table's green felt surface.

He took a deep breath and sighed "Bet they all came for a piece of him, like flies on shit."

"Stinky shit," Albert added.

Claudio chuckled.

Across the room, Tony Scalfaro stood a few feet from the dart board, darts in hand. He was tall and thin and wore Buddy Holly wayfarer style glasses that rested crookedly on his gaunt face.

"Bulls-eye baby," he implored and threw the dart. It smacked against metal edge of the target and fell to the floor.

"Shit!"

"You suck," Albert said. "Don't you know when you suck at something? Now have a seat and a drink."

"Twenty bucks I hit the bulls-eye," he said.

"You degenerate gambler," Albert said. "You got it. Twenty."

Tony squinted, threw the next dart and it stuck in the board but way off center. Albert shook his head.

"Ah shit." Tony walked over and swung himself into the chair across from Albert and Claudio.

"Give me a friggin' drink."

"It's those eyeglasses you got," Claudio said. "Maybe you should clean them."

Tony got out a twenty.

"Easy money baby, easy money" Albert grabbed the bill.

Joey, a confidant man with striking blue eyes, stepped into the room and stood a moment, surveying it.

"Shut the door and sit down," Claudio said. "We're having a drink in honor of Jack — his special reserve."

"Sorry I'm late, Boss." Joey shut the door and took his seat.

"Now," Claudio continued. "I want to have a quick toast to celebrate our good friend's wonderful demise."

Roman slid a tumbler full of ice toward Tony, who pushed it to Joey. Starting with Albert, Claudio poured the scotch, carefully filling each glass half way. He poured his glass last and sloshed the scotch around the ice cubes.

"Yes, this is quite a day, quite a day gentlemen." Claudio smiled, savoring this moment.

"Salud!" he lifted his glass.

"Salud!" the men cheered and clinked their glasses high.

"It's about time that retard is gone," Roman said.

"Heyyyohhh!" Albert joined in.

Joey stood and raised his glass up, "To Jack," he said, feigning a serious tone, but then added, "You dumb fuck! Sleep tight motherfucker!"

A raucous outburst erupted.

"Hey, hey . . ." Claudio said, trying to control his own laughter, and pressing his hand down in the air, "Shoosh . . . keep it down."

"Oh, man. Ahhh . . ." Roman said, "Sorry . . ."

"Damn, that's good . . ." Claudio looked up. "Thank you Jack!"

"To Jack, you son-of-a-bitch!" Roman said.

Claudio took a swig of his scotch, and puffed his cigar again. Then he leaned forward and looked at his men.

"OK guys, here's the deal," he said. "I want you all to know how this is gonna go."

The men fell silent, eager to hear what he had to say. They were like a pack of hungry wolves, relishing the scent of fresh blood and warm meat, elated by the thought of the enormous opportunities presented by Jack Romano's death — such a large kill.

Claudio gathered his thoughts a moment and surveyed his men again, taking a deep breath and puffing out his chest.

"First, with Jack gone . . ." he paused, "I'll be taking

over the operations at the casino. And Albert." He nodded to Albert. "Being my go-to guy and right hand man, will be my second in command—as usual." He placed his hand on Alberts shoulder. "Shit, how long have I known you? Since we were kids, how old were we?"

Albert shook his head, "Longer than I can remember—we were little twerps."

"Yeah," Claudio said. "Back on South Lowe Avenue in Chicago. Those were the days—shit, the things we did."

"Yeah, but we were smart," Albert said. "We were always smart, that's the thing. We always knew what we were doing. We were careful and we survived. Shit, even stayed out of prison."

"Yeah," Claudio laughed. "And look how far we've come. What a great team we make, huh? All that hard work—it all pays off, huh?"

"It pays and pays," Albert smiled.

The other men sat silent, waiting to hear of their coming rewards.

"And now," Claudio said. "It's gonna pay off *big*, for all of us. You'll all have executive positions at the casino. You'll all have a piece of it. Shit," Claudio smiled. "We got nothin' but blue skies ahead, baby!"

He could see that Roman was eyeing him and about to say something.

"And Frances?" Roman said, leaning back in his chair. "She's giving it to you?"

"Giving it to me?" Claudio smirked and shifted his weight.

"No, not like that," Roman said.

"Yeah." Claudio straightened up. *"She's giving it to me*

good!" He burst out laughing, and the men laughed with him.

After a moment they settled down and Claudio looked at Roman, waiting for him to finish his question.

"The casino," Roman said. "That's what I'm talking about. She's giving you the casino? Just like that? And putting you in charge?"

"Look," Claudio shot back. "Don't worry about it. She wants me to do it. I've been working with Jack for the last year. I know the operation."

"Well, yeah," Roman said. "But what about Jack's guys? What about what's-his-name? Lawrence? Larry? And Bill, what about them?"

"What about 'em," Claudio said. "You worry too much. Look, they don't know *shit*. I'll take care of them and Frances."

"And what about Nick?" Joey said.

"You too now!" Claudio said louder, raising his hands, "What the fuck about him?"

"Look," Albert said. "We don't have to worry about Nick. He's never been involved in the operation. Doesn't even know nothin' about it. Nothin. He's fucking clueless."

"That's right," Claudio said. "He's as green as they get, and he's in college."

"Anne Marie," Tony piped up. "What about her?"

"Are you kidding?" Claudio laughed. "Shit, she's too busy drinking, getting stoned and getting laid."

The men snickered.

"And as for you . . ." Claudio stomped on the table. "My brothers! Well, we are gonna rock and roll, baby!"

Claudio grinned and puffed his cigar.

"To Claudio!" Albert raised his glass.

"To Claudio!" They all concurred, raising and clinking their glasses in unison.

Claudio took a sip, his face aglow. It was a special moment, and the men felt it too, relishing the thought of the riches to come.

"Boss," Joey broke the silence. "What about those rumors?"

"What rumors?" Claudio said. "The treasure?"

"Yeah, Jack's silver. Is it real?"

"Don't know." Claudio raised his eyebrows. "Jack never mentioned it."

"Come on." Roman leaned forward. "There must be something to it. For all we know there could be tons. It could be a freakin' gold mine!"

"I don't know," Claudio said to Roman. He took a deep breath and leaned back in in his chair. "Nobody fucking knows."

Roman seemed unimpressed. "Somebodies gotta know," he said.

Albert looked at him, "Look, he said he don't know. What more do you want?"

"OK." Roman raised his hands in surrender. "That's OK, I'm just askin'"

"I'm sure we'll find out soon enough," Albert said.

"Yeah," Claudio puffed his cigar. "If it's true, well, then we're even more golden, huh? If not, then we still got plenty of skim, and everything else too, right?"

Claudio stood up.

"Patience my man, patience," he said. "Now, remember to behave yourselves out there. You know? This is a funeral and we've got to keep up appearances. We're sad, mourning the dead, mourning that poor old bastard. Got it?"

"No problem, Boss," Joey said. "We got it. *He was such a good guy, such a loss, a pity, poor Jack, such a shame, a damn shame!*"

"Alright, alright," Claudio said. "Don't overdo it either!"

"No problem."

———

ON THE FLOOR with their ears to the vent, Mario said, "I told you, what a bunch of snakes!"

"Shoosh . . ." Nick waved his hand.

He could hear the men getting up to leave—the rustling of jackets, jangle of keys and their loud banter quickly fading as they marched out of the room. Then silence.

Nick noiselessly rolled on his back and stared at the plastic glow-stars on the ceiling.

"Shit!" he said through clenched teeth.

Mario stood up and held out his hand to Nick.

"Come on, man," Mario said.

Nick grabbed his hand and pulled himself up.

"This is unreal, I can't believe it," Nick said.

"I can," Mario said. "I told you. I knew he was a fucking snake. They're all snakes."

"Fuck," Nick shook his head. "This it totally fucked."

He made a fist and punched into the palm of his other hand with a crack.

CHAPTER 6

Guests crowded the house. A group of Jack's old friends talked in the living room and a line of people waited in the kitchen at the buffet. In spite of the heat, a few people waited out at the bar for their drinks. Many guests were Nick's relatives—aunts and uncles, cousins and their raucous kids. Some had flown in from Texas, some from Florida, others from California and Montana. Most hadn't been at the house for years, and some had never been there at all. Jack's business associates, staff and other employees, politicians, the mayor, the chief of police, and even Jack's competitors from other Vegas casinos—they were all there. Most came out of great respect for Jack, but some because of obligation, opportunity, or simply good public relations. And the kids, they came because they had to.

In the back yard Nick and Mario sat at one of a dozen tables, in the shade, under a large white canopy tent. Mario drank a frosty Heineken and Nick an ice-cold rum and coke. Nick sipped his drink and gazed over to the in-ground pool where Claudio was smiling and carrying on with a few of his crew. A bunch of kids frolicked in the pool, splashing and screaming.

"There he is," Nick said. "Partying. I ought to throw him out."

"You'd have to chuck all of them out," Mario said.

"Yeah." Nick took another sip. "I don't trust that fuck at all, or his posse of degenerates. You heard them in the game room—unfuckin' believable."

"Yup." Mario looked him in the eye. "And I'm telling you, I know he was up to no good when I seen him at the casino that night."

Nick leaned back in his chair.

"You don't think he did it?" Mario smirked.

"No, I think he did it," Nick said thoughtfully. "But, what if we're wrong?"

He watched Mario consider the question. The low afternoon sun glistened off the Heineken. Mario seemed flummoxed. Nick leaned forward in his chair.

"Let's go check it out," Nick said, practically whispering.

"Check what?"

"The casino, tonight. To my dad's office. We gotta check it out."

"But the police already checked everything, right?" Mario said.

"I don't know, I don't think the police did anything," Nick said. "They thought it was just a heart attack—an unattended death, right? All they probably did was cart my dad's body away. We've gotta take a look, and the sooner the better."

"Shit," Mario said.

Nick shifted his chair to face away from the pool and back towards the house. He had never seen so many people at his house. The whole property was packed with guests. There must have been a few hundred people there. Some stood in small groups chatting, some laughing, some talking loudly, and most waving their cigarettes around, smoking. Nick recognized the mayor of Las Vegas—the honorable Mr. Duane Thompson talking with his dad's good friend and associate,

Lawrence Adams.

Even though this was the funeral reception, it didn't appear to be a very subdued atmosphere. From time to time laughter and boisterousness rose up to fill the hot afternoon air. This random jovialness seemed weird—it was his dad's funeral after all.

While these thoughts occurred to him Nick focused on the sea of guests mulling around up by the bar, near the house. In the crowd something suddenly caught his eye—a subtle movement, a step, a gesture, a face, a certain face. Was it her? Could it be? Shit, not now, he thought. His heart raced but before he could turn away, their eyes met and within a single slow motion micro-second it was too late.

It wasn't that he didn't want to see her, it was just that he didn't want to see her now, on this sad day and in front of all these people.

She smiled, her eyes fixed on his. She walked confidently through the crowd toward him. Rosalie Messina, how she had grown! And so much taller! She wore a black satin blouse with a ruffled fringe and a short black skirt.

Nick immediately stood up and nearly knocked his drink over.

"Rosalie!"

She grabbed his hands. Hers were smooth and warm. Her eyes locked on his.

"Nick," she said. "I'm so sorry to hear about your dad."

She rose up on her toes and kissed his cheek. Her soft touch and the wisp of her breath tingled his skin. Flowery perfume filled the air. He was such an idiot—it hadn't even occurred to him that she might be there to pay her respects.

"It's so great to see you," she spoke close to his ear, then pulled him in, wrapping her arms around him and rubbing his back, her breasts pressing against his chest.

When she released him her perfume lingered in the air. Nick smiled and held her hands at arm's length, his heart racing.

"And look at you," he stammered. "It's really great to see you, too."

Mario stood up with his Heineken. "Rosalie," he said and leaned in.

"Mario, good to see you," she pecked his cheek.

"Jeeze, how long's it been since we've seen you?" Mario said.

"Too long," Rosalie said.

"You been at college too, right?"

"Yeah," She said. "But I miss it here."

"Well," Mario said. "I'll let you two catch up."

Before Nick knew it, Mario was gone.

Rosalie looked at him.

"So, how you doing?" she said.

"I'm OK." Nick pulled the other chair for her. "Have a seat. Want a drink?"

"Sure."

Nick glanced around, searching for one of the waitresses.

"So, you're OK?"

She was so beautiful.

"I'll survive," he said.

"You must be devastated. Your dad passed away so suddenly. Everyone really loved him, even my dad and his friends."

"You think so?" Nick asked. "Even Claudio? You think he liked my dad?"

Rosalie hesitated.

"I'm sure he respected him," she said. "You know, for everything he accomplished."

Nick inadvertently raised his eyebrows at Rosalie's answer.

"Look," she said. "You know those guys talk tough but they're not so bad as you think."

"I'll take your word for it."

Rosalie smiled.

"So, how's school?" Nick asked.

"Not bad, better than being here in Vegas, that's for sure."

"I agree," Nick said. "This place is crazy. It's all about money and partying."

"What's wrong with partying?"

"Nothing, just not all the time." Nick smiled.

He couldn't stop smiling. And Rosalie was smiling too, and her face, it was glowing. She was there. How could he have forgotten about her?

"So," Nick said. "You got a boyfriend at school?"

The waitress suddenly arrived. She was a friendly, older lady. "What can I get for you two?" she asked with a smile on her face.

Rosalie looked up at her, "A rum and Coke, please."

"Make it two." Nick held two fingers up.

"Sure thing." The waitress winked at Nick and walked away.

"What about you?" Rosalie said, locking her eyes on his. "Are you with anyone?"

"Actually, no," he said. He had forgotten how beautiful her eyes were—green, sparkling! He slid his hand across the table to hers.

"It's really great to see you," he said.

She smiled and the air came alive.

He slowly began caressing her hand. Unable to tear his eyes from hers, he suddenly felt something on her finger. It was a ring, a diamond ring.

"You're married?"

Rosalie shook her head. "No, not yet. It's an engagement ring."

"Engaged?" Nick heart sank.

"Yes."

"*Shit*," Nick mouthed the word. "When are you getting married?"

"We haven't set a date yet."

"No date? Who's the guy?"

"Someone from school. Actually he's at law school. He's real nice."

"Huh, what's his name?"

"Greg, but I'm not marrying him until he graduates, gets a job and starts paying back his student loans. That's why we haven't set a date yet. I want to wait. He owes a ton of money for the loans, but he's a spendthrift. He used some of the loan to buy an expensive stereo, with some super fancy turntable. And now he's telling me he wants to buy a Corvette. So I'm going to wait until I see that he can actually make some money after he graduates."

"Is he here, in Vegas?"

"No, he couldn't leave school. He's got finals."

"Huh," Nick said, a bit of good news.

The waitress arrived back with their drinks and smiled when she placed them on the table.

She looked at Nick and Rosalie. "Newlyweds?"

Nick released Rosalie's hand.

"No." He felt himself blushing.

"Engaged?" the waitress pressed, noticing the ring.

Rosalie smiled.

"I knew it!" the lady said. "Congratulations!"

She turned to Nick, "You're very lucky."

"Thanks." Nick was surprised at her candor, and at the same time saddened that it wasn't true.

The waitress walked away with a bounce in her step.

"That was sweet," Rosalie said.

"Yes, it was."

"We should have dinner," Rosalie offered.

"That'd be great."

"Yeah," Rosalie smiled.

She stood up and held her hand out to shake. Nick stood quickly and pulled her into a quick hug.

"Where ya going now?" he said.

"I gotta go say hi to my dad's friends." She pulled away.

"I'll call you," Nick said.

"No, better if I call you. That way we don't have to worry about my crazy dad answering the phone."

"That's right, OK you call me. Don't forget!"

Rosalie held her hand out and Nick shook it.

"See ya." She smiled, picked up her drink and spun away into the sunlight.

CHAPTER 7

By evening most of the guests had left, including Claudio and his crew. Nick walked into the living room, with Bill Andersen trailing him. Frances, Anne Marie, Mario and Lawrence Adams, were all sitting around talking.

Bill Andersen was Jack's longtime, loyal accountant and business advisor and had been with Jack since the beginning in Texas. He was a small, squat man, even shorter than Jack. He knew more about the ebb and flow of money through the casino than anyone else. He was all business and numbers and had helped Jack with everything from IRS audits to dealing with the Nevada Gaming Commission. He even helped Jack figure out a percentage skim that would fly under the radar and be effectively un-auditable.

Bill wore a white shirt, navy blue tie and a black business suit—an outfit that was indistinguishable from his normal office attire. Wire-rimmed glasses framed his gaze while thin, frazzled white hair billowed from the sides of his balding head.

"It's a nice evening out there," he said.

"Yeah," Nick said. "Now that everyone's finally gone."

"Yup." Lawrence looked up from the armchair. "It's nice and peaceful now, with just . . ." he motioned wide with raised arms, "the family left."

And he was, just like Bill, practically part of the Romano family, having known Jack and Frances since they were kids in Texas too. Lawrence had also worked with Jack from the beginning, when they were all just starting out and had their first illicit gambling operation in a basement of a deli in Lubbock. He remained Jack's right-hand man throughout the years and even today he still served as Jack's V.P. of casino operations.

Lawrence was a tall and well-built man. Nick had heard stories about him and his counter-intuitive approach. There were occasions when Jack had gotten into confrontations with disgruntled gamblers, petty criminals, hoodlums and other riff-raff. Lawrence would show up and diffuse the situation simply by quietly but firmly asking the troublemakers to leave. Perhaps it was his Clark Kent like appearance that dissuaded them.

Mario stood up to offer the armchair he was sitting in to Bill. "Have a seat," he said. "I'll get another chair."

Bill took the seat while Nick chose to plop himself down, squeezing between Anne Marie and Frances, right in the middle of the couch.

"Decided to come in?" Frances said to Nick.

"Yeah, we were just sitting out there talking about Dad and everything. It's weird without him here," Nick said.

"I know." She patted his hand. "It's been such a long day. I'll be glad to get some sleep."

Anne Marie, inebriated but still somewhat engaged, said "Mom, you're tired, and uptight. You need to relax. Have another drink, that'll help."

Lawrence looked at Frances, "I know you'll be glad when things settle down."

"I will," Frances said. "We have a lot to do now without Jack here. God, we were together forever. He did everything. Always took care of me, took care of the casino, took care of it all. Even though we had our differences. You know how difficult he could be sometimes, but he would do anything for me and the kids."

Lawrence began to tear up. "Man, I loved that man," he said. "We all loved him."

Nick sat engulfed in the couch, lost in his own thoughts.

Lawrence gazed at him and said, "Nice bolo tie. Looks like one of Jack's."

"Yup," Nick said. "He gave it to me years ago, but I never wore it. Forgot I even had it 'till today."

"Really?" Bill said. "Well, it looks good."

"Thanks."

"What coin's on it?" Bill asked.

"It's an 1884 double strike Carson City Morgan silver dollar. Dad said it was his favorite."

"Let me take a closer look." Bill stood up.

Nick leaned forward and pushed himself up off the couch. Bill took the bolo's slider in his hand and examined it.

"It's mounted in a silver horseshoe clasp," Bill said.

"Nice tie, huh?" Mario said.

Bill raised his eyebrows. "Very nice," he said. "You know, this is a very special bolo. I remember when Jack wore it, years ago. He wore it all the time and I used to joke with him that he didn't own any others. Haven't seen it since, shoot I forgot all about it too. But it's good to see it again. It's valuable, too; that coin's worth thousands of dollars you know. It's very rare. Take good care of it."

"Well, I'm never selling it!" Nick patted the bolo and sat back down.

He turned his gaze towards the front door. "Feels like Dad will be walking through that door at any moment, bringing us somethin' good. Remember that, sis?"

Anne Marie squinted at the door.

"Yeeaahhh," she said. "Pops would come stumblin' in, struggling with a big old bag of silver dollars, just like he robbed a bank! And he'd be hollerin' 'I got the treasure! I got all the treasure! Kids, come help your pops. Help me count it! We gotta count it all!'"

"Yeah." Nick laughed. "He used to tell us he robbed some pirates for it! And those were big coins—all silver dollars. Our fingers would get black from all that silver. I could hardly get that metallic smell out of my hands, not for days afterward."

"That's why I stopped helping to count 'em," Anne Marie said. "At first it was fun, but then it became a real job. Too many coins! I figured I'd just let you and Pops do it."

Frances smiled. "You know," she said. "When he first started bringing those coins home I thought, *'Great, we're rich.'*" She laughed. "He could sit for hours examining them—sorting, stacking, weighing. He'd even examine some with his loop, like a jeweler, studying the coin as if it were a diamond."

She shook her head and said, "Ahhh . . . those were the days."

"Yeah," Nick said. "Pops would get so excited."

"Well," Lawrence said. "I remember, going way back, when Jack and I were just kids. We didn't have nothin'. We were always scrounging around trying to make money. Of course we had our paper routes, but we also had work at Rigby's farm too. We thought he was rich. Man, he had a tight operation and we learned a lot from him. And we saved all our pennies, everything. We'd make money any which way we could and from whatever mischief we got ourselves into. We were always looking for an angle. Once at Davenport Feed Supply, Jack and I found a few coins under the Coca-Cola machine. After that, every day we'd race each other to see who could get to that machine first and check under it and in the coin return too. You'd be surprised how often we found nickels and dimes, and sometimes even quarters there. One time that machine broke and all you had to do was hit the coin return lever and coins would pop out. We kept hitting that thing 'till it was empty—our pockets ended up so full of change our pants nearly ripped!"

Lawrence took a drag from his cigarette and lifted his gaze toward the middle of the room, as if he were searching his memories.

He blew the smoke up in a steady stream, "That was just the start," he added. "We wondered where else else did people drop change? The answer: at Adair's."

"Adair's?" Nick said.

"Adair's Saloon. That was the only bar in town and on Friday and Saturday nights, it was jumpin'. That was our best nights. We'd make believe we were looking for Jack's dad or my dad and we'd push past the crowd, all the while looking down at the sawdust on the floor, looking for glints of coins or sometimes even dollars. We'd stay in there scrambling back and forth through the crowd—Jack would take the left side of the place, and I'd take the right. It became another contest. And we'd always find something there. Shoot, that whole summer was one big long contest to see who could make the most money. I was pretty good, but Jack was relentless. And he always got lucky too. At the end of the day we'd sit in the old barn out back of his house, with the roosters and horses and we'd look through all our coins, searching for the oldest ones. 'Cause we knew those were worth more. We'd save them, then at the end of summer we'd take them to—what the hell was his name? Sam, that's it old man Sam Smith, that's what we called him—Old Man Sam. He was a grumpy old man, but I guess he liked us 'cause he'd buy our coins. He collected them old coins. And Jack was good at the negotiations. Only thing was that after he'd buy a bunch of coins from us, he'd turn around and try to sell us some of his coins. And sometimes Jack would buy one or two. That's how he started collecting. I guess it's only natural that with all the coins flowing into the casino, he would still end up searching for the best coins. Who knows, you might find a really rare one right? One that could be worth thousands."

"Huh." Frances smiled. "So it's your fault, then? You encouraged him? That's how we ended up with so many damn coins in the house?"

"Don't know." Lawrence shrugged.

"Well," Frances sighed. "At one point he had so many coins in the house that every damn drawer or closet I opened had rolls of dimes, quarters, or silver dollars—you name it, we had it, stuffed in there. He filled up our bedroom safe with those silver dollars. Couldn't even fit his guns in there anymore. You know, he had two Remington 12-gauge shotguns and two Smith and Wesson handguns under his side of the bed, all loaded and ready for action?"

Lawrence laughed, "Wouldn't want to be a burglar in this house."

"I'll say," Bill said.

Frances continued, "But boy, was he mad that day I

told him my house wasn't Fort Knox and to get all of it out. I told him, either it went or I went. Well, Jack was steaming when I said that. But you know what, it didn't take him but a few seconds thinkin' about it, when he smiled and looked me right in the eyes. 'Well then honey,' he said, 'guess I gotta get rid of the loot.' That's right, and just like that the next day, wouldn't you know it, there was a Brinks truck right there in the driveway, right outside the kitchen door. Took them over an hour to load up that truck and haul it all off to the casino vaults. Well, you know there was no way he'd take it to a bank!"

"Yup," Lawrence said. "Jack never trusted the banks."

"That's for sure," Bill added. "I suppose he really didn't trust many people."

"He trusted us," Lawrence said.

"And rightfully so." Bill smiled and nodded.

"He trusted his own ingenuity and intuition too," Lawrence said.

"Yeah, that's right," Bill said. "And it served him well."

"Huh," Nick said. "I guess that's true, now that I think about it, he really didn't trust many people."

"Of course not," Bill said. "This is a tough racket. I guess he just got burned too many times—they call that experience! But I don't blame him—with so many lying, cheating, greedy scoundrels around. And growing up during the depression too—that didn't help him foster any trust in banks or in the government, that's for sure."

Nick listened carefully—he'd never heard these stories before.

"Jack certainly believed in cash only—no credit, no

loans, no debt, everything cash," Bill said. "He never liked taking out loans. He'd rather work hard, save up, then buy what he wanted or put the money back into the casino. He didn't like dealing with banks."

"Yup," Lawrence said. "'Cause he always thought they'd take advantage of him."

"Shoot," Frances said, gazing in the near distance. "I remember when we had to leave Texas, you know, after they shut you guys down."

Lawrence gave Frances a certain look and said, "The deli gambling hall?"

"Yeah, remember the new sheriff and his cronies. When they got elected they wanted that business for themselves."

"Oh, yeah," Lawrence said. "I remember that. That was bad. But you know, it's a good thing we didn't wind up in jail. And, it was probably the best thing that ever happened to us. Shoot, we'd never have made it to Vegas and gotten out of that backwater dirt of Texas."

"And boy, did we get out of there quick," Frances said. "And to think, I didn't want to leave. I was afraid to go to Vegas, but Jack kept saying it was the golden city and we had to go. Well, we loaded up the car with everything we had, including two suitcases full of cash — it was all the money we had in the world!"

"Yeah," Lawrence said, "and I remember me and Bill followed you in our car with all our stuff too. What else were we gonna do? I remember thinking you weren't going to make it in that old '47 Buick Electra of yours — it was so packed and sunk so low to the ground, I thought the tires might pop. And me and Bill had my old Pontiac filled to the brim too."

"Those were the days," Bill said. "Before I was even married."

"Yeah," Frances chuckled, her eyes bright with fond reminiscences. "But it all worked out for the best, huh?"

"Remember when we got to Vegas and Jack wanted to buy that old decrepit gambling hall, what was the name of it?" Lawrence said.

Frances looked at him. "I don't remember either," she said.

"It was the Gold Club or something," Bill said. "He was itching to get back in the business. But I convinced him to wait 'till we knew what was what in Vegas. We were new, how were we to know if something was a good deal? Good thing he didn't buy that place. But then, we got lucky and somehow found out that the El Dorado was in trouble and losing money. God, and it was a dump too! Maybe we didn't know how risky it was. But that was Jacks good luck. Somehow his gut told him he could turn it around. And he did. The rest, as they say, is history."

"And, we lived poor back then," Frances said. "At least until he started bringing those coins home." She paused and looked in the distance. "That was a long time ago."

"I was a little kid then," Nick said.

"And you know what happened?" Bill asked. "The damn casino vault was so big that Jack ramped up his coin buying, because now he had more storage space. And of course, the casino kept doing better too. Jack knew what he was doing. Maybe it wasn't such a bad idea, I don't know."

It was getting late, and Anne Marie's head was getting heavy on Nick's shoulder. And, he noticed, her breathing was rhythmic — she was fast asleep.

"Looks like she's had enough," Lawrence said.

"She's out again?" Frances leaned forward and looked around Nick to Anne Marie. She reached across Nick's lap and shook her.

"Wake up and get to bed. It's been a long day."

"Huh? I'm fine," Anne Marie raised her head.

"Time to get to bed." Nick poked her in the side.

"OOOhhhh, Oooaakayyy Dooaakayyy," she said, and clumsily grabbed for her glass of white wine. "I'll go in," she said, then turned to her mom, lowered her head, made a frown and waved her fist like a boxer.

"I don't like that man," she scowled. "I don't like him at all. You tell him I don't like him. I'll punch him right in his nose if he bothers you. I'll break his freakin' nose!"

"Who's face?" Nick said.

"That man — the one in the limo . . ."

"Claudio?"

"She's drunk." Frances stood up and grabbed Anne Marie's wrists, to pull her off the couch.

"Whooo's drrrunk?" Anne Maria said.

Nick and Mario helped Anne Marie up.

"Let's go," Nick said.

She turned to him and said, "I don't like that man!"

Then, as if she hadn't even realized Nick was back, said, "You're back home! Brother, it's good to see you." She leaned in to hug him, but instead ended up hanging from his neck.

Nick pulled her up and Mario helped to steady her.

"Mario?" she said. "What are you doing here? Where's Barbara, you still with Barbara? She's such a nice girl."

"We broke up," Mario said.

"Ohhhhh . . ." she said as if greatly saddened by this news. "I liked her. Tell her to call me."

"Holy shit," Nick said. "Can you take it easy? You need to get to bed."

"Bathroom first." Anne Marie looked at him.

"Fine," he said, and they all headed to the bathroom.

Nick and Mario waited for her outside in the hallway.

Mario whispered to Nick, "She don't like Claudio. I wonder the fuck why."

"Ha, yeah. Very perceptive, huh?" Nick said. "What's not to like about Claudio? Shit, Bill just told me in the backyard how Claudio actually muscled his way in."

"Really?"

"Yeah, they freakin' made my dad the proverbial offer he couldn't refuse. Some mob boss from back east, Crotchettie or something, that was his name, right there in my dad's office."

"Crocetti," Mario said. "I think he's from Chicago. He was in the papers a few months ago about the mob in Vegas."

"Shit," Nick said. "Well, Bill said those guys came out here and caused all kinds of trouble at the casino — must have gone on for weeks. Then, like they're trying to help, they generously offer protection, but for a price of course. You pay, and you keep paying, and all the trouble magically stops."

"Shit, ain't that how it always goes?" Mario shook his head.

"Yeah, but it gets worse. Bill said they insisted that Claudio join my dad's management team. It ends up my dad never actually hired him. But what the hell was he supposed to do? Bill said the final straw was when they threatened our family. Then my dad had to bring him on, he was forced to! How's that, huh?"

"Nice guys," Mario leaned closer. "That's why we gotta get that fuck. Scumbag that he is, we gotta get him."

The bathroom door swung open and Anne Marie stumbled out. When they got her to her bed she crumbled down on it.

"What a freakin' pain in the ass," Nick mumbled. "Now, let's get the key to my dad's office."

Nick went to the den to his dad's desk, where he knew the key had been before, in the top drawer under the box that contained a small loupe. But it wasn't there.

In the living room, he asked his mom for the key.

"You're going to his office, now?" Frances asked with a look of consternation on her face.

"Yeah, just to check it out, take a look around." Nick said. "I don't remember the last time I was in his office."

"It's late, why don't you just go tomorrow?" Frances said. "You know the police were already there."

"Yeah I know, but I want to see it. I want to see where Dad worked."

"The hardest working man I ever saw," Bill said.

"Yup," Lawrence said.

"OK." Frances tilted her head. "But you know we'll need to clean out his office soon."

"One step at a time," Lawrence said.

"I know," Frances said. "But there's no sense dragging things out. We have to move on."

"I know . . ." Lawrence sighed.

"Do you have the key?" Nick asked again.

"Yes, I'll get it," Frances stood.

CHAPTER 8

I n the game room, Mario played the Drop-A-Card pinball machine. He frantically pushed on the flipper buttons, twitching and leaning into the machine, grunting and huffing amid the flashing lights, ringing bells and the clicking of the score ratcheting up.

"On tilt again?" Nick said.

"It's about time. What took you so long?"

"My mom had trouble finding the office key." Nick held up the key. "Hey man, you're addicted to that game."

"Just gotta get to 10,000 points. Gotta get my fix while I'm here, right? Beats feeding quarters into the machine at the bar."

"Let's go Mr. Pinball Wizard." Nick put his hand on Mario's twitching shoulder. "You can play this anytime. It's getting late and we got work to do."

"Gimme one second, this is my last ball."

Nick watched the ball hit one of the bumpers and Mario push hard into the machine. The flashing lights and ringing suddenly stopped, and the flippers collapsed like dead fish. The ball rolled helplessly down the middle and into the hole. TILT!

"SHIT!" Mario threw up his hands. "See what you made me do?"

"What I made you do?" Nick smirked.

"I was rushing."

"Never rush," Nick said in a philosophical tone. "Now let's go check out my dad's office."

Nick turned to go, then stopped. He felt around in his pants pockets.

"Shit," he said. "Wait for me outside, I forgot to get my car keys."

"No problem," Mario said.

———

MARIO SMOKED a Marlboro and casually leaned against Nick's practically brand new white '73 Trans Am, with a screaming chicken emblem spread boldly across it's hood.

"Hey, watch the paint." Nick walked over with keys in hand.

Mario looked at him, "The paint's fine."

He flicked his cigarette to the ground and crushed it, twisting his foot over the butt twice to make sure it was out.

"Let's blow this scene," he said.

Nick cranked the engine and the beast came to life, shattering the dead-still evening air. Nick smiled. He reached for the stick shift and it was good, good vibrations. Is that what the Beach Boys meant?

"I don't like these automatic windows," Mario said. "If the switch breaks, then your window's stuck, right? What's people too lazy to crank the window down?"

"Progress," Nick said. "You know, they always have to make things more complicated."

"Yeah." Mario turned the radio on. "And more prone to breaking too."

Led Zeppelin's "D'yer Mak'er" came on with its heavy reggae bass. Mario turned it up.

"Looky what I got," he said and held up a joint.

Nick glanced over but didn't say anything. He maneuvered the car slowly out of the driveway. By the time they reached the corner, Mario had already lit up.

At the stop sign Nick paused, took a quick look at the empty avenue, then slammed the gas pedal to the floor and let the clutch up. The hood of the car rose as the fat rear tires grabbed the pavement, screeching and burning a trail of rubber in an arc across the road—the car fishtailing in a fit of raw power.

"Wooo-hooo, baby!" Mario yelled, slamming against the door. "But take it easy, man. I don't want to loss this joint out the window."

"Hold on," Nick said and floored it.

With each power shift the car lurched forward with boundless energy. Within just a few seconds they were flying up the avenue at well over 70 miles per hour. Ahead, a couple of cars were waiting a red light. This dictated that Nick quickly brake, downshift, and brake again—which he did with expert precision. The Trans Am came to a stop within inches of one of the cars at the light.

"How's that?" Nick looked over at Mario.

"Cool, how the hell can you shift so fast?"

"Practice baby, practice."

"Well, I tell you, you got fast reflexes, that's for sure."

"Like Bruce Lee, man, like water."

"Yes, grasshopper. Now, chill and have a toke."

Mario held the joint out to Nick.

"Hold on," Nick said. "The lights about to change."

On the green, and with the clutch pedal down, he revved the engine, and revved again. The car in front turned away and now the street was cleared. Nick popped the clutch and the hood lifted, tires screeching, launching the car in a mad, wailing rage of fury, leaving behind a thick cloud of burned rubber. Nick immediately shifted to second, and with hardly lifting his foot off the gas, to third. They were moving at breakneck speed again and quickly approaching slower traffic. Nick waited to the very last second to slam the brakes, downshift, and slam the brakes again. The light turned green and the traffic moved out of the way just in time for Nick to cut the wheel hard to make the turn at the intersection. The rear swerved out and just barely avoided clipping an oncoming car.

"Oh shit man!" Mario screamed, "Take it fucking easy!"

Nick could hear the terror in his voice and looked over to see his pale face.

"Holy fucking shit man, you goddamn nut job," Mario continued.

"Oh, relax," Nick said. "I missed that guy by at least two inches!"

"Here." Mario held the joint to Nick. "Take a hit, you need to chill out."

Nick hesitated.

"Come on man," Mario said. "Time to relax, it's been a rough day, right?"

Nick grabbed the joint.

"Alright," he said. "Everything's so fucked up already, it can't get any worse."

Nick took a good toke and held it a moment, then coughed, exhaling a large cloud of smoke.

"Damn, that's good shit," he managed to say between

coughs.

"Thai stick," Mario grinned. "Only the best."

They rode a few blocks without saying a word, passing the joint back and forth, smoking it down until it became just a roach. Mario smashed it on the back of a matchbook cover and dropped it in a tiny manila envelope.

"Hey," he said. "Rosalie was looking pretty smokin' today huh?"

"Yyyyyup," Nick nodded.

"Hadn't seen her in a while. Man, she's matured!"

"Yeah," Nick smiled. "She looked great."

Under the 15, and at a much slower pace, Nick passed the Double Luck Casino. He made a left, then pointed the car straight for a few blocks to East Ogden Avenue where he turned into the Cornetto Club Casino's parking garage. The sound of the Trans Am's headers reverberating off the walls was otherworldly. Its rumble felt so good that Nick revved it a couple more times.

"How's that?" he said to Mario.

"Nice."

Nick maneuvered the beast into his dad's reserved spot and shut the engine.

"Let's go," he said.

———

THE WEED had settled in. They stepped through the glass doors and into the hall that lead to the casino. Nick noticed the familiar smell of stale smoke and beer, probably from the well-worn and stained carpet. It'd been over a year since he'd last stepped foot in the casino. It was a strange place. Canned music played from the hallway's overhead speakers. Was it a homogenized remake of a Frank Sinatra song or the real thing? He couldn't tell. The muffled sounds of ringing bells and clinking coins dropping from slot machines became louder as they approached the casino floor. There were no voices though—it was like entering some kind of weird mechanical machine, running on automatic. A money machine. What a wicked place.

But Nick was anxious to see his father's office, to see where he had died, to see where he took his last breath, to see where he suffered his last humiliation. His dad, his dead, really gone dad.

He gulped hard and lifted his chin. They entered the smoke-filled casino floor. Bells rang from random directions seemingly continuously. A mix of elderly players sat here and there, hunched over, feeding their pennies or nickels mechanically into the machines, pulling the handles, getting another nickel or penny ready. Every so often the sound of coins dropping in quick succession onto the slot's metal trays signified a small jackpot. Ching ching ching ching, ding ding ding, ching ching ching, ding, ching ching, ding . . .

A lot of hoopla for perhaps 50 cents! Or maybe even a few dollars in nickels? Did these people not have a life? Why would someone do this, and in such a smoky place?

A young couple sat at a blackjack table, probably on their honeymoon, studying their cards, the dealer waiting patiently with his hand outstretched to the table. A group of seasoned middle-aged men in sports jackets stood leaning over a craps table, the last table still going, the last hangers-on, smoking and drinking, mumbling, shaking the dice, placing their bets.

"I don't know," Nick said. "This place, it's so fucking depressing, it's pathetic. How can people stand it here?"

"You got me," Mario said. "Maybe they're all in hell and don't even know it—like something out of the Twilight Zone."

"Shit." Nick took a deep breath. "Let's find Alex and see what he knows."

They walked from the main casino floor to the dismal poker area. It was quiet and dark there, almost as if the room had been shut down, except for two active poker tables packed with players, each illuminated brightly and each with a cloud of rising cigarette smoke that glowed amid the dead still and dark sea of thirty or so empty poker tables. The only noise was the faint ruffling of chip stacks at the two tables, and it sounded almost natural, like crickets in a forest.

This was serious business. None of the players even looked up or noticed Nick and Mario standing there. Across the room, near the exit to Freemont Street, a couple of security guards stood.

"There he is," Nick said.

Alex Rubinstein, a tall solidly-built man, had already seen them. They must have seemed out of place standing there looking around.

Alex walked over.

"Nick, how are you?" he said with a warm smile and hand extended.

"Hanging in there, otherwise good." Nick reached out and shook his hand.

"Hey, sorry about your dad. I still can't believe he's gone. It's not the same without him here."

"Yeah, I know," Nick said. "It's tough."

Nick motioned to Mario. "This is my friend, Mario, you remember him?"

"Sure." Alex shook Mario's hand.

"Well," Nick said. "I'm glad you're here. We want to check out my dad's office, see what it looks like. I got a key."

Alex shook his head, "Well it ain't no good because I changed the lock. But I'll let you in."

Nick knew Alex for practically his whole life, as Alex had worked for Jack for over 20 years. He was the head of security and was one of the few people his father had complete trust in.

"Sorry I missed the get-together at the house," Alex said. "But I know that Jack would have wanted me to stay here and keep an eye on things, especially now."

"Yeah," Nick nodded.

They headed to Jack's office.

Nick said, "So, how is everything going over here?"

Alex lowered his head and leaned toward Nick.

"Tense," he said almost in a whisper.

"Tense!" Mario blurted.

Alex put his hand on Mario's shoulder and gave him a stern look, signaling to be quiet.

"Things are quiet for now . . . tense, but quiet," Alex said. "A couple of FBI guys were here snooping around today, but that's nothing unusual. They try to blend in, but my guys know them. But things here are tense, you can feel it. Nobody knows what's going to happen now that Jack's gone. Claudio's cronies have been prowling around, like wolves."

"Really?" Nick said.

"Yup, and I don't like it," Alex said.

"Shit," Nick muttered.

"That's why I've kept Jack's office locked up. I haven't let anybody in there since he passed."

"Nobody?"

"Nobody, including Claudio. He wanted to get in but I told him it wasn't his office. He was pretty pissed off, but too bad. What's he gonna do?"

"Huh, well good job then!" Nick reached up and patted Alex on the back. "Don't let that fat fuck in there."

The entranceway to Jack's office was at the back of the cash cage, just past the three refrigerator-size safes and reception area. Two chairs sat on one side of the waiting area below a large black and white photograph of Jack, Lawrence, and Bill standing in the middle of Freemont Street, right in front of the casino.

Alex looked at the picture of Jack and shook his head. "It's just ain't the same without him!"

He frowned and handed his key to Nick.

"You have the honor of opening it," he said.

Nick took the key. A brass plaque on the door read *Chairman of the Board*. Nick turned the key and pushed the door open.

A wave of cool, musty air hit him. The room was pitch black except for a streak of light shining through a gap in the window curtains. It came from a streetlight just outside and it hit a shiny brass ashtray on Jack's desk like a spotlight, reflecting a shimmering gold pattern on the ceiling above.

"Where's the light?" Nick asked.

"It's over here somewhere." Alex stepped around Nick, into the darkened office.

Nick and Mario followed.

"Is this it?" Alex flicked a switch on the wall. Nothing happened. He flipped another one and the florescent ceiling lights stubbornly flickered and buzzed to a dull orange hue, barely illuminating the shadows of the objects on the desk. A column of dust particles began to rise in the golden light reflected off the ashtray.

Nick squinted at the desk. "Look at that!" he said.

"What?" Alex said.

"Whoa." Mario stepped back.

A floating amorphous apparition of innumerable dust particles sparkled in the golden light, rising up, taking shape and drifting over the desk.

"It shimmers!" Nick said.

"What?" Alex said. "The dust?"

"It's rising up above my dad's chair!"

"That's flipped out," Mario said. "It's like it just came to life".

"Yes." Nick's mouth hung opened. "All of a sudden. Like . . ."

All three men stood transfixed, watching.

"Like . . ." Nick repeated, "Like my dad did it. His spirit!

Nick stepped closer. "Dad!"

The illuminated shaft of dust particles seemed to rotate and slowly swirl. The men stood frozen. Cool, musty office air chilled their skin. Goosebumps rose on the back of Nick's neck.

"It's just a reflection," Alex said. "Where's the damn light?"

"Don't touch the lights!" Nick raised his hand. It wasn't real, was it? Was it his dad?

"Do you see it?" Nick said. "It's moving toward me!"

Nick stepped back.

"I see it!" Mario said.

"Dad!" Nick shouted.

Alex reached for the desk lamp and snapped it on. The light flashed, then a pop and the room was darkened again.

"Wait!" Nick pushed Alex's hand away. "What happened? Where is it, where'd it go?"

Suddenly the overhead florescent light flickered on all the way.

"It's gone," Mario said. "Just like that! Poof! Gone! Spooky shit man."

Nick gasped and fell back into a chair that faced the desk.

"Dad . . ." he mumbled and slunk down. A shiver ran through his body.

"See, it was nothing," Alex said.

"Wow," Mario shook his head. "I don't know man, I don't know."

"Well," Alex said. "What you see here is pretty much just as Jack left it."

"Huh?" Nick looked up at him.

"This is just how everything was, exactly as Jack left it."

Even with the light on, the office felt cold, the air still dank and stale. Nick rubbed his eyes, and took a deep breath. Alex pulled the heavy curtains open, then reached down and yanked open the window. Nick could swear he felt the air pressure release, as if the room had exhaled. It was surreal. Fresh, cool evening air rushed in. Nick wondered if he should have smoked that joint on the way over. He turned his gaze back to the desk.

Jack's large red leather armchair sat back a bit from the desk, askew, as if his father had just gotten up from it and walked away. On the desk sat several small bronze statues of cowboys on horses, and one larger bronze of a bull. Jack had an affinity for bulls, and even had bull horns mounted on the front of his white Cadillac convertible. A flat desk calendar sat across the center of the desk, with various papers tucked under the leather holders on either side. Some dates on the calendar were circled with arrows and notes scribbled in his dad's handwriting. A pen holder with a marble base and a bronze horse running in the wind, sat just above the calendar. A Las Vegas tourist cup held a bunch of pens and pencils next to the phone. And next it an intercom. The shiny bronze ash tray, with a half-smoked Partagas cigar still resting in it, sat next to the intercom. A wood-grained desktop Zenith AM/FM radio the size of a breadbox sat to the side. It had a fabric covered speaker and two knobs, one for the volume and one for the FM dial.

The wall to the right of the desk had a custom-made rosewood bookcase which had been built around an oil painting of Jack and Frances. The portrait was bright and sunny as if it were painted on a summer day. Jack wore a blue cowboy-style jacket, a white ten-gallon Stetson hat, white cowboy shirt with copper Indian head penny buttons, and a leather bolo tie with a silver steer clasp. Frances stood next to him, her hair puffed up with short banana curls flowing from the side and front. She wore a pink dress with ruffles and lace. In the background, a gazebo with white and purple flowers running up the sides to its top offset a bright pastel blue sky.

On the shelf below the painting sat a real pair of

mounted bull horns that stretched half the length of the bookcase. A few books had been placed on the other shelves, along with more cowboy, horse, bull and Indian knickknacks and sculptures. There were also 5x7 and 8x10 family photographs in stand-up frames.

Nick glanced at two large photographs on the other wall: one of the Cornetto Club Casino, probably taken just after Jack had opened it, and one of the building when it had been the old El Dorado Club, before Jack purchased it.

Nick sat up in the chair and glanced at the floor. He noticed something under the desk. It was in a shadow, next to one of the legs. Nick leaned down and picked it up. A cigar butt. He took a closer look.

"What's that?" Alex said.

Nick held it out to Alex.

"It was on the rug under the desk," he said.

"Let's see." Alex took his flashlight from his belt.

"Padron," he said. "Who smokes Padron's?"

"Hmm, don't know," Nick said. "My dad always smoked Partagas."

Mario shrugged his shoulders. "Don't know either. But, whoever was in this room with your dad probably smoked this cigar."

"Yeah," Nick said. "Alex, do you have something we can wrap this in? I want to hold onto this, as evidence."

"I can hold it if you like," Alex said.

"No, I got it," Nick said.

"Sure." Alex shrugged and handed Nick a neatly folded handkerchief.

Nick carefully wrapped the Padron cigar butt and put it in his pocket.

"Anything else under the desk?" Alex said.

"Let's take a look," Nick said.

Alex knelt down and pointed his flashlight under the desk. Nick knelt too. There were some bits of ashes next to a burnt spot in the carpet.

"Is this where the cigar was sitting?" Alex asked.

"Yup, it was right there," Nick said. "It burned a hole in the carpet?"

"Yeah, good thing it didn't burn the whole place down." Alex pointed the flashlight around under the desk then stopped and looked at one of the legs.

"The desk is off kilter." He turned to Nick. "It looks like it was jarred forward a bit."

"What do you mean?"

"Take a look at the indentation in the carpet where the desk used to sit. It's been shifted. Something happened here."

"And look at this," Mario said from above. "The sculptures were also moved. Look at these dust shadows."

Alex and Nick stood up. There were faint dust outlines that revealed where the sculptures and the pen holder had usually sat.

"Something definitely went on here," Alex said.

"Were you here working the night my dad passed away?" Nick asked.

"Actually," Alex said. "I was off that day."

"You were off?"

"Yeah, I was at home watching *Johnny Carson*, and I get a call from Frances asking me if I know where Jack is. She said he was supposed to be home a few hours earlier but hadn't showed up. She tried calling his office but kept getting a busy signal, so she just figured he was on a long call. But an hour and a half later, she starts to get really worried. That's when she called me."

"So what'd you do?"

"What'd I do? I drove down here right away. I went straight to Jack's office. But the door was locked. I figured he probably left and maybe he left the phone off the hook, or something. But of course I unlocked the door anyway, just to make sure. Then I see him on the floor, lying right there."

Alex pointed down next to the desk by Jack's chair.

"He's lying right there, practically under his chair, and the phone is still in his hand. I thought maybe he was passed out drunk, I was hoping that, even though I know that ain't like him, but that's what I thought—or hoped. I don't know."

Alex paused and shook his head.

"I called his name and shook him, then shook him harder. Nothing! I felt his neck. His skin was cold. I kept shaking him, but nothing. He was gone!"

Alex looked at Nick and Mario with wide eyes.

"Le'me sit down," he said.

"Take it easy," Nick said. "Have a seat."

Alex continued, "I took the phone from his hand and hung it up. It rang immediately. I had just set it down and boom, it starts ringing. I knew it was Frances. I had to pick it up."

"Jack?" she said.

"'Frances, it's Alex', I said barely able to speak. 'Something's happened here. I'm sorry . . . he's. . . gone . . .' I heard her gasp and I started crying. Then I heard something like a thump on the line and thought she must have dropped the phone. But I could hear her sobbing in the background, and I kept repeating her name but she didn't respond.

Eventually, I had to hang up."

Alex looked up at Nick.

"I'm sorry," he said.

Nick felt tears coming to his eyes but held them back.

"So . . ." Nick stammered, "he was right here?"

"Yeah," Alex said.

"He fell off the chair?" Mario asked.

Alex nodded. "I think so."

Nick took a deep breath and tried to regain his composure.

"And the room was like it is now," Mario said. "Like there wasn't even a struggle?"

"Yes, it looked like Jack just keeled over while he was working. Like he just had a heart attack or something."

Nick put his hand on Alex's shoulder.

"He was on the floor," Nick said. "With the phone still in his hand. And nothing fell off the desk?"

Alex thought for a moment. "Yes, he just had the phone in his hand. I didn't see anything on the floor. I would've noticed it."

"And the phone cord, stretched across the desk?" Nick asked.

"Yeah."

"So, Dad falls with the phone in his hand, the cord stretching across half desk and nothing gets knocked off, or even out of place? Doesn't seem to make sense to me."

Nick considered the desk again. The phone sat on the far side, where it would have been on Jack's right. If the cord had been stretched across the desk with the phone in Jack's hand, on the floor on the left, then it should have knocked something down. The cup with the pens and pencils?

"You're sure it looked like this?" Nick asked Alex.

"Yes, it did. This is exactly what it looked like. I didn't touch anything. There was nothin' on the floor, and I didn't let nobody in here either. This is what it was like, just like this."

Nick stared at the desk and rubbed his chin. "It don't make sense. It just doesn't."

CHAPTER 9

I
t had been a few days since the funeral, but Nick still dressed in black. He sat in the living room at the white grand piano, his head slung down. He pressed a single bass note, holding it down, his foot on the pedal, until the tone's very last whisper faded away.

From the corner of his eye he saw his mom approach from the kitchen.

"What is it?" Frances put her hand on his shoulder.

He didn't answer, but turned and lowered his head into his hands.

She rubbed his shoulders.

"Please." He flinched and looked up.

"What is with you?" she said. "It's like you're still in mourning, still wearing black, moping around the house."

Nick turned away, his eyes watery.

"I understand your pain," she said and sat next to him.

He felt her hand on his shoulder again.

"I know it's rough," she said. "But it's *over*, Dad's in a better place now. He walked this wonderful earth with us, but now he's gone . . . and we'll all be gone someday, but that also means we'll all be together someday, too."

She massaged his shoulders and neck.

"I don't know," Nick mumbled.

"Don't know? What don't you know?" she said. "Why are you acting this way?"

Nick shot her a piercing glance.

"*Acting?* Is that what you think I'm doing? He's gone now—and I didn't even see him. I didn't even say goodbye before I went back to school."

Tears pooled in his eyes.

"I should have been here," his voice quivered. "I should have *freakin'* been here."

"Look," Frances said. "Don't beat yourself up over this. It's not good to go on like that—to dwell on something you can't change. It'll drive you crazy. Look at me, I've tried to move on. Dad would want it that way."

Frances stood up. Nick's fingers struck a few random, discordant notes.

"This is a natural thing," she rubbed his shoulder again. "It's over, he's moved on. We'll all be together with him someday."

"Natural?" Nick said. "There's nothing natural about it. Don't you see? It's wrong, it shouldn't have happened and he shouldn't be dead. It wasn't his time!"

Nick pushed her hand away, stood and turned to leave.

"Get some rest," Frances said.

Nick headed across the living room to go up to his room just as Anne Marie entered, the two nearly colliding.

"Sorry!" Nick stepped to the side.

Her breath smelled of alcohol, as usual.

"What's with him?" Anne Marie asked.

"If only I knew," his mom said. "Another one of his funks, I guess."

"Hey, Nick!" Anne Marie shouted after him. "What's up?"

Nick lay in his bed staring at the day-glow green stars and planets on the ceiling.

The door opened slowly. It was Anne Marie.

"Can't you leave me alone?" he said.

"Nope," Anne Marie hopped in next to him. "Move over!"

Anne Marie pressed against him but he only gave an inch.

"What poster's that?" she said.

"Which one?" Nick lifted his head to see.

There were two posters on the wall, one of an astronaut holding up a scientific instrument while standing in bright sunlight on the gray dusty landscape of the moon, and the other, all black except for the outline of a pyramid or prism in the center with a thin beam of white light shining up into it and a colorful rainbow splitting out the other side.

"The black one with the pyramid and colors, what's that?" Anne Marie said.

"Pink Floyd. It's their new one, it's called Dark Side of the Moon. It's pretty cool, huh? The album's really good too. It's spacy. You have to smoke a doob before you listen to it."

"Cool," she said.

They lay there a moment, staring at the ceiling stars.

"Shit," she said. "Why can't we get away from here? Far away, like that guy on the moon? Our troubles would be over. This place is so messed up."

"Yup," Nick said. "Everything is certainly fucked. With Dad gone and Mom just doing her thing. I don't know why she likes Claudio so much. He's nothin' but trouble."

"I don't like him either," Anne Marie said. "But what can we do? It's all fucked up, the world is fucked up. Let's go have a drink. Come on, let's have a glass of wine and relax."

"No," Nick said. "I'll pass."

"Ah, Nick, you need to loosen up. You're all bottled up, too tense. You gotta chill out. Have a drink, man. It's not cool to be so uptight. You gotta release that shit before you explode. Do some Transcendental Meditation or something. You gotta let it go."

"And bury myself in booze like you're doing?"

"No," Anne Marie whispered. "It's more like a warmth that decends over my head. I can feel it, soothing and relaxing. It flows down over me, protecting me—from all the bullshit."

She took a deep breath.

"Look," she said. "How do you think I feel? I'm in just as much pain as you. What am *I* supposed to do? Who's helping me? Nobody. It hurts me, too. But Pops wouldn't want us hurting, would he? No, of course not. He liked his whisky too, right?"

"You're burying yourself," Nick said. "Numbing yourself. You've given up. Just when Mom needs your help, you're drowning yourself in booze and who knows what else."

"Mom doesn't need my help. She's fine. She wouldn't even want my help. At least I'm not all uptight like you. Why not be happy? Instead of being a drag and a downer like you are?"

"Can you leave me alone?" Nick shoved her off the bed. "That's all I ask. Just leave me alone."

Anne Marie slid to the floor.

"That wasn't very nice," she said.

"I didn't ask you to come in here."

"Fine! Be alone!" She stood up. "I'm getting a glass of wine!"

She left and slammed the door after her.

Nick closed his eyes and pressed his face into the pillow. Darkness settled in all around.

———

LATER THAT NIGHT Nick lay in bed sweating, and turning from one side to the other. His thoughts raced on and on and round and round in a torturous, ceaseless parade. Claudio, his dad, his dad's office, his dad on the floor, Claudio, did he really do it? His mom, her chumminess with Claudio, his hand on her leg, his cronies, their game room celebration, the casino, the office, his dad, the bolo tie, and on and on.

Minutes passed into hours. Finally, Nick found himself lying down on the warm desert sand, the weeds tumbling by, a cool night above, a crisp canopy of stars. Millions of sparkling pinpoints of light, dazzlingly alive against the velvety blackness . . . the cool, clear blackness . . . stillness . . . not a sound . . . and a super bright star . . . a blazing, blue one . . . Dad's light . . . warmth raining down . . . a blessing . . . Dad's blessing.

But that feeling of benevolent warmth lasted only for what seemed like a fleeting moment before the brightness of the day lit up the room and Nick squinted open his eyes. He sighed and pulled the pillow over his face.

CHAPTER 10

When Nick walked into the kitchen, Frances and Anne Marie were at the kitchen table drinking coffee and smoking cigarettes.

"At least you're not wearing black this morning," Frances said.

"Yeah."

"How 'bout some coffee?"

"Sure."

Frances took a mug from the cabinet shelf.

"You know," Nick said. "I don't think he just died."

Frances fumbled the mug, clunking it on the counter top. "Sorry. What are you talking about now?"

"I don't know, I've been thinking about it and I just think there's more to Dad's death than we know."

"Oh brother," Anne Marie said.

The doorbell buzzed.

"I'll get it." Anne Marie stood.

"We'll talk about this later." His mom frowned.

Nick shrugged and sat down.

"Talk about it now," Nick mumbled. "Talk about it later . . . frigg's the difference?

Anne Marie came back into the kitchen and announced, "It's Lawrence."

Lawrence strode in holding a white pastry box.

Frances smiled, "Lawrence, you're just in time for coffee."

"Perfect, I've got some delicious butter rolls,

doughnuts, and crullers here."

"Sounds good." Frances grabbed another mug from the cabinet.

"Nick, how are you?" Lawrence said.

"I'm OK." Nick looked away.

"He's in a funk," Anne Marie said.

"A funk?" Nick glared at his sister.

"Yeah, you're in a freakin' funk," she said. "You're all *funked* up, admit it."

"I guess we're all funked up then," Lawrence said. "I miss your dad terribly too, but what can we do?"

Anne Marie took a last drag of her cigarette then pressed it into the ashtray and reached for the box of pastries.

"Thanks," Nick stirred his coffee. "But that's not it."

Lawrence gave him a quizzical look.

"If I thought he died naturally, then that'd be fine. But I don't think that's what happened. I don't think he went, just like that, all of a sudden, *naturally*."

"It was a heart attack." Frances tapped her cigarette against the edge of the ashtray. "That's what they said."

"It could happen to anyone," Lawrence agreed.

"But he wasn't that old, and he was healthy. It's just too fishy," Nick said.

"What do you think happened?" Lawrence sat down.

"Well," Nick said. "I don't know exactly—I just have a bad feeling."

"A bad feeling? Like he was killed or something?"

"*Lawrence*," Frances shot him a look.

"We gotta have out with it Fran." Lawrence looked back at Nick. "What do you think?"

Nick shrugged, "I don't know."

Anne Marie grabbed a glazed doughnut, "Who would murder Pops?"

"Lots of people, maybe," Nick said.

"Like who?" Frances placed a cup of coffee in front of Lawrence.

Lawrence studied Nick, "So . . . you think someone might have really murdered Jack?"

"I don't know," Nick said. "Maybe. There would be a lot to gain."

"How so?"

"Well, the casino."

"But your family owns the casino."

"Yeah, but who's gonna run it now? Who's gonna be in charge and, *have control over it?*"

"Bill and I are running it," Lawrence said.

"But who's going to step into Dad's shoes? Who's gonna be the boss, the head of the casino?"

"I don't know," Lawrence said. "But does it matter? It practically runs itself. Why would anything change? It's up to your mom if she wants to appoint me or Bill. She's the owner now."

"Exactly." Nick turned to his mom. "And have you thought about it yet?"

Frances seemed taken aback by the directness of the question and took a quick drag from her cigarette.

"Look," she said. "It's a beautiful morning. We shouldn't be discussing business right now. Have a donut."

"Why not?" Nick said. "I'm not allowed to talk? This is important. I can't sleep thinking about what might have happened to Dad. And what might happen now with the casino and everything he struggled for."

"Rest assured," his mom said. "Nothing's going to happen. You're getting all worked up over nothing."

"He's uptight," Anne Marie said.

"What if Claudio gets more involved?" Nick blurted and noticed his mother actually flinch a bit.

"Claudio's not getting involved," Lawrence chuckled. "In fact, Bill and I are going to reduce his role over there. He's a loose cannon — too unpredictable."

Lawrence turned to Frances, "Right?" he said.

"Look." she stood up. "Can we talk about something else? This isn't the time or place to be discussing business."

"Huh?" Nick said. "But we're already discussing it! Can't we just finish the conversation? If I've got nothing to worry about then tell us what your plans are."

"Leave her alone," Anne Marie said. "Why are you always so paranoid?"

"What?" Nick said.

"Look," Lawrence said. "Let's drop it."

Lawrence motioned to Frances to sit back down.

She shook her head and smiled, "It's OK. I'll tell you what I'm thinking. Nick is right, I might as well clear the air now."

She sighed, sat down and took a drag from her cigarette, then smashed it out in the ashtray. Nick waited, his attention focused on her as she gathered her thoughts. Lawrence sipped his coffee and Anne Marie broke off another piece of doughnut.

"Well," Frances finally said. "I was going to let you know as soon as I work out the details, but I might as well tell you now, if you all insist."

"Tell us what?" Lawrence put his coffee down.

Frances looked at him.

"Claudio's going to run it."

"What?" Lawrence raised his eyebrows and jerked his head back. "Claudio?"

"Fuck . . ." Nick slapped his hand on the table.

"But we were just going to reduce his responsibilities at the casino and even demote him!" Lawrence said. "How can you let him run it now?"

"Because," Frances said. "He's got more experience than anyone else and I'm convinced he'll do a great job. He worked very closely with Jack, so he knows the operation well."

"Holy shit," Nick said. "What about Lawrence here? Or Bill?"

"I've already made up my mind," Frances said firmly.

"Yeah, but Claudio? Frances be sensible," Lawrence pleaded. "You know Jack never liked working with him."

"I hope you're not offended," Frances said. "I told you I didn't want to talk about it now."

"Oh my God," Anne Marie said.

"Look," Frances said. "Strategically, I think it would be for the best. You and Bill will keep your present responsibilities. You continue to be in charge of operations, Bill stays in charge of accounting, and Claudio oversees it all."

"He'll be my boss?" Lawrence said incredulously.

"Yes, he's got the clout and influence to run things best. He'll be able to grow the business even more than Jack did. He's got lots of experience in Vegas and is well-connected."

Lawrence stared at her in disbelief.

Nick shook his head, "This is exactly what I mean.

Now what?"

"You know," Frances said. "Sometimes Jack was too nice to people. I think it slowed things down and he lost opportunities—I mean he missed a lot of opportunities."

"What?" Nick said. "Lost opportunities? Dad freakin' started the whole thing and it was his smarts that made it so great. What do you mean he lost opportunities? Where?"

"I don't know," Frances said. "But things have changed. Vegas is changing now. It's growing fast. I want Claudio to run it because his guys are out there and really know what's going on, and nobody dares to mess with them. If I put you in charge," she looked at Lawrence, "or Bill, or even you, Nick, Claudio could cause plenty of trouble. And I don't need trouble right now. I want things to run smoothly, without any problems. I want the business to grow and don't want us to be left behind. We have a golden opportunity. Don't you want to be part of that?"

"Yeah, but Claudio!" Nick stood up. "Are you crazy? It'd be better if a *fucking* chimpanzee ran the place."

"Nick . . . that's enough!" Frances said.

"What about me running it?" Nick said. "I could do it. Shit, I even went to college."

"You're still in college though," his mom said. "Don't you want to at least finish and graduate? Also you never wanted to be involved when your father was alive. Why would you want to be now?

"Now's different," Nick said. "And I'd do it just for Dad because that's what he wanted. Why do you think he gave me this bolo tie?" Nick grabbed the silver dollar of the bolo, "He wanted to pass the torch to me. He told me that."

"It's not so easy as you think," she said. "And, I want

you to finish school, then you can come back and help at the casino. You can't just quit school now."

"Who said I'm quitting? I'll just take a leave of absence for a semester."

Frances shook her head and Nick glared at her.

"Mom," Anne Marie said. "I think you should give Nick a chance."

"Look, you can't just step into it," Frances said. "How are you going to learn to deal with all the ins and outs? All the people? The tough people? Those problem people that caused so much trouble for Jack?"

"Nick might be better than Claudio," Lawrence said. "And we could bring him up to speed pretty quickly, and protect him too."

"Look," Frances said to Nick. "If you'd like, I'll make you Claudio's assistant. You can be his right-hand man."

"What, and shine his shoes?" Nick said. "This is crazy, who even gets along with Claudio? Do you have any idea what you're doing?"

Frances bit her lip. "I do," she said sternly. "It's my decision and for now it stands."

Nick shook his head and Lawrence let out a sigh.

"And," Frances said smugly. "Claudio and I get along fine."

"Well, I certainly don't like him at all," Anne Marie said.

"That slime-ball will milk us dry," Nick smirked.

Frances' face suddenly lit up. She was looking past Nick and into the living room.

"Well, speak of the devil," she stood up.

Nick spun around to see.

It was Claudio, standing there in his bathrobe! He seemed as surprised to see them as they were to see him.

"I was wondering when you were going to get up." Frances walked over to him. "We were just talking about you."

"Oh?" Claudio smiled. "Hope you only talked about the good parts."

"Don't worry," Frances said. "It was only the best."

Nick's head was spinning.

"What's for breakfast?" Claudio kissed Frances' cheek.

"What the hell's going on here?" Nick took a step toward Claudio. "How'd you get in here?"

"Take it easy," Claudio held his hands up. "Nothing's going on. I just woke up, that's all. And now I'd like a cup of coffee. And breakfast too."

"What?" Nick said.

"Hey," Lawrence stood. "Take it easy. I'm sure there's some logical explanation."

Nick's eyes burned at Claudio. Frances grabbed Claudio's arm and pulled close against him.

"What the . . ." Nick said.

"Oh my God." Anne Marie rolled her eyes. "You slept over?"

Frances looked at Claudio.

"We should tell them," she whispered.

"Tell us what?" Nick glared.

Frances nodded to Claudio.

"What exactly *are* you up to Claudio?" Lawrence took a step closer. "Yes, please tell us."

"I'm ducking for cover!" Anne Marie said.

"Calm down everyone," Frances said. "I invited him over."

"Cool it," Claudio said to Nick and Lawrence.

"Cool it?" Nick was incredulous.

"We have an announcement to make," Frances said.

"Yes," Claudio said. "Take a seat."

"I'll sit when I'm ready," Nick glared at him.

"Sure." Claudio placed his arm around Frances.

"Well," Frances said. "This is as good a time as any to tell you."

Nick's thoughts raged so fiercely he wasn't even sure what Frances was saying. Frances looked nervously at Claudio.

"We're engaged," Claudio said.

"Engaged?" Nick said. "In what?"

"You know my boy . . ." Claudio chuckled. "To be married!"

"Isn't it wonderful?" Frances smiled.

"Aaahhh . . . shit!" Nick fell back in his chair and grabbed his leg in agony.

"Oh!" Frances said. "Are you OK? What happened? Rub it!"

"Ah shit!" he grimaced. "I don't know. It's my leg, it's knotting up, a muscle cramp. Shit!"

"Rub it!" Frances said.

"What?" Anne Marie said to Claudio. "Did you say you're engaged to my mom?"

"Yes, we're engaged," Claudio repeated more firmly this time. "To get married, that's what I said. Frances and I are getting married."

"What?" Nick scowled at Claudio.

Lawrence sat down, all the while focused on Frances, and said, "That's ridiculous. I can't believe it. Why would you do that?"

"Because we're in love," Frances said.

"That's nuts." Nick rubbed his leg. "Only a few weeks after Dad passed away? My god, he's still warm in the ground. The damn worms haven't even gotten him yet, and you're getting married? Already? Just like that!"

"We didn't want to wait," Frances said.

"Yes, we're getting married in three weeks, on June 21st in fact, the start of summer. It's a Thursday. That'll be enough time for old Jack to settle into the ground, don't you think?" Claudio smirked. "Now, where's my cup of coffee?"

Nick pushed himself up and stormed past Claudio, avoiding his glance.

"I can't believe this shit," he mumbled as he left the room.

CHAPTER 11

Nick drove to meet Mario at the Star Diner, a neighborhood favorite. He thought that maybe there was an infinitesimally small chance he could be wrong about Claudio. Maybe he hadn't killed his dad. Maybe Nick was just imagining things—how many times had he jumped to conclusions before? And been dead wrong? It was crazy, he knew, but just for the hell of it, he wanted to play this through in his head. Maybe Claudio actually did love his mom. Maybe his mom was right and Claudio really was the best man to run the casino. He kept people in line, after all. Yeah, he's not the smartest guy, and he's a thug, but he gets things done. He's damn effective. Right?

Wrong. He's a fat fucking slime-ball, a snake. Not to be trusted. That's what he is, *a fat fuck!*

Black Sabbath's "Paranoid" came on the radio.

Nick turned up the volume and hit the accelerator. He shook his head and tapped the steering wheel as the car entered beast mode. If Claudio really did it, he was going to kill him. That was that. He would exact his revenge, plain and simple, one way or another. Claudio would be a dead man.

At the diner, in mid chew of his lumpy hamburger, Nick mumbled to Mario, "This is a total bummer."

Mario looked at him, "I'm with you, man, but you're not gonna let him get away with this, are you? You're not gonna let him ruin your life, man, right?"

Nick grabbed a grease-saturated french fry.

"I don't know, man," he said, waving the fry.

"Don't know?" Mario said.

Nick shoved the fry in his mouth and devoured it.

Mario stared at him, waiting patiently for his reply.

Nick licked his fingers and wiped them with his napkin. "Look," he finally said. "I just don't know. I mean yeah, he probably did it. Ninety nine percent he did it. But what if he didn't? What if we're wrong? Nobody actually saw him do it, right?"

"I saw him."

"But that was afterwards."

"What about their little celebration in the game room?"

"Maybe they were just celebrating that my dad died. And not that Claudio killed him."

"No way, man," Mario said. "Wake up, Nick. That guy is guilty. I know it. And what about your dad's office being all messed up? What about that? I think you're trying to find an excuse for that schmuck."

Nick took a sip of his coke. "I have an idea. A way to test Claudio, to see if he really did it."

"What?" Mario said. "How we gonna do that? Ask him nicely? *Claudio, did you do it? Pease tell us. Will you swear on your mother's grave?*"

"No, of course not."

"Then how?"

"Ever heard of *Hamlet*?"

"Hamlet?"

"From Shakespeare, man. You never heard of *Hamlet*?"

Mario smirked, "Yeah, I heard of that guy. *To be or not*

to be and all that crap?"

"Yeah, all that crap. It's a play, a Shakespeare play."

"So what's that got to do with anything?"

"Listen." Nick waved a fry at Mario.

Mario shifted uncomfortably. "You're scaring me man. Are you nuts?"

"Quiet," Nick demanded. "What we do is we trap him."

"Trap him?"

"Yes, just like in the damn play," Nick said. "It's really weird, but in the play, the main character, *Hamlet,* comes home from school—just like I did, right after his dad also just died. Then he discovers that his uncle killed his father, just like we're finding out, that Claudio probably killed my dad. It's fucking weird man, his uncle marries his mom right after his dad is buried, just like Claudio is doing!"

"What?" Mario looked confused. "You're insane."

Nick leaned forward.

"Claudio announced this morning that he's marrying my mom."

"Get the fuck outta here!"

"No shit," Nick said. "It's totally fucked up."

"What? That's crazy."

Now Nick had Mario's full attention.

"Yup, so here's my plan. We find Claudio, and you tell him about the story of *Hamlet.* I'll bet he never even heard of it, and when he does, if he's guilty, he'll make the connection and freak out. Simple as that. We'll know from his reaction if he did it."

"How'm I gonna do that?" Mario said. "All I know is *'To be or not to be'.*"

"I'll help you," Nick said.

"And how we even gonna bring up the subject of *Hamlet* with Claudio?"

"No problem. I think Claudio and my mom went out shopping this morning. We go back to the house, and when they return, we'll be ready for them. I'll give you a copy of the book—I have it in my room. You just walk in with it in your hand, like you're reading it, and lay it on the kitchen table. As long as the doofus is sitting there, he'll ask you what it is. Then you launch right into how great you think it is and start telling the story. Then we'll see if he flips out!"

"Why don't you do it?" Mario objected. "I don't even know the story."

"I can't," Nick said. "I need to be carefully watching him for his reaction. I can't do that if I'm telling the story."

Mario thought a moment.

"Well alright, but we'll have to rehearse it," he said. "The whole thing, a few times."

"No problem," Nick said. "It'll be easy to remember."

"Yeah, sure." Mario seemed uncertain.

"Don't worry," Nick said. "You can do it."

"OK . . ."

"Hey, if that son-of-a-bitch did it, then he's dead meat."

"I'm with you, man," Mario said, and high-fived him.

"Good," Nick said. "And listen, one more thing. I need you to come with me to the casino, to check the vault. But you can't tell anyone, you dig? You've got to keep it a secret. Can you do that?"

"Of course man, what are you kidding? I'm solid, man."

"Good, I need to check it out and I want you to see it too, like a witness. You know, just in case anything happens to it, or to me. Understand?"

"Alright, sure, no problem. Whatever you need, man."

"There's a lot of coins and silver." Nick lowered his voice. "A shitload. Remember the other day at the house we were all talking about how my dad hoarded silver coins?"

"Yeah."

"Well, it's all in the vaults, in the basement of the casino. But I haven't seen it in years. I have to make sure that Claudio and his pack of snakes don't touch it."

"But how we gonna get in? You got the combo?" Mario said.

"Yeah, I got it."

"Alright." Mario smiled. "Let's do it then."

"Good."

"I always wondered if those treasure rumors were true," Mario added.

Nick wiped his mouth with his napkin. "It's not exactly treasure," he said. "But you'll see."

———

MARIO FOLLOWED CLOSELY behind Nick's white Trans Am in his own red Ford Mustang. At the casino they quickly found Alex who escorted them over to the cash cage.

"Nick!" one of the cashiers said. "Well, look at you, haven't seen you here in ages." She was an older lady whose hair was stiff with hairspray and face pasted with makeup. "So sorry about your dad, we all miss him so much. It's so sad."

"Thanks," Nick said. "Good to see you."

"Are you going to be taking over?" she asked. "We're all on pins and needles because nobody seems to know what's going on."

"Sit tight," Nick said. "You girls are the best cashiers in all of Vegas. Everything's gonna be fine. Don't worry, nobody's losing their job."

Alex led the way through the short hallway to the elevator. It went only one flight down to the basement vaults and was used to move carts full of chips, coins, cash, or silver. Next to the elevator, a locked door led to a stairway, which also led down to the vaults. Alex unlocked the elevator control and they all squeezed inside.

The doors opened to an empty room. The heavy steel door of the walk-in vault was located on the far wall.

"Wow, that looks like a bank vault," Mario said.

"Come on," Nick said and led the way.

It took a few tries to enter the combination, but the vault lock finally clicked open and Nick pulled down on the handle. The massive door slowly swung open.

"Let's take a look," he said.

"I've got to get back on the floor," Alex said and headed for the stairs.

Nick stepped into the vault first and flicked on the lights. The air was cool and musty. The vault was large, at least fifteen feet wide by twenty feet long. Rows of carts held locked Plexiglas boxes full of neatly stacked chips. A path between the chip carts ran the length of the vault like the narrow aisle of an airliner. There were also shelves along the left and right walls, also full of racks of chips, each in locked

Plexiglas cases.

"This is the main casino safe," Nick said. "But we want the other safe."

"The other safe?"

"The family safe, at the back of this one."

"A vault within a vault?" Mario asked.

"Yeah, heavy security."

Nick made his way up the aisle to the back of the vault and to the family vault door. He took the piece of paper from his wallet that he had scribbled the combination on. Alternating glances from the paper back to the dial, he turned it right, then left, then right, back and forth. He yanked down on the latch handle. It clicked open.

Nick pulled the heavy door open, then anxiously stepped in. He flicked on the lights and stood a moment. It wasn't what he expected and he didn't immediately comprehend what he was seeing.

"Holy shit." His jaw dropped.

"You mean *holy freakin' shit*, man." Mario held his palm out. "Slap me five."

"Motherfucker!" Nick said and wacked Mario's hand. "Look at all of this. Can you imagine?"

This vault was even larger than the first, maybe thirty feet long. The air had a distinct metallic tinge to it. Another airline aisle-wide path led from the door to the back wall. It was defined by neat stacks of silver bars, carts packed with racks of casino chips stacked high, bags of coins piled on heavy metal shelves, and stacks of rolled coins, all on metal shelves that reached to the ceiling. The vault was jam-packed.

Nick stepped slowly, gazing at the incredible treasure before him. A few steps in, and it suddenly occurred to him that maybe he shouldn't have brought Mario there. He hadn't realized the extent of the hoard—it had obviously grown since his dad had last shown it to him years before. How long ago was that? Five, six years? Seven? Nick couldn't remember, but he had been much smaller then and the whole vault seemed smaller too. Could his dad have expanded it? One thing was for sure, Nick had no idea his dad could have squirreled away so much. And what was it? All silver, coins and chips? Or maybe even some gold too?

Did his mom even know the extent of what was down here? As for Mario, it was too late, Nick would have to hope for the best and just trust him.

"Look at all this shit!" Mario said. "This is fucking incredible."

"Yeah," Nick said. "There's a lot of stuff here. I had no idea."

He slid his hand across an opened canvas sack full of what appeared to be silver dollars.

"There must be millions here," Mario said. "Tons!"

Nick glanced at Mario, then back across the stuffed room. It could easily be worth tens of millions of dollars or maybe even hundreds of millions. Who knows?

"It's all here, I guess," Nick said. "That's all I wanted to find out, that it was still here."

"It's here, baby," Mario said. "It sure is here. Man-oh-man, baby. It's fucking here."

Nick snapped around and grabbed Mario's shoulders.

"Hey, man. Take it easy, you look fucking crazed."

"Listen," Nick gritted his teeth. "This can't get out. This is a fucking secret, understand? The biggest fucking secret of your life!"

"Nick, man, no problem. No fucking *problemo*. I'm not going to say anything to anyone . . . ever."

"*Ever?*"

"Yeah, *ever*. Shit, you invited me down here, I respect that. There's no way I would ever say anything to anyone."

"Never *fucking* ever. I will kill you. I will cut your heart out and chop your fucking dick off."

"Yo, man, no problem. I'm telling you, why would I ever say anything to anyone? Don't fucking worry about it." Mario pushed away. "I'm solid. I'm telling you, you're like my brother, I'd never turn my back on you!"

"Shit," Nick said "I'm sorry . . ."

"No problem. You're a brother to me. Got it?"

"Yeah, thanks, man," Nick said. "When this is all over I promise to take care of you. I fucking promise. You have my word."

"You have my word, too," Mario said.

"Alright then," Nick slapped his back. "Let's get out of here."

Mario turned to lead the way out, but after a few steps Nick stopped and called to Mario, "Wait!"

Nick looked around, then squeezed past some pallets stacked high with large silver bars. He headed over to one of the shelves that lined the wall. It held loose stacks of chips. Nick grabbed a few green chips and examined them, reading their value printed below his dad's portrait. He put them back and grabbed a yellow chip, examined it too, and put it back. Then he grabbed a black chip with a gold striped edge—it read $5,000. He grabbed a handful of these.

"OK," Nick smiled and held one up to show Mario. "I'll cash one of these chips and then we can go relax a bit."

"Alright," Mario squinted at the chip. "I always loved that your dad is on the chips."

"Yup," Nick said. "Always the promoter."

He stuffed the chips in his pocket and they headed out.

CHAPTER 12

Mario held a dog-eared copy of *Hamlet*.

"He should be here soon," Nick said.

Mario stopped at a random page and studied it.

"How can you read this shit?" he said.

"What? What do you mean?"

"I can't even understand what they're saying. Here, what's this?"

Mario puffed out his chest, held the book out with one hand, and waved his other hand dramatically in the air as if he were on a stage playing to an audience. He lowered his voice and read from the book.

> *Here is your husband, like a mildewed ear*
> *Blasting his wholesome brother. Have you eyes?*
> *Could you on this fair mountain leave to feed*
> *And batten on this moor? Ha, have you eyes?*

"What the hell does that mean?" Mario glared at his friend. "Can *you* tell what it's saying? *'Batten on this moor'*? Is that even English? A mildewed ear?"

"I know, it's a little weird." Nick said. "But that's how people talked a few hundred years ago. Maybe hundreds of years from now, people will have no idea what we're saying either."

"Ha! I'm sure they'll have no problem with my simple words."

"Who knows? Anyway, in that part, I think Hamlet is

yelling at his mother because she's married the brother who is such a damn louse. He's asking her why she can't see that he's such a loser."

Nick grabbed the book from Mario's hands.

"I think," he continued, pointing at the words on the page, "'feed and *batten on this moor'*, I think that means to shack up with and latch onto, and especially with such a rotten person."

"Huh." Mario nodded. "Like your mom and Claudio. Your dad was such a great guy, and now your mom is falling for such a fat fuck."

"Yes, unfortunately," Nick said. "That's exactly right. It's freaky how similar the story is."

"No shit."

"Now, you got it straight?"

"Yeah sure, I think so—or close enough," Mario said, still holding the thin book in his hand. "The guy sees a ghost who tells him that he was murdered with poison poured in his ear by the kid's lousy uncle, and . . .'"

"No," Nick said. "Not poison. That's in the play, but we need to change that to suffocation—like a forced heart attack. In fact, say that. Say *'suffocated, to make it look like a heart attack'*."

Mario held his hand out, "The prince killed him by suffocation—made it look like a heart attack!"

"No, not the Prince. It was the brother. The broth . . ."

The kitchen side door swung open and Frances walked in carrying two armfuls of groceries. Mario threw the paperback of Hamlet on the table. "Hi, Mrs. Romano," he said. "Need some help?" He grabbed one of the packages from her arms.

"We got it, Mom." Nick stepped up and grabbed the other bag.

"Thanks, dear. I think Claudio's got the rest," she said.

Mario sat down at the table and pulled a pack of Marlboro cigarettes from his jacket pocket.

"Whew, it's been a busy afternoon," Frances. "What are you guys up to?"

"Nothin', just hanging out," Mario said.

"Yeah," Nick said. "Just talking about this book I was reading at school, *Hamlet*. And now Mario's reading it."

"Oh," Frances said. "*Hamlet*? Shakespeare, huh."

"Yeah," Nick said. "Shakespeare."

The door swung open again and Claudio stepped in carrying a small package.

"Look who's here," he said, clearly surprised to see Nick and Mario.

"Hello, Claudio." Nick stood up. "How's the shopping?"

"She shopped," Claudio said. "I was the chauffeur, but I did buy one thing." He pulled a bottle of wine from the brown paper bag. "A bottle of fine red wine, to go with tonight's prime rib."

"Sounds great," Nick said.

"Unfortunately." Claudio sneered. "There's not enough for all of us." He held the bottle at arm's length and studied the label. "It's a fine French Cabernet."

Claudio put the bottle down next to the book. Nick was just about to say something and point it out when Claudio suddenly announced, "I'm bustin', gotta go . . ." and promptly turned and rushed from the kitchen.

"Wow." Nick looked at his mom. "How can you be

'Battened to that moor'?"

Mario chuckled.

"What?" Frances said, unpacking the groceries.

"Nothing," Nick said.

Frances shrugged.

Nick sat down and grabbed the book. Mario took a drag from his cigarette. Nick looked at the three line-drawn faces on the book's cover. One was the father, one Hamlet, and one the mother. Nick put the book down, leaned toward Mario and whispered, *"suffocation"*.

"Got it," Mario whispered back.

A moment later Claudio strolled back in, still adjusting the belt around his pants.

"Guess all that coffee and waiting in the car caught up to you," Frances said.

"Yeah," Claudio said. "I didn't realize I had to go so bad until I walked in the house."

Nick looked up at Claudio.

"Funny how that works, huh?" Nick said. "You know, that's your subconscious working. It suppresses the urge until it sees you getting closer to a bathroom, then it goes nuts. It knows what's going on before you do. There's no hiding from it."

"Don't give me that psycho-babble bullshit," Claudio said.

Nick shrugged, "It's not bullshit."

Mario held up the paperback conspicuously.

"Hey Claudio, check out what I'm reading."

"What?" Claudio smirked. "You're reading a whole book? Good for you."

"It's a small book, see?" Mario held the book on edge

to show Claudio how slim it was. "Not many words, just like I like it. Nick recommended it. He read it at school. It's Shakespeare. I'm freaking reading Shakespeare! *Hamlet*, it's really good. Ever read it?"

"No, but I saw some of it on TV once. Laurence Olivier? Boring as shit. Couldn't even tell what they were saying."

Claudio rested his hand on Frances's shoulder and kissed her.

"I gotta go," he said.

He turned to Nick and Mario.

"Some of us don't have time to sit around reading books," he said. "Some of us have work to do."

"Well," Nick said. "You're missing out then on all the murder and intrigue and power-fighting struggles, and Kingdom-building adventures."

Claudio smirked and started to walk out when Nick added, "You know there's even a King in this play that I'd swear Shakespeare modeled right after you."

Claudio stopped, "Really, a King? How so?"

"Oh, I don't know," Nick said. "But he's even got almost the same name as you – Claudius!"

"Really?" Claudio said.

"That's funny," Mario said, as if just making the connection. "You're right, that's crazy."

"Maybe I was named after a King!" Claudio smiled and sat down.

"Well, let us tell you about it," Nick said and raised an eyebrow to Mario.

"I'll tell it." Mario stood up, and in dramatic fashion, continued. "Well, the story! It's a great story, a thin little book, just a few words on a few thin pages, but what a great story! Wait till you hear it. It's got murder, intrigue, everything!"

"Well get on with it," Claudio said impatiently.

"Ok, ok," Mario said. "Here's how it goes . . ."

Claudio fidgeted in his jacket pocket and pulled out a cigar. Nick kept a close eye on him. Mario took a deep breath.

"Well," Mario said. "First of all this takes place at a castle in the middle ages."

"Middle ages?" Claudio said. "I like the Middle ages. No guns or bullets back then."

"Yes," Nick said. "But daggers, they still had daggers that could slit a man's throat!"

Claudio looked confusedly at Nick. Nick looked back at Mario.

Mario cleared his throat. "OK well, this kid, the prince, was away studying or something at school, and he comes home because his dad, the King suddenly dies. Nobody suspects anything fishy happened to the dad, but this kid, the prince, gets a visit from his dad who tells him who did it."

"What?" Claudio said. "His dad's dead. How can he get a visit from him?"

"Ahh," Mario said. "It was from his dad's ghost."

"What?" Claudio said. "A ghost? Is this a freakin' ghost story now?"

"Not really," Nick said, then to Mario, "Hurry up, let's get to the good part."

Claudio fidgeted with his unlit cigar.

Mario sat down again and pulled his chair closer to Claudio.

"OK," he said. "So his dad's ghost tells him, you know tells his son, the prince, this kid Hamlet, the ghost tells

Hamlet."

"Get on with it already," Claudio barked. "I get it, what am I an idiot!"

"OK," Mario continued. "The ghost tells Hamlet that his brother, Hamlet's uncle, actually murdered him. And the ghost orders the son to get revenge and kill the brother!"

Claudio seemed to be getting uncomfortable now, crinkling his brow and sitting up as if he wanted to leave.

Nick watched him closely.

"Great story," Claudio said. "But I gotta go."

"Wait!" Mario said. "See, the brother purposely murdered the king so he could take over the castle and the kingdom. But that's not all, not only does he murder the king by suffocating him, and making it look like a natural heart attack, but then he turns around and marries the queen, just like that. He marries the dead king's wife! So now he becomes king and is in charge of the whole goddamn kingdom! And the son, why he just goes nuts and is left with nothin'!"

"That's it!" Claudio blurted and stood up, his face and neck fuming red. "I don't have time for this."

Nick stood up.

"Wait," he said. "You haven't heard it all."

"Let him finish, dear," Frances said. "It's just a story."

"He is finished, I've heard enough," Claudio said, and promptly rushed from the room.

"Bye!" Frances called after him.

The kitchen door slammed shut. Frances threw a dishtowel down and rushed out the door after him, letting it slam again.

"Bye, asshole!" Nick said.

"Holy shit," Mario said. "Did you see the look on his

face?"

"Yup," Nick grinned. "I saw it all. Guilty as shit. We definitely got our man."

He held out the palm of his hand to Mario.

"Gimme five, brother!"

Mario slapped Nick's palm, then turned his hand over and Nick slapped him back.

"Hoo-ha!" Mario said. "Oh yeah, damn, that worked perfectly! You're a freakin' genius."

"Unbelievable." Nick shook his head. "Just un-fucking-believable!"

CHAPTER 13

L ater that night, Nick and Mario headed over to the Red Lion disco. The club was a local favorite with Vegas's corrupt officials, aspiring casino moguls, Mafioso and other shady businessmen and hangers-on. It was a club that perhaps didn't have the spit and polish it once had, but that didn't matter, as its rough edges added a certain charm to its ambiance. Locals went there to be bad, to be seen and to be among the movers and shakers of the glittering city of Vegas. The Red Lion was also an enclave, considered safe from the reach of legitimate law enforcement. FBI agents had been known to stake the place out, but they were obvious and easily avoided. They seemed sometimes to just be going through the motions of their job, sitting across the street all night in their black Ford LTDs and dark suits, lazily observing the patrons coming and going, and sometimes even sleeping.

Even though it was a Thursday evening, a crowd of people stood on the sidewalk in front of the club waiting to get in. A small sign hung above the black steel doors, "Red Lion" painted in gothic red letters with gold trim. The crowd was cordoned off from the entrance with rope sheathed in red leather that hung on polished, brass posts. Two thick-armed bouncers stood guard in front of the doors, just inside the roped-off area.

Nick and Mario pulled up in the Trans Am. Nick went to open his door but the valet had already swung it open for him. Nick stepped out. The valet was a short pudgy man with baggy black pants. His grizzled face round and sweaty, his hair disheveled and greasy.

"Hey man, Nick." The valet smiled up at him. "Good to see you, man. Sorry about your dad. Where've you been?"

"Carl, buddy." Nick patted him on the back and handed him the key. "I'm a been busy man, out of town — at school. How are you? Still working the club, huh?"

"Yeah." Carl nodded. "It's good money."

Nick straightened his jacket and slipped him a ten-spot.

"Thanks, man," Carl said.

A few people in line glanced over in their direction. As soon as the larger bouncer, dressed in all black, saw Nick approaching, he unlatched the rope.

Nick wore a light blue jacket over a white polyester shirt and white bell-bottom pants. He casually buttoned his jacket and approached the club entrance. The faint sound of disco music thumped from inside and mixed with the chatter of the crowd. The scent of marijuana, Yves St. Laurent perfume, and Drakkar cologne drifted through the warm night air.

"Nick baby, how are you?" the bouncer said. "Too bad about your dad, that fucking sucks."

"Thanks, man." Nick said.

"Paulie," Mario said. "Holding up the fort, huh?"

"Yeah, man. Gotta keep things under control, you know."

"Paulie, buddy." Nick slipped him a rolled-up ten-spot as he shook his hand. "It's good to see you man."

Paulie ushered them past the line. People glanced curiously at them. Who were they and why were they special?

"Don't worry, you'll get your chance," the shorter

bouncer announced to the crowd.

Nick and Mario strode in as if they were kings. The music thumped louder and the smoke thickened with each step they took down the short hallway to the main club ballroom. The walls and ceiling of the hallway were painted in flat black with small mirrors and sparkles embedded in the paint. It was as if they were going through a portal and leaving the harsh, cruel world behind. Nick pushed through the disco's flappy doors. The pounding beat hit them full force. They paused to take in the scene — spinning and flashing colored spotlights cut through the thick cigarette smoke. The walls of the club were covered in floor to ceiling mirrors with gaudy stamped marbled gold leaf patterns. The room looked larger than it was.

They headed towards the bar, making their way around the cocktail tables that surrounded the dancefloor. A mirrored disco ball spun from the ceiling above the writhing dancers and a million stars swirled and the music pumped.

Nick squeezed through the crowd at the bar, and leaned in to try to catch the bartender's attention. As soon as the bartender saw him, he immediately came over.

"Two Heinekens," Nick said.

"No problem."

Nick turned and surveyed the scene, trying to spot an empty table.

Shit, there were members of Claudio's crew sitting at a table across the room. He recognized Albert Lorenzo and his cousin Roman, Claudio's chubby, bossy daughter Marla DeVito, Tony Scalfaro, and was that? Yes, it was. Rosalie Messina. Rosalie was there too. She was there.

"Don't look now," he said. "But guess who's here?"

"I don't know," Mario said. "Elvis?"

"No, Rosalie's here. But with half the DeVito tribe — to your right at 2 o'clock."

"Really?" Mario raised his eyebrows and casually turned to see. "Yup, there they are. Don't see Claudio though."

"No," Nick said. "He's probably in the back room doing lines."

The ice cold beers came and Nick handed one to Mario, then took a quick swig of his.

He patted Mario on the back, "Let's find a table."

There was one across the room from the DeVito faction, a couple of rows from the dance floor. They made their way back through the bar crowd and up the aisle to the table.

"Maybe we should have gone to the Fountain Club instead," Mario suggested and he took his seat.

"Relax, we'll be fine. And Rosalie's here. What more could I ask for?"

"You should go over and ask her to dance."

"I don't know." Nick shook his head. "If it was just Rosalie and Marla, I'd be there in an instant, but with the goons there too, I don't know."

"Just go ask her, man," Mario said. "You know fortune favors the brave!"

Nick glanced over to their table, then back at Mario.

———

ACROSS THE ROOM, Albert Lorenzo stood up. "Did you see who the fuck just walked in?"

"Huh?" Marla said, straightening up her posture,

looking around the room. "Who?"

"It's Nick," Rosalie said. "And his friend, Mario."

"What a drag," Tony said and took a swig of his beer.

"The dad just died, and now he's out partying. Pathetic." Albert sat back down.

"Yeah, pathetic, man," Marla said. "Freakin' losers."

"Give 'em a break." Rosalie glanced over at Nick and Mario. "The funeral was over a week ago."

"If it was my dad I wouldn't be out partying so soon afterward," Marla said.

"Yeah, give the body time to cool, right?" Roman elbowed Albert.

Rosalie pushed her chair back and stood up.

"Well, I'm going to go say hello," she announced.

"You're what?" Albert said. "Sit down."

"No, I'm going to go say hello. I can say hi if I want to." She promptly grabbed her purse and defiantly walked away.

"Holy shit," Tony said.

"What the hell?" Albert said.

"Want me to go stop her?" Roman stood up.

"Too late," Marla said.

Rosalie was already crossing the dance floor, heading in Nick's direction.

———

"AH, FUCK IT!" Nick stood up, "I'm gonna go ask her. It's a free country, right?"

"Right on," Mario said.

Nick turned to leave and saw that Rosalie was already on her way over to them. He practically ran to meet her on the dancefloor.

"Rosalie," he said. "It's great to see you. How are you?"

"Fine," she smiled. "It's great to see you again too."

She lifted up on her toes and kissed his cheek.

He stepped back to look at her. Her shining green eyes were surrounded by heavy mascara and white eye makeup with silver sparkles and an orange trim. She wore orange polyester bell bottom pants, a thick white belt, one-inch white platform shoes, a white ruffled blouse with a flared collar, and a thin gold chain necklace with a cross pendant. She also carried a small white leather purse with a gold hoop chain strap. And there was her flowery fresh scent—it was as if the air had suddenly come alive. As if everything had come alive.

"Ready to boogie?" he asked.

"Boogie?" she said. "Definitely."

"But first ask Mario to hold this." She handed her purse to Nick.

"Sure," he said. "Stay right here."

He ran back to Mario and threw the bag on the table.

"Watch this."

"No problem," Mario said.

He hotfooted it back to Rosalie.

"Let's dance," he said.

The music suddenly changed to a primal, driving drum beat. The dance floor filled up and they found themselves surrounded.

Rosalie and Nick twisted and shook to the beat, dancing a few feet apart. But the crowd of dancers closed in, and they were pressed close. Rosalie stumbled forward, into Nick, and for a moment, pressed against him.

"Oh man, I love this song," Nick shouted above the music.

"Me too." Rosalie flashed a smile.

Nick moved his arms to the beat and pulled Rosalie's waist in close. She reciprocated, grinding her hips against his, her arms raised and rocking.

It was like a dream—the scent of her body, her warmth and softness, her hair flying free. And the music pumping, pushing them on. She looked up at him and her eyes said everything.

This was too good and he hoped the next song would keep them moving on the dance floor. And it did, it's percussion sneaking up, with a driving syncopated bass line and incomprehensibly hypnotic lyrics. It was "Soul Makossa" by Manu Dibango. Hips moved and heads shook. After four and a half minutes the music transitioned to Barry White's Love Unlimited Orchestra's 'Love's Theme' and the dance floor began to empty. Nick and Rosalie were sweaty and semi-exhausted. Nick hesitated and looked at Rosalie. He held her hand. Was that it, the last dance? She looked into his eyes. Neither one of them were going anywhere. Only a few other couples remained on the dance floor. Then she smiled and pulled him closer.

"I love this song," she said softly into his ear.

Nick realized that they were in full view of everyone in the room, but it didn't matter. Nothing mattered but this moment. His hands slid up her back and hers over his shoulders and around his neck. Her waist swayed from side to side. It all felt so good, so right. She was amazing. It didn't matter that people were watching them.

Then Rosalie fell into him, resting her head gently on his chest. He closed his eyes and snuggled his cheek against her forehead. They swayed back and forth, their hot bodies melting together as if in a dream.

———

"WHAT THE HELL are they doing?" Albert said.

"Looks like Rosalie's dancing, and having a dynamite time by the looks of it," Marla said.

"Wow." Roman smiled. "Slow dancing."

"Are they kidding?" Tony said. "Has she lost her *fucking* mind?"

"Leave 'em alone, Tony," Roman said. "They're just kids, let 'em have a good time."

Albert stood and with his hands on his hips, he glared at them on the dance floor. They'd all been there for over an hour drinking, and all were a bit drunk.

"Better go rescue her from that cretin!" Marla said.

"Go get 'em, Boss," Tony said.

"Geeze . . ." Roman shook his head and shrugged. "This ain't gonna be good."

Albert looked across the room at the DJ booth, then back at the dance floor. "I'll fucking fix this," he said and stormed toward the dance floor.

———

MARIO had been sitting there drinking his beer, watching Nick and Rosalie on the dance floor. He had seen Albert across the room standing and looking at the dance floor, then looking over towards him.

Then Albert walked around the dance floor and right up the aisle towards Mario. Mario automatically stood up and pushed his chair back taking a reflexive step getting ready to duck or block a punch. But Albert walked right past him and up toward the DJ booth. Mario watched in disbelief.

He saw Albert trying to open the door to the booth. But it must have been locked, and Albert suddenly stepped back then bulldozed himself through the door.

———

THE DJ jumped back.

"Shut the fucking music!" Albert shouted.

The DJ put his arms up and shouted back, "Yo man, take it easy. What song do you want?"

"Shut off the fucking music!" Albert shouted into the man's face.

"I can't shut it off, this is a disco! You want a different song? I'll give you a different song."

Albert reached over to grab the turntable but the DJ tried to shove him away.

"You fucking . . ." Albert grabbed the man and threw him against the wall, jolting the turntables.

The needle bounced across the record, popping, crackling, and crunching in a horrific cacophony of sound. Everyone in the club let out a collective "Ohhh." A few people glanced up at the DJ booth to see what was going on. But the needle landed on the record again and the music continued playing.

"I said shut the music, asshole!" Albert punched the DJ in the gut and he bowled over and slid to the floor. Albert turned to get the needle off the record, but instead tripped on the man's leg and stumbled into both turntables. This time it sounded like a truck had crashed into the building. The crowd glanced around, startled. Some held their ears. Albert ripped the records off the turntables, but they continued to turn and the needles bounced along the rubber mat creating explosive popping sounds that thundered throughout the club.

Albert stumbled out of the booth. Everyone was looking at him, wondering what the hell was going on. He headed back toward the dance floor. Mario followed. Nick and Rosalie stood in shock. Albert was coming right at them. He grabbed Rosalie's arm. Nick reached to intervene, but Albert easily shoved him away.

"Party's over, we're getting out of here now," Albert announced.

"What the hell are you doing?" Nick shouted. "We were just dancing!"

"I said, the party's over. You're coming with me." He tugged hard on Rosalie's arm.

"Get your hands off me," she screamed, struggling to pull herself free.

"Let's go." He wrapped both arms around her and pulled her off her feet. "We're leaving."

He turned to Nick, "Don't ever touch her again, understand? Don't *fucking* touch her!"

Albert dragged Rosalie kicking and screaming off the

dance floor.

Nick and Mario stood in shock. Nick lunged to grab Albert, but Mario held him back.

"Shit, calm down, man," Mario said. "Cool it."

Nick tried to break away, but Mario held him tightly in a bear hug.

"You don't want to get involved in this!" Mario said.

Albert carried Rosalie, still kicking and flailing, toward the exit.

"Shit man." Marla slammed her drink down on the table.

Roman stood up, "Let's get out of here."

Marla and Tony didn't immediately follow his lead.

"You heard me," Roman said. "It's time to go."

"Shit!" Marla stood up and grabbed her bag.

They all headed down the aisle following Roman's lead, toward the dance floor.

Roman stepped right up to Nick and poked his finger in his chest.

"Better watch yourself there, tiger."

"It's a free world, buddy," Nick seethed.

"Free for some," Roman said. "But not for you. You'd be smart to leave her alone."

Roman turned away toward the exit and the others followed.

Nick said under his breath, "Fucking retards!"

"Assholes," Mario added.

"What a bunch of shitheads." Nick's hands were shaking.

The music was still off and the house lights had been turned on. Nick and Mario made their way back to their table.

Some patrons were on their way out of the club, but others just stayed, looking around, waiting to see what would happen next.

"This is bullshit, man," Nick said. "I mean, what the fuck?"

Mario grabbed Rosalie's bag. "Let's get out of here," he said. "It ain't worth it."

"No, let's wait. If I go out there now I'm going to kill that motherfucker."

Nick sat down and reached for his beer, his hand still shaking.

CHAPTER 14

Outside the club there was no sign of Albert, Tony, or anyone else from Claudio's crew. Nick and Mario stood by the curb waiting impatiently for the Trans Am. Nick was angry. How could the night go from one extreme to the other so quickly? He'd been so happy with Rosalie and then *WHAM!* —total chaos. If he had a gun he could have killed someone.

"Hey, man," Mario said. "Looks like our friends."

"Where?"

"Up the block."

Nick turned to see. There they were, on their way. And Marla and Rosalie looked like they were in some kind of argument.

"Maybe I should just stroll over there and grab Rosalie," Nick said.

"Na, fuck 'em," Mario said. "Let's get the hell outta here, Nick. Call her tomorrow, take her to dinner or something."

"I'll bet you Rosalie is saying the same thing and wants to be with me right now instead of those retards."

"Fuhgeddaboudit, man," Mario said. "Things are too hot right now. Just see her tomorrow. Let's go."

The valet pulled the white Trans Am up to the curb.

"Ahhh . . . fuggin' . . . shit . . ." Nick mumbled under his breath.

They jumped in the Trans Am and Nick slammed his door, glanced over his shoulder, then spun the wheel and floored it. The car made a sharp, screeching U-turn and Mario crushed against his door. But Nick felt good punching the gas pedal to the floor and feeling the front of the car lift and erupt like a beast. In a moment he would be flying past Claudio's crew, and they would see him rocket by, burning rubber, with the screaming chicken wailing in glorious rage. Should he flip them off as he went by? Maybe.

ALBERT LED the way across the street. Tony and Roman followed closely behind with Marla and Rosalie trailing. But as Rosalie stepped off the curb, her ankle twisted and she tumbled into the gutter.

"Owwwweee . . . *SHIT!*" she screamed.

Tony and Marla both stopped.

"Whoa, take it easy, woman," Marla said, stumbling a bit herself. "Are you OK?"

Roman rushed back to help too, but Albert kept walking into the street.

Tony and Roman pulled Rosalie up to her feet.

"Shit," Rosalie said again, hopping on her one good foot.

Tony put her arm around his shoulder. "You OK?" he said.

"No!" she cried.

Roman held her other arm.

"Oh shit." Albert stopped in the middle of the street and shouted back at them, "What the hell are you guys . . ."

NICK HAD IT NAILED to the floor when he noticed a shadowy figure standing up ahead in the middle of the street. Did the guy not see them coming? Was that Claudio? It looked like his fat pot-bellied physique. What's he doing here? Meeting up with his cronies at the club?

"Watch it!" Mario yelled.

But before Nick could avoid it, the car was upon the man and there was a bone crushing blow. It felt like they had hit a tree. The guy flew in slow motion across the hood and smashed into the windshield, then bounced off it, up over the car. A bloodcurdling scream whooshed by from the sidewalk. In the rearview mirror, Nick caught sight of the body falling from the night sky. He struggled to see through the bloody, shattered windshield and regain control of the Trans Am as it sideswiped two parked cars.

"Holy shit!" Mario cried.

"Oh fuck!" Nick wrestled the steering wheel.

The car careened insanely up the street.

"You hit him!" Mario shouted at him. "You *fucking* hit him!"

"Claudio? Was it Claudio!" Nick yelled back.

"I don't know man. It looked like Albert to me."

"Albert?" Nick's eyes widened.

"Yeah, I didn't see Claudio, man. I saw Albert standing there. What the fuck was he doing in the middle of the road? And Rosalie, I think that was her screaming."

"What?" Nick said. "Rosalie?"

"This ain't good, man. We gotta get the fuck out of

here."

Nick slammed on the brakes.

"No," he said. "We gotta go back."

"What?" Mario said.

"I'm going back for Rosalie."

"Fuck that, man. We gotta get the hell out of here. Our ass is grass. That was a hit and run. Don't be a fool, we gotta go."

"No." Nick gripped the steering wheel. "I'm going back."

———

TONY AND ROMAN rushed to help Albert, whose twisted body had landed on the hood of a parked car.

"Shit, you alright!" Tony yelled.

A pool of blood was already forming in the dent under Albert's head.

"Holy shit!" Roman said.

"Fuck, fuck, fuck . . ." Tony repeated.

Rosalie and Marla turned away in shock. They sat at the curb. Marla suddenly doubled over and began puking into the gutter. Rosalie was shaking and rubbing her swollen ankle.

People started running over from the club. Tony shook Albert but got no reaction.

"Shit, don't just fucking lay there," he cried.

Roman stood frozen in place looking blankly at Albert's body.

"What's going on?" someone from the crowd yelled.

Tony looked at Roman, "Call an ambulance!"

"He's dead," Roman muttered.

A crowd quickly formed around them.

"Someone call a damn ambulance!" Tony yelled at them, but nobody moved.

"Shit!" He stormed past the onlookers and headed back to the club. He'd call an ambulance himself.

By the time he got back, Roman was sitting by the curb with his face in his hands.

"What the hell are you doing?" Tony said.

Roman looked up at him, "He's dead. It's too late."

Tony bit his lip and looked across the crowd.

"Dead?" someone said.

"Who did it?" another said.

"A white Trans Am, I saw it—had a screaming chicken on the hood."

Tony walked over to the person who said that. "You saw it?" he said.

"Yeah, looked like he was gunning for him."

"Were there two guys in the car, could you see?"

"I think so, they just left the club, made a wild U-Turn too. It was fucking nuts!"

"Thanks." Tony turned away.

"Fuck!" he cried. "I'll get him, I'll fucking get him. I'll torture and bury that fuck."

He leaned down to Roman and laid his hand on his shoulder.

"Nick's, a fucking dead man."

Roman looked up and nodded. In the distance, sirens wailed.

A BLOCK away from the commotion, Nick pulled the Trans Am up onto the sidewalk. He jumped out. The grill and hood were smashed, the windshield shattered and bloodied. He ran back, toward the accident.

Mario ran after him, yelling "Shit . . . Stop! What the fuck are you doing!"

Nick just ran. He approached the crowd, and pushed his way through.

"Who is it?" he hollered.

"Don't know, some guy," someone replied.

Nick squeezed closer, and raised his head over the crowd to see the victim sprawled on the hood of the car. *It was Albert!*

"Shit." Nick turned away, his eyes shifted left and right. He saw Mario arrive, out of breath, at the edge of the crowd. Nick went to meet him but Tony Scalfaro cut him off and now stood right in his face. Nick wiped the sweat from his forehead.

"You fuck!" Tony grabbed him by the collar and cocked his arm to crack him.

Nick pushed away and ducked.

"It wasn't my fault . . ." he tried to say, but Tony caught him with a left hook in the stomach.

"Uuufff . . ." Nick stumbled backward and doubled over. Tony reloaded his arm, ready to strike again, but Mario grabbed it from behind and pulled Tony backwards, causing him to fall into the crowd and down onto the sidewalk. The crowd retreated.

Mario grabbed Nick, "Let's go man!"

Nick straightened up and they both ran.

Tony pulled himself up and fought his way through the crowd, sending a couple of the bystanders to the ground.

Nick and Mario tore back up the block.

"Nick! Nick!"

It was a female, shouting.

Nick spun around. It was Rosalie, balancing on one foot in middle of the sidewalk.

"Nick!" she shouted again.

But it was too late. Nick saw Tony coming up quickly behind her, gunning for him. He had to keep running.

"I'll call you!" he shouted to her.

When they reached the car, Tony was practically upon them. They jumped in and Nick threw it into gear. But Tony was already there, reaching in to grab him through the open window.

Nick floored it and the car swerved wildly across the sidewalk. Even though he was getting dragged on the side of the car, Tony held on, choking Nick's neck. Mario reached over and frantically tried to pry Tony's hands off Nick.

Out of control, the car smashed into parked cars in a crescendo of scraping and crashing steel. Mario dug his fingers into Tony's hand, struggling to release his iron grip. Finally, Tony flew off, falling and rolling back in the street. Nick took a gulping breath and straightened the wheel.

———

"YOU DEAD FUCK!" Tony shouted after them.

In a moment he was in his black Caddy, burning out after them, fishtailing up the street.

Nick and Mario had gotten hung up behind traffic stopped at a light. Tony quickly caught up. As he came to a screeching stop he slammed into them, ramming the Trans Am and sending it crashing into the car in front.

Nick threw it in reverse, hit the gas and slammed back into Tony's car. But the guy from the first car had gotten out and was stumbling towards Nick's window and screaming a tirade of curses. The guy lunged for Nick but Nick cranked the wheel and sped out from between the two cars. The guy fell forward onto the pavement.

Tony slammed the gas and cut the wheel also, his car lifting and accelerating forward. But the car suddenly bounced violently up and down, as if it hit a speed bump.

"Holy shit," Tony said. "The poor sucker, shouldn't have gotten out of his car."

Ahead, Nick sped onto the freeway. Tony followed. Nick's Trans Am held the road nicely, weaving around cars traveling much slower. Tony's Caddy swayed and bounced as he tried to keep up. Within moments they were both going over one hundred miles per hour, and Tony was catching up, getting closer, until he was only a few car lengths behind. But as Nick approached the next exit, at the last second, he slammed on the brakes and cut the wheel sharply to make the exit ramp. By the time Tony realized what happened, it was too late, Tony had been going too fast and the exit was upon him too quickly. He hit his brakes and cut the wheel, trying to make it anyway but instead overshot the exit and slammed over the grassy ravine. The Caddy shook violently as it went airborne and came in for a crash landing. Dirt flew in a cloud of debris. The car came to a slanted, crooked stop, steam billowing from its radiator. Tony's skull had cracked the steering wheel and blood flowed from his forehead.

"Fuck." He raised his ringing head and pounded his fist into the dashboard.

"*Ohhh . . . SHIT*, my shoulder! Mother fucker, he's dead, he's fucking dead."

CHAPTER 15

With so much on his mind lately, Claudio had been having trouble with anxiety, continually reviewing in his mind the various things he and his men had to do in order to solidify their position at the Cornetto Club Casino. It had taken Claudio decades to get to this point, having slowly worked his way up with his mob brethren in Chicago. If he could just stick around, then eventually things would fall his way. He was given the chance to make inroads in Vegas, just when it was beginning to really boom. That was only a few years earlier, and now it was all coming to fruition. With Jack gone, he was now the de facto boss of the Cornetto Club Casino. This clearly represented the biggest opportunity of his life and he didn't want to blow it. Wealth, power and respect—Claudio could taste it all. Even if he didn't actually own the Cornetto Club Casino, there were numerous ways that he and his crew could control it and siphon off barrelfulls of cash.

There was also the not so small matter of the rumors of silver bullion and coins, that Claudio hoped, were stored in the casino vault. He hadn't known for sure, and Jack had never directly spoken of it with him.

Over the years the legend of the silver persisted. People often speculated about it, but now that Jack was dead, speculation and interest grew. The Las Vegas Sun even mentioned it in the newspaper article about Jack's passing:

And if the legend of Jack's treasure trove were true

*– decades of collecting silver bullion and coins – it
would represent one of the largest treasure hoards
ever squirreled away.*

With all that was at stake and all that was happening,
Claudio couldn't sleep well, even though he was taking
valium, drinking every day, and receiving late afternoon
masseuse sessions. Nothing seemed to relax him or quell his
anxiety enough to enable him to get a good night's sleep.
However, on this particular night he somehow had slept
deeply. So deeply, that when he awoke, he was especially
groggy and felt as if he had emerged from a damp hole in the
ground. He sat on the edge of the bed and rubbed his face.

"Shit," he said and staggered to his feet.

It was already mid-morning and the sun was high in
the sky. Claudio sipped the coffee that Frances had just made.
She stood behind him, rubbing his large, lumpy shoulders.

"Friggin' delicious darling, just perfect," he said. "Oh,
and that feels good, a little harder."

He rolled his shoulders up and down, then tilted his
head from side to side, stretching his neck.

The phone rang and Frances answered it.

"It's for you," she said.

"Who's bothering me already?"

Frances shrugged and handed him the phone.

"Yeah," he said.

Tony's voice rambled through the line.

"What?" Claudio said. "Slow down. Who . . .? Albert?
Nick?"

"Nick what?" Frances pulled her hands from his

shoulders.

Claudio stood up and turned away, waving her off and stretching the cord across the room.

"*Shit!*"

"Huh?" Frances said. "What about Nick? What happened to him?"

Claudio waved her off again.

"OK, OK," he said. "What hospital are you at? I'm on my way."

Claudio hung up the phone.

"What!" Frances grabbed his forearm. "What happened? Is Nick OK?"

He looked at her, "Albert's dead."

"Dead?"

"He was run over. And Tony's in the hospital."

"What? And what about Nick? You said something about Nick too."

"Nick?" Claudio said. "Is he here?"

"What do you mean? Tell me what happened?"

"I have to go."

"But what happened?"

"I don't know what happened, but I gotta get to the hospital."

He quickly left the room.

"*What?!*" Frances was about to chase after him when the kitchen door flew open.

It was Nick.

She grabbed him, "Are you OK?"

"I'm fine, Mom."

But he knew he looked like hell. He was sweaty and

probably smelly, his hair disheveled and his clothes wrinkled as if he had slept them. He took off his leather jacket and threw it on the back of the kitchen chair.

"What happened? Was there an accident? Tony called and he's in the hospital."

"Tony called you?"

"No, he called Claudio."

"Claudio? *Shit*," Nick said. "Is he here?"

"He's upstairs, getting ready to go see Tony in the hospital. What's wrong?"

"Nothing, but don't let him know I'm here."

Nick opened the sliding glass door to the patio.

"I'll be out back," he said.

"What? Why? But he'll see your car."

"Mario just dropped me off. My car's at his house."

Nick closed the door and crouched down by the side. He heard Claudio come into the kitchen and peeked up to see.

Claudio gave Frances a quick peck on the cheek. "Gotta go," he said and left.

"Bye," Frances called after him.

Nick turned away and cringed. The kitchen door slammed shut. He closed his eyes and took a deep breath—he was out of harm's way for now. But suddenly, the kitchen door swung open again. He turned to look. It was Claudio, and he was holding up Nick's leather jacket.

"Where is he?" Claudio shouted at Frances.

"Who?"

"Nick, goddamn it!"

"Nick?"

Nick slid open the patio door and stepped in.

"I just got back home," he announced.

Claudio glared at him.

"It was an accident," Nick said.

"*Albert's fucking dead*," Claudio growled.

"It was an accident," Nick repeated. "A freakin' accident. He came out of nowhere — didn't even look where he was going. I'd have stopped if I could."

"All I know," Claudio said and came right up to Nick's face sputtering and spitting and jabbing a finger into his chest. "Is that he's dead, and you *ffuu . . . you ran him over!*"

Nick pushed Claudio's hand away and wiped the spit from his eye.

Frances jumped between them.

"Cut it out!" she yelled and pushed them apart.

Nick stepped back, with outstretching arms and hands raised.

"What do you want from my life?" he said. "It was an accident. I didn't do it on purpose. *I don't kill people on purpose.*"

Claudio shuffled around Frances and lunged at Nick with an awkwardly thrown punch. Nick ducked. Claudio lost his balance and plunged down into the kitchen chairs.

"Ahhh!" Frances shouted. "You're wrecking my house!"

She pushed herself between them again.

"Get out of here!" she shouted at Claudio. "Get out of my house!"

Claudio wrestled himself up, huffing and puffing. He adjusted his suit jacket and sleeves.

"I'm not the one you have to worry about," he snarled at Nick.

"What?" Frances glared at Claudio.

"I wouldn't do anything to hurt him. But I can't say that for anyone else." He turned to Nick, "You'd be wise to take off for a while, go someplace far away. Someplace safe, like Hawaii."

"You mean run away?" Nick said. "Like a coward?"

Claudio smirked but didn't answer. Instead he said, "I'll see you later."

His lower lip quivered and sweat dripped off his brow. He turned and stomped out, letting the kitchen door slam behind him.

"Bastard," Nick sneered.

Frances grabbed Nick's shoulders and looked him in the eye.

"Now, tell me what happened," she said.

He righted the chairs and they sat down. Nick told her about being at the club, dancing with Rosalie and the accident. When he was done, she looked at him and shook her head.

"This isn't good," she said.

"What am I gonna do?" Nick said.

She was clearly concerned.

"Well," she said. "First, I don't want you to get arrested. And second, I don't want anything to happen to you."

She looked into Nick's eyes, "Maybe it would be best if you went away for a few weeks. Maybe Hawaii would be good."

"Hawaii?" Nick said. "But what about Claudio?"

"Don't worry, I'll take care of him. Albert was standing in the middle of the street, right? It was an accident; he can't hold that against you—it wasn't your fault. And I'll have him take care of the police too. We don't want any trouble. Everything will get straightened out and then you can come back. For now, you just go and lay low, and be safe."

"*Shit . . .*" Nick mumbled.

———

AT NORTH VISTA Hospital Tony sat in a yellowish-brown Naugahyde recliner, leaning forward over a plastic food tray. He ate a thin tuna fish sandwich and watched a rerun of Bonanza. With his right arm in a sling he struggled to eat. He had a black eye and a white bandage stretched across his forehead. As he took another bite, a good portion of the tuna spilled from the sandwich and onto his blue hospital gown.

"Fuck," he cursed, ejecting a few more tuna pieces from his mouth.

At that moment, Claudio walked in, wearing a white knit golf shirt, a loose fitted blazer, a white belt, and brown Haband polyester pants.

"How you doin'?" Claudio said. "You OK?"

"I'm fine. It's just my head." He pointed to the bandage in the middle of his forehead. "Ten stitches. And my shoulder, it's a bit messed up."

Claudio sat himself down on the edge of the bed.

"So what happened?" he said.

Tony briefly explained the night's events to Claudio, then finished by referring to Nick as 'that asshole,' and saying, "I'll fucking kill him."

Claudio listened, then rubbed his eyes and exhaled. "I can't believe Albert's gone." He shook his head.

After a moment of staring into space, Claudio stood

and said, "Let's go. We got work to do."

In his gold Lincoln Mark IV, with white vinyl roof and small oval carriage windows on each side, Claudio reached into his jacket pocket and pulled out a single cigar tube. He unscrewed the top and took a half-smoked cigar from it. Tony sat next to him on the plush and supple leather seat. A thick armrest separated them and Dean Martin played in the background on the stereo.

While Claudio lit his cigar with his torch lighter, Tony took out a pack of Pall Malls and pressed in the cigarette lighter knob. Claudio took a puff on his cigar and Tony lit his cigarette. They smoked a moment then Claudio turned on the air, and flipped the switch down for the power windows, to crack them a bit so the smoke could escape. Then he maneuvered the car slowly, like a boat, sailing it through the hospital parking lot and out onto East Lake Mead Boulevard. As the car accelerated the smoke inside swirled.

"Listen," Claudio said.

"Yeah," Tony answered.

"Nick is heading out of town. I told him to go to Hawaii."

"He fucking kills Albert and now he's going to fucking Wak-kiki?"

"I said listen," Claudio raised his voice. "Do you know what that fucking that means?"

Tony turned away and Claudio took a few puffs from his cigar.

"OK, so . . ." He glanced over at Tony. "Nick is going on hiatus for a while until things settle down here. I don't want anything to happen to him before he goes. Everything should be copasetic for now, you know, status quo. But when he's gone, I want you to go and find him." Claudio paused. "And, I want you to make it look like an accident, like he drowned or something."

Tony smiled, "No problem Boss. It'd be my fucking pleasure."

Claudio puffed his cigar again, "With him out of the way, I can focus on Frances and more important things."

He glanced again at Tony, "Got it?"

Tony nodded.

———

AFTER NICK FINISHED packing his suitcase, he sat at his desk with a Morgan Silver dollar. He held vertically on the surface of the desk, with one finger on top, then flicked it, sending it spinning across the desk. He watched it fly almost to the edge of the desk, then spin back to the middle. It circled round and round and he watched, waiting for the moment when it would finally lose its momentum, wobble, and fall.

Exactly at what point did the silver dollar lose its equilibrium and fall helplessly, with a final last gasp and drop, with a ping, onto the desktop?

It seemed everything in his life was spinning out of control. Would it be only a matter of time before he fell, like the coin, to the ground? But did it all really matter, in the end? What difference did it make? He felt like he could be going crazy.

He spun the coin again and watched. What would he do when they came for him?

The spinning silver dollar finally lost momentum, did a few quick revolutions in a small circle, wobbled, then fell to a pinging dead stop. The sound lingered for a moment. What echoes would resonate after he was gone?

He laughed and stood. Of course he'd have to fight now. He had no choice. He'd have to take care of Claudio, no matter what. He stretched his arms over his head and sighed, then picked up his bag.

CHAPTER 16

Rosalie spent most of the night in an uncomfortable and regrettable alcoholic slumber. At some point in the dark, a feeling of nausea dragged her to queasy wakefulness. She got out of bed and tried, but failed, to throw up in the toilet. Now she lay staring at the ceiling in her room. How could it be that Claudio's friend Albert was dead, having been hit by Nick's car? Maybe it was good for him and he got what he deserved. But maybe it was actually her fault. Would they even have left the club if she hadn't danced with Nick? Would Albert have been standing in the middle of the street if she hadn't twisted her ankle? It was all too much.

And what about Nick? Was he OK? She'd had such fun seeing him at the club, dancing so close, touching him. But all the trouble, the fight, and her twisted ankle, and then that horrible accident. It was her fault. No, it wasn't. She didn't do anything wrong. It was Albert who flipped out. The events of the night cycled endlessly through her head as she lay in a torturous, sweaty purgatory caught between the living and the dead. It was only when dawn began to break that she finally succeeded in slipping off to sleep.

All too soon, though, she was awakened by a faint but distinct tapping. She squinted her eyes open to a blazingly bright bedroom.

Tap tap tap tap tap . . . from the window?

Sunlight beamed through the opened curtains. She could see a person's face pressed against the glass, hands cupped around eyes peering in at her. It was a man.

"Huuuhhh . . ." she gasped and was just about to scream when she though she recognized him. He held his finger to his lips, signaling to be quiet.

Nick? What the hell?

She rubbed her eyes and sat up. Wearing only her panties and bra, she slid out of bed and immediately felt pain in her ankle. She winced and hobbled over to the window. Nick motioned to her to unlock it, which she did.

He yanked the window up and popped his head in.

"Listen, I've got to talk to you," he pleaded. "It's important. And, I've got your purse."

He held up the white purse and offered it to her. She hesitated, then grabbed it and stepped back. Nick had on the same clothes and leather jacket he wore the night before. He seemed nervous and rushed too.

"What's going on?" she demanded. "You look like you've been up all night. Are you OK?"

Nick smiled and climbed, head first, through the opened window. He fell straight onto the floor. From his back, he said, "I've got to talk to you."

He held out his hand and Rosalie helped him to his feet.

"Thanks," he said and wiped his sweaty brow with the back of his hand.

Rosalie stepped back again. He seemed crazed and hyped-up. Maybe he was on uppers? Speed?

"Rosalie!" He grabbed her shoulders and pulled her in, like he was about to hug her. She pushed him away.

"What's wrong with you? What are you doing here?"

"Your room smells like flowers." He smiled excitedly.

She was confused. Was he OK?

"I just wanted to see you before I go," he said. "I need to get out of here, fly away, go somewhere safe." He sighed. "Everything is so fucked up."

"What do you mean?"

"I'm freakin' out," he said.

"Albert's dead." Rosalie turned away.

"It was an accident." Nick said. "An accident, I swear. He stepped right in front of my car. I couldn't avoid hitting him."

Rosalie's stomach suddenly began feeling woozy and she placed her hand on it. She turned back to Nick. His eyes were wide and crazed.

"I feel sick," she said.

"Take it easy," he said. "Sit down. You look pale."

He guided her to the disheveled bed.

"Are you OK?" he said.

Rosalie looked at him. "I'll be fine, I think."

Nick sat next to her.

"Oh shit," he muttered. "How did I get myself into this?"

He lowered his head. Rosalie put her hand on his shoulder, rubbing her fingers gently into his muscles.

He straightened up and looked at her, his eyes aflame with an intense and unnerving urgency. Was he going to try to kiss her?

"I don't know if you should be here," she said. "It's not safe. Do you know what my dad would do if he found you here?"

"What?" Nick said.

"He'd probably kill you."

"Ha!" Nick laughed. "You think so?"

"Yeah," she said. "I don't know."

"Listen," Nick said. "I wrote you this letter."

He reached into his pocket and pulled out a folded envelope. "I want to give it to you before I leave."

He held the letter out to her.

"What does it say?"

"Here . . ."

Rosalie hesitated, then took it. Instead of opening it though, she placed it on the nightstand, on top of her book, "*The Chariots of the Gods*".

Nick's desperate eyes remained fixed on her.

"I want to be with you." He pulled closer to her. "Just you and me. We should be together, you know that? You and me. Don't worry about anything. In fact, forget everything. Don't you see, we can do this. Come with me! Can you come with me?"

"Where? What are you talking about?"

"I'm going to Hawaii, to Waikiki. White sandy beaches and blue skies. Just for a little while!"

"Hawaii?"

"Yes," Nick said. "Until things cool down."

"What about school?" she said. "Aren't you going back?"

"I can't, I gotta disappear. Claudio thinks I killed Albert *on purpose!*"

There seemed to be genuine terror in his eyes.

"Well, I . . ." she turned away. "I can't think. This is all happening too fast."

"Come with me Rosalie!"

There was a sudden knock on the door and they both looked up.

"*Shit!*" Rosalie turned Nick.

The knocking got louder.

"Who's in there? Is everything OK?" It was her dad.

"I'm fine Dad, just getting up."

Rosalie grabbed Nick's arm. "Hurry, get under the bed!"

"Who's in there? Somebodies in there with you."

"No, Dad, it's just the TV. Give me a second."

Nick headed around to the other side of the bed, but his sneaker caught on the edge of the shag carpet and he stumbled into the vanity.

The door flew open.

"What the hell!" Joey Messina shouted.

———

NICK BARELY MADE IT through the open window when Joey grabbed at his ankle and tore his shoe off. The shoe flew back across the room directly at Rosalie. She screamed and ducked, and it went flying by. Joey cursed after Nick as he ran away across the lawn.

"Don't ever come back here, you fuck!" her father shouted.

Rosalie stood watching in shock, her weight favoring her one good foot.

"I'm gonna kill that fuck," he turned and yelled at her. "What the *hell* was he doing in here? You let him in?"

He was about to slap her, but she dove onto the bed and pulled the pillow over her ears. He ripped it from her hands.

"That stupid fuck!" He shook his finger at her. "Don't you ever let him step foot in this house again. Do you freakin' understand?"

Rosalie let out a wild scream and he smacked her with the back of his hand. She tumbled off the bed to the floor.

Tears streamed down her face.

Her dad knelt down beside her.

"Baby, I'm sorry," he said. "Take it easy, I just don't want that guy bothering you. You're my little girl."

He attempted to put his hand on her shoulder but she pushed away.

"Leave me alone." She kicked at him. "Get away from me."

"Shit, I'm sorry," he said. "Are you OK?"

She rubbed her eyes and glared at him.

"Here, get off the floor." He reached for her hand.

She hesitated.

"Come on," he said.

She reluctantly gave him her hand and he pulled her up, hugging and squeezing her as she got to her feet. She couldn't move.

"It's OK, sweetie," he said, patting her back. "It's OK. I'm going to kill that fucker. Don't worry, I'll get him."

"Please," Rosalie said into his ear. "Don't do that. Don't hurt him."

"Baby," he said. "I don't want him to ever lay a hand on you again. Don't you see, he's nuts, he's unstable. And he's a killer — he just killed Albert, for Christ's sake!"

She broke away and tried to gather her conflicted thoughts. Nick had scared her, yes, but it was almost as if he were the only sane person she knew. What was wrong with everybody?

"He's just going through some changes," she said. "He'll get over it."

Her dad grabbed her by the shoulders again, "What did he want? Tell me what he wanted!"

"Let go of me!" she shouted and pounded her fists on his chest.

"Tell me what he wanted."

"You can't hurt him, you can't!" she kept punching his chest.

"Nobody's getting hurt," he smirked and released her.

She stepped back and glared at him.

"Now tell me why he was here."

She shook her head.

Her dad sighed. "Just tell me what's going on. That's all I want to know. Is he bothering you?"

Rosalie shook her head again, "No, he just came to see me. That's all."

"And?"

She hesitated. "And he told me he's going away, that's all."

"Going away?

"Yes, because of what happened."

"Where?"

"I don't know, someplace safe."

"Safe?" her dad said. "Like where?"

"Who knows, far away, like Hawaii maybe."

"Hawaii?"

She wiped her tears, "I don't know. He didn't finish what he was trying to tell me before you barged in."

"Hmmm, well," her dad said. "He's all fucked up. Just

as well that he disappears. I don't want you seeing him, understand? He's trouble."

He looked straight at her and pointed his finger, "And I don't need trouble."

"I'll see him if I want," she suddenly shouted. "It's my life and that's for me to decide!"

He stepped back.

"What about your fiancé, Greg?"

She looked at him but said nothing.

"How can you . . ." He looked at her with indignation.

"How can I what?" Rosalie yelled back at him. "How can I live my life? How can I look at myself in the mirror? What about you, Mr. holier-than-thou? You and your slime-ball friends. What about that?"

She could see her dad was about to slap her again.

"I hate this . . ." she turned away. "I hate it . . . I'll do what I want. Leave me alone. Leave! Get out! Leave me alone, goddamn it!"

She attempted to push him out the door.

"Hey, take it easy."

She pushed him harder and he threw up his hands.

"OK, fine, I'll leave. Just don't let me see you near that fuck again."

She slammed the door and locked it.

"Understand!" her dad yelled.

"Frigg you!" she screamed back.

Rosalie threw herself on her bed and pulled the pillow over her head. She was so confused. Why was her dad such a prick? Wasn't it enough that she liked Nick? Wasn't that enough for him to back off? Why couldn't he just leave her alone? Why couldn't they all just leave her alone? None of this would have happened at the club if Albert hadn't intervened. Asshole! Maybe she'd be sleeping at Nick's place now instead of being back in her own room and nursing a hangover and a sprained ankle.

But Nick did show up, at her window, and he tumbled in. He literally tumbled into her room—how sweet! He was stressed, yes, but what was he saying? He was leaving, to Hawaii?

The letter.

She looked toward the night stand. It was sitting right there, on top of that crazy book, "The Chariots of the Gods". Aliens, that's what she needed to save her now. She pushed herself up and wiped her eyes.

Her hand shook as she held the envelope. Inscribed across it in big letters . . .

* Sweet Rosalie *

She pulled out the letter and unfolded it.

Sweet Rosalie,

I'm not that good with words, but first I want to tell you that I'm sorry for all the trouble I've caused. I had a great time dancing and being with you last night. I wish we could do it again. Too bad Albert had to flip out! That was crazy, what a moron! I feel bad about running him down, but believe me, it was, one hundred percent, an accident. Somehow he was just standing right in the middle of the street, and in his dark suit, I couldn't see him. I really didn't mean to hit him! And now things have gotten out of control. Claudio is after me, and he doesn't care if it was an accident or not. He just wants me dead!

So I have no choice but to leave. But before I go, I want to tell you this and I don't care what anybody else thinks. I'm in love with you, and I've always been in love with you. Even if you don't want me, then at least you know where I'm coming from.

I Love You!!!

Rosalie's hands stopped shaking. She read and reread the words:

. . . I'm in love with you . . .

and

. . . I Love You!!!

Her face flushed and she rolled onto her back, holding the letter up. *He was in love with her. He really was.* She continued reading.

I have to leave tonight and get out of here. Everything is too crazy and too risky for me to be here around your dad's friends. So, for now, I'm going to Hawaii. Can you come with me? Can you meet me at the airport later today? Pack a small bag and just go, we're

adults after all! Just go. We can be together on the islands!
Think of how great that would be, together and away from
all this bullshit. Just you and me on a beach in Hawaii! I'm
taking TWA flight 95 — it leaves at 5 this afternoon.

I'll wait for you there at the gate.

xxxooooxxx

Love,

Nick

Rosalie read the letter a few more times, then put it down and hugged her pillow. He wanted her. *He actually wanted her.*

CHAPTER 17

For the rest of the day Nick stayed out of sight at Mario's place, waiting for his flight and for Mario to take him to the airport. They sat on the couch together smoking weed, drinking beer, and watching Mario's small black and white TV. They watched Bewitched and the Beverly Hillbillies.

They were in a melancholy mood, passing the joint back and forth, sipping their beers, not saying much of anything, and allowing themselves to be transfixed by the TV.

A True cigarette commercial came on. A dapper man, dressed in a suite, confident, and clean-cut, sat at a desk, smoking. He casually held his cigarette out and talked directly to the audience. "Man, this is a good tasting cigarette. 12.5 milligrams of tar, zero point seven milligrams nicotine. Air filtration system… True gives you everything you want!"

"Ah shit." Nick put his hand over his eyes and rubbed his brow.

"Huh?" Mario responded.

Nick rested his head back on the couch and stared at the ceiling. "Everything is so fucked up," he mumbled.

"Hey," Mario said. "Be cool, man."

"I can't. I fucking killed that guy."

"It was an accident," Mario said.

"I shouldn't have been going that fast. I should have slowed down."

"Don't beat yourself up, guys are always pealing-out in front of the Red Lion. Look, what idiot is gonna just step right out in the middle of the street there? It was his fault."

"You don't understand, man." Nick shook his head. "I thought it was Claudio. I knew it was his crew down the block, and I thought he somehow showed up with them. I thought I got him!"

"What are you talking about? There was no way to avoid it."

"I keep replaying it in my head. I keep seeing him smash into the car, rolling across the windshield. I can't get that bone snapping crush and jolt out of my head. If I didn't know I hit him I would have thought the engine blew up."

"Look, man, just chill out. You'll get over it. Get some rest down there in Waikiki—the land of Aloha! The trade winds, the sand, the beautiful girls, all on vacation, just wanting to get laid. Oh, yeah, you'll get over it soon enough."

"Shit, I don't know'" Nick said.

Mario suddenly straightened up and looked at Nick. "And the weed, man. Don't forget the fucking weed—they got the best in the world down there. Maui-Wowie! It's gonna be like you died and went to heaven."

"Alright," Nick said, but he knew it wasn't alright, he had just killed the wrong man, and Claudio was still out there. Things were going from bad to worse.

On the ride over to the airport, Nick said, "Keep an eye on Claudio. I'll call you when I'm down there."

"No problem," Mario said. "Call me when you get there and let me know where you are."

"Sure," Nick said.

He gazed out the window, at the cars zipping by on the expressway, all going somewhere.

Before he knew it, they were at the gate. Mario waited a few minutes before saying his goodbyes. Nick hadn't told him about going to Rosalie's, or that he was hoping she would already be at the gate waiting for him. But she wasn't there. It was one more let down, one more disappointment.

Nick hardly even looked up as Mario walked away. After a moment, Nick jumped up and ran across the waiting area. He grabbed Mario from behind, and spun him around.

"Hey, man," he said. "Take it easy."

"You too, man."

"And let my mom know I'll call her."

"Sure," Mario said. "Don't forget to call me too. And try to chill out."

"I'll be fine." Nick hugged Mario. "Take it easy, man."

Twenty minutes later only a few passengers remained in line waiting to board the plane. But Nick still sat at the gate, waiting and losing hope that Rosalie would show up. He kept his eyes fixed on the open concourse that led up the gate. As each shadowy figure appeared in the distance, he scrutinized them, searching and hopping for Rosalie. But, it was not to be. Over and over again, it was not to be. Where was she? What was wrong with her? What was wrong with him? Was this another one of his screw-ups?

———

NICK TWISTED the volume all the way down on the hotel's color TV and stood in front of its flickering image, a glass of vodka in hand. It was his third glass, or maybe his forth — he didn't know. A jet roared to life close by, shaking the room's windows. It didn't matter. Nothing mattered. Everything—so messed up. His dad? Dead. Albert? Dead. *And he killed him—murdered him!* And Rosalie? Gone. Away. Far away gone. Probably ran as far away as possible. Probably the last thing she would have done was show up at the airport to be with him. And he waited until the last minute, right up until they shut the doors and the plane left the gate. Had she even read his letter? If she did, she probably thought he was mad. What was he thinking? That he had a chance? Ha! Stupid dumb-ass idiot! Idiot!

He stepped around the small dining table and desk to the window and slid it open. The heat of the fading day blew into the cool room. From this high up, he could see the wide expanse of the Mojave Desert and the mountains far in the distance. Over by South Las Vegas Boulevard the McCarran International Airport Hotel sign flicked on and off—Color TV. He looked down at the asphalt of the parking lot, five stories below. There were only a few cars parked here and there scattered around—and none directly under the window.

Nick leaned out and stared down. The fresh air, tinged with the smell of jet fuel, brushed his face. He didn't think he could really jump. Could he? That'd be the coward's way out. But it'd be so easy and simple! A quick escape from all the insanity. He couldn't even stand up to Claudio, after all. Just so fucking useless. What a waste of life he was. How far was it? So easy. Let them clean up the mess.

He leaned further out, hanging onto the window with just his fingertips, his weight forward, tempting fate to intervene and tip the balance once and for all, and just throw him over, and throw his troubles to the wind.

Why put up with all the bullshit this life has to throw at you? Why be afraid of dying? What's to fear in that undiscovered country? Just end it now, right here. It's so simple. Just so simple!

He hung down and the pressure built in his head, while his chest compressed against the windowsill. He started getting light-headed, but didn't try to take a breath. Maybe he would just pass out and fall, and that would be that.

His skin tingled and his heart felt like it was going to pound right out of his chest. This balancing act—this life! Shit, at any moment it could be over. The struggle for survival, for existence. The struggle to *exist* among the living and among the dead, was that it? The honor of existence? Of just existing? Could you hold your head up high because you'd already won—because you simply still existed?

All the misfortunes, all the struggles, all the bullshit—all just minor inconveniences! You stand and are still breathing—that's what mattered. Everyman thinketh that his burden is the heaviest. Yeah, each the heaviest! But that can't be.

He lifted his eyes from the asphalt, but he was losing his equilibrium. His fingertips were in icy pain from holding the window frame, their energy sapped and about to release. He tried to groan but couldn't—he was breathless and mute. His face turned blue, and veins popped in his neck and across his temples and forehead. His grip slipped and he tried to lift himself up, like a plank, but started to fall forward instead. A rush of adrenaline flashed through his body. It was happening, surreally, in slow motion, and there was nothing he could do about it. It was too late, sadly, all too late.

His face and hands smashed down against the brick of

the building. And then . . . *bang!* The heels of his feet caught the underside of the desk just behind him, the desk dragging toward the window, following him out. He instinctively grabbed back at the windowsill and with a vice-like grip struggled to pull himself up, his shirt buttons scraping against the brick, his muscles burning, and the desk, seesawing slowly up behind him. He couldn't die now, it wouldn't be right. He pulled with every ounce of energy he had and slowly began to rise up, back up to the window frame, then promptly fell back into the room, flat on his back.

He gasped and stared up at the popcorn ceiling.

"Shit . . ."

The room spun as he caught his breath. After a moment, he closed his eyes.

What was wrong with him? What was he doing? Shit, he might as well fight—the righteous fight. And if he died trying, so be it, he tried. That's what mattered. He tried. Better to try and die then to fold up like a lawn chair and walk away like a wimp.

He got to his feet and stared out at the horizon and the pastel colors of the desert dusk.

He lifted his chin and vowed, "I will fear no fucking evil as I make my way through this valley of unrelenting bullshit. No one ever said it would be easy, and I'm not gonna make it easy for anyone either. Now, I stand up, and I fight—or I die trying!"

He took a deep breath and stretched his arms wide over his head. He stood like that for a moment, then curled the fingers of his right hand, making a fist, and punched into his palm.

He straightened up the desk and pulled shut the

window. Then he poured himself another drink. He stirred the ice and figured a few days at the hotel would be sufficient to lay low, strategize and think.

He shut the TV, sat down and took a sip. The vodka tasted very good. No, it tasted great.

CHAPTER 18

Two FBI men sat in their black Ford LTD Crown Victoria snapping pictures of guests arriving for Albert's funeral. They were parked across the street from the steps of the St. Joan of Arc Church on South Casino Center Boulevard. While each guest walked through the church parking lot, or walked on the sidewalk, or walked up the church's short steps, the agents snapped away. Some of the guests turned away, and a few even flipped them the finger. But others smiled and nodded when they noticed the surveillance. The FBI guys weren't too discreet, probably because most people expected they'd be there, just as they were last month at Jack's funeral at the very same church. It was all par for the course.

Everyone except Nick was in attendance at Albert Lorenzo's funeral. Albert's widow Jackie, his cousin Roman Lorenzo, Claudio DeVito, Frances Romano, Claudio's daughter Marla, Joey Messina and his wife Mary Ellen and their daughter Rosalie, the rest of Claudio's crew and the rest of their friends and business associates too. Frances sat arm in arm with Claudio. Anne Marie was there too, but no other family or friends of Jack's were there.

The minister read the eulogy in a dreary, monotone voice. Guest fidgeted impatiently. Anne Marie fanned herself with the program, which had a grainy picture of Albert on the cover. In the picture he was, as usual, dapper in his custom-fitted suit, and smiling, with cigar in hand. The photograph was taken as if he had been caught off guard in a rare moment of levity.

The minister went on about faith, God and forgiveness. The guests continued to fidget and to gaze around the church. Only a few elderly guests seemed to pay any attention to the eulogy.

It was just another funeral and the mood was that of impatient obligation and duty, rather than true sympathy or grief. In life, Albert Lorenzo was not the most likeable person and even his own wife, Jackie, didn't seem very mournful. She sat motionless, a veil hiding her face and a cotton handkerchief clasped tightly in her hand.

At the podium in front the white casket, the minister glanced down through his bifocals at his script.

"Albert was a faithful husband and . . ." He glanced up at the audience. "Had he any children, he would have been a loving father."

He looked down again at the paper, "He was cut down by a senseless accident. But it is not ours to judge the moment or circumstances as to when we will be returned . . ." He paused and looked up at the audience again. ". . . to dust. Ashes to ashes and dust to dust, that's what the good book says. It's a club, but not an exclusive club, it's a club that's opened to everyone, and we're all going to join someday. We must remember that, we will all be dust someday, in the dirt, with the slithering worms." He seemed to smile at those words, as if he were revealing some great secret. "And so, we must live each moment, as Albert surely strived to, with our faith in God. It doesn't matter who you are; the dust and worms won't discriminate between you and a king or a queen, a prince or a pauper or . . ." He paused and glanced down at the coffin. ". . . a criminal or a priest." A murmur spread fleetingly through the audience.

Claudio sat there gazing around, hardly hearing anything the minister said. He was up next and was thinking over the main points he wanted to make at the podium. Albert and Claudio had gone back many years and it was difficult for him to comprehend that Albert was actually gone for good. As selfish, egotistical, ruthless and hard-assed as Claudio was, and as feared as Albert had also been, there were pangs of regret and sympathy that welled up in Claudio's thoughts as he couldn't help but reflect on his own life and his own mortality.

Coming back to earth, he wondered what this meant for business. Albert was taken in an instant and that wasn't in the plan. He would have to appoint a new right-hand man, someone he trusted. This was bump in the road, and Albert would be sorely missed.

The minister finished and walked down to the casket.

"May God bless you," he said and made the sign of the cross. "In the name of the Father, Son and Holy Ghost. Amen."

A few half-hearted "Amens" were repeated from those in attendance. The minister walked off to the side and for a moment nothing happened. A few people coughed, and there were some murmurs and restless glancing around.

Then Claudio stood up, shrugged his shoulders and straightened his jacket. He walked past the casket and cleared his throat, then stepped up to the podium. After adjusting the microphone height, he grabbed the podium with both hands and glanced around the room. He looked down at the casket and took a deep breath, before returning his eyes back up to those in attendance. He cleared his throat again.

"As most of you probably know, Albert and I have been good friends for over thirty years. In fact, he's always been one of my most loyal and trusted friends. His sudden death has shaken me, as I'm sure it's shaken many of you and especially shaken his wife, Jackie."

He paused and looked at Jackie.

"He was a good friend, and a good man . . ."

He turned toward the casket and took another deep breath.

"He was a good man . . ."

His stared at the casket and his lip began to quiver and eyes water. His face flushed red. He had more to say, but now he was unable to continue.

"That's all . . ." his voice faltered. "He was a good man. I'm gonna miss him . . ."

He hurriedly stepped down and made his way back his seat. Frances grabbed his arm and patted his wrist as he settled into the pew.

Joey Messina was up next to say a few good words about Albert. He talked quickly, and Claudio could hardly pay attention.

A few minutes later, after he settled down, Claudio turned to Frances and whispered, "Have you heard from Nick yet?"

"No." She shook her head. "I hope he's OK."

CHAPTER 19

A Few Days Later

A t the dimly lit Nico Salvatore's Italian Steakhouse, Claudio sat with his hands clasped, resting on the clean white cotton tablecloth, his menu pushed to the side. Jackie Gleason's 'Days of Wine and Roses' played in the background. Roman Lorenzo sat across to his left and Joey Messina to his right. The waiter had just placed a basket of warm bread on the table, and now stood ready to take their orders.

"Well?" Claudio looked at Roman.

"I'm not sure," Roman said. "What about you Joey?"

Joey looked up from the menu and slapped his hand on the table, "I'm gonna have the fettuccini!"

"Fettuccini, you always get the fettuccini," Roman said. "I'll have ravioli and meat balls."

"Very good, sir," the waiter said.

"And I'll have the usual," Claudio said.

"Chicken marsala, excellent. How about some garlic bread and calamari? And maybe a little anti-pasta too?"

"Sure," Claudio said. "And also a bottle of Chianti."

"Certainly." The waiter left with a spring in his step.

Claudio lit a Parliament cigarette and took a deep, much needed drag. A cloud of smoke drifted over the table. He flipped his Zippo lighter opened and closed a couple of times while gathering his thoughts.

"So Boss." Roman reached for a piece of the warm Italian bread. "Any word from Tony? Did he find Nick yet?"

Claudio snapped his lighter shut and said, "Haven't heard anything from him yet."

"You mean Tony's been down there for three days and hasn't even found him yet?" Joey said.

Claudio took a drag from his cigarette. "That's right."

"Wow," Roman said. "He's probably lounging on the fucking beach drinking Mai Tai's with his feet in the sand and his head up his ass."

"Ha," Joey laughed. "Tough friggin' assignment, huh?"

"He wants Nick dead as much as I do," Claudio said.

"So what the hell is going on then?" Joey said.

"Don't know." Claudio took another drag.

The waiter returned with a carafe of Chianti and began pouring each a glass.

Claudio exhaled. "Let's call him then. Bring me a phone," he said to the waiter.

A moment later the waiter unraveled the long cord and brought the red rotary-dial phone over to the table. Claudio grabbed it and slapped it down, with a ding, in front of Joey.

"Get him on the line," he said.

Joey dialed the operator.

"I'd like to make a collect call from Joey Messina to Tony Scalfaro at the Outrigger Waikiki, room 709."

After a minute, Joey said into the phone, "Yeah, sure."

"He's not there?" Claudio said.

"Not in his room, but maybe at the Blue Dolphin Room, they're checking."

"What the fuck is the Blue Dolphin Room?" Claudio said.

"It's the bar," Joey said. "Here listen there's freakin' Tiki music playing."

Joey reached the receiver over to Claudio's ear. It was Martin Denny music, with romantic steel guitars, bird calls and all.

"Shit." Claudio grabbed it, then suddenly heard Tony answer, "Alooooooohhaaa!"

"Will you accept a collect call from Joey?" the operator said.

Claudio waited.

"Yeah, sure, charge it to my room," Tony said.

"Thank you sir, your party is on the line."

"Joey, how the fuck are you?" Tony said. "Too bad you ain't down here with me, it's fucking crazy. Pina Coladas, you know the ones with the little umbrella, sunset on the beach, bikini-clad chicks, best fuckin' marijuana you ever had, and the sand, it's so fucking white. Shit, I'm tellin' ya, I got it made here, I ain't never comin' back . . ."

"You stupid fuck, it's Claudio! What the hell are you doin' down there?"

Claudio could hear the exotic Tiki music in the background suddenly fade away. Joey had probably cupped the receiver with his hand.

"Sorry Boss."

"Do you fucking think you're on vacation?"

"No Boss. I've been trying to find him but he's not here."

"Maybe you're not looking hard enough?"

"I have, nobody's seen him Boss."

"You checked with Macho?"

"Macho ain't seen him and none of his guys have either. He's not at the hotel."

"Well," Claudio held the receiver away from his face and shouted at it, "Where the fuck is he then!"

"I don't know Boss, maybe he's on another island?"

"What other island?"

"Maybe he skipped Waikiki and went to Maui, I don't know," Tony said.

"Shit," Claudio said, and took a last drag of his cigarette before crushing it in the ashtray.

"Wherever he is, I'll find him Boss. Don't worry, I'll find him."

"If you don't find him by tomorrow afternoon then get your ass back here, we got better things to do."

"Sure thing Boss."

"And bring me back some Kona coffee and chocolate covered macadamia nuts. And a couple of fresh pineapples too."

"And what about us?" Roman held his palms out.

Claudio smirked, "Bring some for the boys too."

He hung up the phone, and shook his head. "Shit."

The waiter marched over with a large tray of food balanced on his shoulder. He set it down and the men immediately perked up. The waiter slid a large dish of Chicken Marsala in front of Claudio first. The sweet smell of the Marsala wine, butter, olive oil and mushrooms filled the air.

"Ah, Madrone!" Claudio said and inhaled the aromas, "Beautiful!"

"Yes, it is Boss," Roman said. "Smells great."

Claudio said to the waiter, "Bring us some more garlic bread too and another Chianti."

With the corner of his cotton napkin tucked into his shirt collar, Claudio carefully sliced off a piece of chicken and spun his fork a few times to wrap some pasta around it. After chewing, he looked up and said, "Delicious."

The men fell silent and dug into their food. Dean Martin music played merrily in the background, and the restaurant, felt warm and cozy. Life was good and the food tasty.

After a few bites and a few sips of his Chianti, Claudio put his fork down.

"What's up?" Roman said, through a mouthful of ravioli.

Claudio leaned forward. Roman and Joey stopped eating, their attention set on him.

"So," Claudio said quietly. "I talked to our brethren on the east coast about Albert's replacement."

"You spoke to Crocetti?" Joey said.

"Yes, I spoke to the man himself."

Roman smiled and straightened his posture.

"Huh? Well," Roman said. "What'd he say? Good news?"

Claudio looked stone-faced at Roman, and his smile abruptly disappeared.

"I'm sorry," Claudio said. "But Mr. Crocetti says he's sending out Angelo to replace Albert."

"What?" Joey said. "Angelo 'The Nut' Lombardo?"

Roman smirked.

"Unfortunately for us," Claudio said. "Yes, that's right, The Nut."

"Angelo the fucking Nut!" Roman threw his napkin on the table, "What the fuck about me? My cousin Albert is dead—I'm next in line to fill his shoes."

"That's what I thought too. And I told him that."

Claudio took a sip of his wine.

"And?" Roman said.

Claudio wiped his mouth and placed his cotton napkin on his lap.

"He said no."

"No?" Roman said incredulously. "Who the fuck am I? They think I'm a piece of shit?"

"Take it easy," Claudio raised his voice. "There was nothing I could do."

"Shit," Roman said. "This is bullshit. I'm the guy. I'm the one that's been here with you all these years, not him, he's just a thug. And that's all we need, some fucking maniac comin' down here. How many fucking guys has that psycho wacked up there? He's a goddamn one-man wrecking crew."

"Look." Claudio pointed his finger at Roman. "I went to bat for you, and for me." He pointed back at himself. "How do you think I feel? I'm running things here. I'm the one that busted my goddamn ass getting everything setup here, and now it's fucking perfect, it's a dream—it's golden. But now here's The Nut, coming in from left field, muscling his way in!" Claudio paused. "But you know what? I can't do a fuckin' thing about it. We got no choice. We gotta do what we're told and we gotta do our job."

Roman's teeth were clenched and face red.

"Look," Claudio continued. "I tried to talk Crocetti out of it, but he won't have it. He wants more feet on the ground, period. And The Nut is his guy. He said Angelo *deserved* it, for his loyalty, for his goddamn hard work. Fuck, I'm just as pissed as you. Shit, I did everything I could to convince him, but it was a no-go. A big fat fucking NO-GO!"

Roman held his words, then looked over at Joey and said, "What do you think?"

Joey shrugged his shoulders and shook his head. "What do I think? Nothin'. If that's the way Crocetti wants it, that's the way it is. Period. We can't do nothin'."

"That's right," Claudio said. "But don't worry, you're still my go-to man. Even when The Nut is out here, you're still my man, understand?"

Roman slouched back in his chair, unbelieving, defeated. "I got it," he said.

"Good," Claudio said. "I knew you'd understand."

"Yeah, well let's not forget," Roman added. "We got the Gaming Commission breathing down our necks and the damn FBI lurking around like vultures." He lowered his voice, "And we got a fortune right under our noses, practically at our fingertips. And now The Nut is coming to town? The fucking Nut. That's all we need."

Claudio raised his eyebrows and took a deep breath.

"There's nothing we can do," he said. "He's coming out next week and we gotta make him feel welcome. All we can do is apprise him of the situation and keep him out of trouble and off the radar. That's all we can do."

Claudio looked at the men and took a sip of his wine, signaling that that conversation was over. Then he cut into his chicken marsala.

After they ate for a few minutes, Claudio wiped his mouth, folded his napkin, and looked at them.

"I've been thinking," he said. "With this new twist, we

should get the stuff out of the casino."

Roman and Joey both stopped chewing.

"You know," he continued. "Before The Nut gets here. For safe keeping. We don't want him to ruin it for us, right?"

"What?" Roman said. "Are you kiddin', take it for ourselves? What if Crocetti finds out?"

Roman looked at Joey, but Joey didn't say anything.

"Yeah," Claudio said slyly. "We take it for ourselves, then we change our names, run to Mexico and live a fat, dumb and happy life with all the beautiful little chiquita's that we want."

Claudio slapped Roman's back. "Isn't that a great fuckin' plan?"

Roman looked at him in disbelief.

"I'm kidding, man." Claudio smiled.

Roman chuckled nervously. "Well," he said. "You had me going there for a second."

"No problem," Claudio said. "But, seriously. I'm just brainstorming. Don't you think maybe we should get that stuff outta there before trouble starts? You know, before The Nut gets out here and the shit hits the fan?"

Joey leaned forward. "How much you think is there?"

"A lot." Claudio raised his eyebrows. "Two large walk-in vaults. Maybe they're full, I don't know. Frances told me Jack collected silver coins practically his whole damn life. Once I heard him arguing with his accountant, Bill, about buying too many coins and too many silver bars. Bill wanted him to diversify and put the money into other stuff—stocks, bonds. He even told Jack his life would be in danger with that much shit lying around. Fuck, guess he was right, huh?"

"Yeah, no shit," Joey said.

Claudio smiled. "There's gotta be tons down there. I'm gonna get the combo from Frances, then we can take a look."

Claudio leaned back and took a sip of his wine.

"Alright Boss," Roman said. "I'm with you. If it's anything like you say man, holy shit, we're in big baby. And there's no harm in taking precautions, especially before the damn Nut gets here."

"Yeah," Claudio said. "Here's what I'm thinking. There's a guy in way over his head at the casino. He has a ranch up in Mesquite. We get him to dig us a nice big hole out there in the middle of nowhere, and then we bury the shit."

"Mesquite?" Joey said.

"Yeah." Claudio said. "We get the shit outta here, and we protect it. Away from Nick and the rest of the Romano clan, away the Gaming Commission, away from the FBI, away from everyone–except us, of course."

"Well, alright then," Roman said. "Sounds good to me."

"Yup," Claudio said. "First, we check the vault, then we go talk to the rancher."

He stood up from the table. "I gotta use the little boy's room. I'll be right back."

Roman waited until Claudio was gone, then turned to Joey and said vehemently, "I don't trust that *fuck*!" Particles of food ejected from his mouth.

Joey smirked and shook his head. "You talk too much, you know that? He told you what happened, right? It wasn't his fault. You'll get over it."

"He didn't try hard enough," Roman said. "He threw

in the towel too early. Gave up! And that's if he's telling the truth. How the fuck do I know if bringing out the Nut wasn't his goddamn idea to begin with?"

"You really think so?" Joey shook his head again in disagreement. "That's a pretty fucked up accusation."

"I'm telling you, it's his fault." Roman looked down at his plate of congealing fettuccini. "Shit, I can't even eat anymore."

He pushed the plate away.

"Waiter!" he yelled. "Bring me a scotch on ice."

In the bathroom stall Claudio pulled out a small mirror, steamed it up with his breath, then wiped it clean on his shirt. He placed it face up on his thigh, then reached into his jacket pocket and removed a small plastic zip-lock bag. Within a moment he held a rolled up twenty-dollar bill pressed into one nostril and the sparkling white lines on the mirror in front of his face. He leaned forward and with a swish whiffed one line, threw his head back, sniffled and shook. He considered for a moment the other line before him, then lifted the small mirror to his face and with another whiff it was gone. Only a few flakes remained. He wiped them up with his finger and rubbed them on his gums.

"Ooohhh baby . . ." he whispered.

CHAPTER 20

Frances threw her head back and swallowed a couple of pink 5mg Valium. Accidentally, she plopped the glass down too hard, splashing water onto the kitchen counter.

"Shit," she said and reached for the dish towel.

It wasn't so bad. The glass could have easily broken. Her nerves were a wreck—the wedding planning was getting more hectic, and Nick hadn't called yet. Did he even make it to Hawaii? Could something have happened to him? She should have heard from him by now. It was almost five days, but there was nothing, not even a post card. She knew he would be laying low down there, but didn't think he would completely disappear. It was disconcerting and worrisome. Why hadn't he at least called?

She picked up the receiver of the kitchen's yellow Bell System wall phone and began dialing Mario's number, each number pulsing in her ear as she swung the dial around her finger. She hadn't called him yet today and was anxious to hear if he had any news.

"Mrs. Romano," Mario said. "I haven't heard anything from him, but I'm sure he's OK."

"Why don't you go down there and look for him? I'll pay for your airfare."

"I'd love to go to Hawaii," he said. "But I'm sure he's OK. He's a smart guy. He probably just doesn't want to take any chances. Let's give him a couple more days. If we don't hear from him by Saturday, then I'll go. OK?"

"But it's been almost a week," Frances said. "Why hasn't he at least called?"

"I'm sure he's OK. He's probably chilling out on the beach. I'll let you know the second I hear anything."

"Thanks," Frances said.

"Don't worry. He'll turn up soon."

"Call me right away, even if it's the middle of the night."

"No problem, bye Mrs. Romano."

"Bye."

Frances hung up the phone, sat down and slumped back in the chair. She slipped a Kool cigarette from its box and tapped it a few times on the kitchen table. Her fingers shook while she lit it. She exhaled and watched the smoke drift away. Her eyes fell toward the living room, to the piano. The valium was beginning to settle in like a warm blanket, insulating, protecting and calming her.

She heard a sound from the garage and stood up. It could be Nick. She opened the kitchen door to see, but it was only Claudio pulling his gold Lincoln into the carport. She closed the door and slid down in the chair again, then gazed at her cigarette, not even wanting to lift it to take a drag.

A few moments later Claudio walked in carrying some packages.

"What's up honey?" he said cheerfully.

"Nick." She looked up at him. "Where is he? Why hasn't he at least called?"

Claudio put the packages on the table and said, "I'm sure he's fine."

He proceeded to take off his jacket and hang it on the back of a chair. Then he sat down and grabbed Frances' hand.

"Honey," he said. "Nick's probably having a great time soaking up the sun on Waikiki beach."

He rubbed her hand. "Hey, look what I got for you."

He reached into one of the bags and pulled out a small pink box with a white ribbon neatly tied in a bow. He placed it in front of her.

She stared at the box a moment, then put her hand over it. She looked at Claudio.

"Have you heard from Nick?" she said.

"Nothing," Claudio raised his eyebrows and shook his head. "Not a thing. It's like he disappeared. Nobodies' heard anything."

"You don't know where he is?"

"No."

She placed her hand over his and looked him in the eye. "You wouldn't let anything happen to him, would you?"

"Of course not, don't be ridiculous." He pulled his hand away.

"You'd tell me if you heard anything, right?" she said.

"Of course I would, now open it." He pushed the box at her. "You worry too much, I'm sure he's fine."

She stared at him.

"Look," Claudio said. "When he comes back, I'll make sure nothing happens to him, you have my word. Guaranteed."

She smiled.

"Now open the box."

"OK, what'd you get me?"

She picked up the box and pulled the ribbon off.

"You didn't have to," she said and opened the box.

It was a pearl necklace.

"Thank you," she said and held it up. "It's lovely."

———

LATER THAT AFTERNOON, Claudio sat at the bar with a glass of whisky and gently swirled it around. He also held a new Padron cigar, but hadn't yet reached the right moment to light it up. He smiled and swirled the ice in the glass, then brought the cigar to his lips as if he were going to take a puff. He glanced across the casino floor at the moving crew while they carried box after box out of Jack's office. His smile grew wider.

"See this?" he waved the cigar in the air. "Is this not trippin', my man?"

"It's . . ." Roman Lorenzo nodded. "It's, right on. definitely happenin' man."

They laughed, and Roman took a drag from his cigarette.

Claudio swigged the rest of his drink and pushed the glass toward the bartender. "One more round, sir. Dewar's on the rocks."

The bartender delivered their drinks, placing them down on fresh coasters, which had a portrait of Jack in his 10 gallon Stetson printed on them, the same as on the chips.

"Gracias." Claudio turned to Roman, smiled and patted him on the back.

"I'm glad you got no hard feelings about this thing with The Nut coming down." Claudio looked at him. "I mean that. Really. I'm glad you understand. You're my man, not the Nut, you. You are my main man."

"I know, I know." Roman nodded again. "And I appreciate it."

Claudio smiled again, and so did Roman.

"Here's to you sir." Roman raised his glass.

"No, to us, and . . ." Claudio raised his glass and waved it at the noisy, smoke filled casino floor. ". . . and to our new location!"

They drank and savored the moment. Then Claudio put his glass down, and became serious.

"Can't wait to sit in that office at Jacks desk," he said. "Life is good, very good. It's taken me a long time to get here Roman, you know that. It's been a long road."

"I know," Roman said. "And I got your back all these years."

"Yes you do," Claudio said. Then lowered his head and leaned toward Roman. He had his full attention.

"First, I want you to get rid of these damn coasters that have Jack's face on them." He motioned toward the coasters with the unlit cigar.

"No problem."

"Then," Claudio said.

"Yes sir."

Claudio cleared his throat.

"I want you to get rid of all the security here and replace them with our guys. I'm gonna be in that office over there and I want my own security."

"Absolutely." Roman took a drag from his cigarette. "No problem, I'll get it done."

"Good." Claudio smiled.

He clipped the cigar and with his torch lighter carefully rolled the fat Padron cigar tip in the flame. Then he brought the cigar to his lips and drew in a few puffs to get it well lit. A thick, satisfying cloud of smoke rose around him.

Claudio looked at Roman and said, "You know that foxy chick?"

Roman gave him a quizzical look.

"You know, the new girl, the 'light my fire' girl?"

"Oh, Nichole," Roman said and took another drag from his cigarette.

Claudio gave Roman a sly look and with a subtle upward flick of his chin said, "Send her up in ten."

Roman smiled. "You got it Boss."

Claudio stood up and took a deep breath, then adjusted his jacket sleeves. He grabbed his whisky, and with his chin up, he proudly strode, like a king, toward the elevator.

CHAPTER 21

I t was late evening and "Live and Let Die" played on the radio. Mario had just taken a toke from his joint and now sat with his head back on the couch. He exhaled and watched the smoke push through the dust that floated in the dim light of his apartment.

His mellow repose was suddenly interrupted by a knock on the door. He immediately grabbed the Glade Forest Fresh off the coffee table and sprayed it around the living room. More banging on the door.

"Just a minute," he shouted.

He grabbed a dirty T-shirt off the back of a chair and flapped it in the air. Another rap rap rap at the door.

"Mario!" someone called.

He stumbled over a pile of Rolling Stone and Playboy magazines.

"Mario, man, it's me, open up!"

He swung opened the door. It was Nick—a suitcase at his feet and a knapsack on his shoulder.

"Holy shit, man," Mario said. "Where the fuck have you been?"

Nick stepped in and hugged Mario, patting him on the back.

"Good to see you man," Nick said.

"Shit, why didn't you call?"

"I couldn't."

Nick looked around the living room. "Wow," he said. "Haven't been here in a while, don't you ever think of cleaning up? What's that smell? Smells like pine trees and funk."

There was a pile of dirty laundry spilling out from the hallway, crusty dishes piled in and around the sink, potato chips strewn across the floor, newspapers and magazines piled around, empty cigarette boxes, Zig Zag and EZ-Wider rolling papers on the coffee table, and an ashtray full of cigarette butts.

Mario shook his head, "Cleaning's a low priority, man."

"You need a permanent girlfriend, man. Someone to help you with this place."

"Yeah, I know." Mario looked at him, "So, what the hell? Why didn't you call me, or at least call your mom?"

Nick navigated through the mess and threw his knapsack on the couch, then sat down next to it.

"Oh man." He stretched his arms over his head and took a deep breath. "I was going to call, but then I thought that would be stupid."

"Shit," Mario said. "Your mom's been calling me every day. She's a wreck. I've got to call her right now—now that you've materialized."

Mario reached for the phone on the coffee table.

"Hold on." Nick straightened up.

"I promised I'd call her as soon as I heard from you."

"Chill out, man. If you call her and Claudio finds out I'm back, then what? Then I gotta worry about that, right? Now I don't have to worry. I can relax and we can get our act together."

"But you know, she's really freaking out."

"Yeah, but I'm sure she'd be happier if I'm safe and nothing happens to me, right? So for now, you haven't seen me, understand?"

Mario raised his eyebrows, "OK man, but you gotta let her know it wasn't my fault."

"Don't worry. Now, where am I sleeping in this dump tonight?"

"The couch, I guess," Mario said.

Nick looked at the cushions and brushed a bunch of crumbs off them.

"Do you have a vacuum?"

"Yeah man, it's in the closet. But shit man, so how was Hawaii?" Mario grabbed the partially smoked joint from the ashtray.

"Don't know," Nick said. "Never went."

"*What?* You got on the flight, didn't you?"

Nick shrugged. "Not exactly, man. I was so pissed off, I decided not to go. Why the fuck should I be the one running away?"

Mario sat down. "Yeah, so where you been?"

"At the airport hotel, thinking, going stir crazy."

"Well." Mario lit up the remainder of the joint and passed it to Nick. "It's good to see you man."

Nick held the joint. "Listen," he said. "I did a lot of thinking. We gotta do something about Claudio, we gotta get rid of him."

Nick took a hit.

Mario didn't say anything and Nick continued. "He killed my father. And now he's got my mom fucking brainwashed. How the *hell* did this happen?"

He took another hit, then passed the joint to Mario.

"Maybe they're in love?" Mario said.

Nick coughed, "What?"

"I'm kidding." Mario took a hit. "What about going to the police? Maybe we should just do that."

Nick smirked. "Gimme a break."

"Shit." Mario passed the joint back to Nick.

"No, now it's up to us," Nick said. "We gotta do it, ourselves."

Mario raised his eyebrows, "I got it. What if we gave him a massive hit of acid!"

"Oh man." Nick chuckled. "That'd be crazy. I could just see it, Claudio going nuts in the casino."

"Yeah, he'd be runnin' around like crazy through the casino with all the noise and bells ringing in his head, and all the old ladies laughing at him. Shit, that'd be great."

Nick laughed again. "Yeah, it'd be what he deserves. But it wouldn't kill him. Seriously man, we gotta do something. Something that'd make my dad proud."

"Absolutely, man," Mario said.

Nick gaze around the room. There was a poster of the album cover of L.A. Woman, which hung on the wall above Mario's small Panasonic black and white TV. Jim Morrison. Nick took a deep breath. Yeah, L.A. Woman, you're my woman.

"By the way." Nick sat up. "Have you seen Rosalie around? Is she still in town?"

"Haven't seen her, but everyone knows you're after her."

"What? What do you mean?"

"Well," Mario said. "After I left you at the airport I stopped back at your house to let your mom know that you got off alright on your flight. So when I stopped by to tell her, Claudio and Rosalie's dad, what's his name? Joey. Anyway, he was there, and he said that he had to throw you out of their house."

"What?" Nick smirked.

"He said you broke into Rosalie's room and was bothering her. So he threw you out."

"Are you kidding me, man?" Nick said. "I went there to see her and return her purse. We were just talking. It's her dad that flipped out. He was going to kill me. So, I had to high-tail it outta there."

"Shit," Mario shook his head.

"I was hoping to convince her to come to Hawaii with me. Then I would have gone, and maybe never come back. But as I'm talking to her, her dumb-ass dad comes busting in on us before she could even answer me. I thought she'd meet me at the airport. But shit, I don't know what her deal is now."

"Think she really likes you, man?"

"Don't know. She told me that she was already engaged."

"Huh, shit," Mario said.

Yeah, Nick looked up at the LA Woman poster again, *you're my woman.*

They sat quietly for a minute, then Mario said, "So, what's the plan?"

"The plan," Nick repeated. "The big plan! What's the plan?"

Nick shook his head. "The plan, brother," he said in a whisper. "Is to get Claudio."

Nick straightened up and looked at Mario. "We kill him!" he said louder. "A king no more, a made-man made dead! And we take his old stinking rotting flesh and bones out to that vast desert wasteland, and dump him, in a nice dusty old hole in the ground, where the tarantulas, lizards and insects can feast on his greedy bones."

"OK, man." Mario raised his eyebrows and stared at Nick with wide open eyes.

"What's a matter, man?" Nick said. "You're not getting cold feet, are you? You're the one that freakin' told me what Claudio did. Shit, if it wasn't for you I wouldn't have a clue. I would have thought my dad died naturally, like everybody else, like it was his time. But it wasn't his time. *We proved that.* And that's not fucking right. It's wrong. And now we gotta fix it." Nick eyed him closely. "So, are you in?"

"Yeah man, of course," Mario stammered. "I'm in. I'll do whatever I gotta do to help. Just let me know."

"All you gotta do is help me dig the hole and push him in."

"Cool," Mario said. "No problem!"

"Alright man," Nick said. "Let's have a beer. Got any beer?"

"Yeah, sure."

After getting a couple of cold beers, they sat back down on the couch. Nick popped the pull tab on his can.

"A toast," he said. "To us, and to my dear Pops!"

"Toast." Mario clicked cans with Nick.

Nick took a sip. "Ahhh," he said. "That's good."

He put his head back and gazed at the ceiling and chuckled.

"So," Mario said. "What's the plan? I mean, the actual plan."

Nick sat up. "OK," he said. "First, you gotta shave off that mustache. Then, tomorrow, we stake him out. See what he's up to, see what his routine is. We can go by my mom's house early and wait for him to leave. Then we follow him."

"In my car?" Mario said. "That'd be a little risky."

"Shit, yeah, you're right. Where can we get a car, that nobody will recognize?"

Mario thought a moment. "Maybe I can get Barbara's car."

"Barbara?" Nick said.

"Yeah, she owes me a favor."

"Think she'd do it?"

"I don't know," Mario said.

"You don't mind seeing her again?"

"No, it's fine. She's OK."

"Alright man. Let's call her in the morning then."

"No problemo," Mario said, then looked at Nick. "Shit, it's fucking good to see you, man."

"Good to be back," Nick said. "Now let's smoke another doobie."

CHAPTER 22

J ack's old office bore no resemblance to what it once looked like. Claudio had redecorated it to the extent that only a few items of Jack's remained — his desk, chair, phone, intercom and Zenith radio. The rest of Jack's stuff now sat in boxes in the car port at Frances's house. A photograph of Claudio and Frances, now hung on the wall in the office, in the same spot where the oil painting of Jack and Frances had previously hung. On the desk a picture of Claudio's daughter Marla sat lounging in a bikini, on their house boat, her dog Chip on her lap, a beer in her hand and sunny Lake Mead in the background.

Outside the office, there was an empty space in the cashier cage where Jack had previously left three refrigerator-sized safes opened and on display to reveal their treasures to customers. Claudio had them closed and moved to the side, out of view. All that was left now were bright red rectangles of fresh carpet under where the safes had been.

Claudio leaned back in Jack's old chair and put his feet on the desk. Roman Lorenzo sat across from him, looking at him in disbelief. Joey Messina sat next to Roman.

"How can you do that?" Roman said.

"Very easily, just do it," Claudio said. "What's the problem?"

"If you just switch out all the chips . . ."

"Hold on." Joey stood up and raised his hand as if to signal to stop.

Up-tempo jazz played softly on the desk radio.

Joey leaned over the desk and whispered, "I just wanna turn up the radio."

"You're too damned paranoid," Claudio said.

"Just takin' precautions." Joey said.

With the volume up, he sat back down.

"So," Roman said. "You just switch out the chips and bring in new ones, is that it? What about all the people that are gonna wake up and find out their old chips ain't worth shit? And what about that guy, what's his name, Sy Zeldin? He's gonna flip out when he finds out his chips are no good. And how much is he sitting on, hoarding them at his mansion? Half a million?"

"Probably at least that much." Claudio puffed his Padron cigar. "Seymour Zeldin, fool. Fuck him — what the hell do we care?"

Roman shook his head, "I don't know. That guy Sy, he's friends with the mayor, and his cronies. What do you think he's gonna do when we announce this thing?"

Claudio pulled his feet off the desk and leaned forward.

"Look, we don't have a choice. That's what The Nut said we gotta do because that's what Mr. Crocetti wants, right?"

"The Nut said to replace the chips?"

"Yeah, do you think I'd do something so fucking stupid?"

Roman scratched his chin, "Nah, of course not, Boss."

"Yeah, well I don't like Jack's face on every goddamn chip anyway," Claudio said. "So we might as well replace them. But like I said, we got no choice. And I did express my concern to Angelo, but he said he'd take care of any trouble.

Said he'd be looking forward to it."

"Yeah, well, trouble's all we'll have around here then," Roman said.

"He also said to get it done before he arrives too. Look I know it's gonna be tough for you to pull off, but you'll get guaranteed brownie points for it."

Roman shifted in his seat.

"Plus." Claudio smiled. "We're all gettin' a percentage. Gross is gonna be over a million, and we'll get a few hundred thousand of that to split."

Roman raised his eyebrows.

"But," Claudio said. "We won't know until after everything settles down and we figure out the net."

"What's the percentage?" Roman asked.

"Fifteen."

"Sounds good to me," Joey said. "Split four ways, that could be 75 grand each."

"Yeah, that's not bad." Roman lit a cigarette. "But you know all hell's gonna break loose."

"Well," Claudio said. "Maybe, maybe not. We'll have some trouble, from some people. Like Sy. But for those that ain't hoarding tons of chips, it won't matter."

Roman took a drag on his cigarette and exhaled. "Yeah, I guess so. It may not be so bad," he said. "Anyway, let The Nut clean up the shit. That's his job right?"

"Damn straight," Claudio said. "Also, one other thing. They want us to stop all Jack's payola to the mayor, the police and the guy on the gaming commission. Mr. Crocetti wants us to stop everything, at least until The Nut gets here and has a chance to review it all. Wants to make sure that Jack wasn't overpaying."

"What?" Roman said. "That's crazy, we'll have so much heat we won't know what hit us."

"Just put the word out to them that we're reassessing everything before we resume payments. Make it sound like the payments will go up."

"I don't know, man," Roman said. "That's really risky."

Claudio looked him in the eye. "Don't worry about it. Just do it. Like you said, let The Nut deal with the bullshit. He's gotta have something to do, right?"

Roman raised his eyebrows. "Oh, yeah, and he'll have plenty to do, that's for sure."

"You'll score some points on this too buddy," Claudio said. "Just keep that in mind too."

"Yeah," Roman said.

The intercom on Claudio's desk buzzed.

Claudio flinched and hit the button, "Can't you lower the buzzer on this damn thing, it almost knocked me off my chair."

"I'll call for service on it, Sir," his secretary answered. "Tony Scalfaro, here to see you."

"Send him in."

Tony walked in, his arm still in a sling.

"Guess what Boss?"

"Don't give me that shit. Have a seat and tell me what's happening."

"We found Nick," Tony said.

Claudio immediately sat up straight and smiled.

"Really?" he said. "You didn't take care of him, did you?"

"No." Tony took his seat. "We just found him last

night."

"In Hawaii?" Joey laughed. "You leave Hawaii and now somebody finds him there?"

"No, he's here. Two of our guys found him last night, at his friend Mario's apartment. I had a hunch he might show up there, so I had them stake out the place. And sure enough, Nick arrived there last night, with his bags and all. Guess he must've just got back."

"Wow, good work," Claudio said, as he considered the implications.

"Great, man," Roman said. "Who found him?"

"The two kids," Tony said. "Mike and Ralph."

"Good," Roman said. "Have them come and see me. I'll give them their due reward."

"I can do it," Tony said.

"No." Roman smiled. "That's OK, just send them to me, so I can congratulate them."

"Alright." Tony shrugged.

"So," Tony said, turning to Claudio. "What do you think? Let me take care of him, you won't have to worry anymore. I'll make sure he disappears, nice and quietly."

Claudio leaned back, puffed his cigar, and thought for a moment.

"Let's not rush into anything," he said. "For now, just leave him alone."

"What?" Roman said. "He fucking killed my brother. What do you . . ."

"Whoa!" Claudio interrupted. "I didn't say we weren't gonna whack him. I just said to cool your jets. That's all. Let's see what he's up to first. We gotta make it look good, like an accident. We gotta be super careful and it's gotta go right. If

Frances suspects anything then we're screwed, and that's it, our whole enterprise would be fucked. Remember, she still owns it all—and we ain't even married yet."

Roman leaned back in his seat.

"Shit," Tony said. "Just let me know. I'm ready when you are."

"Good," Claudio said. "Just keep an eye on him for now, and don't touch him."

"Sure." Tony nodded.

CHAPTER 23

By the time Nick woke up the sun was already streaming through the kitchen window and onto dirty piles of dishes that sat in and around Mario's sink. Dust drifted in the stale air. Nick stumbled to the refrigerator and yanked it open. He hoped there was at least milk for coffee.

An overwhelming stink of rotting and putrefied food and gunk assaulted his nostrils.

"Oh, shit!" He slammed the door and turned, about to throw up. "Mario, where's the damn coffee?"

Mario grumbled something incomprehensible from the living room.

"What?"

"The top cabinet."

Nick grabbed the coffee. "Damn," he said. "How the hell do you find anything in this house? There's piles of shit all over. How can you live like this?"

"Hey man, I know where everything is. And I told you, cleaning's a low priority."

"Whatever."

Nick sipped his black coffee, then said, "So, you gonna call your girlfriend? We gotta get going, we got work to do today."

"She's not my girlfriend anymore, but I'll call."

Mario brought the phone to the table and dialed.

When Barbara answered, Nick could clearly hear her through the receiver and he could even hear some Grateful

Dead music playing in the background — *Casey Jones*.

"What's up?" She sounded surprised.

"Not much, but listen, I got a favor to ask."

"What?"

"Well . . . I need to borrow your car."

"What? What's wrong with yours? And when are you going to bring me back my waffle maker?"

"I'll bring it back." Mario smiled. "But only if you'll make me waffles again."

"Not likely. So what's wrong with your car?"

"Nothin. Umm, I mean . . ." Mario hesitated. "It's not good. It's overheating. It'll only drive like a mile before it gets too hot and stalls. I got a guy coming over to look at it, but in the meantime, I need a car. Can I borrow yours just for the afternoon?"

Silence. Mario looked at Nick and waited.

"What the hell am I gonna do for transportation then?" Barbara said. "I got an appointment this afternoon to get my hair done."

"How 'bout we drop you off?"

"We?"

"Sorry, yeah, me and my friend Nick. You remember him? His dad just passed away last month, he owns the casino, the Cornetto Club."

"Huh."

"Look, you gotta lend us your car, it's an emergency. I'm screwed if I don't get a car."

Silence again, and then, "What's in it for me?"

"I don't know, I'll take you to a Dead concert. How's that?"

"Really?"

"Really."

"OK, fine. They'll be in L.A. in a couple of weeks, at the Universal Amphitheater. How about that show?"

Mario hesitated, but Nick nodded and gave him a thumbs-up.

"OK, no problem," Mario said.

"Floor tickets."

"Fine."

"Great," Barbara said. "It's yours, but just for today."

"Beautiful," Mario said.

"And you better take care of it, it's only a few months old."

"No problem, don't worry."

———

MARIO PEEKED through the curtains just as the bright lime-green Pinto pulled up in front of the house. "She's here," he said.

"Great, let's go," Nick said and grabbed his knapsack.

Mario snatched a joint off the coffee table and shut the light. In a moment Barbara stood at the door, her frizzy, wavy hair parted down the middle, a head band wrapped around it. She wore a loose fitting tie-dyed shirt, bell bottom jeans, and clog sandals. She held her hand out.

"Waffle maker," she said.

"Oh, shit, give me a second."

Mario ran back into the kitchen.

"Are you Nick?" she said.

Nick nodded.

"I heard about your dad. That's too bad."

"Yeah, thanks." Nick looked toward the small, funky car.

"Wow," he said. "That's a pretty wild color."

"Like it?" she asked.

"It's different."

"It's alive, that's what it is," she said. "With energy. Not like every other drab car on the road. I call it my *peace & love* car."

"That's Cool," Nick said.

Mario came back with the waffle maker in a shopping bag and handed it to Barbara.

"Here it is," he said.

She grabbed it and smirked. "I see you haven't even cleaned yet, since I left."

Mario shut the door.

"Let's go," he said.

———

BARBARA PULLED the car in front of the hair salon and turned to Mario.

"You better take care of my car," she said.

"Don't worry," Mario said. "What are you worrying about?"

"Nothin'. Pick me up in an hour, and can you fill up the tank, too."

"No problem, thanks."

Mario squeezed in behind the wheel and Nick jumped in the front seat. Nick's knees were hitting the dashboard, so he repositioned the seat as far back as it could go.

"That's a little better," he said. "Damn, this car is tiny. I guess nobody will think it's us in it."

"But the color, man, that's gonna attract attention."

"Nobody notices a Pinto, man," Nick said. "So, what's with you and Barbara?"

"Nothin', we had our thing. You know, she's a hippy flower child Dead-Head. Can't cook, except for some waffle recipe she got from her grandmother—which is actually pretty damn good."

Mario drove slowly. "OK," he said. "So, where are we going now?"

"Let's swing around my house first to see if anyone is there."

"Sure."

Nick flipped through the stations on the radio. Hey Jude came on and he turned it up.

"This is good song," Nick said. "But it goes on forever."

"Definitely," Mario said. "But why'd they break up? The Stones are still together, why not the Beatles? Freakin' Yoko, that's why!"

Nick shook his head. "Nah, I don't believe that crap."

"You don't?"

"Nah, that's bullshit. They broke up because of something else. It couldn't have been because of her."

"OK," Mario said. "But it still sucks. They should have stayed together, like the Stones. I'm sure the Stone's will stay together for at least a couple more years."

"Yeah, let's hope so," Nick said. "That'd be great."

A few minutes later Mario pulled up to Nick's house.

"Should I park in the driveway?" Mario said. "Doesn't look like anyone is here."

"No, let's drive around the block first and scope out the scene."

"Sure."

Mario drove slowly. He and Nick checked for activity on the block, but in the crushing heat of the late morning sun, there was nobody around. They passed the house again. The driveway was empty.

"Park over there and wait for me," Nick said. "I'll run in."

Mario parked down the block from the house. Nick grabbed his knapsack from the back seat and pulled out a Mets baseball cap, gold-rimmed aviator sunglasses, and a dungaree jacket. After he struggled to put the jacket on in the cramped car, he said, "Give me five minutes."

"OK," Mario said. "But, you gonna wear that jacket? In this heat?"

"Sure, gotta keep disguised, right? And the house is air conditioned anyway."

Nick walked up the block, past the neighbor's house, then along the empty driveway to the side of his house, all the while glancing in each window he passed. He made his way to the expansive back yard and to the sliding patio doors. He looked in. Nothing. He walked back to the carport and the kitchen's side door. His pulse quickened. He inserted the key in the doorknob and turned it. He knew where his dad had kept his guns and hoped they were still there. He carefully opened the door and stepped in. He paused to listen.

Nobody seemed to be home. On the kitchen table, the

newspaper was open in mid-read, a cup sitting next to it, with a dry coffee ring at the bottom. Nick made his way upstairs to his mom's bedroom.

First, he checked the nightstand drawer next to the bed. His dad had always kept a gun there, loaded and ready. He pulled open the drawer but it was too light; the gun wasn't there. Instead, he saw receipts and three matchbooks — one from The Fabulous Flamingo Hotel, one from The Stardust, and one from The Vegas Club.

There were also two ticket stubs from the Lido De Paris at the Stardust Hotel. Who had gone there? He examined the stubs. They were dated just a few days earlier, June 15, 1973. Had Claudio taken his mom there? To a topless dinner show? *Shit.*

He continued to rummage through the drawer. Under the matchbook covers, a small magazine. TV Guide? No, it had a drawing of a girl on the cover bending her head back, her neck and skin showing down to the tips of her breast, her nipple just barely covered by an orange sarong.

FORUM
The International Journal of Human Relations

The Sexual Advantages of Being Plump
Plus 35 Pages of Readers' Letters

He stood with the magazine in hand. Claudio's? Fucking perv, he thought. He glanced at the bed, still disheveled from the night before. He tried to put the magazine back into the drawer, but it hit something. It was a box, a box of Ramses Condoms. Nick cringed.

"Oh shit," he said out loud.

He threw the magazine and condoms back in the drawer, slammed it shut and stormed out of the bedroom.

Alright, the guns, Nick thought, where else had Pops kept his guns? The safe? The piano bench? Yes, the piano bench. Claudio couldn't have even guessed there might be a gun there. Nick dashed over to the living room and pulled opened the top of the white piano bench. Inside, a piled of sheet music. He grabbed it and there, underneath, was a beautiful, huge silver revolver. He considered it a moment, then picked it up. It was heavy and solid in his grip. His heart raced. The gun had a brown wood grain handle and gleaming silver barrel, inscribed "Python .357".

Perfect. He held the gun up and pointed it. He slowly turned around the room as if he were stalking someone. It felt good. But something in the room was different. What was it? He glanced around and there, the spot where his favorite photograph of his dad had hung, the one with him standing in front of the casino next to his Cadillac, the one with him wearing the bolo tie that Nick now wore around his own neck, was gone. *What the hell?* Instead, in its place, hung a large Sears and Roebuck type, cheesy, studio photograph of Claudio and Frances.

He stepped to the hallway to see if the other pictures were still there, the ones of his Dad with the politicians and dignitaries. They were all gone, too, except for the shadows of their frames that remained as outlines on the wall.

Nick grabbed his bolo. *Dad, he's erasing your memory!*

Nick ran to the game room, gun still in hand. The portrait above the stereo, the one of his dad with the colorful casino lights, roulette wheel, and show girls in the background. It was gone! Instead a garish painting of the *Welcome to Fabulous Las Vegas* sign, with Claudio standing in front of it with his hands on his hips, like Superman. Nick raised the gun up with both hands and pointed it at the figure of Claudio in the painting. He pulled the trigger. It clicked.

Damn!

Nick checked the gun's chamber. No bullets, it was empty.

He turned to leave but something caught his eye. There was a cigar butt in a heavy red glass ashtray sitting on the rail of the pool table. He picked up the butt and read the label. *Padron*. That was the same type of cigar he had seen under his dad's desk, and even smoked down the same amount. He grabbed a napkin from the wet bar, wrapped the evidence in it, and put it in his jacket pocket. Then he slid the 357 Python into his waistband and left.

"What took you so long?"

Nick fell into the front seat of the Pinto and slammed the door. "Just drive. Get me out of here."

"What happened?"

"DRIVE!"

Mario cut the wheel and tried to peal out, but the car only whined as it struggled to come to life. The steering was loose, and Mario barely missed hitting a parked car.

"I got the gun, Nick said. "Now we need some ammo."

Mario glanced at him.

"OK, man, sure," he said. "But what happened in there?"

"Nothing, let's go to that gun store, the one on

Tropicana. What's it called? Survival Guns & Ammo or some shit."

"Sure," Mario said. "No problem."

A few minutes later Nick stood at the counter of the gun store, a bag of bullets in hand, waiting for his change.

"Thanks, man," he said to the clerk and left.

He held up the bag as he approached the Pinto.

"Alrighty baby!" He smiled. "Got two boxes worth. Now, let's get to the casino."

Nick jumped in the car.

"What the hell are we gonna do at the casino?" Mario said. "It's the middle of the day."

Nick pulled out the gun and placed it in his lap.

"Just go," he said. "Start the fucking car, man, let's go."

"But what's the plan?"

"The plan, the fucking plan, I'll tell you the plan. See this gun?"

Nick held up the gun, pointing toward the ceiling.

"Yeah," Mario said. "Nice gun."

"See this bullet?" Nick held up a bullet.

Mario didn't say anything. Nick put the gun down.

"See this finger?" He held up his finger and pointed it like a gun.

"This trigger finger and this ten-cent bullet, this tiny fucking piece of lead will do its job, and Mr. Fat Fuck won't know what hit him. And justice will be served, baby! Today!"

Nick raised his eyebrows and smiled wide.

Mario shook his head.

"Look, I don't know what you're doin', man. You

can't just march into the casino and kill him. You'll get busted man, everyone will see you."

"They won't know it's me because I'll have the hat and the sunglasses and this shitty dungaree jacket on."

"Yeah, but you think he's going to be alone in there? What about his cronies? They'll fuck you over. You'll get killed."

"I don't care. Now drive to the casino, so I can get this over with."

"I can't let you do that, man," Mario said. "I won't let you throw your life away for Claudio's fat ass. You'll either wind up dead or arrested. And I'll be arrested too, as an accomplice!"

Nick opened the door and looked at Mario. "I'll take a fucking cab then."

"You can't take a cab! Are you nuts?"

Nick stepped out of the car and began walking across the parking lot toward the avenue.

"Wait, man," he heard Mario yell from the car. "You're out of your fucking mind. You can't do that, man. Oh shit!"

Mario scrambled to drive up next to him.

"Yo, man," Mario shouted out his window. "Don't be so freakin' ridiculous. Let's go, get in."

Nick stopped and Mario stopped.

"You taking me to the casino?"

Mario took a deep breath, "Ah shit, man, sure, just get in. You're going down, I'm going down with you." Mario shook his head. "Shit, who the fuck knows, you might just get away with it."

Nick jumped in. "Don't worry about it, man."

"Shit," Mario said. "I thought you were going to have a real plan, instead of just some kind of blind fucking rage. What the hell happened back at the house?"

"Nothin'." Nick pulled a handful of bullets out of the box and started loading the gun.

Mario gassed it all the way to the floor, but the Pinto only whined miserably again as it struggled to gain speed.

At the casino Mario parked across the street from the side entrance.

"Wish me luck." Nick tilted the Mets baseball cap down over his sunglasses and got out.

"You're fucking crazy man." Mario shook his head. "I wouldn't don't do this."

Nick leaned into the window. "I gotta," he said. "That's just the way it is."

"Alright, good luck then, man. You fucking nut-job."

Nick laughed. "Thanks, man, for helping."

He stood and put the gun securely in his belt, making sure it was well covered behind his unbuttoned jacket. Then he pulled up the collar around his neck and smiled nervously.

"I'll just be a few minutes," he said.

He held his chin up, and with his senses on high alert, he strode as casually as he could into the casino.

Even though it was the middle of the afternoon, there were still diehard slot players, here and there, taking their chances, yanking on the machines as they clicked, binged and buzzed. A lone security guard, whom Nick didn't recognize, stood across the floor, at the far end of the casino. But the place was mostly empty, and that was good.

At the cage, Nick stepped up to the first window. He asked the cashier, a young, attractive woman, "Howdy, you new?"

"Yes." She smiled. "We're all new. New management you know. This place is really shaping up now."

"Claudio DeVito?" Nick said.

"Mr. DeVito?"

"Yes, is he the new management?"

"As a matter of fact he is." She smiled again.

"Well, I have an appointment with him, is he here?"

"Oh," she said. "I don't think he's here, but I can check. What's your name?"

Nick hesitated.

"Johnny Shafter."

"Shafter?" She gave him a curious look.

"He'll know who it is."

"OK, Johnny Shafter." She stood and spun away.

Her hips rocked as she walked in her short and tight, red skirt to Claudio's office. Jack's old office. Bastard. Nick clutched the gun under his jacket. His jaw tightened. He tried to remain calm. If Claudio suddenly appeared should he just shoot him in front of all the cashiers? Wait till he gets real close. Wait till he just recognized him, then pop! Just like that, right in the face. Blood would splatter everywhere. It'd be messy. Nick pushed up his Mets cap and wiped the sweat from his brow. Nobody would recognize him. He leaned on the counter and tried to compose himself. He took a deep breath. He glanced left. He glanced right. The wide hallway was empty. If Claudio was there, he could do it. He could finish this thing. He could end it. He'd just have to run, fast, right up the hall and out the door before anyone even knew what happened. It'd only take a second. Had Mario kept the car running? Nick felt his chest pounding, blood rushing, eyes darting. What was taking so long?

The young woman suddenly appeared, sauntering back to the window, alone.

"I'm sorry'" she said. "But Mr. DeVito's not here. Are you sure you had an appointment with him?"

"That's OK." Nick flashed a smile, and quickly turned away.

He walked quickly down the hallway toward the exit, all the while staring down at the carpet — the metallic sounds of the casino clinking and clanging and ringing in his head. He pushed the exit door opened and squinted in the bright afternoon sun.

He jogged to the Pinto and Mario looked up at him, clearly wondering if he did it.

"He's not there." Nick got into the car. "He's one lucky mother fucker, I tell you that much. He'd be dead right now if he were there. Fucking dead!"

Mario shook his head. "Well, I'm glad you didn't do it here, in broad daylight. They'll be better chances later."

"Yeah," Nick said. "I guess so."

Mario turned down Freemont Street, neon lit, even in the middle of the afternoon.

"So, why this sudden craziness to get him?" Mario said. "What'd you find back at the house?"

Nick looked out the window, his hand resting on the gun under his jacket. The lights and the color, the reds and yellows glided by in a blur.

"You're not going to tell me what happened?" Mario

said.

Nick took a deep breath. "Nothin' happened. I just didn't like what I saw. Fucking Claudio took down all my dad's pictures and put up his own instead. He's obliterating my dad's memory. He's brainwashed my mom and he's replaced everyone at the casino. He's taking over everything. I can't even stand to think of staying back at my own house now. It's totally fucked."

"Shit," Mario said. "That is pretty fucked up. But you can stay at my place as long as you like."

"Thanks," Nick said and reached into his jacket pocket. "Take a look at this. I found it at the house, on the game room table. It's Claudio's."

He held out the cigar butt so Mario could see.

"Padron," Mario said. "I knew it. I fucking knew it."

"Yup, exactly the same one as from under my dad's desk. Same brand, same shape, and smoked down the same amount."

"Fuck . . ." Mario said.

"Let's swing by the hardware store and get some duct tape, a pick-axe and a couple of shovels."

"I'm with you, man," Mario said. "I'm fucking with you."

CHAPTER 24

J ust off Highway 170 in Mesquite, a small town north of Las Vegas, Claudio brought his gold Lincoln Mark IV to a stop. A cloud of grit and dust rose up around the tires. He and Tony were in front of the *El Rancho De Milagro* sign at the entrance to Miguel Rodriguez's ranch. Claudio stepped from the car and stood in the blazing sun. He glanced around at the windswept landscape.

Tony stretched his one good arm over his head.

"Ahhh . . ." he said. "That was a long drive."

"Yeah," Claudio said. "Time for a leak."

"Yup."

Claudio stepped to one of the posts that held up the sign.

Tony went to the opposite post.

"Man, there ain't nothin' out here," Tony said.

"Why do you think I picked this place," Claudio said over his shoulder.

They drove up the ranch road, pebbles scrunching under the tires and kicking up a trail of dust. In the distance, Claudio could see a few metal farm buildings, a tractor, a backhoe, other farm equipment, and a decrepit faded yellow house trailer. It sat crookedly in the dirt as if it had been settling into the earth for some time. Claudio pulled the car up to the trailer. Three mangy dogs barked wildly from their kennel, just next to the trailer.

"Alright, alright!" a man with a heavy Mexican accent shouted from inside.

Claudio stepped from the car and adjusted his suit jacket and shirt sleeves. Even with the man's scolding, the dogs kept barking.

"Quiet!" another shout came from the trailer.

A short stocky man stepped from the flimsy trailer door and rubbed his weathered eyes. He squinted at Claudio, then crouched down and picked up a few stones, which he flung at the dogs.

"Quiet I said!"

A small stone hit one of the dogs. It yelped and retreated to the back of the kennel. The other two dogs immediately stopped barking but kept up their agitated pacing back and forth.

The man came up to Claudio and Tony. Claudio towered above him. Tony stood next to Claudio, chewing a small piece of paper, his arm in the sling under his suite jacket, its sleeve hanging empty.

"I am a US citizen," the Mexican said.

Claudio eyed him.

"We're not from immigration; we're from the Three-C's, you know, *the Cornetto Club Casino*. You owe us two thousand dollars, and we want it."

Claudio noticed the curtains pull back from one of the grimy trailer windows and a woman peek through. A baby cried from inside.

The man's face turned sullen. "I'm very sorry," he said. "Very sorry. I will pay you the money. But not today. I will pay you, you don't worry about that, in a few days. Miguel is good for da money."

But Miguel withered and shrunk, even as he tried his best to negotiate.

"Well, we can't wait any longer." Tony spit the piece of paper to the ground and stepped toward the man.

"Please sir," Miguel said with his hands opened, as if begging for mercy. "Give me a chance to get the money. I will repay you, I swear to it, with interest too."

Claudio placed his hand in his jacket as if he were reaching for a gun. A woman's scream came from the trailer, but Claudio only pulled out a white handkerchief and wiped his sweaty brow. "How can you live out here in this heat?" he said.

"I'm just an old gringo, scraping together a living from the dirt and my animals. Please sir, give me a chance."

"Damn," Tony said. "It is hot as hell here."

Claudio loosened his tie and took off his suit jacket. He handed them to Tony, then stepped up to Miguel and put his hand on his shoulder.

"Let's go," he said. "Get in the car."

"NO!" The woman shouted from the trailer.

"Tell her not to worry, we'll be right back," Tony said.

Miguel was shaking and yelled something in Spanish at the woman. The baby in the trailer kept crying and the dogs started barking again. Miguel made the sign of the cross and shuffled toward the car.

Tony grabbed a pebble off the ground and threw it with his left hand, awkwardly, at the frenzied dogs. But they kept barking and kicking up dust as they scrambled around their cage.

"Take it easy." Claudio pushed Miguel into the back seat.

Miguel seemed to be mumbling his prayers.

Tony jumped in and drew his gun on Miguel. The

lady from the trailer came at them yelling, cleaver held high in hand.

"You leave my husband alone!" she shouted. "You leave him alone!"

The baby wailed louder from the trailer and Claudio pealed out, creating a cloud of dust that engulfed Miguel's frantic wife. He headed a good way back down the long dirt road and stopped the car halfway between the trailer buildings and the *El Rancho De Milagro* entrance sign. They were in the middle of the wide opened fields, which stretched dry and barren on each side.

"Let's go." Claudio got out of the car.

The men walked into the dirt field until they were a good distance away from the road and the car.

Miguel was shaking. "Where are your taking me?"

"Just relax," Tony said.

Claudio stopped and looked around. "See this spot?" he said.

"Yes sir, this spot," Miguel's voice trembled.

"I want you to take that backhoe of yours and dig a big hole right here. We're gonna dump some garbage here, understand?"

"Garbage?"

"That's right, garbage."

Miguel thought for a moment. "Alright, yes sir, garbage."

Claudio looked at him. "It's medical. From the hospital. Maybe some diseased shit, you know what I mean? It's contagious. So don't touch it. It'll get you sick. Needles and stuff. Maybe a little radioactive too. Who knows? What do you think of that?"

Miguel seemed confused.

"Look," Tony said. "You dig the hole, we dump our shit, and you cover the shit. That's it. Simple, right? And you don't worry about nothin', and you don't owe us anything. We forget about the two grand you owe us. How about that?"

Miguel smiled, "I dig, I cover, I will dig, sir, yes I dig for you, and bury your junks."

"Good," Tony said.

"I dig, right here?"

"Yes," Claudio said. "Right here."

"But how big you need?"

Claudio turned to survey the field.

A blood curdling wail let out just behind them and the wife was almost upon Tony with the cleaver held high, her eyes livid.

"No, stop!" Miguel jumped between them and grabbed the cleaver.

Claudio stumbled to the side.

"I will kill you!" she yelled.

"Wait!" Miguel held her wrist. "It's OK! Oh my God, it's OK."

She glared at the men. "What do they want?"

"They just need some work done, they are good men. They are giving us a job."

She leered at him.

"It's OK," Miguel said. "I promise, go back to the trailer, the baby is crying."

"It's OK?"

"I promise," Miguel said. "Now go check the baby."

"Hmmmfff . . ." She turned and stomped away with the cleaver.

"Sorry sir," Miguel said. "My wife can be . . . you know . . ." He spun his finger around, "Loco . . ."

"It's OK," Tony said.

Miguel smiled nervously. "Thank you sir. So, how big for the hole sir?"

Claudio looked around the dirt.

"I don't know. What do you think?" He looked at Tony.

Tony lifted his eyebrows and swept his good arm around indicating a large patch of land, "Big, baby."

Miguel frowned, "That's really big."

"Just dig it," Claudio said.

"Yes, of course sir, sorry, Miguel can do that for you. Not too much for me. For you it is done."

Claudio surveyed the ground again.

"Here's exactly how big I want it," he said, then started pacing around the imaginary perimeter of the pit. He took measured steps to about a hundred feet away from Tony and Miguel, then turned and shouted, "To here. A nice big fucking hole."

"Yes sir, yes sir." Miguel shouted back. He grabbed a long twig from the dirt and stuck it in the ground, then ran to where Claudio was standing and stuck another twig in the ground. "Like this sir, is here good?"

"Perfect," Claudio said. "And go about twenty feet that way too."

Miguel followed his orders and marked another corner.

"Very good sir," Miguel said.

He and the men walked back toward the car.

"And . . ." Tony said to Miguel. "Keep this a secret.

Don't tell anyone about it, not even your wife. Comprehendo?"

"Yes sir," Miguel said.

"If you tell anyone, we'll be back here, and you and your family will be at the bottom of that hole, with the worms. Understand?"

"Oh, yes sir, I understand." He motioned with his hand, zipping his lips closed. "I will keep it top secret sir, you can count on Miguel. I am a man of honor, my word is good sir. I dig, you dump your stuff, I bury it and no one will know, I promise and swear to you, sir."

"You swear to God?"

Miguel nodded and made the sign of the cross. "In the name of the Father, Son and Holy Ghost."

"Amen," Tony smiled. "Good."

"And," Claudio said. "You have two days to get it done. We'll be back by Friday."

"Oh," Miguel said with a look of concern on his face. "I don't have enough diesel, gasolina, sir and have no money. I will need to fill it up a few times."

Claudio looked at Tony, "Give him a hundred bucks for gas."

Tony pulled out a wad of cash and peeled off five twenties. "That should be enough," he said. "Wait, one more for good measure. Buy some beer and burritos for yourself after you're done."

"Oh, yes sir. Thank you very much. I will get working today."

Claudio put his arm around Miguel's shoulder.

"And remember," he said. "No one knows but us."

"Of course sir, no one but us, you have my word."

"Good." Claudio squeezed his shoulder. "Two days. Got it?"

"Two days, yes sir, I know," Miguel smiled nervously. "And then we are even sir, right?"

"Don't worry about it," Tony said.

"Thank you, sir."

"Just get it done," Claudio said, and climbed into the driver's seat.

Miguel gave them a half-hearted wave, and they drove off.

Tony pulled out his pack of Paul Mall cigarettes, packed them down and pushed the lighter in.

Claudio looked over at him and said, "This is a big deal, you know that?"

"Yeah," Tony said.

"Don't *fucking* screw it up. Make sure you get the trucks ready."

"It's as good as done Boss, there's nothin' to worry about."

Tony lit his cigarette, took a drag and gazed out his window.

"Look how friggin' beautiful this is." He waved his cigarette across the landscape.

"How beautiful?" Claudio glanced out at the endless expanse of desert racing by, then turned back to Tony. "Look, I don't give a *fuck* how beautiful it is. You just get the shit out here, in the ground, and safe. That's all I want. *Then* everything is beautiful."

Tony nodded.

Claudio suddenly slowed down and pulled over to

the shoulder.

"What are you doin'?" Tony said.

"Your turn to drive."

"With my bad arm?"

"You got one good one, right? So use it, I've been doing too much damn driving. I wanna relax."

"OK Boss, no problem."

They got out and switched places.

With Tony behind the wheel now, Claudio reclined his seat back. He took a deep breath and closed his eyes. Treasures would soon be flowing his way—silver bars, coins, chips and who knows what else. Maybe even gold! Bag-fulls, piles, and maybe pallet-fulls! A dizzying array of wonderful, sparkling riches flew through his head.

CHAPTER 25

"Shit," Mario said. He and Nick exited the Cornetto Club Casino parking lot for the third time. "We need to bring the car back to Barbara. It's late."

"What?" Nick said. "It's still light out. Let's just swing by the house one more time. Then we'll call it a day, go back to your place, have a beer and smoke a doobie."

Mario sighed, "Alright, last time."

They still wore their baseball caps and sunglasses. But now, in the trunk were two shovels, a pick axe, heavy duty garbage bags, a thick plastic drop cloth, duct tape, towels, three gallons of water and a bar of soap. And still in Nick's jacket pocket, the loaded Python .357.

Ten minutes later, they turned down Nick's block again and Mario drove slowly passed the Romano house one more time. The only car in the driveway was Frances' '71 white Eldorado convertible. As they drove by, Nick felt bad that he hadn't told his mom that he was back. She could be sitting in the house that very moment worrying about him.

"Still no Claudio," Mario said. "Back to my place then?"

"Yeah, I guess so."

At the end of the block a car turned the corner, coming toward them. It was a gold Lincoln.

"Is that them?" Nick said.

"Could be."

Nick lowered his cap and slunk down in the seat. His heart raced as the Lincoln approached.

"Oh, shit!" Nick sat up. "That was Claudio and Tony."

"Yup, you think they saw us?"

"No way, Claudio looked like he was sleeping and Tony wasn't even paying attention."

Nick turned, keeping his eyes on the Lincoln.

"They're turning into your driveway," he said. "Finally, we got him." He pumped his fist. "Yeah baby!"

At the corner, Mario made a U-turn and drove back toward the house.

"Park over there," Nick said. "Let's hang out for a few minutes. Maybe they're just stopping by before they head out again."

Mario parked across the street a few doors down from the house. He pulled out a Marlboro cigarette and lit it.

"I need one of those," Nick said.

Mario handed him the box.

"What'd ya think?" Nick said. He fixed his gaze toward the house and lit his cigarette.

"Don't know," Mario said.

"Did you notice how dirty the car was?"

"No," Mario said.

"You didn't see it? It was filthy, like they were driving out in the desert, off-roading or something."

"Huh."

"They're up to something." Nick took a drag.

After a few minutes of waiting, Mario flicked his cigarette into the street. "Let's go, man," he said.

"Wait, let's drive by one more time."

They drove slowly past the house once again. Tony was in the driveway, holding the garden hose, washing down the Lincoln. He was dressed in his white shirt, suit pants and black leather shoes — and one of his arms was in a sling. He glanced over at them as they passed.

"Oh shit, man," Mario said. "Did he see us?"

"He definitely saw us," Nick said. "But he couldn't possibly recognize us, not in this car."

"He was cleaning the Lincoln," Mario said.

"Yeah, where the fuck did they go?" Nick said. "Maybe out to the desert, to bury someone?"

"Who knows!"

"And why's his arm in a sling?" Nick said. "Did you see that?"

"Oh yeah," Mario snickered. "I forgot to tell you. Apparently, he broke his shoulder when he crashed while chasing us."

"No shit?"

"It's true, man."

"Wow, serves him right." Nick said.

The Rolling Stones' *Sympathy for the Devil* came on the radio. Nick turned it up.

———

"HONEY, are you home?" Claudio called out.

"I'm here," Frances said weakly from the living room. "Resting."

Claudio walked in to see Frances lying across the couch, her head hanging back, off the side of the cushion.

"Sweetie, what are you doing?" He rushed over.

Her arm slipped off the couch and her hand fell to the rug.

"Resting . . ." she whispered.

He pulled her up to a sitting position and sat down next to her. An empty bottle of wine stood on the coffee table next to a half full wine glass.

"What did you do?"

She leaned her head toward him, her eyes rolled back and closed.

"What'd you do!" Claudio shook her.

She opened her eyes, smiled and motioned toward the end table where a bottle of prescription pills sat. Claudio leaned over and grabbed the bottle. He held it at arm's length to read the label.

"Valium? How many did you take?"

"A few," she smiled.

"Shit," Claudio muttered.

"Where have you been?"

He pulled her close, examining her half-opened eyes.

"Can you stand?"

"Sure . . ." she said half-heartedly. "I'm just a little dizzy."

She leaned forward to try to stand.

"Wait," Claudio said.

He stood and pulled her up. She wobbled to her feet and threw her arms over his shoulders.

"I'm think I'm going to throw up." She crumbled back to the couch.

Claudio sat down and pulled her close, touching her face. It was pale and cool.

"You don't look good, babe." he said.

She lifted her eyelids a bit, "I'm glad you're home, it's spooky by myself. It was dead quiet."

She glanced down at his shoes.

"They're so dirty."

"Yes." Claudio stood up. "You sit tight, I'm going to get you some water."

"OK."

Claudio watched as she leaned her head against the back of the couch and stared up at the ceiling. He shook his head, then went to get the water.

When he got back, she appeared to be sleeping.

"Come on babe," he said. "Sit up and drink."

He pulled her head up and she opened her eyes.

"Where's Nick?" she said.

"Don't know." He brought the glass to her lips.

She took a sip and looked at him.

"What do you mean you don't know?"

"Don't worry, I'm sure he's fine," Claudio said.

"Why doesn't he call me? Why doesn't he call his mother?"

She tried to stand but stumbled backward again.

"Hey take it easy there." Claudio grabbed her.

"Leave me alone." She pushed him away and stood again. "Where is he?"

"Look, he's an adult. He'll call when he's ready. I'm sure he's fine."

"But it's been over a week."

"Don't worry." Claudio took her hand. "I'm sure he's OK. You'll probably get a postcard from him soon."

Frances looked him in the eye. "Anything happens to him—it's your fault." She poked him in the chest.

"Babe, Babe." Claudio sighed. "I wouldn't do anything to your boy, I promise. Nothin's gonna happen to him. Do you understand?"

Claudio shook his head and continued, "Shit, I don't know why he hasn't called. You know, maybe he's gone crazy, he's a little nuts sometimes, right? Maybe he's gone AWOL?"

Frances smirked at him and looked like she was about to fall over.

"Shit, sit down." Claudio grabbed her and guided her onto the armchair. He rubbed the back of her hand and considered her half-opened eyes. He kissed her cheek.

"Now," he said. "We need to talk some business for a second."

"Business?"

"Yes." Claudio launched right into it. "One of my associates is coming out from Chicago, to replace Albert and help with the casino operations — Angelo Lombardo. He's a good guy. He'll oversee casino security, which includes the vaults. I worked with him back in Chicago and he's someone we can trust. I hand-picked him for this job. He's my top security expert, and runs a super-tight ship."

Frances looked blankly at him.

"So?" she said, her eyelids falling lower.

"So," Claudio continued. "He'll need to have access to the basement vaults so his men can transport the cash, do counts, you know inventory everything. I need the combos. Do you have them?"

Frances lifted her eyelids.

"Didn't I already give it to you?" she said.

"That was for the upstairs vaults, I need the one for the downstairs vaults now."

"Combos?"

"Yeah, for the vaults," Claudio said. "I need them now

because Angelo is coming in tonight and I need to get everything ready for him."

"Shit," Frances said. "Help me up."

Claudio pulled her gently to her feet and shuffled her to the den.

"Pull that off the wall." She motioned toward a picture of Jack hanging on the wall next to the desk.

Claudio grabbed the picture and placed it on the floor against the wall. Frances stood unsteadily staring at the combination dial on the small wall safe. Claudio looked at her.

"You remember the combination?" he said.

"The combination, yes."

Claudio held her. She began dialing. Left, then right, then left, then stopped. Claudio helped her push down on the handle. Nothing. It didn't budge.

"Try again," he said. "Take your time."

Frances leaned against the desk, her head down, pondering. Then she tried again. Right, right, right, left, right, left and . . . Claudio pushed the handle down again. Click, it opened.

Frances reached in and pulled out an index card with Jack's hand-written numbers on it.

"Alright." he grabbed it from her and kissed her forehead.

"Copy the numbers down," she said. "I want to keep that card in the safe."

"Absolutely," Claudio said.

Frances watched him copy the numbers.

"Pour me another glass of wine," she said.

"Absolutely, Babe." Claudio could hardly contain his glee.

CHAPTER 26

The Lincoln and a Buick Riviera fastback pulled into adjacent parking spots at McCarran Airport. Claudio DeVito and Tony Scalfaro, his arm still in the sling, emerged from the Lincoln. Roman Lorenzo and Joey Messina emerged from the black, with white vinyl roof, Riviera. The four dapper men stood in the parking lot a moment and adjusted their suit jackets and ties. Then they walked quickly to the gate, being that they were a bit late.

A TWA 707 pulled into the gate just as they got there, its engines whirling and whining down. The ground crew rolled the stairs over to the front exit door. A small crowd stood waiting, including limo drivers, taxi drivers, a few business people, and a lady with a couple of kids that wouldn't stop running around in circles.

"Haven't seen Angelo since last year, in Chicago." Roman commented.

"That was a year ago, already?" Joey said.

"Yeah, crazy how time flies." Roman said.

"Just relax," Claudio said as he watched the plane's door open. He adjusted his suit jacket, tie and shirt cuffs again.

An attractive stewardess, dressed in a short-skirted and form-fitting uniform, with a tapered cap, stepped from the gleaming jet. She stood to the side at the top of the stairs waiting for the passengers to emerge.

Amazingly, Angelo stepped out first. He stopped and stood on the platform a moment as if he were a dignitary about to wave.

"There he is," Claudio said. "Straighten up."

"The Nut," Tony whispered. "The Nut is back."

Claudio shot Tony a look. "He hears you call him that and you'll be dead. So, shut the fuck up."

Tony zipped it and the other men kept quiet.

Angelo was impeccably dressed in a finely tailored suit, and his hair was greased perfectly back. His professional demeanor belied his cruel reputation. He stepped, ceremoniously, down the stairs. His polished black patent leather shoes glistening off the gates spotlights. He casually walked across the tarmac toward the men.

"Angelo . . ." Claudio held his arms out wide and hugged him. "Welcome to Vegas!"

Angelo raised one arm half-heartedly around Claudio's shoulder and shook his hand with the other. Claudio pulled him closer.

"How are you?" he said. "How was the flight?"

"Good," Angelo said. "Too bad about Albert, huh?"

"Yeah," Claudio said. "I miss him already."

"Mr. Crocetti was very upset about that. How's Albert's wife doing?"

"Jackie?" Claudio said. "What can I say? She's holding it together."

"Yeah, it's been tough," Roman added. "Welcome to Vegas sir. We got big plans here."

"Really?" Angelo said. "I'd like to hear them."

"Good to see you." Joey shook Angelo's hand. "Hope you had a good flight."

"Wonderful flight," Angelo said. "First class, steak and lobster, wonderful stewardesses. What more could I friggin' ask for, huh?"

Angelo led the way, a half step in front of Claudio. The crowd parted as the entourage followed.

"You drive with me," Claudio said. "They'll get your bags, and meet us at the Cherry Orchard Club."

Angelo smiled, "Good."

Claudio turned to his men. "Meet us at the club. Tony, find a pay phone and give them a call—tell 'em we want their best table, right down in front."

"No, no." Angelo waved his hand. "In the back. Too distracting in the front."

"You got it, sir, no problem," Tony said.

Joey looked at Roman and Tony, "I can only carry something light. I messed up my back while chasing Nick out my daughter's bedroom window."

"And I only got one arm," Tony said. "Also because of Nick!"

Claudio shook his head and escorted Angelo to the car.

"I've got you set up with the best room at the casino," Claudio said. "It's got its own whirlpool hot tub, wait till you see it."

"Good." Angelo stopped to look at Claudio's car. "This yours?"

"Yup, she's brand new."

"Geez, it' a bit flashy," Angelo said. "Kinda like a pimp-mobile."

"A pimp-mobile?" Claudio said.

Angelo slapped his back. "Yeah, if you put a TV antenna on the back, chrome wire-spoke wheels and whitewalls, *shit* . . . you'd be all set, a pimpin' motherfucker!"

Claudio laughed, "Yeah, I guess this baby's got flash. I call it my golden chariot. Don't I deserve a goddamn golden chariot?"

"In Chicago they'd think you were a pimp." Angelo chuckled.

"Yeah, but we're in Vegas baby," Claudio said. "And everything here is glitz. Shiny silver and gold. Neon lights. Shit, if I had a typical black Caddy I'd look like an undertaker."

Claudio got in and Angelo followed.

"Interior's nice," Angelo said as he settled in to the plush leather seat.

He struck a match and lit his unfiltered Camel cigarette. Claudio grabbed his half-smoked Padron cigar from the dashboard ashtray and lit it too.

"So." Angelo took a drag. "What's the story here?"

"Things are good."

"Good?"

"Very good. I mean, you know, things are finally paying off."

"That's good," Angelo said. "I give you credit."

"Yeah, as the cash flows through, we get the skim, the whole thing now, every penny. It's practically a fucking gold mine. Mr. Crocetti should be very happy."

"He's happy." Angelo took another drag on his cigarette. "Word is you've done a great job here."

"Thanks." Claudio was surprised that Angelo would actually complement him like this.

They drove in silence, then Angelo casually said, "And what about the silver?"

Claudio hesitated. "I don't know, there's been a lot of

rumors and Jack never spoke of it."

"All that time you worked with him, and you don't know?"

Angelo stared at Claudio.

"Nobody knows. I'm getting the combo to the vaults to check. Frances is going to give it to me."

"And she trusts you?"

"We're getting fucking married, she better trust me." Claudio laughed.

"You really are getting married?" Angelo said. "Mr. Crocetti told me that and I couldn't believe it. How'd you pull that off?"

"Yup, well." Claudio took a deep breath. "You better believe it."

"Crocetti and I were trying to figure out if it was all a brilliant plan of yours, or if you're really in love with her?"

"Ahhh . . ." Claudio smiled and puffed his cigar.

"The Boss was concerned, you know." Angelo waved his hands in a swirl.

"Don't worry about it," Claudio said. "You guys worry too much. How's everything back home? I heard there was trouble with the Grason family, infringing on our business."

Angelo looked at him. "There's no trouble, not anymore, not as of last night anyway."

He took a drag from his cigarette.

"Great," Claudio said. "That's good."

"Yes."

"And how's my house back home? Charlie keep it nice and neat for me in the front?"

"Oh yeah," Angelo said. "You know how he is, your

front yard is immaculate."

"And my Virgin Mary statue? Did he paint it up good?"

"It looked brand new when I drove past there last week."

Angelo took a drag and blew the smoke out in a steady stream.

"Guess who I saw?"

Claudio glanced at Angelo.

"Who?"

"Your ex," Angelo said. "Cynthia."

"Really, what's she up to?"

"I seen her at Stella's restaurant. She was with some sharp-dressed guy."

"Hope she's happy. Maybe she'll get his money, too. Thank god she ain't got no claim to nothing else of mine. Marla's knows what a freakin' pain her mom was."

"Yeah, how is your daughter? She's out here with you too, right?"

"Yeah, she's good, real good," Claudio smiled. "Maybe she does a little too much partying though and likes Vegas a little too much, I don't know. But she's good, shit, if it wasn't for her, I don't know what I'd do. Know what I mean?"

"Yeah." Angelo nodded and took a last drag from his cigarette. "Well, she's your only one," he said. "I bet you spoil her."

"Yeah, she's definitely spoiled, but what am I gonna do?" Claudio laughed and puffed his cigar.

They drove a few more blocks, then Angelo said, "So, you got some good blow for me?"

"Sure," Claudio said. "The best."

"Good."

"I'll have it waiting for you in your room. How 'bout a nice babe, too?"

"Busty and cute?" Angelo smiled.

"No problem, wait 'till you see. Vegas has the best chicks in the world, and they know how to please."

Claudio took a last puff on his cigar, then pushed it in the ashtray.

———

THE CHERRY ORCHARD CLUB was comfortably cool. Disco music thumped and the girls on stage writhed and spun on their poles. Claudio sat with Angelo at a dimly lit back table that was just far enough from the stage that they could still hear each other. He sipped his scotch on the rocks and watched the dancers swing around, lift their legs, squat and caress their butts and breasts. One of them caught Claudio's eye and slowly, provocatively licked her lips at him.

Angelo smiled.

"Holy shit," Claudio said with an uncontrollable grin on his face.

"She's real cute," Angelo said and took a sip of his drink.

Tony, Roman, and Joey walked in, Roman practically stumbling into one of the empty tables while craning his neck to look at the dancers.

"Oh, man, how's that?" he said. "I'd like to lick her."

"Cool your jets, take a seat," Claudio said.

The three men sat, but Roman and Joey turned their

chairs toward the stage to get a better view.

"Hey," Angelo said. "They'll be plenty of time for that later."

"No problem." Roman shifted his chair back around.

Joey frowned but did the same. The men were now huddled, their attention focused on Angelo and Claudio.

"So, Claudio," Angelo said, patting him on the back. "You're really getting married? Again?"

This caught Claudio off guard.

"Well, yeah," he said. "We're getting married."

"That's freakin' wonderful," Angelo smiled, his hand still on Claudio's shoulder.

"Yeah."

"You gonna give up the single life and settle down again." Angelo raised his empty glass in a mock toast. "Well, congratu-fucking-lations!"

"More power to ya'," Tony said.

Claudio grinned and laughed. "She's my new old lady."

"Huh." Angelo chuckled. "But seriously, I gotta say, that's quite a stroke of fucking genius. I gotta hand it to ya'. Pure genius!"

Claudio straightened up and shrugged his shoulders, loosening his suit jacket. He glanced around. "Where's the waitress?"

Angelo continued. "You're not fucking in love with her, are you buddy?"

"Waitress!" Claudio called. He turned to Angelo. "You know I got everything under control. I'm gettin' freakin' married, man. That's all. What do you want from my life?"

"That's *fucking* great," Angelo rubbed Claudio's neck

hard.

Claudio winced and glanced toward Tony, Roman and Joey.

Tony piped up, "Life is good Boss!"

"It certainly is." Claudio turned to Angelo. "And you're coming to the wedding, right?"

"I'll be there," Angelo said. "And what about the kid? Did you guys find him yet? Where is he, Hawaii?"

"We found him," Tony blurted.

Claudio shot him a look.

"Yeah." Claudio hesitated. "We just found him today, back here in Vegas."

"Well, what the fuck?" Angelo said.

Claudio gathered his thoughts.

"Well?" Angelo pressed. "When the fuck were you going to tell me? I hope you took care of him."

"No, see," Claudio said. "We can't do anything yet. Frances is pretty upset that he's been missing — for over a week now. And he hasn't even called her. She don't even know he's back yet. I don't know what he's doing."

"Really?" Angelo looked confused.

"Yeah. It's weird, he just got back. He's hiding at his friend's house. Tony found him. Guess he don't want to show his face. I haven't said anything to Frances yet. That way our options are open. She might as well think he's still M.I.A."

"What's the delay?"

"Nothin'," Claudio said. "We just gotta make it look good. You know, like an accident or something. Something not obvious."

"Obvious? You're in Vegas, baby. I'll take him out to the goddamn desert and do it myself. What's the problem?"

"My guys are gonna handle it." Claudio lifted his chin slightly in Joey's direction.

"A couple of days," Joey said. "That's it. Then, the problem is solved."

"It fucking better be solved," Angelo said. "For Albert's sake."

"Don't worry," Claudio said. "We'll get him."

The waitress finally bounced over. She wore a thong bikini-bottom and silver-starred pasties with glittering tassels, that hung and swung off her perky breasts.

She smiled at the men. "What can I do for you fine gentlemen?"

CHAPTER 27

They had been sitting in the Pinto, in a shadowy section of the garage parking lot, for over an hour, with their baseball caps on and collars pulled up. The buzz from the joint they had smoked on the way over had well-worn off. The radio was off and windows open so they could hear the activity in the parking lot. They had a clear view of the lot's entrance to the casino.

It had been a long day, and it was almost midnight. Mario had convinced Barbara to let them keep the car overnight and Nick wanted to make the most of it. He sat slouched back in the passenger seat with his baseball cap visor pulled low over his eyes and arms folded. With his eyelids heavy, he struggled to fend off sleep. Mario also fought to stay awake, his chin resting on his hands over the steering wheel.

Every time there was any activity, they would lift their heads to watch. A patron leaving the casino dejected, a couple leaving the casino arm in arm, a group of drunk friends staggering away. Cars arrived, doors slammed, and tires screeched on the polished garage floor. Although there had been a few stretches of dead silence, it seemed amazing to Nick how much activity there was at this time of night.

He thought of his dad parking here every day, walking into the casino at this very spot, working in his office, making his calls, signing papers. Nick's eyelids fell lower. His head slumped forward.

He was in the casino, in his dad's office talking to him about getting rid of Claudio. Nick would pop him like a balloon, with a pin. His dad said it wasn't that easy, even with a big pin, the size of a nail. It would take more than that, but if he were pricked in the ear, that might work to deflate him and bring him down. Even though this was crazy, it seemed to make perfect sense and would work.

"Nick!" Mario jabbed his elbow into his arm. "You sleepin'?"

Nick looked up.

"Check it out. Claudio's Lincoln."

Nick sat up and wiped his eyes. The Lincoln had just pulled into the first reserved spot next to the casino entrance. That was his dad's reserved spot. The driver's side door opened and Claudio stepped out. From the passenger side, a stocky, sharply-dressed man emerged. The man glanced around then walked to Claudio. A black Buick Riviera fastback with a white vinyl roof, pulled in right next to Claudio's car. Roman Lorenzo got out of the driver's side, Joey Messina from the other side and Tony Scalfaro from the back seat, his arm in a sling.

Claudio and the new guy stood for a moment waiting by the entrance. The other men arrived and they exchanged a few quick words and then all headed into the casino.

"Who the hell is that?" Mario said.

"Don't know." Nick held his cap down.

"A high roller?"

"Don't think so," Nick said. "He'd have to be a pretty big fish to have Claudio personally chauffeuring him around. Looks like another crony, maybe from out of town. Something's going on."

———

IN HIS PENTHOUSE SUITE, Angelo 'The Nut' Lombardo smiled and looked up from the bed at the spectacularly well-endowed young lady that stood over him. Tracy, that's what she said her name was, spun around on her red spiked high heels and flipped her hair back.

"Ooh La La," Angelo said.

She began peeling off her black satin mini-skirt negligee, but then stopped, frowned and said, "What's that noise out there? And at this hour?"

"Huh?"

"I'm gonna check."

She sauntered, with hips rocking, over to the open window. She bent over to look out, arching her back and raising her plump butt to Angelo's view. The negligee's ruffled edge fluffed gently from the window breeze.

"What the hell is that?" Angelo stood and pulled his robe closed. He walked over to Tracy and slid his hand over her ass. She cooed and not-so-subtly pressed herself upwards against his hand.

"Look at that commotion," she said.

"What commotion?" He leaned next to her to look out the window.

Down below, on the casino's back street, diesel trucks rumbled — the noise echoing off the canyon walls of the surrounding hotels. A man shouted directions at one of the trucks while it backed into a loading dock.

"Must be a late-night delivery," Tracy said.

Angelo pulled her away from the window and closed it shut.

He smiled, "That's better now, isn't it?"

"Sure is." She turned and knelt in front of him. His robe opened. She smiled slyly, turning her eyes up at him. He ran his fingers through her hair.

"You're so good," he whispered.

———

DOWN BELOW, in the alley, two trucks sat in position, backed up against the loading dock. They were heavy duty straight trucks with large axels and double wheels. On their sides, billboard-sized graphics of a globe that read: World-Wide Moving Services – *We Get the Job Done.*

Two drivers stood waiting on the loading dock smoking cigarettes.

"Where are we taking this stuff?" one said.

"Don't know exactly," said the other. "They haven't told us yet, probably some warehouse."

A steady stream of men loaded the cargo onto the two trucks. They man-handled their heavy-duty hand trucks, piled high with boxes, and covered over with moving blankets.

"What do you think this stuff is?"

"Don't know and don't care."

"Let's go, let's go," Joey Messina prodded the men as he trailed alongside them. They carefully strapped the boxes, still covered with the moving blankets, against the walls of the truck.

"Tie it down good," Joey said. "We don't want anything shifting around in transit."

"Yeah, this shit's pretty heavy," one of the men said.

Joey glared at the guy. "Just make sure you tie it down good. That's all you gotta fucking worry about."

"Yes sir." The man pushed his empty hand-truck back inside the casino for another load.

————

NICK LIFTED HIS HEAD and squinted across the parking lot at Claudio's Lincoln and the black Riviera.

"Shit," he said. "They're still here."

He turned to Mario.

"Hey." He nudged him. "Wake up! They're still freakin' here."

"Oh, crap, I dozed off. Sorry," Mario said.

"It's alright. Let's go, I'm tired of waiting, they might be here all night for all we know."

Mario drove the Pinto out of the parking lot to the street, passing the two delivery trucks in the loading dock. Mario slowed down and he and Nick turned to look at the trucks and activity.

"Shit, what the hell?" Nick said. "It's after midnight and there's trucks delivering shit?"

"Maybe they work at all kinds of hours," Mario said. "Maybe they're delivering new poker tables or something. You know when the casino is empty."

"Huh," Nick shook his head.

————

CLAUDIO sat in his office smoking a cigar and watching the laborers roll their loads past his office and out to the trucks. It was late and Claudio was tired. But he was upbeat about the 'extraction,' as he put it to Roman.

Roman sat across from him smoking a cigarette and sipping a scotch on the rocks. They had been discussing the plan and contingencies and speculating on the value of all the silver bars and coins.

Tony stepped into the office, sweating.

"You won't believe this," he said. "We're only about halfway through."

"That's great." Claudio smiled and puffed his cigar.

"Holy fuck," Roman said. "There must be tons. How long do you think it'll take?"

"I don't know, another hour or two maybe. There's a hell of a lot of shit down there, it's crazy."

Tony high-fived Roman, then leaned over the desk and high fived Claudio. "Unfugginbelievable, Boss!"

Claudio smiled and said, "OK, go get Joey, we need to have a quick pow wow,"

"Sure thing," Tony said and quickly left.

Roman looked at Claudio. "This should be good."

Claudio shifted uncomfortably in his chair.

A minute later Tony walked back in with Joey.

"Have a seat, boys," Claudio said.

Tony sat down on the chair next to Roman and Joey settled onto the couch.

Joey wiped his sweaty forehead with his handkerchief and said, "What's up? We're making good progress, huh? Let's make this quick; I don't want to leave those guys out there alone for too long."

"Yeah, well," Claudio said. "We've had a slight change of plans."

Joey and Tony looked at him. Roman picked at his teeth.

"This may come as a shock," Claudio said. "But we want to leave some behind, in the vault. You know, not take all of it."

"Huh?" Tony said. "Why leave some behind? For charity? I thought we were emptying it?"

"No," Claudio said. "It'll look strange if it's all gone."

"Yeah," Roman said. "We need to leave some there. Maybe a few piles and pallets, maybe to fill about ten feet by ten feet or so? You know to make it look legit."

"Huh?" Joey said. "For what?"

Claudio leaned across his desk and looked at Joey and Tony.

"Shut the door," he said.

"Sure." Joey swung the door closed. "So, what the hell's up? Why leave some of the loot?"

"To look good." Claudio took another puff. "Like Roman said."

"Look good?" Joey squinted his eyes.

"Yeah, to look legit." Claudio waved his hand in the air. "We gotta leave some behind to look good. You know, for," he cleared his throat. "The Nut."

"Huh?" Joey gasped.

Claudio continued, "Think about it. He knows that Jack had a hoard of some kind of treasure, but he don't got know idea of how much. *Shit*, everybody and his brother knew the rumors about the stash, but nobody knows exactly how much. So, we leave a good amount, for him to see. And that'll be Jack's treasure hoard."

"I'm still not following." Tony stood up.

"Holy shit man, relax." Roman stood up and walked over to the wet bar to pour himself another drink.

Tony sat down again.

"Don't you see?" Roman waved his empty glass at Tony and Joey. "We leave a decent amount here, maybe a ton or so, then we tell The Nut that *that's all the loot — the whole fucking thing*. It's still a ton and he won't know anything's up. How's he gonna know? He's never seen it — nobody's ever seen it! He won't suspect anything, but there will still be a shitload there."

Roman put his hand on Tony's shoulder.

"It's still a hell of a lot left over," he said. "And the Nut will be so fucking happy — he won't even know what he don't know."

Tony's eyes widened and eyebrows lifted. "Really?" he said. "What if he finds out there's fucking five or six tons more? Then we're dead meat."

"No shit," Claudio said. "But grow some balls. We got this whole thing covered. We're gonna leave a lot behind, a whole lot. Then we cover our tracks, clean up the vault, make it look good, spread out the remaining stacks, you know, take the empty shelves out, etc. And when I show it all to the Nut, he'll be fucking astonished. Like Roman said, he don't know what he don't know."

Tony began to grin.

Claudio went on. "You, Joey and Roman go with the drivers halfway to Mesquite — but obviously don't tell them where you're going. Then let them out at the truck stop just outside of Vegas. Tell them you'll be back the next day with their trucks. Buy them a room and some whores. Then take it to hole in the ground at the ranch in Mesquite."

"Sure," Tony said. "But how we gonna unload all this stuff ourselves? I only got one arm."

"And my back's fucked up, no thanks to Nick," Joey said.

"Yeah well, it's a piece of cake," Roman said. "We got the hand-trucks right? We'll back the loads right to the hole. All we gotta do is move the shit just a few feet. We can take our time."

Tony shook his head, "I don't know man . . ."

"It's gonna be a tough night," Joey said.

"I'll move it myself if I have to," Roman said.

"Look," Claudio said. "This is par for the course. We're hard working motherfuckers, right? All you gotta do is remember the millions we're gonna split."

Claudio could see Joey getting excited.

"Now," Claudio continued. "Don't let Miguel see anything. He thinks it's some kind of medical waste. Wait till you got the shit covered with blankets and tarps before you tell him to start burying it all. Comprehendo?"

"Yeah, sure," Tony said. "And we'll all either end up rich or dead."

"I'd rather be rich," Joey laughed.

"Me, too," Roman said. "Dead ain't option."

"After things settle down, we'll dig that shit outta there and split it up, just among us four." Claudio smiled and puffed his cigar.

"Shit," Tony said. "It must be millions."

"Oh yeah," Roman said. "And the split will be 24 percent for each of us three, and 28 percent for Claudio.

Anyone got a problem with that?"

"No," Tony shook his head. "He's the boss."

"And that's fine with me too," Joey added.

"OK then," Claudio stood up and smiled. "Now you guys get back out there and get this thing wrapped up."

"Sure Boss." Joey said. "No problem."

He and Roman and Tony left—all with smiles on their faces.

Claudio sat back in his chair, alone. He put his feet up on Jack's desk, smiled and took another puff on his cigar. He blew the smoke over his head and watched it swirl through the air.

"Jack" he nodded and held his cigar up. "It's a damn good thing you didn't put your money in the bank, buddy. A damn good thing!"

CHAPTER 28

U nable to sleep, Nick lay on the couch, eyes wide open, staring at the ceiling. There was a bad smell in the air, something dead, like a rat or mouse somewhere in the room amid the piles of junk and clothes. Maybe it was right there under the couch. Nick pealed his blanket off and sat up. He felt light headed.

He stood from the couch and stumbled across the room toward the sink. At the faucet he took some water in his hand and slurped it up. He felt sweaty and his skin clammy. Maybe some fresh air would do him some good.

Even though he was only in his boxer shorts, he stepped outside onto the sidewalk in front of the house. The concrete was cool and course on the soles of his bare feet. He took a deep breath and immediately felt better. The sinking crescent moon had a bright star, maybe a planet, next to it. He could even see the craters along the moon's shadowy inside edge. Hard to believe men were walking on that dusty orb just a few months earlier. Crazy shit. In another twenty years they'll probably have a colony on Mars — *hope I live that long!*

Then he caught a glimpse of someone in a car parked across the street. A Chevy Impala? At this hour? Nick stepped a little closer. It looked like two people. They were sleeping.

Young guys. Maybe Claudio's crew? Shit, they must have been staking out Mario's place. Claudio wasn't fooling around.

Nick turned and scampered back to the house. He dressed quickly and grabbed Mario's car keys from the coffee table. He grabbed the gun too and slipped it into his jacket pocket.

Mario's red Mustang purred to a mellow rumble. Without turning on the headlights, he let the car drift down the driveway and into the street. He drove slowly up the block, glancing in the rear-view mirror, checking that the Impala was still parked and not making a move. At the corner he made the turn, then hit the gas.

It would be a relief to see his mom. He'd call Mario later. If Claudio saw him at the house, so what. Claudio must have already known he was staying at Mario's.

Fishing around in the glove compartment, he grabbed a random cassette tape. Janis Joplin. *Pearl*. Perfect. He slipped it into the console.

Cry Baby started right in the middle of the song.

He turned it up. Poor Janis, so young. Morrison and Hendrix, too. Shit, everyone was dying! Such a waste. Who knew, *he could maybe even be joining them soon!* They'd have a concert—a Woodstock in the clouds, on the moon, on a star, far away from the world and all its shitty and insane problems.

Vietnam—what the fuck are we doing over there? Dropping bombs on peasant farmers—and we gotta go all the way over around the world for that? Moving the whole fucking military—all that equipment, and all those people? To some country, who knows where! Dad was right, it's the government you have to watch out for. *Assholes!* The world sucks and we're all going to hell. The hippies are right. Flower power, man, the age of Aquarius. Peace and love in the universe, the goddamn universe. Yeah, that's what it's all about. Peace and fucking love—it'd be nice, but it ain't happenin' — not on this planet, not in this universe, not in this lifetime. What a freakin' mess.

Nick laughed and drove faster singing as loud as he could along with Janis. *"CRY CRY BABY!"* He drummed his fingers hard on the back of the steering wheel. *Oh, she was so good, so freakin' good.*

A hint of red and pink spread across the desert horizon. Thin high clouds floated over the mountains. Nick made a quick decision to take a detour, to the edge of Vegas, out to the desert. He was free and felt relieved and relaxed — even light. *Why not?* A few minutes later the endless expanse of desert stretched out before him.

His was the only car on the road. Peter Max colors spread across the distant sky. He pulled to the shoulder and cut the motor. The only sound, his own breathing and the clicking of the engine as it cooled. He stepped into the brisk, earthy air and took a breath. The sagebrush vibrated lightly in the breeze. There was something primordial about the place. The flat expanse of the desert stretched to the horizon — and the road, pencil straight, lead to the mountains, their craggy silhouette against a psychedelic sky of iridescent reds, pinks, purples and blues.

Nick took another deep breath, and slowly let it go. The thin crescent moon and star still visible, hung low behind him. He was alive — a creature, alive on a planet, in the universe. Yes, he chuckled, the honor of existence. *Hamlet had it wrong.*

He heard a sound in the distance, down the highway. A lone eighteen-wheeler was barreling toward him, its lights bright like a freight train against the blackness of the receding night. He stepped away from the road and into the desert. The truck flew past, roaring and kicking up a burst of dust, leaving the car and sagebrush rocking in its wake. The dust drifted past Nick and he could taste the earth. He knelt down and grabbed a handful of the sandy grit, and rubbed it between his fingers. Maybe it was a dry lakebed eons ago? He patted some of it on his tongue. It was salty. He stood back up and spit, then smiled and tossed the dirt in the air. It was going to be a good day.

Twenty minutes later the sun was up and the morning in full swing. Nick pulled into his driveway. Claudio's gold Lincoln Mark IV was parked on the left and his mom's white Cadillac El Dorado convertible parked on the right. He pulled the 'stang right to the back of the Lincoln and cut the engine. He exited the car as quietly as he could and stood a moment, and listened. Nothing. He carefully opened the kitchen door and slid in, as if he were breaking into his own house. Then he tiptoed to the living room.

He heard a noise and turned. *Snoring?* He looked down, at the couch. Someone was sleeping there. He stepped closer. It was Claudio, cozied up in a semi-fetal position with a light blanket thrown over him—sound asleep, snoring and drooling on the cushion.

Nick froze and took a step back, hardly able to believe his luck. His mom and sister must be upstairs sleeping. He reached into his pocket and pulled the hammer back on the gun. It made a muffled *click*. He gingerly stepped around the back of the couch and raised the gun. He aimed it down, inches from the back of Claudio's head.

A man no more!

He pushed the gun closer, until it almost touched Claudio's slicked-back hair. He held the barrel steady. All he had to do was pull his finger back just an eighth of an inch, Claudio's head would be blown to bits. He could just do it, do it — *right now!*

But while the man slept? While the man's in dreamland and defenseless? He'd get all that bad karma. And it would be bad karma, very bad. That's the truth. Did he want that heavy shit in his head, dragging him down, for the rest of his life? Shit, Claudio probably wouldn't even end up going to hell, having gone out defenseless like that.

Shit.

Nick pulled the gun away and stepped back. He stood a moment looking at Claudio, a huge bear of a man, sputtering and drooling like a baby.

Disgusting.

He walked quietly up to his room and placed the gun in his desk drawer, next to the box that had held the bolo tie from his dad. On his bed, he sat a moment, staring at the Jimmy Cliff *Harder They Come* poster — a pistol in each of Jimmy's hands.

He lay back and closed his eyes, then he felt for the bolo on his chest and rubbed his fingers over it — over his dad's Carson City silver dollar.

He hoped that this wouldn't be his last chance with Claudio and his last chance to make his dad proud.

———

LATER THAT MORNING, Frances made Claudio toast and coffee.

"My neck is stiff from sleeping on that damn couch."

Claudio rubbed his neck.

"Next time don't come home in the middle of the night," Frances said.

"Shit." Claudio smirked.

He sipped his coffee.

Frances pulled a Kool from her pack and lit it. She sat with her elbows on the table and blew the smoke hastily.

"Look," Claudio said. "I know you're worried, and I don't like it any more than you do."

Frances bit a fingernail and looked at him, "Where is he? You don't know?"

Claudio shrugged and shook his head, "I really don't, but I gotta go. It's going to be a busy day."

He stood up. Frances took another drag and turned away. Claudio grabbed his suit jacket from the back of the chair and slung it over his shoulder.

"I'll let you know as soon as I hear anything." He kissed the top of her head. "I promise."

He left and quickly got behind the wheel of his Lincoln. His thoughts were focused on whether or not the silver had gotten to Mesquite OK. He was so anxious to get going that he fumbled the ignition key.

"Shit."

Finally, he cranked the engine, threw it into reverse, and hit the gas. Then he turned to look behind. A sudden crushing crash of steel and glass whipped his head violently sideways.

"OHHH . . . FUCK!" he yelled and grabbed his neck. "SHIT!"

A bolt of pain ran through his neck and spine. He cut the engine and closed his eyes.

"FUCK!"

He struggled to pull himself out of the car.

Frances ran out from the kitchen.

"What the hell happened, are you OK?" she said. "Did you hit my car?"

He had to turn his whole body to look at what he hit. "No. Whose fucking car is that?"

Frances looked, "Wow, is that Mario's?"

"Mario's? What the hell could he doing here?"

Frances shrugged. "Are you OK? How's your neck? Come inside and put some ice on it."

Claudio grimaced and held his hand on his neck. Sweat beaded up on his forehead.

Just as Frances opened the kitchen door, Nick stumbled out and fell right into her arms. They both smashed backwards into Claudio.

"AH, SHIT!" he yelled as he held them up. "My neck!"

"Nick!" Frances shouted.

"Mom!"

———

WITH FRANCES INTERCEDING between them, Claudio and Nick stood directly across from each other in the driveway.

"Is that . . ." Claudio stammered. "Your fucking car?" Spit ejected from his mouth and landed right below Nick's eye.

Nick wiped it. "Mario's," he said. "And it was parked when you hit it."

Frances looked up at Nick with tears in her eyes. "It's

so good to see you," she said and hugged him. "Where were you? I was so worried."

"Don't worry, I was fine." Nick rubbed her back as he kept an eye on Claudio.

"I gotta sit down," Claudio said, and pushed past them to the kitchen door. "My neck."

Frances looked at Nick, "I was so worried, why didn't you call?"

"Sorry Mom," he said. "I didn't want to bother you."

She looked at him and frowned, "Well, I'm just so glad you're OK."

"I'm fine," Nick said. "Shit, look at what he did to Mario's car, he's gonna be pissed."

"I'm sure he'll pay for it," Frances said. "I better check on him."

Frances went back in the house and Nick surveyed the damage. Claudio's Lincoln didn't have much damage at all, only one of its tail lights was broken. But the Mustang's grill was smashed, its hood crinkled and one headlight shattered. Glass was scattered over the driveway. Nick tried to open the Mustang's hood, but it was jammed. He looked under the front end. The radiator was leaking—a green puddle forming on the driveway.

"*Dammit.*" He went back into the house.

"You really did a number on Mario's car, you know," he said to Claudio. "He's gonna kill me."

Claudio looked at Nick.

"I don't give a fuck," he said. "I practically broke my neck because of you."

"Why don't you look where you're driving? His car is completely fucked up now."

Claudio's face reddened.

"Here's some ice." Frances handed Claudio a towel wrapped around a handful of ice cubes. "Hold this on it."

"I am," he barked and grimaced in pain. "I gotta go." He tried to stand up.

"Take it easy," Frances said. "Where you gonna rush off to in that condition?"

"I gotta get to the casino." He looked at Nick. "You wanna try to move your friend's car so I can get out?"

"Sure," Nick said and left.

Frances sighed. "What about your neck, maybe you better lie down?"

"I'll be fine," Claudio said. "It's nothing. I'll take another cup of coffee though."

"Aren't you glad Nick is back and OK?"

Claudio watched Frances pour the coffee.

"Well?" she said. "Aren't you glad?"

"Sure," he said. "Now you don't have to worry anymore."

She placed the coffee in front of him.

Claudio added some milk and sugar. He tried to take a sip but couldn't tilt his head.

"Shit," he said.

"Take it easy," Frances said.

Claudio tried again, this time getting a half-sip of the hot coffee. He put the cup down.

Nick came back and without saying anything went out the kitchen door.

"I gotta go." Claudio pulled himself up.

"Are you sure you're OK?" Frances said.

"I'll be fine," he said.

"And you can drive?"

"I'll be fine," Claudio repeated and left.

———

NICK IGNORED Claudio as he passed him on his way back into the house.

"Shit," Nick said and sat down. "Mario's gonna kill me, his car's a wreck."

"Just have it towed out of here when you get a chance." Frances grabbed his hands. "So what happened?" She looked him square in the eyes. "You have no idea what that did to me. I thought the world was coming to an end. With Jack gone, then you disappear, and Anne Marie drunk all the time. I was beside myself."

"Sorry," Nick said. "I just didn't know what to do. And I didn't want anyone to know where I was. Why should anyone know? Especially Claudio and his goons?"

"I'm just glad you're OK." She rubbed his hands. "So, what did you do in Hawaii?"

"Nothing. I never went. I just stayed at the airport hotel, all by my lonesome old self—just me, myself and I!"

"You were here the whole time?"

"Yeah." He smiled guiltily.

"You should have called me."

"Sorry, he said, and looked her in the eye. "So, are you still getting married?"

Frances grabbed her box of Kool's.

"Yes, we're still getting married." She pulled out a

cigarette and lit it. "Anne Marie, Barbara and Marla have been helping with the plans and arrangements. They've been doing a lot. But I've been so worried about you, I couldn't do anything, I couldn't even think straight. But now that you're OK, I can get the wedding back on track. Isn't that wonderful?"

Nick's mouth fell open.

"Well?" she said. "Isn't that wonderful?"

He raised an eyebrow, "Yeah, I guess."

"And you know, Claudio's been really good. He's doing a great job at the casino."

"Really?" Nick said. "That's not what I heard. I heard he's screwing everything up."

"No, he's doing a great job. We're going to make more money than ever. He knows what he's doing."

"I can't believe you'd say that. He fired everyone, you know that? Alex, Bill, Lawrence, the cashiers, the security! Now he's got all his own people over there."

"But they're good people, they're professionals and they know what they're doing. Sometimes you have to clean house to get results."

"Shit!" Nick smirked. "I can run the casino better than he can."

Frances took a quick drag of her cigarette.

"But you never liked the casino business," she said. "Your father tried to show you the ropes, but you didn't want anything to do with it."

Nick shook his head. "That was then and this is now. I was just a kid then. Now I've been to college, and now Dad's gone. There's nobody else but me. Anne Marie can't do it and neither can you."

Nick grabbed the bolo tie and held it up. "Why do you think he gave me this? Because Dad wanted me to do it, that's why."

"You worry too much," Frances waved her cigarette. "Things will be fine. You'll see, and we'll have record profits. Dad would be proud of what I'm doing."

Nick bit his tongue.

His mom took a measured drag on her cigarette, held it for a second, then exhaled slowly.

"Have you heard about Rosalie?" she said.

Nick straightened up, "What do you mean? Is she OK?"

"You haven't heard?"

"No, of course not, what happened?"

Frances looked at him, "She OD'd."

"OD'd? What do you mean? Is she OK?"

"Well, she's alive, but she's at the hospital, in a coma. She took something a few days ago."

"Holy shit," Nick said. "I can't believe that, and you didn't tell me? Rosalie's not a drug addict."

"Well, whatever she did, it practically killed her. They think she may have even been trying to kill herself."

"What? *Why?*" Nick stood up.

"Nobody knows, that's the big mystery."

"What hospital is she at?"

"North Vista."

"My god," Nick said. "I gotta get over there. Can I take your car?"

"I don't know if you should go there now. What about her dad, Joey?"

"I have to go. I have to see her."

CHAPTER 29

In one way Claudio was glad that Nick was back and his whereabouts were no longer a mystery to Frances. He was off the hook, now that Frances knew he had nothing to do with Nick's disappearance, and that she knew he was safe. Claudio could rest easy, there was no chance that Frances would pull the plug or do something crazy like bring back Bill and Lawrence to work at the casino.

But, the problem with Nick being back was . . . Nick.

Claudio held his head stiffly tilted while he drove his banged-up Lincoln into the Three-C's parking garage. He couldn't even turn his head to back up, so he parked crookedly in his reserved spot. He took his jacket and cigarettes and stepped from the car, slamming the door behind, rattling something loose by the back bumper.

"Damnit." He turned to look and rubbed his neck.

"What the hell happened to you?" someone shouted, their voice echoing off the parking lot walls.

Claudio turned to look but a shot of pain ran through his neck.

"Shit." He said between clenched teeth. It was Joey. "Ah, fuck, had a slight accident."

"What?" Joey said. "What's with your neck?"

"It got fucked up, I backed into Nick's car. He's back at home now."

"No shit, so he's not hiding out like a pussy at his friend's house anymore?"

"Nope. He parked right in back of me at the house

and I slammed right into him as I was leaving. Sprained my fucking neck."

"Shit, want me to take care of him now? Look at the condition that Rosalie's in." Joey shook his head. "And, he fucked up my back when I had to chase him from her room. Let me get him now that he's back home. I'll just make him disappear."

"No, don't do anything yet," Claudio said. "Like I said the other day, we need to be careful and do this thing the right way."

"Sure," Joey said.

They headed into the casino.

"So, how's Rosalie doing?" Claudio asked. "She wake up yet?"

"No, I just came from the hospital. She's hanging in there. It's damn depressing. I don't know what to do."

"Shit, you just gotta hope for the best," Claudio said. "All her vital signs are good, right? She'll pull through."

"I hope so."

They walked onto the main floor of the casino. It was early and only a few diehard players were hunched over the slots. The usual stale smell of cigarette smoke hung in the air.

Claudio stopped and rotated his body toward Joey. "So," he said. "How'd it go last night?"

"Good," Joey said. "Took us all night, but we did it."

Claudio tried to nod his head, but instead grimaced and groaned. "Good," he said.

They continued toward his office, Claudio with a bit more bounce in his step.

"Morning," he said to the cage girl who buzzed them in.

In his office, Claudio threw his jacket on the couch and took his seat behind the desk.

"So, what happened? How'd it all go?" Claudio said.

"It was a lot of work," Joey said. "Fuck, it almost killed us. There was more stuff than we thought—practically filled up both freakin' trucks. Can you imagine?"

Claudio smiled, "Shit, really?"

"Yup, there's gotta be tons. Silver bars and coins. But mostly silver bars. I'm telling you, it's the goddam mother-load, a fuckin' mother-load."

Claudio smiled. "Holy shit, I knew it was huge. This is going to be freakin' great."

Joey continued, "Went without a hitch. We gave the truck drivers the night off, then me and Roman drove the trucks up there ourselves. Tony followed in his car. When we got there, we had the Mexican unload the truck with his backhoe."

"The Mexican?" Claudio asked. "He didn't see nothin', did he?"

"No, it was all wrapped in moving blankets. For all he knows, it's just garbage."

"Good."

"He covered it all up too," Joey said. "We made sure to wait for him to finish the job. Now you can't even see anything from the road, it's just one big-ass farmer's field."

"Great. Let's go check on the vault—make sure it looks good down there before The Nut comes by. How much stuff did you leave behind?"

"Well, we didn't want to leave too much," Joey said. "But it should be plenty to make a good impression. Don't worry."

"I am worried. Let's go."

They stepped into the elevator to the vaults. Claudio leaned forward and looked at the floor.

"Looks clean," he said.

"Yeah, I had the guys lay cardboard down so the floors wouldn't get scuffed or have hand-truck marks all over them."

"Perfect."

The room outside the vault looked clean, too. Claudio put on his reading glasses, and carefully dialed the combination. He turned the handle and the vault door clicked open.

He surveyed the room-sized vault swiveling his body left, then right, his head remaining stiffly tilted. Some of the steel shelving was empty. But there were piles of silver bars neatly stacked on the floor in front of them. There were also carts full of chips parked in each isle of the vault, between a few small stacks of silver bars.

Claudio thought for a moment.

"What do you think?" Joey said.

"I don't know, it looks a little sparse. What about the back vault, is that all emptied out?"

"No," Joey said. "We left a bit there, too."

"Let's have a look."

Claudio opened the second, inner vault door. There were a few stacks of silver and a single pallet piled with bags of coins. But it was mostly empty too.

"You know what?" Claudio said. "I think it'd be better to move all this stuff to the front vault. Then we close this one and say it was always empty."

"You sure?"

"Yeah," Claudio said. "What else are we gonna do? Put some of the shit back?"

"I don't know," Joey said. "He might be suspicious. A whole vault empty?"

Claudio pondered this a moment.

"Alright," he said. "How bout we just cover over this vault door? Like plaster it over or something. Then the Nut won't even notice it. Make it look like it's just another wall."

"Sure, no problem, that sounds good," Joey said. "But it might take me a few days because I gotta do all the work myself, right?"

"Yeah, shit." Claudio rubbed his neck again. "I'll try to stall The Nut and you just hurry up with it. And don't make it look brand new either. Put some dirt and dust on it and make it look legit. Make sure he won't notice. Hollywood it up, you know?""

"No problem." Joey looked at him. "And you should go to the damn doctor. You don't look too good."

Claudio rubbed his neck again. "Yeah, it's fucking killing me now. I think it's getting worse."

CHAPTER 30

Nick raced his mom's white Cadillac Eldorado up freeway 15 to the North Vista hospital. Rosalie, sweet Rosalie. She could be dead or worse, stuck in a coma for years. What the fuck happened? He wasn't prepared for this. And was it his fault? Did he let her go while he was hiding in his hotel room like a coward, while she OD'd?

Before he knew it, he was pulling into a parking spot at the hospital.

"Rosalie Messina," he blurted at the information desk attendant. "What room is she in?"

The elderly lady smiled warmly and looked down at her blue mimeographed sheet. She moved her finger down the page as she searched the name.

"Room 312A," she finally said.

Nick immediately started walking to the elevator.

The lady hollered after him, "Make a right, right and a left when you get out of the elevator, then it's down the hall."

"Right, right, left," he repeated.

He stood in front of the elevator watching the numbers. 5, then 6. Shit, he shuffled back and forth, turned and considered taking the stairs. Finally, the elevator doors opened. A group of nurses and a doctor pushed a patient out on a rolling bed, with one nurse holding an I.V. bag alongside. Nick stepped back to let them pass.

He just barely reached his arm to the doors in time to stop them from closing. He hit the "3" button, then hit it again, then again. Another visitor stepped in and held the door. A nurse escorted a thin, emaciated old man who looked like death itself toward the elevator. Shit, they were moving at a snail's pace, the man hanging his head down low and barely sliding one foot in front of the other.

"Take your time," the person holding the door said.

The nurse smiled. Nick stepped to exit the elevator to bolt up the stairs. But as he passed the old man, the man glanced up at him. Nick took another step then stopped and turned.

The doors began to close.

"Yuri?" Nick reached his arm to stop the doors from closing, then stepped back into the elevator. The old man's eyes lit up, then a subtle smirk appeared on his face.

"Nick?" he uttered.

"Yuri! What's happened to you?"

"Nicky boy," Yuri said in a raspy whisper. "You're all grown up."

The elevator doors closed and the nurse hit the button for the second floor.

"Yuri, you crazy Russian, what happened to you? Are you OK?"

Yuri smiled. "I'm on my way out, boy."

He lifted his frail hand and grabbed onto Nick's arm.

Yuri leaned in and winked, "It's been a good run."

Nick smiled. "My God, Yuri, I can't believe it's you. You used to carry me on your shoulders when I was just a little kid. Always so full of life! And now . . ."

The second floor came and Nick held the door for them.

"I know," Yuri said. "I'm a walking shadow now, but

you take care and keep your chin up."

Yuri lifted his hand to wave goodbye.

"Take care, Yuri!" Nick said and the elevator doors closed. Nick stood staring at the back of the doors, and saw, in their polished silver finish, his fuzzy, muted, reflection. The elevator groaned and began to rise.

"You knew him?" the person in the corner of the elevator said.

"I knew him well." Nick nodded. "I knew him well."

At the third floor Nick stepped from the elevator and headed right, down the hall.

302AB, 306AB, 310AB and . . . 312A.

"Messina" was scribbled on a yellow card over the room number plaque.

Nick peeked into the half-opened doorway. He could see the bed behind a half-closed curtain. He stepped in. What if her dad Joey was there? It didn't matter. Only one thing mattered. He stepped over to the bed. Rosalie's mother, Mary Ellen Messina, stood by the side, her startled look indicating that she didn't immediately recognize him. Rosalie lay under a white hospital blanket.

"How is she?" he said.

"Oh," Mary Ellen said tentatively. "She's hanging in there."

Nick stepped to the opposite side of the bed and looked at Rosalie. She had an I.V. connected to her, some wires, more tubes and various bandages. Her face was pale and her hair had been brushed back.

"You're Nick?" Mary Ellen said.

"Yes."

"You're the one who broke into her bedroom?"

"I didn't break in."

"No?"

He stared at Rosalie sleeping, dead still. He wished he were here alone with her.

"She invited me in," he said. "She was glad I came to see her. It's just that your husband wasn't too happy to find me there."

"You're lucky he's not here."

"I know. But I had to see Rosalie; will she be OK?"

Nick leaned over the bed's railing, closer to Rosalie. Her eyelids were spookily half closed and her mouth hung open. Her lips were chapped and dry.

"She's been like this for two days," Mary Ellen said.

"But is she going to be OK?" Nick lifted his head and looked directly at Rosalie's mom.

"The doctors don't know."

"They don't know?" He stood up straight. "What do you mean, they don't know?"

Mary Ellen shook her head, "We just have to wait and see. That's what they said." She paused, then added, "You know, my husband thinks she'd be OK if it wasn't for you."

"Me?"

"Rosalie was *distraught*—over you." She glared at him.

"Distraught?"

"We saw your letter."

Shit, he'd forgotten about the letter.

"But, what happened to her? Why's she like this?"

Mary Ellen looked at Rosalie and ran her hand through her daughter's hair.

"She took sleeping pills, three nights ago. When I went to wake her in the morning, she wouldn't move. We rushed her here and they pumped her stomach. But it was too late. She's been in a coma ever since. They said she may never come out of it."

"Why would she do that?"

"Look, you better go," Mary Ellen said. "There's no telling what my husband might do if he finds you here."

Nick reached for Rosalie's limp hand. It was cold. The hospital was cold too, but Rosalie's hand felt unnaturally cold, the skin pulled tightly over her thin fingers.

Nick leaned down, close to her face. She was breathing, but very lightly.

He whispered, "Rosalie . . ."

He wanted to look into her eyes and tell her he was there for her, that he'd never ever leave her again.

"It's no use," Mary Ellen said. "We've been talking to her and rubbing her hands but she hasn't moved a muscle."

Nick heard what she said but didn't want to believe her. He moved closer to Rosalie's face, his breath light on her cheek.

"Can she move her muscles?" He searched Rosalie's face for any signs of life.

"Yes, she has feeling in her fingers and toes," her mom answered. "But hasn't moved."

Nick brushed Rosalie's hair back from her forehead. He touched the back of his hand against her cheek, his skin tingling against hers. His lips started to quiver and eyes tear. Now he pressed his hands against her cheek and slid his fingers across her lips. A single tear slid down his cheek and fell to her blanket.

"I'm going to step out to have a cigarette," her mom suddenly said and left.

Nick tears began to flow uncontrollably. He pressed his wet face against Rosalie's, grabbing her head in his hands. *This wasn't right. Why did this have to happen?* His eyes were closed but the tears kept coming.

After what seemed like minutes he began to regain his composure. Rosalie's skin felt so soft against his face. He held his cheek against her forehead.

A few of his tears rolled against her face. He wiped them from her cheek, and pushed them back through her hair. One fell directly onto the tip of her tongue.

He took short breaths, trying to calm himself. *Why, why?* He touched his finger to her lips again.

A weak spasm, a cough? *Was it a cough? Or did he imagine it?* He searched her face.

Another cough, it was definitely a cough. Nick pulled back to look at her. Suddenly her hand rose toward her mouth, trying to cover it.

Another weak cough.

Nick pulled her head close, pressing his cheek against hers.

"Rosalie!"

One of her eyelids seemed to rise a bit.

"Rosalie!"

Both eyelids lifted a bit and her lips quivered.

Nick kissed her lips.

"Rosalie . . ." he cried.

She coughed again. Both eyelids slowly lifted.

She gazed blankly at him.

"Nick . . ." she whispered, almost imperceptibly.

CHAPTER 31

Angelo "The Nut" Lombardo sat in Claudio's office calmly examining his nails. He looked surprisingly refreshed to Claudio, who sat across from him at his desk, his head uncomfortably tilted. Claudio leaned forward, opened his Padron humidor and pulled out two cigars. He handed one to Angelo. They took turns lighting their cigars in silence.

Claudio rubbed his neck and puffed his cigar.

"You really did a number on it, huh?" Angelo said.

"It's nothing," Claudio said.

"Maybe you better go see the doc? It's gonna feel worse tomorrow, you know? It's always worse the next day."

"I'll go later."

Angelo puffed his cigar and leaned back in his chair.

"Well, don't it feel just fucking great knowing you're about to make a huge score? You know, like when your horse is coming down the stretch and there ain't another horse near it—and you know you're going to win a fucking fistful of dollars?"

"Sure," Claudio watched the smoke rise and swirl off his cigar. "Like a fucking gift."

"Exactly my point," Angelo said. "But that's as long as we don't screw it up."

Claudio looked at him.

Angelo continued, "I like the idea that you're marrying Frances," he puffed his cigar. "But Nick, he's a problem."

Claudio sat up, "Don't worry, I got a plan for him. I'll take care of him in a few days, after the wedding of course."

The Nut leaned forward, "That's too late," he said. "We gotta move quickly, before something goes wrong."

"Nothing's gonna go wrong, what's gonna go wrong?"

"Things gotta be moved up," Angelo said. "We gotta wrap up these loose ends fast, we can't leave shit like this hanging."

Claudio searched Angelo's face. He pulled rank on Claudio, and based upon his previous history and the fact he was a certified and unpredictable psychopath, Claudio knew there was little point in arguing with him.

"Sure." Claudio rubbed his neck again. "No problem, I'll take care of it."

"Fuck!" Angelo slapped his hand on the desk and stood up. "No, I'll take care of the Nick problem today, and it'll go away." He snapped his fingers. "Just like that."

Angelo stepped over to Claudio and hovered over him. "You don't want to jeopardize the silver that you say is piled high like a mountain, right? All that money! You don't want to jeopardize it, do you? You fucking snooze you lose. What do *you* think that fucking means?"

Claudio looked at Angelo incredulously, which he knew was a mistake. But it was too late. Claudio could see the crazed look of anticipation in Angelo's eyes. He knew the man couldn't wait to smash someone's brains in.

"Wait a minute." Claudio stood from his chair and faced Angelo. "We can't just whack him right before the wedding. If Nick goes missing, Frances will be a wreck. Who knows what she'll do. She could end up calling the whole thing off."

Claudio hoped his argument held. Angelo turned and stepped to the wet bar. Claudio knew he was buying time, thinking of what to say. Angelo poured himself a drink, and Claudio sat back down.

"Want one?"

"Sure." Claudio kept his eyes on him.

Angelo casually put the ice in the glasses and poured the scotch. He walked around the back of the desk and handed Claudio his drink.

"Nick," Angelo snarled.

"Yeah, Nick . . ." Claudio repeated.

"Well what da' fuck are you gonna do about him then?" Angelo yelled at Claudio while leaning over him. "You can't fuck this up."

Claudio tried to look up at Angelo. "Yeah, ahhh shit." He rubbed his neck. "I know." He pushed the chair back to get some distance between them.

Angelo lunged at Claudio, slapping him on the head, *"What, you stupid fuck!"*

Claudio cowered. A bolt of pain shot through his neck.

Angelo stared at him. "Tell me what the fuck are you gonna do?"

"I'll take care of him." Claudio held up his hand in surrender. "Sit down so I can tell you my plan."

Angelo smirked. "I'm all ears."

"I have an idea." Claudio reached for his whisky and noticed his hand shaking.

He took a sip, "First, we gotta make it look like an accident . . ."

When Claudio was done he smiled and said, "And, I'm gettin' fucking married!"

"Well, *congratu-fucking-lations*," Angelo said.

"Toast," Claudio held up his tumbler.

Angelo lifted his glass.

"To Sex, Drugs, and Rock and Roll baby!" Claudio said enthusiastically, "and, to the silver and gold, too . . ."

Claudio immediately realized that he shouldn't have mentioned the loot.

"Silver and gold!" Angelo echoed.

They clinked glasses and took sips, then leaned back in their cushy chairs and puffed their cigars.

Angelo stared at Claudio. "So," he said. "There's gold too?"

"Gold, I don't know," Claudio tried to be as casual as possible and puffed his cigar. "Silver bars and coins, yes."

"That's what I thought."

"Yeah," Claudio continued. "Wait 'till you see it. It's a fucking boatload!"

Why say that? The pain in his neck tightened. He tried his best to smile.

Angelo looked at him. "When where you planning to show it to me?" he said.

Claudio briefly turned his attention down at his drink and its floating ice cubes.

"Whenever you want," he looked up. It was the only good answer. Call his bluff, head on, don't raise any suspicions.

"Let's go fucking check it out right now." Angelo smiled. "What are we waiting for!"

Shit, Shit . . . Claudio heard himself say in his head and wondered if he may have even mistakenly mouthed the words. He laid his cigar in the ashtray.

"Sure, no problem," Claudio said. "I got the combination right here."

He opened his desk drawer and rummaged around. Angelo scrutinizing his every move. He searched as earnestly as he could through the drawer. Then he abruptly stopped and shut the drawer.

"Shit," he looked at Angelo. "I don't have the damn combination here. It's freakin' back at the house."

Angelo looked at him quizzically, "You don't have it here with you, in the casino?"

"Shit," Claudio tried to show as much surprise as possible. "Frances just gave it to me the other day and it's in my other jacket. At the house."

"You *gotta* be kidding me? You left the combination to tons of silver in your fucking jacket pocket?"

"I'll just bring it tomorrow," Claudio said as casually as he could.

Angelo stood up and pointed his cigar at Claudio.

"Go home and get it the fuck now! Get the fucking key. I wanna see the hoard, this mountain of silver. I want to see it *now*."

"Ahhh, fucking shit!" Another bolt of pain shot through Claudio's neck.

He rubbed it.

Angelo looked down at him and turned for the door. He was about to leave but stopped and turned back to Claudio.

"Maybe you should go to the fucking doctor first," he said. "Then meet me back here later tonight with the key, or the combo, or whatever the fuck you got."

"Sure, no problem, I'll meet you back here later." Claudio rubbed his neck and watched Angelo leave.

"Shit," he said, under his breath.

CHAPTER 32

Nick left the hospital elated. In the car the radio was tuned to one of his mom's stations and the Partridge Family's *I Think I Love You* was playing. Nick began singing along, "*I think I love you!*"

He turned it up. Rosalie was going to be OK and *he* had snapped her out of it. Her mom, Mary Ellen, was ecstatic, and he hoped that when her dad, Joey, found out about it, maybe he wouldn't be such an asshole to him anymore. And the doctors, they were amazed that she was awake now. They said she'd probably fully recover and might even be out of the hospital in just a few days.

"*I think I love you!*" he shouted while tapping the steering wheel. The car glided on, over the cracked pavement and over the troubled earth. Everything was going to be alright.

He pulled into his driveway and saw Mario's smashed red Mustang where he had left it parked on the side. Barbara's lime green Pinto was there also, and one other car—a blue Thunderbird with a white vinyl roof. Was that Marla's car?

He parked behind the Pinto. The Partridge Family tune was still in his head as he headed into the house, beaming, ready to share the news. In the kitchen, he was surprised to see Mario and Barbara, Anne Marie, Marla, and his mom, at the table making some kind of angel-winged party favors.

"About time you showed up, man," Mario stood up. "What'd you do to my car?"

"Nothin'," Nick said. "Claudio did it. My mom didn't tell you?"

"She told me but what happened?"

"Later man. What are you guys doing?"

"Making decorations for mom's wedding," Anne Marie said. "Aren't they pretty?" She held one up.

"Yeah," Nick said.

On the table, piles of pastel-colored cut paper angels, pieces of ribbons, glitter, glue bottles, wine bottles, a glass of white wine in front of each of the women, and a pile of cigarette butts in the ashtray. Mario held a Michelob in one hand and a Marlboro in the other.

"You helping too?" Nick said to Mario.

"Yeah, somehow they got me and Barbara roped into this."

"It's no problem," Barbara said. "And he's having fun."

Mario smirked.

"How's Rosalie?" Frances said to Nick.

All eyes turned to him.

"You went to see Rosalie?" Marla interjected.

Nick looked at her, "Yeah."

"Why can't you just leave her alone?" Marla said. "You're not doing her any favors you know."

Nick turned to his mom. "You're not going to believe this."

"What?" Marla interrupted. "What aren't we gonna believe, how she's so messed up because of you?"

"Let him talk." Anne Marie nudged her.

Even though Marla irritated him, Nick couldn't hold back the huge smile on his face.

"What happened?" Frances said.

"She came out of the coma."

"*What?*" Anne Marie said.

"Sit down and tell us what happened," Frances said.

Nick sat down.

"I spoke to Rosalie and I guess when she heard my voice, she came out of it. It was crazy. Her mom was there too, she saw it. The doctors couldn't believe it. They said she's going to be OK."

"Wait a minute, tell us everything," Anne Marie said. "From the beginning."

Nick picked up one of the paper angels and started fiddling with it.

"OK well, first of all, I get there and on the elevator, believe it or not, I see Yuri, freakin' Yuri. Remember him? I could hardly recognize him. It was like seeing a ghost, he's nothing but skin and bones. But he remembered me, imagine that? It blew my mind, I didn't even know he was still alive, and here is was on death's door! It was crazy."

"Yuri," Frances said. "Such a great guy, we always had so much fun with him."

"Wow," Anne Marie said. "I remember him. That was a long time ago."

"What about Rosalie?" Marla said. "Tell us what happened."

"Yeah, well I get to her room, and only her mom was there with her. She wasn't too happy to see me but she didn't exactly kick me out. But poor Rosalie, she was really in a stone-dead coma. She had all kinds of tubes and wires on her and everything. It was sad to see her like that, just sleeping. But I talked to her, and touched her cheek. Then her mom left to go smoke a cigarette, and I was there alone with Rosalie. It was so sad. I talked to her, and I think she heard me because something happened, and all of a sudden she coughs, just a bit. I could hardly hear it. It was weird, I think she knew I was there. And then she woke up."

"You're a *fucking* hero, Nick," Marla said. 'You know that?"

"No shit?" Mario said.

"That's absolutely wonderful." Frances placed her hand on Nick's cheek. "My boy."

"Cool," Barbara said. "You got good karma, man."

Marla stood up, "I'm going to head over to the hospital right now to see her."

"That's not a good idea," Nick said. "The doctors don't want her to have any extra stimulation or excitement right now. It'd be better if you visit tomorrow."

Marla huffed and sat down again. "Alright," she said. "I can dig it."

"That's wonderful news, Nick," Frances said. "She's such a sweet girl."

"She is," Anne Marie said. "Better not let her get away this time!"

Nick smirked.

Mario took a swig of his beer, "Cool, now what the *hell* happened to my car?"

"Freaking Claudio was rushing to get out this morning and backed right into it. Didn't even look where he was going."

"Maybe you shouldn't have parked right on his ass," Marla said.

"It was an accident," Frances said.

"Maybe he should've looked where he was going," Nick said. Then to Mario, "Let's go shoot some pool."

Mario stood up, "Great idea. I've done my share of folding party favors."

"What's the matter," Barbara said. "You don't like making these groovy little angles?"

"Not exactly." Mario shook his head.

At the fridge, Nick grabbed a couple beers and he and Mario left.

"Thanks for your help, Mario!" Frances called after them.

"No problem." Mario raised his half-empty beer in mock salute.

As they walked down the hallway, which was now lined with all of Claudio's pictures, Mario said, "Now, who's gonna pay for my car?"

Nick stopped and turned to Mario.

"Shit," he said. "I forgot to call a tow truck. My mom wants your car out of the driveway."

"No problem, I'll call, where's the yellow pages?" Mario said.

"In the kitchen. And don't worry, we'll get the retard to pay." Nick said, then whispered, "before we kill him."

Mario went to the kitchen and Nick continued to the game room. At the pool table, he took a few balls from the chute and placed them on the green felt. He selected a stick off the rack, chalked it, and studied the table. He placed the cue ball behind the line, aimed and took a shot. His technique was relaxed and smooth. The seven ball dropped in the corner pocket and the cue ball stopped, spun backward and stopped again. It was perfectly setup for his next shot.

Nick took a swig of his beer. Why couldn't his life be like that? Every step perfectly planned, every action perfectly executed, lined up, positioned, and ready for the next step? He walked around the table and studied the alignment of the cue ball with the other balls.

What did Einstein say? 'God doesn't play dice with the universe?' No, he plays pool, that's what he does—plays pool with our lives. Sometimes he makes a shot, sometimes he misses, and we all roll around, bouncing off each other, bouncing off the bumpers, and dropping down holes.

He slammed the cue ball into the one ball, smashing it into the corner pocket which ate it in one swift bite.

"Tow truck's comin'" Mario walked in. "Half hour, it'll be here."

"Great," Nick said. "Let's rack 'em up."

"Alright," Mario said. "But you're gonna lose."

"Eight ball?"

"Sure," Mario grabbed a ball from the chute and looked at Nick. "So, what the hell is going on with you, man?"

"Me?" Nick gently hit a ball to the far bumper of the table and watched it return and slowly stop a foot away from the near bumper.

"Nothing. Let's see ya' beat that."

Mario positioned his ball right up to the line and hit it a bit too hard. The ball bounced off the far bumper, came back, and bounced off the near bumper.

"Shit." Mario grabbed the rack. "So . . ." He started loading the balls. "Why the hell did you leave this morning?"

Nick chalked up his stick as he walked to the other side of the table to set up his break shot.

"So?" Mario carefully lifted the rack off.

Nick stopped, holding his stick like a staff. "You didn't see the two goons parked outside, staking us out?"

"What? No."

"Well I couldn't sleep, so I stepped outside for some air, then I see these two guys, maybe about our age, sleeping in a Chevy Impala across the street. Probably from Claudio's crew, staking your place out, looking for me. They could have been hitmen!"

"Shit," Mario said. "I wonder if they knew you were here?"

"I don't know but I wasn't going to take any chances. I figured it'd be best to split. And I didn't want to wake you up, who knows what might have happened. They're after me, but they could have gotten you too."

"Huh."

"So I split. Figured there's no sense hiding anymore. I came back home. My mom was thrilled to see me. She was a little pissed at me, but thrilled anyway."

He placed the cue ball down and lined up his shot.

"Yeah, she told us about it, and how relieved she was."

"I know." Nick took his shot, hitting the cue ball hard, cracking the other balls, scattering them across the table and dropping two of them.

"But you think you're safe here?" Mario said.

"Sure," he said. "Claudio's can't do nothin'."

"I don't know man." Mario shook his head. "He's unpredictable."

"What's he gonna do?"

Nick leaned in for his next shot.

"Maybe like, kill you?"

Nick took his shot and missed. "I don't think so," he said. "With the wedding just a few days away, he can't do nothin'. My mom would call it off if anything happened to me. So everything's cool, for now."

"Huh," Mario said.

"And," Nick leaned closer to him. "It's easier to keep tabs on Claudio. I'll call you when everything looks good. Then we can get on with it."

Mario raised an eyebrow and nodded. "Alright man, just let me know. I've got all the shit ready. Whenever you say go, we go."

"Right on," Nick said.

Mario lined up his shot.

"Seven ball, side pocket."

"You don't have to call it."

Mario cracked the cue ball, slicing the seven ball into the side pocket and smashing the cue ball into a cluster of balls, scattering them around the table. He smiled. "How's that?"

"Not bad."

"So." Mario was nonchalant as he took a swig of his beer and surveyed the table, "What's up with you and Rosalie?"

Nick cleared his throat.

"Well?" Mario said.

"Well what?"

"You're in love, man!"

Nick smiled. "I admit it, I dig her. And I think she digs me too. I was there and she woke up, just like that!" He snapped his fingers. "It was unbelievable."

"What about her boyfriend? Fiancé?" Mario said. "Didn't you tell me she was getting married or something?"

"Shit man," Nick said. "He never even came down to see her. Too busy. That's what her mom told me."

"Really?"

"Yup," Nick said. "He must be a fucking douchebag."

Mario took his shot and sunk the next ball.

"I'm going back over there tonight to stay with her."

"What?" Mario frowned. "Are you crazy? What about her dad, ain't he gonna kill you too? Man, you got Rosalie on the brain."

"Don't worry, I'll be fine, Nick laughed. "It's a fucking hospital after all. Anything happens to me there, well then I'm in the right fucking place, ain't I?"

"OK man." Mario shook his head and lined up his next shot. "Just be careful."

"I'm always careful, man," Nick said.

Mario took his shot and missed.

"Ha!" Nick chalked up his cue stick. "My turn. You're dead now."

CHAPTER 33

Frances yelled from the hallway, "Tow truck's here."

"Finally." Nick put his pool stick down. "Let's go."

Mario followed Nick out. "He better pay for this. I ain't, that's for sure." Mario said.

"Don't worry about it, if he don't pay, I'll pay."

In the driveway, a *Sin City Roadside Service* tow truck reversed up towards Mario's smashed car. While it positioned itself closer to the car, Claudio's gold Lincoln Mark IV turned into the driveway. Claudio pulled right up to the front of the tow truck, blocking it. The driver raised his hands in complaint.

Nick looked at Mario. "Great," he said. "Now Claudio's here to cause more accidents!"

"No shit," Mario said.

The tow truck driver jumped out of the truck. He was a brawny, tattooed man with rolled up T-shirt sleeves that accentuated his massive arms. He swaggered over to the Lincoln.

"Aye! What the fuck? You don't see me doin' my job here?"

The man raised his arms again.

"Is that Claudio in a neck brace?" Mario asked Nick.

"Yeah, that's from the accident," Nick said. "He gave himself a major whiplash. Serves him right. Looks like he's with that guy from the casino we saw him with in the parking lot. This should be good."

Claudio wore a white plastic neck brace and struggled

as he leaned and turned his body, trying not to twist his neck while he exited the car. Angelo "The Nut" emerged from the passenger side, slammed the door and stared at the tow truck driver.

Frances, Anne Marie, Barbara and Marla had already come out from the house.

"What's your problem?" Angelo approached the man.

"Nothin.' Except you're blockin' me. How I'm supposed to do my goddamn job with you blockin' me?"

Angelo got right up in his face, "You know, you got a messed up attitude. I see you cursing like that, and there's ladies over here?" Angelo glanced toward the women. "I got a problem with that, a big problem."

The tow truck driver took a half step back. "What are you, some kind of nut?"

"Nut?" Angelo turned red and sucker punched the guy in the solar plexus. The guy keeled over and stumbled backward into the tow truck. Angelo sprang forward and threw a left hook to his jaw, then an upper cut, and finally a cracking jab squarely to his nose. An explosion of blood splattered over the front of the tow truck. The driver moaned but stayed on his feet a moment before beginning to crumble.

"Claudio!" Frances yelled. "I don't want no trouble at my house."

Anne Marie and Barbara covered their faces and turned away. But Marla, Nick and Mario stood transfixed as the beating progressed. Marla even encouraged Angelo, yelling, "Fuck 'em up! Teach 'em a lesson! Dumb fuck!"

"Oh, shit, what the fuck is he doing?" Nick said.

"Yeah, who's gonna tow my car now?" Mario said.

Angelo continued pummeling the guy until he slid

down against the front grill of the truck and hit the pavement, gurgling, wheezing and sputtering blood all over the driveway.

Claudio stood by but didn't say a word.

"You want some more?" Angelo shouted. He adjusted his pants and turned toward the house.

The man's head was a deformed mass of blood and hair.

"Don't you ever come here and disrespect this family, you fuck," Angelo said. His homicidal assault over, he shook his head, and turned to Claudio. "Got what he deserved."

Frances ran back into the house, her hand covering her mouth. Anne Marie and Barbara followed in.

Angelo pulled out a handkerchief and wiped his face with it.

"Good job!" Marla said.

Angelo smiled at Marla.

Claudio walked over to the fallen driver.

"You better get the fuck out of here," he said to the man.

The truck driver could barely get back to his feet. He pulled up his T-shirt and wiped his bloody face.

Claudio stood like a robot staring at him, his neck in the white plastic and foam brace. "You ever come back here again, we'll bury you in the back yard."

The man crawled back into his truck.

"Are you OK?" Marla asked.

"I'm fine," Claudio said. "Here, pull my car out of here so the douchebag can get out." He gave her his keys.

Claudio and Angelo headed into the house.

"Man, that was crazy," Mario said.

"Yeah," Nick said.

They headed back into the house. Angelo was at the sink washing the blood off his hands. Nick stepped up to Angelo and caught a glimpse of the blood spinning in a candy cane swirl down the drain.

"Where the fuck do you get off causing that kind of trouble, at my house, and in front of my mom?" Nick said.

Angelo smirked, and continued washing his hands.

"Hey." Claudio stepped up to Nick and put his hand on his shoulder. "It was a mistake. My friend Angelo's got a short temper."

Claudio looked at Angelo.

"Sorry about that," Angelo said. "I just can't take disrespectful idiots."

Frances stepped up and pushed Claudio.

"Shit," she yelled. "I don't need to see that kind of thing in my house. Go beat the crap out of people someplace else!"

"Hey, hey, we're sorry." Claudio said, almost sounding earnest about it. "It won't happen again. He just got a little carried away."

Claudio handed Angelo the dishtowel.

"Shit," Nick backed off.

Mario grabbed the yellow pages from the shelf by the phone. "Let's call another tow truck company."

They headed back to the game room.

———

IN THE LIVING ROOM, Claudio made Angelo a drink.

"Nice place you got here," Angelo surveyed the room.

"It's not bad. Nicer than my apartment."

"You still got that?"

"Oh yeah." Claudio lowered his voice and nodded toward the kitchen. "If she ever kicks me out I got a place to go, huh?"

He handed Angelo his drink.

"You ain't even married yet," Angelo said.

"Just a few more days, baby." Claudio raised his drink.

"You gonna have to keep wearing that thing?"

"Yeah, it's is a pain in the ass," Claudio frowned. "I look like a goddamn invalid. Doc said I gotta keep it on for at least a week."

"Maybe you can take it off when you're saying your I do's and promising to honor and obey." Angelo sat down with his drink.

"Yeah, we'll see, my necks killing me even with this thing." Claudio lowered his voice again. "Now, gimme a second to get the combo. I'll be right back."

Angelo smiled.

———

IN THE UPSTAIRS BEDROOM, Claudio sat on the edge of the bed and dialed the casino office.

"This is Claudio. I need to talk to Joey Messina. Can you page him? I'll hold on."

Claudio picked up the Penthouse Forum magazine that he had left sitting on the nightstand next to the phone. He held it up to look at the cover, "The Wild Wonderful Age of Aquarius" and "Sex for the Hell of it."

"Claudio?" It was Joey.

He threw the magazine down. "Listen. How's it going over there? Did you move the stuff yet?"

"Almost done Boss, I'm bustin' my ass."

"What about blocking that other vault door?"

"Can't do that 'till tomorrow."

"*Shit,*" Claudio said. "I got The Nut here at the house and he wants to see the shit now."

There was silence on the other end of the line.

"Well?" Claudio said.

"Boss, I got most of it moved, and it looks good. Maybe I can block off the other door with something else. I'll figure it out. What time you think you're getting here?"

"Shit I don't know, maybe half hour?"

"Make it an hour," Joey said. "Stall him, get dinner or something. I'll have everything ready by then."

"Thanks." Claudio hung up the phone and stared at the wall. "Damn-it."

He stood from the bed.

"*Ahhh shit!*" A sharp pain shot through his neck again. "*Goddamn it!*"

———

ANGELO LOOKED UP from his chair. "Got it?"

"Yeah," Claudio said. "But let's get something to eat first. I'm starving."

Angelo leered at him.

"I got the perfect place," Claudio said. "Carmine's—it's on the way, it'll be quick. You gotta eat too, right? Let's go."

Claudio made a move toward the door.

Angelo stood up and grabbed his arm, "We can eat afterward. I ain't got that much of an appetite right now. After I see the shit, then I'll feel like eating. Now, let's get to the casino."

Claudio saw that Angelo wasn't in a negotiating mood.

"Sure," he said. "No problem. Shit, wait 'till you see this fucking thing, man-o-man."

Angelo smirked, "Let's go."

CHAPTER 34

"So," Angelo said. "How big is it?"

Claudio moved his head slightly in Angelo's direction until he felt pain. "It's big, baby."

Angelo shot him a look. "How big? Did you count it?"

Claudio shifted in his seat and drove as slowly as he could without making it too obvious.

"No, not yet." Claudio tried to be as vague as possible. "But there's lots. You'll see, it'd probably take a day just to count it all."

"What's there? Silver bars, coins?"

"Everything." Claudio slowed and stopped for a light that had just turned yellow.

"Hey, what the fuck are you doing?" Angelo said. "Think you could go any slower?"

"It's my neck. I think it's getting worse, and I don't want it jerking around if I don't have to."

"Fuck your neck," Angelo said. "I wanna see the loot. Your neck will survive. Drive faster."

"Don't worry, the shit ain't goin' nowhere."

Claudio heard Angelo mumble something under his breath and could see him turn away and look out the window. He knew Angelo could flip out at any moment and lose control.

Sweat began to bead on Claudio's forehead. He drove faster, and more erratically, accelerating, then jerking to a stop behind some traffic. His neck hurt, but the casino was just a few blocks away. He hoped Joey was finished with the setup.

"Almost there." he wiped his forehead with the back of his hand.

"Good," Angelo said.

Claudio made a hard left at the next intersection, whipping the car around the turn.

"Shit," Claudio shouted, his head tilted a bit too much. "Ah, Fuck!" He held steady.

"Take it easy! I told you to go faster, but we still wanna get there in one piece."

Claudio pulled the car over, stopped and began massaging his neck under the brace.

"What the fuck are you doing?" Angelo erupted. "Let's go. I can't fucking believe you're stopping!"

Claudio was sweating profusely now. He couldn't even turn to look at Angelo.

"Gimme' a moment, I'm in fucking severe pain here." He clutched the steering wheel with one hand and rubbed his neck with the other.

"Shit, let me drive. I'll fucking get us there."

"Just a second." Claudio clenched his teeth.

"You're sweating like a pig, you know that?"

Claudio pulled out his handkerchief and wiped his face.

Angelo shook his head. "Didn't the doctor give you anything for that?"

Claudio sat up. "Yeah. He did. I got some freakin' valiums."

Claudio dug in his jacket and pulled out a prescription bottle. He held it up, and rattled it at Angelo. "I forgot all about these babies!"

Claudio twisted open the bottle and shook a bunch of

the tiny pink pills into his hand. He popped them all in his mouth.

"Hey go easy on those," Angelo said. "They'll fuck you up, especially if you've had a few drinks."

"I'll be fine," Claudio said. "I only had a few."

He pulled away from the curb, his head tilted now more than it had been before.

"You look ridiculous, you know that?" Angelo said.

Claudio ignored him.

At the casino, Angelo walked at a quick pace, ahead of Claudio. "So, you think millions?"

"Don't know, but it's a lot." Claudio hoped Joey wasn't in the middle of working in the vault.

As they came upon the restrooms, Claudio said, "Give me a sec, I gotta go."

Angelo rolled his eyes then followed Claudio into the men's room. Claudio went into one of the stalls and shut the door.

"Give me a couple of minutes," Claudio said.

"Ahhhh shit. Hurry the fuck up," Angelo said, relieving himself at the urinal. "I ain't got all day!"

"Sorry." Claudio sat there.

He heard The Nut rinse his hands and leave. If he screwed this up, he was as good as dead. Unless of course he wacked The Nut first. He reached under his jacket for his handgun in its shoulder holster. If anything went wrong he could just do it. But that wouldn't work very well when the Chicago guys came around asking questions. It would at least buy him time though, to flee and take what he could with him. But what about the buried treasure? Leave it for another day? He could come back for that later. It was in Mesquite after all, a dot on the map in the middle of nowhere—his Chicago compadres would probably never set foot in Mesquite in a million years.

"Come on, man!" the Nut barked, his voice booming off the bathroom's tiled walls. "I ain't got all fucking day for you to sit there contemplating life! We gotta get on with the show baby! You got me waiting out there like a goddamn moron."

"Alright, I'm done." Claudio stood and flushed the toilet. He struggled to pull his pants up and leaned his head forward in his neck brace to get a better grip. "Sorry," he said. "I got a little problem here with my neck. I'll be right there."

"Hurry the fuck up."

A minute later, Claudio emerged into the smoke-filled casino.

Angelo was sitting near the slot machines.

"About fucking time!" He jumped up and tossed his cigarette in the ashtray.

"Buzz us in," Claudio said to the cashier at the cage.

The buzzer sounded and Angelo shoved the door open. Claudio followed. He began to feel very relaxed now, muted and dizzy. His neck was uncomfortable, but not as painful as it had been.

As they walked down the hall to his office, Joey Messina turned the corner and practically walked right into Angelo.

"S'cuse me, sir," Joey said.

"Take it easy," Angelo said.

"Sorry, man." Joey stepped back. "How you doin', Angelo?"

Angelo ignored him.

"Boss!" he said. "What's happenin'?"

"Nothin' buddy," Claudio said.

"How's your neck?"

"It's fine."

"I'm glad you're here," Joey said. "Got a minute?"

"Sure . . ."

Angelo held his hand up to Joey, "It'll have to wait. He don't got a minute."

Joey looked at Claudio.

"Yeah," Claudio slurred. "We're in a rush."

"Sure," Joey said. "No problem. You don't look too good Boss."

"Where's the vault?" Angelo said.

"Right there, down the elevator," Joey said.

Angelo turned and led the way. Claudio followed, then stopped and turned back to Joey. "Why don't you come with us?"

"Sure," Joey said.

"It's OK," Claudio said. "He's already seen it."

Angelo glanced at Joey but didn't argue. He hit the button for the elevator.

"Angelo hasn't seen it yet," Claudio said.

Joey nodded. "It's pretty fucking impressive, I tell you that."

Angelo lifted his chin and adjusted his tie. "Can't fucking wait, Mr. Crocetti's going to be very happy."

The elevator door opened and the men stepped in. Its cables creaked as it began to drop.

"So," Angelo said. "The rumors are true then? Jack had his own little Fort Knox here?"

"You could say that," Joey said.

Claudio felt himself fading. He stared blankly at Angelo.

The elevator door opened and the men stepped toward the vault door.

Claudio took the paper from his suite jacket pocket, unfolded it and held it at arm's length. He spun the combination dial right, then left, then right, left and right again. He pulled on the handle and it clicked. "There we go," he said.

Joey pulled the heavy door open. A musty smell emanated from the dark vault. Claudio flipped the light switch.

"Alright!" Angelo pushed his way past Claudio, and smacked his hands together. "This is it." He glanced around.

"Yup," Claudio said and swiveled his body carefully around on his heel, surveying the room, looking at the work Joey had done. He felt a bit wobbly. "What'd you think?"

There were piles of silver bars on pallets and piles of coin bags on more pallets, all about waist-high and arranged toward the middle of the room. By the narrow paths between the pallets stood the chip carts. A few racks of chips in their Plexiglas cases sat on shelves against the wall.

"Cool, huh?" Joey said.

Angelo didn't say anything but continued to look around, walking slowly through the aisles, inspecting.

Claudio checked the wall where the entrance to the second, interior vault was. There were now curtains along that wall, covering its entrance. But the curtains were held up haphazardly on what looked like lamp posts. Shit. Not a great solution, Claudio thought.

"Well?" He patted Angelo's back. "Whaddya think?"

"There must be at least a ton of silver here, probably worth millions," Joey interjected.

"Not bad," Angelo said. "That's what I think. But I thought there might be more. This is all of it, right?" Angelo scrutinized Claudio.

"Oh, yeah," Claudio said confidently. "This is it, unless he's got more buried in his backyard."

Claudio suddenly felt the room begin to spin and dip, down to the left. His knees weakened and the air, where was the air? He glanced helplessly at Joey.

"You don't look too good, Boss," Joey said.

"I gotta sit down."

Joey grabbed an empty cart. "Lean on this," he said and positioned it against one of the pallets.

Claudio leaned back and braced himself against the cart.

"Take it easy, Boss," Joey said. "You look a little pale."

Angelo stepped closer to Claudio. "What about the house?" he said, seemingly uninterested in Claudio's plight. "You checked there? He could have buried some more treasure in his backyard, right?"

"We checked," Joey said. "Didn't find nothin'."

Angelo turned toward Joey. "Nothin' nowhere?"

"I checked the house personally," Claudio said weakly. "And there was nothing there. Frances would have told me if Jack had anything stashed there. She said he used to actually keep it all in the house. Imagine that! But then it got outta hand and she forced him to get it out. That's when he took it all to the casino here."

"It's some load, huh?" Joey said.

"Yeah," Angelo said. "It is. But the rumors made it

sound like it was really huge."

"Just that," Claudio said. "Rumors. This is what it is. All right here. Not bad, huh?"

"Yeah." Angelo glanced around the room. "I guess so."

Claudio raised his hand. "Give me a second." He lowered his head and tried to catch his breath to keep the room from spinning.

"Sure, Boss."

Claudio suddenly realized the longer he sat there and the longer Angelo stayed in the vault, the more chance he would notice the curtain and wonder what was behind it. Claudio took a deep breath.

"Help me up," he said to Joey. "I can't breathe in here."

Joey grabbed Claudio's forearm and they staggered to the door.

"Take it easy Boss, take your time," Joey said.

"You don't look good," Angelo said to Claudio. "It's those valiums you took. I told you they would fuck you up."

"Shit," Claudio said. "I gotta sit down, everything's spinning. Help me get up to my office."

Joey closed the vault door and helped Claudio back to the elevator. It spun as it creaked and climbed, as if it were tumbling off a cliff. Claudio held on as best as he could. He barely made it back to the refuge of his office and Jack's plush leather chair. Joey guided him carefully as he sat, falling back into it.

Claudio gazed blankly at the ceiling and closed his eyes. He felt beads of sweat roll down his forehead, across his cheeks and inside his neck brace.

"You're pale and sweating like a pig again," Angelo said. "Like you saw a ghost."

"Here, Boss, have some ice water," Joey said.

"Sure," Claudio said. "I don't know what the fuck is going on. Everything's spinning."

Angelo stood impatiently by the desk picking his teeth with a toothpick. Claudio sipped the water Joey had given him.

"Shit man," Joey said. "Should I call an ambulance or something."

"No, I'm good," Claudio said. "Just gotta eat something."

"It's all those fucking valiums you took," Angelo said.

"Want me to get you a cheeseburger?" Joey asked.

"Sure." Claudio wiped the sweat from his face.

Angelo leaned over the desk. "Listen," he said. "Nothin' better happen to that shit."

"Yeah, don't worry about it." Claudio looked up at Angelo with half opened eyes. "Nothin's happened to it yet."

"Good," Angelo said, and without another word he turned and stomped away.

Claudio watched his shadow recede out the door.

"Hey," Joey said. "What the hell's his problem?"

Claudio took a deep breath and closed his eyes, the room still spun endlessly dipping and dipping.

"His problem," Claudio muttered. "Is our problem."

CHAPTER 35

In the hospital's elevator, Nick held a brown paper bag that contained a toothbrush and toothpaste and a book of short stories he had read last semester at school, *Ficciones* by Jorge Luis Borges. He wanted to reread one of the stories, *The South*. It was an intriguing story of knife fights, death and destiny.

He made his way through the maze-like hallways to Rosalie's room. The hospital was eerily quiet and empty. He stepped into the dimly lit room and saw Rosalie sleeping on her side, her knees bent up, as if in a fetal position. Light came into the room from the hallway and from the parking lot.

Nick placed his bag next on the floor and went to the side of the bed. He leaned over the tubes and wires and slid his hand over hers. He gazed at her face as she peacefully slept. Even though she had been here for days, she still looked so pretty. How was that so? He pushed a strand of hair away from her eye and kissed her forehead.

He took a deep breath and surveyed the dark room. Lights blinked and equipment ticked, hummed and periodically beeped as if alive. He pushed the large brown, naughide-covered recliner chair next to the bed and sat down to test it. He pulled the handle and the footrest came up and it reclined back. Good enough.

After getting sheets and an extra blanket at the nurse's station, he carefully made his recliner bed. He brushed his teeth at the small sink in the room. Before settling into the chair for the night, he kissed Rosalie on the forehead again. He got in the chair, fixed his pillow and pulled the blanket over himself. Then he closed his eyes.

The equipment beeped and buzzed eerily. It was a cold and lonely place to be. He reached up to the bed and felt for Rosalie's hand. When he found it, he grabbed hold of it and smiled. It wasn't long before he drifted off to sleep.

Sometime in the middle of the night, a light came on. The nurse had come to check on Rosalie. Nick watched her shadowy figure as she took Rosalie's blood pressure and made some notes on her clipboard.

He pulled the chair to an upright position.

"How is she?" he asked.

"Oh," the nurse said, in a heavy Haitian accent. "She's fine. This girl is doing very well now. She's lucky to be alive, you know."

"Really?"

"Sure," she continued. "She could have easily wound up at the morgue instead of ICU. You know how you kids are these days, taking all kinds of drugs."

She waved a finger at Nick.

"Then, all of a sudden, OD and dead! What a shame! But she's been blessed, you know? She's one of the lucky ones."

"Huh," Nick said. "Any idea of what she took?"

The nurse flipped through her chart.

"Hmmm," she said. "Looks like sleeping pills."

She raised her reading glasses and looked at Nick.

"Is she your girlfriend?"

Nick hesitated. "My fiancé," he said, figuring it was better to say that then take a chance that he might get kicked out of the hospital.

"Ohhh," the nurse smiled. "Well, you better take care of her."

The nurse glanced at Rosalie. "Your fiancé looks like she's waking up."

Nick unraveled himself from the blanket.

The nurse leaned over Rosalie, "How you feeling, honey?"

Rosalie looked at her but didn't answer. Then her eyes turned to Nick and she smiled.

"Rosalie."

"Nick," she whispered.

"How are you feeling?" the nurse asked again.

"Thirsty," she replied.

"Take it easy, honey." The nurse grabbed the plastic water pitcher and poured some water in a cup, then held it to her lips. Rosalie drank all of it.

"What day is it?" Rosalie said.

"Thursday," Nick said. "Early Thursday morning, it's still the middle of the night."

At the foot of the bed the nurse checked her clipboard notes, then gently squeezed Rosalie's toes through the blanket. "You're doing very well, dear. You're a very lucky girl, do you know that?"

Rosalie smiled again.

"Well," the nurse said. "I better leave you two lovebirds alone. If you need anything just come get me."

After she left the room, Nick turned to Rosalie. "How are you feeling?"

"Tired," she whispered. "How long have I been here?"

"For the last three or four days, I think," Nick said. "We didn't know if you were going to make it."

"What time is it?"

Nick looked at his watch.

"Two thirty in the morning. I figured I'd stay here with you tonight."

Rosalie held her eyes on him, "Thanks."

Nick smiled.

"But where's my dad? What if he finds you here?"

"I talked to your mom," Nick said. "Everything's fine."

"Are you sure?"

"Yeah, he don't hate me anymore."

Rosalie smiled and Nick leaned in closer, gazing into her beautiful green eyes. He wanted to tell her how much he missed her, and even that he loved her, but he didn't know how to say it.

"You went to Hawaii?" Rosalie said.

"No." Nick shook his head. "I never left. I stayed at the airport hotel, just laying low."

"Oh," Rosalie said. "I wanted to go with you."

"You did?"

"Yes, but by the time I read your letter and decided, it was too late. I couldn't get to the airport on time. I didn't know what to do."

"And I couldn't go without you," Nick said.

"Really?" she said and squeezed his hand.

"Yes," Nick said. "That's why. I just couldn't leave without you!"

He leaned in, his lips practically touching hers. She smiled and pulled him in, her cheek pressing against his.

"I thought they got you," she whispered into his ear. "And I couldn't live without you either."

A tear rolled down her cheek and she pulled him closer.

"I don't want you to ever leave me again," she said.

"I won't, but . . ." He pulled away, just a bit, then wiped the tear gently from her cheek. "But what about your friend at school? What's was his name—Greg? Isn't he your fiancé?"

She rolled her eyes and shook her head. "I broke it off. He was an asshole—a womanizer. He had some girl on the side. That's why he didn't come with me. I don't know what I was thinking."

"Wait a minute. So you don't have a fiancé? Or even a boyfriend?"

Could it be true? Nick's heart leapt in his chest.

"I have you." Rosalie put her hands around his neck and pulled him close, then kissed him gently on the lips.

"And I love you," she whispered.

"I love you, too." Nick heard himself say, as if in a dream.

CHAPTER 36

Nick sat next to Anne Marie, who had just returned from helping their mom make her final preparations in the ready room at the back of the church. They sat in the reserved first row of the futuristic-looking Guardian Angel Cathedral. Nick wore a white tuxedo with bell bottom slacks and white patent leather shoes, but instead of a bowtie, he wore the bolo that his dad had given him. Its pendant lay over his chest, contrasting against his all white outfit.

Nick gazed up at the beams of the A-framed cathedral which rose high to the sky like a rocket blasting off and heading to an alien Flash Gordon planet. Floating above the altar, hanging in mid-air, hung a large modern gold crucifix with a flesh-colored painted Jesus. Rising on the huge triangular wall behind the altar, a colorful, surrealistic mural of bodies floating and swimming toward an ethereal Jesus whose outstretched arms reached over head, as if launching himself off the planet earth like superman. The mind-blowing design of the cathedral allowed Nick to forget, for a moment, the distasteful but unstoppable ceremony that was about to take place.

"I can't believe Mom is marrying him," Anne Marie whispered.

"I know, I tried to talk to her." Nick shook his head and kept his voice low. "She won't listen, though. That's how it is. Inexplicable. Damn inexplicable, man."

"No shit," she said.

"This place is pretty far out, huh?" he said.

"It is groovy. Even kinda psychedelic."

Anne Marie already looked a little sloshed to Nick, even though it was only 10 AM.

Lawrence sat in the row behind them, next to Bill and his wife Eleanor, and Alex and his wife Tina. The mayor, Duane Thompson, was there too, sitting in the third row. Aunt Stephanie and Uncle Bill were there too, dressed in their finest.

Nick looked around to see who else was there. Across the aisle in the front row sat Claudio's daughter, Marla, with Angelo "The Nut" next to her, then Joey Messina and his wife Mary Ellen, and then Rosalie on the end. Tony Scalfaro, his arm still in a sling, with his wife Lorraine sat in the next row. And next to Tony's wife was Roman Lorenzo's wife, Meg, by herself. Roman was conspicuously absent.

Nick heard The Nut ask loudly "Where's Roman?"

"Don't know." Joey turned to Tony and asked, "Is Roman here?"

Tony shrugged his shoulders.

"Where is he?" Joey asked.

Tony turned to Roman's wife Meg and said, "Where's Roman?"

She shook her head, "He's hung up in bed. Sick with the flu or food poisoning, or something. He was up all night. Digestive problems. He couldn't even get out of bed this morning."

Angelo turned to Joey and said, "At least he doesn't have to suffer through this."

Mario and Barbara were there too, a few rows back, next to the Mayor. The church was crowded with other extended family members—cousins, aunts, uncles, nieces and nephews, and also with other friends, businessmen and politicians. A few policemen, who were friends with Jack and Frances, sat in the back row.

When he had arrived at the church Nick had noticed two officers in a police squad car, keeping an eye on the event from across the street. And a few cars away from them, he had seen a black Ford LTD with two FBI agents inside—the same ones he could have sworn he had seen outside the Red Lion disco before. One of those FBI guys had a camera with a telephoto lens and was taking pictures of the guests as they arrived.

"This sucks," Nick said to Anne Marie.

"Oh, lighten up," she said. "Let Mom have her happiness."

"I know, but Claudio?"

"It's water under the bridge now," she said, then added with some drama, "Troubled water under the bridge."

"Ha, very good," Nick said and shook his head.

There was suddenly a noticeable increase of murmur and chatter—things seemed about to get underway. Nick turned to look toward the back of the church just as the booming sound of the pipe organ pierced the air, filling the place with magnificent, bone-penetrating, melodious sound.

"Holy shit," Nick said.

"That's far out," Anne Marie agreed.

At the back of the church a lone altar boy appeared holding a large candle. He proceeded with measured steps down the aisle. At the altar, he stepped up to the platform and carefully lit each candle that stood on either side. The priest came out next with another altar boy following close behind. They proceeded slowly down the aisle and around the kneeler stand that stood in front of the altar platform. They stepped up to the altar and the priest turned and waited. The altar boys took their positions on each side. Large flower bouquets in crystal vases stood atop small pillars on each side of the altar.

The pipe organ intensified and Claudio appeared at the back of the church. He stood a moment and gave a nervous glance around, towering in his black tuxedo, his hair slickened and his bow tie awkwardly attached under his neck brace. He proceeded to walk, step . . . pause . . . step . . . pause . . . step . . . pause . . . down the aisle. About half-way through though, he seemed to give up the formality and just walked casually, but slowly, to the altar. He stopped in front of the kneeler stand below the priest, paused, and turned stiffly in his neck brace, robot-like, to look back up the aisle and wait for his bride.

When Frances stepped through the doors, the priest motioned with his hands for the audience to stand up. The tempo of the pipe organ accelerated. She stood wearing a satin, golden dress with white lace around the neckline and shoulders puffed, and sleeves with ruffles at the cuffs. It was a stovepipe style dress that fit snugly around her hips and accentuated her figure. A short train ran a few feet behind. She held a bouquet of white lilies and smiled, then started to walk down the aisle. She walked briskly, as if in a bit of a rush. When she came up to Claudio she stopped and took his hand, then lowered her head and turned her eyes up to the priest.

Curiously, there wasn't a bridal party as Frances had nixed the idea. It would have been awkward to have Claudio's mobster friends with Frances' and Jack's family and friends, and especially the friends that Claudio had fired.

The organ stopped and Claudio and Frances took two steps up to the altar. They stood before the kneeler in front of the priest. He smiled, surveyed the guests, and told everyone to sit — then he motioned to Claudio and Frances to kneel.

"In the name of the Father, Son and Holy Ghost," he made the sign of the cross.

"My brothers and sisters, thank you for gathering and joining us here today to witness the forging of the holy sacrament and coveted bonds of marriage between Claudio and Frances, who is a widower having lost her beloved husband not too long ago."

There was a slight gasp, and rustling, from the audience. Nick shifted uncomfortably in his seat and grabbed his bolo tie pendant.

The priest read from the Book of Genesis, speaking of the sanctity of marriage, commitment, the house of the lord, and God's love. Nick thought about his dad and how his life was cut short, how Claudio was stealing his mom, and stealing the casino, and stealing his dad's legacy. And yet he was letting it all transpire, right in front of him, and right now — Claudio and his mom, kneeling at the altar of the Lord. Nick took a deep breath and tightened his jaw.

He rubbed the bolo and glanced at Anne Marie, who had a tissue and was wiping tears from her eyes. He turned to look across the aisle for Rosalie but instead caught her dad Joey Messina's glance, which quickly turned to angry glare.

What?! Nick grimaced and surprisingly, Joey turned away.

The priest motioned to the bride and groom stand. Claudio huffed and pushed himself up from one knee. Together they stood again before the priest.

"Claudio DeVito, do you take . . ."

Things were moving too quickly, how did they get to

this? Nick gazed up at the freaky mural above—the flying superman Christ. This marriage would be short lived if he had anything to do with it. He shifted in his seat. The superman Christ rocketed up, into the sky, and off the earthly morass. Just jump away, take off, a super hero, a savior! *I can be a savior too, but do I have the guts?* He smiled and laughed to himself.

"I do," were the words he heard himself say. And then from his mom, "*I do*". And that was it, the ceremony was over!

"I now pronounce you man and wife," the priest said.

Claudio leaned forward in his neck brace and, unable to tilt his head, awkwardly kissed Frances.

The organ music thundered up like a storm. With a smattering of applause Claudio and Frances turned and smiled at the guests. They waited a moment, then began their walk, back up the aisle, toward the exit—a sense of relief upon each of their faces.

Frances beamed as she turned to Nick and Anne Marie. Nick couldn't help but smile. Anne Marie's tears flowed happily down her face. Nick watched them gleefully walked back up the aisle.

Guests on each side smiled and politely clapped as they passed, a few with camera's clicking and flashing. Some guests patted their teary eyes with handkerchiefs and tissues. A man began shouting something—maybe congratulating them with just a bit too much exuberance? Nick got up on his toes to get a better view up the aisle.

"You bastard!" he clearly heard.

A thin, older man stepped into the aisle in front of the newly married couple. He pointed at Claudio.

"I want my money back!" he shouted. "You lying cheating bastard! Scum!"

The two police officers that had been in the back row immediately jumped up and grabbed the guy.

"Officer!" the man yelled. "I want this man arrested!"

Claudio pulled Frances toward the exit. Angelo "The Nut" stepped over just as Nick came up from behind. The two police officers quickly put handcuffs on the guy and held him.

The man shouted, "He took my money! He switched the goddamn chips and now my chips are worthless! He's the one that needs to be arrested!"

"Take it easy, pal," one of the police officers said.

Angelo approached the guy and poked the man's chest hard with his finger.

"Who the fuck are you?" Angelo said.

"Who am I?! I'm Sy Zeldin, that's who. Let me go!"

Angelo poked him again with three stiff fingers in the gut, and twisted them in, hard.

"Ehhh!" the man yelped.

"Don't come around here disrupting the peace, in this church," Angelo seethed.

One of the policemen placed his hand on Angelo's shoulder. "We got this under control," he said. Then to Sy, "You need to come with us."

"He's a fucking slime-ball. Stealing my money! How the fuck do you run a casino like that?"

The two police officers practically had to drag Mr. Zeldin from the church.

"Watch it buddy!" Angelo shouted after them.

"Bastard!" Sy hollered in reply.

Nick hurried to follow them out.

Claudio and Frances were in the sunshine, standing for a picture in front of the long white limousine. The words

"Just Married" were scribbled on the back window in large whitewash letters. As soon as the photo was done they climbed into the limo, and in a moment, it pulled away, cans dangling and clanging from the back bumper, and the driver excitedly honking the horn.

Nick stood there in the middle of the church plaza watching his mom drive off with Claudio. It was frustrating that he couldn't do anything about it right there and then. It was depressing and he felt like a sap—shitty, useless and wimpy. How could he let this happen? But he'd get him, he knew that in time, he'd get him.

Someone suddenly wrapped their hand around his arm. He turned. It was Rosalie.

"Hey," she smiled.

"Hi," he glanced at the crowd exiting the church. "Where's your dad?"

"He left, in the other limo."

"Good." Nick smiled.

"Yeah, I told him not to bother us anymore."

"Really?"

Rosalie looked up at Nick.

"Yup, really," she said. "Told him to mind his own damn business. I reminded him that you're the one that woke me up, and I reminded him that I'm an adult and can run my own damn life!"

"That's exactly how I feel," Nick said, and held her hand.

She smiled and squeezed tightly.

"Hey, isn't this place crazy?" he glanced up to the top of the steeple, which rose next to the cathedral, looking like the futuristic spire from the 1939 NY World's Fair.

"Isn't it far out? Like a space port? I mean look at it, it's like everything is taking off!"

Rosalie laughed, "Yeah. It's cool, I like it."

"Hey, let's go," Nick said. "Ride over to the reception with me in my new car."

"You have a new car?"

"Yeah."

Just then Mario, in a tan tux and Barbara, in a flowery blue dress, stepped up.

"Wow," Mario said. "What a commotion!"

"Yeah," Nick said. "I'm surprised he didn't shoot Claudio."

"Yeah," Mario said. "Hey, I'm gonna catch a ride over to the reception with Barbara."

"Yeah, I'm his chauffer," Barbara said.

"No problem," Nick said. "I'm taking Rosalie anyway."

"Ohhh!" Mario turned to Rosalie. "You get to ride in his screaming new Porsche."

"Porsche?" Rosalie looked at Nick.

"Yup." Nick smiled. "Let's go."

He put his arm around Rosalie's waist and they strode into the parking lot.

"Wait 'till you see it, just got it yesterday," Nick said. "Mario's mad because he only rode in it once so far."

"Wow," she said as they approached the car. "Very cool."

It was a shiny, gleaming, red 911. Nick unlocked the passenger door and held her hand as she sat down into the brown leather bucket seat.

"It's so low," she said. "I feel like I'm sitting on the

ground."

"Lower center of gravity," Nick said. "Makes it handle better. You'll see."

Nick cranked the engine and it purred to life. He put his aviator sunglasses on and pulled away. Once on the street, he hit it, straight up the block, accelerating through first, then second and into third.

"Whhhhooooo," Rosalie said. "Take it easy, I'm still recovering you know."

"You're fine." Nick grinned at her. "And you look great."

Rosalie smiled, the wind whipping up her hair.

CHAPTER 37

The reception was held at the Sands Copa room. Frances hadn't wanted the reception at the Three-C's and although the Copa was a little large, it had a certain mystique and aura about it. All the greats had performed there—Sammy Davis, Jr. and the rest of the Rat Pack, Judy Garland, and even Lena Horne. Claudio wanted the reception there too because it was classy and big. It had a large stage for the band and the entertainment, and it had a nice dance floor, right down in front of the stage.

Claudio and Frances sat at the center table, directly in front of the dance floor and facing the stage. It was a long table with a white cotton table cloth, sparkling place settings, and centerpieces of white and pink roses with the perfectly folded and formed pastel colored party angles rising from the flowers. Claudio sat stiffly in his neck brace with Angelo to his right, then Marla, and Joey and his wife Mary Ellen. An empty seat sat next to them, just in case Roman had a miraculous recovery and could somehow make it. But his wife Meg was there anyway, trying to make the best of it, sitting next to the empty chair. Albert's widow Jackie sat next to Meg, fidgeting with her napkin. Then Tony's wife Lorraine, and Tony, still wearing his arm in a sling. On Frances' side of the table sat Lawrence and Anne Marie, then Bill and his wife Eleanor. Next to them were two empty seats for Nick and Rosalie, who hadn't shown up yet, and next to them sat Mario and Barbara.

On the stage, the band played a decent rendition of Elvis' "All Shook Up." A few guests did something like the twist on the dance floor. Glasses and silverware clinked. Guests chatted and the wine and drink flowed. Mountains of hors d'oeuvres were presented by the many attentive and perky cocktail waitresses. They wore white bustiers that pushed up their breast, jiggling them as they walked. Pink feathers sprang from the small of their backs, just above their butts. Their hair was pulled up in a tight bun, with a tastefully arranged headdress of more feathers amid white hibiscus flowers. They smiled and shook their feathery tooshes as they cheerfully carried trays of hors d'oeuvres and drinks to the guests.

Claudio stared at one of them as she bounced by. He whispered to Angelo, "Just the way I like it."

"Oh, yeah," Angelo smiled.

The stage and ballroom lights cut dramatically through the haze of cigarette and cigar smoke. Every few minutes the laughter and lively conversation stopped, interrupted by the raucous tapping of silverware on glasses, and the chant *"kiss, kiss, kiss!"* Everyone waited impatiently, their attention fixed on Claudio and Frances.

"That's enough of that!" Claudio stood and shouted. "I won't have anything left for tonight!"

"Oh, come on," Angelo shouted back. "You're still a young man!"

More laughter rose throughout the ballroom and the clinking intensified, until Claudio sat down, awkwardly tilted his head as best he could, and he and Frances finally kissed.

It was already late afternoon and the main course hadn't yet been served. Most of the guests felt good as the wine and liquor had been flowing for quite some time now.

"Where do you think they are?" Barbara asked Mario.

"Who knows," Mario said. "Maybe they got sidetracked or something."

"Maybe they're getting it . . ." Barbara leaned over closer to Mario and winked, "on."

Mario laughed and started rocking his head and singing, "Get it on! Get it on! Get it on!" Then he slowed down and said, "Ahhh, but they better get here soon, before the whole thing is over."

"Yeah." Barbara took another sip of wine.

Claudio and Angelo talked, and Frances bit into a piece of prosciutto wrapped mozzarella. "Delicious," she said.

Angelo cut short his chatter with Claudio and looked across the banquet hall toward the entrance. Nick and Rosalie had just arrived and were surveying the room. Nick held Rosalie's hand.

Joey Messina stood up and raised his arms.

"About time!" he shouted and stepped out from the table.

———

NICK COULD SEE they were all annoyed with him.

"Sorry we're late," he said to Frances.

She smiled and wiped her mouth, "It's OK. You made it, right?"

"Right." Nick turned to Joey.

"Relax." Joey smiled and patted him on the back.

Nick tensed up. Could her dad actually be copasetic about him and Rosalie? Joey grabbed Rosalie's head, pulled her close and kissed her forehead.

"My baby," he said. "You take it easy, now. You're still recovering, you know."

"I'm fine, Dad."

He looked at Nick, "You take good care of her, understand?"

"Absolutely, sir." Nick nodded. He couldn't believe he used the word *sir,* it had just popped out of his mouth.

"Now, drink up son," Joey said and walked back to his seat.

"Hey," Mario said. "What took you so long?"

Nick grinned. He held Rosalie's chair as she took her seat.

"Took a detour on the way from the church?" Barbara said.

Nick laughed, "Maybe."

Mario gave him a sideways glance and smirked.

"What?" Nick said. "I had to give her a ride in my new car."

"Ohhhh . . ." Mario said knowingly.

"Nothing happened," Nick said. "Now, let's party, where's my drink?"

For the next hour Nick drank red wine, danced with Rosalie, carried on with Mario and Barbara and had a great time cutting loose and forgetting his troubles. With all the recent pressure and chaos, he just wanted to have fun, and it seemed to him that everyone else did, too. Rosalie drank a few glasses of white wine and seemed to be having great time too. She laughed and smiled. "I like your little red Porsche," she said, touching her finger on his lips.

Maybe things weren't so bad after all.

After dinner was served, Claudio and Frances cut the

first slice of the five-level wedding cake.

The drinks kept coming and Rosalie had another glass. Nick couldn't take his eyes off her. She was having such a good time; his head was in a whirl. She grabbed his hand under the table.

"I'm so glad you're OK," she said. "Maybe we could still go to Hawaii after all?"

She leaned over and kissed him. Her lips were soft and sweet from the wine. It didn't matter who was there and who saw them. He wanted to ask her to stay over for the night. His mom and Claudio would be gone, atop the Stardust in their honeymoon suite.

"That'd be great," Nick said. "Hawaii."

Rosalie smiled and took another sip of wine.

"When are we gonna get a good man?" Anne Marie said to Marla, her speech slurred. "Where are all the good guys? Look at these two happy couples." She waved her arms toward Nick and Rosalie and Mario and Barbara.

"Wait a minute," Mario said. "We're not a couple anymore."

"Wwwelll . . ." Anne Marie slurred. "You could've fooooled me."

"When's the big wedding?" Marla said loudly leaning across the table, almost knocking her glass onto Rosalie's blouse.

Nick reached over and grabbed the glass, but not before half of it spilt on the white cotton table cloth. "Take it easy Marla!"

"I am taking it easy," Marla said. "I *always* take it easy."

"You're an easy girl!" Anne Marie laughed.

"I ain't *that* easy." Marla waved her finger and leaned away from Rosalie. Then she stopped and stared at Rosalie's earrings.

"Hey! Those are nice earrings."

Nick glanced at the earrings. Rosalie wore a series of three silver loops from large to small, with a round piece of turquoise hanging at the bottom.

"Thanks," Rosalie said.

"Silver?" Anne Marie said.

"Yeah."

"Very nice," Anne Marie said. "You know my daddy had lots of silver."

"Yeah," Nick said. "Now, who wants another drink?" He glanced around and stood up. "Waitress!" he shouted, spinning around and snapping his fingers. "Service!" He sat back down and grabbed Rosalie's waist.

She leaned to him and said, "Didn't your daddy, collect silver?" She touched her finger to his lips again, then trailed it down his chin and neck, all the way to his Carson City Silver Dollar bolo pendant. She passed her fingers over it.

Nick took her hand and kissed it, then smiled and whispered, "He did."

———

CLAUDIO LEANED OVER, closer to Angelo.

"Now's a good time," he said quietly in Angelo's ear.

Angelo turned toward Joey. When he caught Joey's eye, Angelo nodded towards the waitress who was taking Nick's order. Joey casually stood up and walked to the bar. A minute later, he returned to the table.

"Congratulations, man." Joey leaned in between Angelo and Claudio, a hand on each of their backs. "This is indeed a very special evening."

"Salud!" Angelo said, and raised his glass, beaming a wide smile.

The band started an upbeat number and a dozen scantily clad girls, with large feather headdresses and colorful snake-like feather boas, danced onto the stage. They kicked their heels high in the air, smiled and shouted their song.

———

NICK GLARED at the stage. The sexy playboy-club-like waitresses were one thing, but now a burlesque show? At his mom's wedding? It was just too much. And Claudio was even whistling and hooting too.

The cocktail waitress returned, wiggling over to Nick with a glass of red wine. She pushed her butt out as she leaned over and daintily set the glass down in front of him, pausing a half second while her voluptuous breasts pushed forward. She winked at Nick and stood up to leave. Rosalie had just finished the last sip of her wine and raised the empty glass to the waitress.

"Another," she said.

"Are you sure?" Nick asked.

"Go ahead," Marla said. "Let her have another, it's a party! She's fine."

"Drink up!" the waitress said. "Anyone else want another?"

"Sure," Mario said.

The waitress nodded, smiled and left for the bar. Nick reached for his glass. Rosalie stood up, but immediately stumbled backward into her chair. Nick put the glass down, grabbed her and pulled her close.

"Where you going?" he said.

"I want to get out of here."

"Where?"

She ran her hand through his hair and smiled. "Let's dance! I wanna dance!"

"Right on!" Nick said.

He helped her up, and followed her to the dance floor.

Mario and Barbara jumped up and they followed Nick's lead to the dance floor, leaving Marla and Anne Marie behind with Claudio and the old folks.

"Go ahead," Marla said. "Just leave us all, just like that. Go dance, who do I get to dance with?" She looked at Anne Marie.

"Yeah," Anne Marie said. "Let's find somebody to dance with."

Marla grabbed her half-empty glass of red wine and drank it down in one gulp, then slammed the empty glass on the table.

"First another drink," she said and glanced around. "Now where's that pretty little waitress bitch?"

"This sucks," Anne Marie said.

Marla stood up and looked for the waitress, then slumped back down again in her chair. "Shit," she said.

"There's Nick's," Anne Marie said pointing to his full glass of wine, which sat right next to his plate. "He hasn't even taken a sip."

"Ooohhhh . . . yeeeaaahhhh . . ." Marla reached over and grabbed Nick's drink.

She quickly guzzled half of it down.

"Whoa," Anne Marie said. "Take it easy! Give me a sip."

Marla leaned back from Anne Marie, holding the glass away from her.

"No way," Marla said. "You can just order one yourself from that little miss hoe. This one's mine."

"Just a sip!" Anne Marie reached for the glass.

Marla quickly took another huge gulp, finishing the whole glass. She smiled in satisfaction at her drinking accomplishment then sat back in her chair and gloated.

"Shit," Anne Marie said.

They sat a moment, watching the guests on the dance floor, the band and the dancing girls, all having a raucously good time.

"What are we, chopped liver?" Anne Marie stood up, shaking her hips and clapping her hands, "I wanna dance!"

She glanced down at Marla, who was just sitting and staring, zombie-like.

The band reached a crescendo as the dancing girls finished their finale. Guests stood in delight to applaud and cheer. Anne Marie clapped enthusiastically too, but the room began tilting. She placed her knee onto her chair and leaned down on it, balancing her weight. She turned to Marla.

"Geeetttt up," she said. "Don't be a drag!"

Marla was pale, frozen in place, her mouth half opened, staring blankly ahead. Her eyes suddenly rolled back in her head, and she fell forward into her plate of cake, and slid down to the floor, dragging the table cloth with her, in a crash of dishes and food. Anne Marie staggered and reached down to Marla as she lay sprawled on the floor, flat on her back, broken glass, wedding cake, flowers, and paper angels strewn over her twitching body. Foam oozed from her shuttering lips.

INSTEAD OF WALKING to the dance floor, Rosalie had led Nick straight out of the ballroom.

"Where we going?" he said.

Rosalie stopped.

"I gotta get outta here," she said, then continued walking. "Let's get some fresh air."

"Sure."

Nick reached his arm around her waist and she did likewise. They bumped their hips playfully as they walked.

Outside the Sands, amid the neon, the flashy cars, the parking attendants, bellhops and crowds of people, all dressed to the nines, Nick stopped and suddenly pulled Rosalie close. They kissed—a long, hot, wet kiss. When the kiss was over, he rested his forehead on hers, and looked straight into her eyes.

"I want you to see it," he whispered.

"What?"

"The silver, my dad's silver."

Rosalie looked confused.

"I want to show it all to you, it'll only take a few minutes. You've never seen anything like it."

"Sure." She shrugged her shoulders. "As long as we don't have to go back in there."

She smiled, and they headed for the Porsche.

CHAPTER 38

Nick drove up the brightly lit and colorful, bustling strip. The fresh evening air brushed cool over his face and the rumble of the Porsche's engine gave him a feeling of power and control.

"So," he said casually to Rosalie. "Wanna stay over tonight?"

"At your house?"

"Yeah."

"Well, sure." She put her hand on his leg and smiled.

"Nobody will be there you know." He tried to maintain his cool. "Except maybe later when Anne Marie gets home. But she'll be so drunk she'll just pass out."

Rosalie turned up the radio. Elvis's "Stuck on You" came on.

"I love Elvis." She shook her shoulders and snapped her fingers. "I don't care what they say. He was the king."

"I can dig it, he's cool," Nick said. "Isn't he playing at the Hilton soon?"

"Uh huh, yeah yeah," Rosalie said. "I'm all shook up. We should go."

"Sure, I can get us tickets."

"Uh huh, uh huh." Rosalie danced in her seat, then she grabbed Nick's arm and pulled closer to him.

Nick shifted into third and the car took off. Rosalie's hair blew wildly in the warm Las Vegas night.

In a moment, they were at the Three-C's. He parked the Porsche in Jack's reserved spot and held Rosalie close as they headed into the casino.

"Wait till you see it," he said. "You have to promise to never tell anyone."

"My lips are sealed." Rosalie mimicked zipping her lips.

After checking his ID and looking his name up on a list, the cashier reluctantly buzzed them into the cage. Nick didn't recognize anyone working there and actually felt like a bit of an intruder.

Nick noticed only a shadow remained of the now missing brass plaque that used to read "Jack Romano - Chairman of The Board" on the door of his dad's office.

"That used to be my dad's office. Now it's the idiot's office."

"Claudio's?" Rosalie said.

"Yeah." Nick pressed the elevator button. "A real bummer."

"Why don't you run the Casino?"

The elevator doors opened and they stepped in.

"I don't know. My mom wants him to do it, 'cause he's supposedly got casino-runnin' experience. But the only thing he really has experience with is being a nincompoop fool."

"And I wish my dad had never gotten mixed up with him," Rosalie said. "I told him he's either gonna wind up dead or in jail behind bars. But he won't listen to me."

"Well, my dad was no angel, but he was smart and fair and knew how to take care of people. People always respected him for that," Nick said. Then in an exaggerated debonair way, said, "What floor, ma'am?"

"Fourteenth floor please, fine dresses."

"Sorry," Nick said. "Only one floor, the *silver* floor."

"*Ohhh . . .*" Rosalie grabbed Nick.

They kissed and before they knew it, the elevator shuttered to a stop and the door opened. Nick pulled her close. The door shut and the elevator headed back upstairs. He reached over and felt for the button again. He hoped he hit the right one, but it didn't matter. Nothing mattered, not the silver, not anything. Her touch was soft and warm, and her lips wet. She paused and peered into his eyes. Everything was spectacularly right. The door opened, then closed and the elevator dropped again.

When the door opened again, Nick stuck his foot out to hold it.

"The combination," he said and fumbled for his wallet, pulling out a small piece of paper.

He was hardly able to think. He held the paper up to Rosalie. "Don't get any ideas. I'm burning this after I show you my dad's treasure."

"Ohhh . . . treasure-schmeasure" she said. "You can just keep all your treasure." She pulled him close again. "I just want you." She linked her hands behind his neck and kissed him again.

He ran his hands across her back and down to her waist. He gazed into her eyes.

"I love you," Rosalie said.

He brushed a strand of hair from her cheek.

"And I love you," he said.

He pressed against her, and pulled her tight. They kissed again.

"Ohhh . . ." she cooed, then pushed away.

"Show me the stupid gold," she said. "Then let's get to

your place."

"Sure." Nick couldn't help but smile.

His fingers shook as he turned the dial, entering the combination. It didn't open. He started again, this time slower, more methodically, turning to one number, then carefully the next. He pressed down on the handle and it clicked open.

———

HE STEPPED into the dark room with Rosalie tagging behind, her hand on his shoulder. There was a stale, metallic smell. He hit the light switch. In the middle of the largely empty room, sat neat stacks of silver bars and coin bags on a half dozen pallets.

"Holy mackerel," Rosalie's eyes widened. "This is crazy, you weren't kidding."

Nick stood in shock with his mouth hung open.

"Your dad collected all this?" she said. "There must be a ton of silver here."

Nick shook his head.

"It's wrong," he said. "It's not right."

"Huh? What do you mean? Look at it all."

"There was more, much more. It's all gone now!"

"More?" Rosalie grabbed his shoulders. "But Nick, look at it all."

Nick shook his head again.

"The vault should be packed," he said. "It should be filled to the brim! I can't believe this. This vault used to be packed."

"What?"

Nick turned pale and began shaking.

"Don't you see? It was freakin' full, so full you could hardly walk in here. And the other vault was packed, too. Shit, let's check that one, oh my God!"

He scrambled to the other wall.

"Why are these curtains here?" he said and yanked them to the side. The whole curtain rod fell off the wall to the floor.

"What the hell?" Nick said. "Looks like somebody just threw this thing up there, it wasn't here before. Shit!"

He quickly entered the combination on the inner vault door and with a heave, yanked it open. It was completely empty except for some steel shelves along one wall and a few empty canvas coin bags laying, deflated, on the dusty floor.

"SHIT!" Nick shouted at the ceiling with clenched fists.

"*SHIT — SHIT — SHIT,*" echoed off the concrete walls.

He turned to Rosalie. She reached to touch his cheek but he stepped aside and staggered back to the front vault.

"FUCK! Claudio, you FUCK! You're a dead man! You stupid fuck! *YOU'RE FUCKING DEAD!*"

He collapsed to his knees and covered his face down in his hands.

"Nick, your white tuxedo!" she said.

Nick looked up at her, "Claudio must have taken it. My dad left us all the silver, and Claudio stole it. He fucking stole it all. That's what he was after! Now there's practically nothing left."

Nick gazed at the mostly empty vault. "But why did he leave this little bit behind?" he said.

Rosalie knelt in front of him and pulled him into her

bosom.

"Take it easy." She rubbed his back. "It's OK."

She kissed the top of his head and ran her fingers through his hair.

"It's gone," he muttered. "I know that fuck took it, him and his goons!"

"It'll be alright," Rosalie said. "We'll get it back. There must be some mistake."

She massaged the back of his head and held him tight against her.

"I'm gonna fucking kill that fuck," he blurted.

"Why don't we just go ask him first? Maybe he transferred it to the bank or something."

Nick looked at her.

"It's possible," she said.

"Are you crazy?" he said.

Rosalie got to her feet and helped to pull Nick up.

"We got no time to waste," he said. "Let's go."

"Where?"

"Back to the reception, to find that fat fuck."

He closed the inner vault door and locked it.

"Can't you just talk to him tomorrow? I don't want to go back there again."

"No way," Nick said. "First that fuck takes over the casino, then he marries my mom, and now he's taken all my dad's silver?"

Rosalie frowned and Nick closed the main vault door.

"Look," he said. "I'm gonna kill that fuck when I see him."

"Nick," she said. "Stay with me. Let's just go to your

place, like we said."

"No, I gotta find him and find out what the fuck he did. This can't wait, we gotta go now."

Nick pressed the elevator button.

"Don't worry," he said. "He can't do anything in front of all those people."

Rosalie folded her arms.

"I am worried," she said. "I don't want anything to happen to you."

"Don't worry," he repeated.

They headed back to his car.

"You don't know what those guys are capable of!" Rosalie pleaded after him.

Nick dismissed her objections with a wave of his arm.

"I'll take care of this," is all he said.

He drove the Porsche like a bat out of hell, whipping around corners and flooring it on the straightaways.

Rosalie held on tight.

————

NICK RIPPED into the parking lot at the Sands. There were flashing lights—an ambulance and police car at the main entrance, a crowd, and some kind of commotion. Probably just some gambler suffering a heart attack—poor guy. Nick grabbed Rosalie's hand and they hurried toward the entrance. More shouting and commotion. A policeman cleared a path. Paramedics rushed a gurney out—the victim, not some guy, but a woman? A young woman on the stretcher?

"Shit . . ." Nick stopped.

One of the paramedics frantically applied CPR to the woman as the other pulled the gurney to the ambulance.

"That's Claudio," Rosalie said.

"Huh? Where?"

"Look, following them."

"What?" Nick said.

"Oh my god," Rosalie said.

"What? Mom and Anne Marie too. What the hell? Who's on the stretcher?"

It was Marla.

Still in his tux and neck brace, Claudio squeezed in between the paramedics, leaned over, and touched Marla's cheek.

"NO!" he shouted

They slid the gurney into the ambulance and Claudio stepped back.

Frances was right behind him, in her wedding dress. Angelo and most everyone else was close behind, pushing and shoving and trying to see what was happening—Joey, Tony, Lawrence, Bill, Mario and Barbara, the wives, the other guests. They were all out in front of the Sands, under its flashing neon, and amid the spinning lights of the ambulance and police car.

"What happened?" Nick said to his mom.

"Nick!" she hugged him. "Thank goodness you're OK!"

The paramedics slammed the doors shut and the ambulance pulled away, its siren wailing.

"Wait!" Claudio shouted.

A policeman grabbed him and wrestled him back.

"She's dead!" Claudio's face contorted in horror. "My

baby girl is dead!"

He reached for Frances, then saw Nick standing there. He froze, his angry eyes locked on Nick. He pushed Frances to the side and lunged for Nick with an overhead cross. Nick ducked and Claudio stumbled into the crowd. Frances screamed, and the crowd turned to look at this new commotion. Claudio stood up and regained his balance.

"You Fuck! You did this," he shouted at Nick. "You knew it, you gave it to her. You poisoned her!"

"What?" Nick stepped back. "What are you talking about?"

Claudio came at him again, "You fucking killed her!"

Rosalie screamed. More shouting. A police officer lunged to grab Claudio.

Frances shouted, "STOP!"

Nick retreated back into the crowd but inadvertently ended up right in Angelo's arms.

"Shit!" Nick tried to wrestle free. "What the hell is he talking about?"

Angelo held him tighter. Claudio pushed the police officer to the ground, and screamed in pain from his neck. He threw a low punch at Nick and hit him hard in the stomach. Nick doubled over and stumbled backward with Angelo still latched onto him. More screaming and shouting rose up. Alex, the security guard, suddenly appeared. The crowd stood back.

"You poisoned my daughter, you fuck!" Claudio came in for another shot.

Rosalie jumped onto Claudio's back, wrapping her arms around his neck brace. He screamed and his head and neck twisted back. Rosalie slid back to her feet and Mario jumped in. He grabbed Claudio's arm and twisting it behind his back. Alex jumped between Nick and Claudio, but Angelo wrapped his arm around Nick's neck and pulled him up off his feet, in a choke hold.

"Don't you hurt my son!" Frances swung wildly at Angelo. "Let go of him!"

Alex pulled Frances away and threw a sweeping kick at the back of Angelo's leg. Angelo stumbled and winced in pain but didn't let go of Nick. Instead he roared and leaned back, lifting Nick even higher in the headlock, Nick's feet dangling helplessly.

Frances and Rosalie kept screaming and shouting amid the jostling and shoving. Alex came in for another shot at Angelo throwing a forearm elbow to Angelo's arm. But he still held his grip around Nick's neck.

"You knew, you fuck, you did this! My daughter is dead because of you!" Claudio shouted at Nick.

Nick's face started turning blue.

"Alright," Alex shouted from behind. "Enough. Let the boy go."

He threw a low kick at the back of Angelo's leg while at the same time yanking him down by the shoulders. Angelo crumbled backward with Nick, and his head hit the pavement. Angelo was promptly knocked out. Nick gasped and rolled off onto his knees. He gulped for air.

Another police officer stepped in and grabbed Alex's arm. Alex twisted away.

"That's your man." Alex stepped back and pointed to Angelo on the ground. "I was just helping to control the situation."

The officer looked at Alex, and turned away. Rosalie and Mario ran to help Nick, still on all fours. The crowd surged forward to see what was happening.

Another officer finally grabbed Claudio and held his arm bent up behind his back.

Alex held Frances. She was shaking. A police officer helped Angelo as he came to.

"Fuck!" Angelo said and wiped blood from his mouth. He struggled to get to his feet and rubbed the back of his head.

Another police officer now stood between Angelo and Nick. Alex stood next to Nick. Angelo glared at them but couldn't do anything. Anne Marie appeared, stumbling forward from the crowd and right up to Claudio's face.

"So," she said. "It was Nick's then? Nick's wine, his poisoned wine? A gift from you I suppose!"

Claudio glared at her but said nothing at the accusation. Frances listened intently.

"Your special gift of death!" Anne Marie shouted. "You fuck, it was meant for my brother! Wasn't it? But he left, and your dumb ass daughter drank it instead! I was there, I almost took a sip! Well, you got what you deserved!"

She spat at him.

Claudio turned away and the crowd pressed in.

Mario and Rosalie helped Nick back to his feet.

"What are you talking about?" Nick said to Anne Marie.

"It was poisoned wine, meant for you!" she said. "But when you left, Marla drank it by accident. Claudio's the one who sent it over to you. Don't you see? He planned it for you, to kill you!"

Frances suddenly fell backward and fainted, right into Anne Marie's arms, causing them both to fall back onto the ground. Luckily Frances' head landed on Anne Marie's lap.

Alex immediately knelt down to help.

"Everyone stand back," Alex shouted. "She needs air!"

Nick stared at Claudio, trying to comprehend what had just happened. He could have been the dead one instead!

"Oh my god," Rosalie said.

One of the police officers tried to get everyone back. The other officer, who held Claudio, also began shouting to the crowd to get back. But the crowd didn't move, so the officer let go of Claudio and began shoving people back with his night stick. Claudio bent over and braced his hands on his knees. He took deep breaths, gasping as if he might be having a heart attack.

His gold and white Lincoln suddenly pulled into the wide driveway and pressed its way through the crowd. It came to a stop next to the squad car. Tony was in the driver's seat, holding the wheel with his one good hand, the other still in a sling.

"Get in Boss!" he shouted through the open passenger side window.

As one police officer was preoccupied with the crowd, pushing the onlookers back, and the other officer attending to Frances, who was sprawled out, laying across Anne Marie's lap, Angelo ran to Claudio.

"Let's get out of here," Nick heard Angelo yell.

Angelo helped Claudio up and hustled him over to the Lincoln. He flung the passenger door opened and shoved Claudio in. Nick watched in disbelief. Why weren't the cops stopping and arresting them both?

Nick ran over and grabbed Claudio's arm.

"No you don't!" he shouted and tried to pull Claudio from the car. "You're not going anywhere."

Rosalie came up behind Nick and grabbed his arm.

"Leave them!" she shouted and tugged, trying to pull him away from Claudio and Angelo.

"But they're getting away!" Nick yelled.

Angelo glared at Nick and shoved him back, into Rosalie. They both stumbled backward. Suddenly Angelo lunged up at Nick and grabbed him by the lapels of his tuxedo.

He yanked him up, spun him around and threw him in the back of the Lincoln. Angelo jumped in after him and pressed his weight against Nick, holding him down. Joey Messina hopped in the other side, trapping Nick and blocking any chance of his escape. Angelo reached to shut the door but somehow Anne Marie had a hold of it.

"Leave him alone!" she shouted.

Rosalie screamed, "No!!!"

Angelo pulled the door, slamming it on Anne Marie's fingers and catching her skirt bottom too.

Alex came to help, but it was too late. Tony hit the gas and the car plunged forward through the crowd with Anne Marie still snagged in tow. Rosalie screamed and the car screeched away.

"STOP!" Rosalie called after them.

Just as Tony made a hard left out of the parking lot, Angelo cracked the door open and Anne Marie tumbled away, rolling and landing up on the sidewalk.

CHAPTER 39

Nick sat in the middle of the back seat, crushed between Joey and Angelo. Joey held a gun poked into Nick's left side. Claudio sat in the front rubbing his neck. Tony drove. The traffic was heavy on the strip and a Frank Sinatra tune, "That's Life", played in the background on the radio.

"Let's get to the desert," Angelo announced.

"No problem," Tony said. "If I can get through this goddamn traffic."

Angelo pulled his neatly folded, embroidered, cotton handkerchief from his jacket pocket and patted the bloody lump on the back of his head.

Tony pressed on the horn. "Get the fuck out of the way, you fucking moron!" he shouted.

"What the hell are you guys doing?" Nick said.

"Shut the fuck up." Angelo wiped blood from his lip.

"Where are you taking me?"

"Nowhere," Joey said.

"What?" Nick said.

"Shut the fuck up," Angelo glared at him.

"Are you crazy? Anything happens to me, you're screwed!"

Nick pushed himself forward in the seat and turned toward Angelo.

"*Watch it!*" Joey stuck the gun hard into Nick's side.

"Ah, shit," Nick yelled. "Take it easy, I ain't goin' nowhere."

Joey eased off, but just a bit.

"You're gonna get what you finally deserve." Angelo scowled at him.

"What do you mean *what I deserve*?" Nick was incredulous. "I deserve this? Is that what you're saying? Shit, he's the one . . ."

Nick indicated Claudio with a node, "He's the one who killed my dad, took the casino, took my mom . . ."

"That's enough!" Angelo raised a clenched fist. "It's because of you Marla's dead!"

"What? Are you kidding me? I had nothing to do with that!"

"Shut the fuck up!" Angelo roared.

Spit sprayed from his mouth and hit Nick's left eye. Nick jerked his hand up to wipe the slime out. In an instant Angelo threw a bone crushing right hook that landed squarely on Nick's jaw. Blood splattered all over Nick's white tuxedo, Joey's tux, and across Tony's forehead. Nick promptly fell across Joey's lap, his eyes staring blankly, and blood flowing from his mouth.

"Get the fuck off me." Joey grabbed Nick's limp shoulders and yanked him off.

Nick keeled forward, his shoulders coming to rest on his knees and head hanging down in between his legs.

———

"THAT SHUT HIM UP, huh?" Angelo rubbed his knuckles and laughed.

"Yeah," Claudio said. "Good for him."

With his handkerchief Angelo patted the lump on the back of his head again. "Shit," he said. "It's all this fucks fault."

"Here." Joey took off his tie. "Let's use this so we don't have to listen to him no more."

Joey reached under and wrapped the tie across Nick's mouth, pulled it back, and tied it tightly behind his head.

"That'll do it," he said.

"Take your belt and tie his hands, too," Angelo said.

"Sure, no problem."

Joey took off his belt and tied Nick's hands behind his back.

Tony adeptly maneuvered the car, with his one good hand, around the tight curve of the on-ramp to the freeway. They headed north on Interstate 15.

Claudio held his hand under his neck brace, rubbing it. Joey rested his gun across his thigh. Nick's head hung down between his legs, blood still dripping from his mouth. Angelo refolded his bloody handkerchief, and stared angrily ahead, into the night. Tony drove on, straight down the lonely desert highway, as the bright lights of Vegas receded behind them.

———

NICK OPENED HIS EYES to see his Carson City silver dollar bolo swaying between his legs and flickering in the freeway's passing lights. The corners of his lips felt like they were about to be split in two by the gag. His wrists were tied so tight that he couldn't feel his hands. He groaned and attempted to lift his head. Blood dripped from his mouth.

"Watch it," Joey poked his gun into Nick's side.

Nick pulled himself up and swung his eyes left, then right. It wasn't a nightmare—*it was real*. Why didn't they just shoot him? He should have listened to Rosalie and just gone home with her. They'd be in bed now, snuggling up together. But instead, he was a fool, he had to go back to the reception to go after Claudio. He had to try to pull him out of the car. He didn't actually think the police were going to do anything to help, or to go after them, did he? They didn't even chase them out of there when Tony practically ran half the crowd over!

He felt a loose tooth in his mouth and the gash on his lip. Then he noticed the blood stains on his tux and the sweet taste of blood in his mouth. He had let everyone down. Rosalie, his mom, and especially his dad. Now he would pay the price, just like his dad. How stupid could he be? His head hurt as it rocked back and forth.

The thought occurred to him that maybe they all wondered how they got there. What were their regrets? Their mistakes? No, don't be a fool, he corrected himself, this was their job, their brutal and obscene job. They'd done it before. It's second nature for them. So where were they going? Far into the desert night, into the wasteland, a real moonscape. Might as well be the moon. A million miles. This was it.

Tony finally pulled off the highway and onto a decrepit old road that was full of bumps, potholes and dips. The Lincoln rocked and bounced and bottomed out. Tony jerked the steering wheel this way, then that. Sparks shot from the car's undercarriage.

"Shit," Claudio rubbed his neck. "Fucking take it easy! I'm in goddamn pain here!"

"Sorry Boss, I forgot." Tony eased up on the accelerator.

"Do you know where the fuck you're going?" Angelo asked.

"Yeah, it's where we always go. We're almost there."

Soon he turned off and onto another road, this time a dirt road. After five more minutes and an even bumpier ride, the Lincoln finally came to a crunching, dusty stop.

"The Eagle has landed." Tony grinned.

"Great," Claudio said. "I gotta take a leak."

Tony left the car running and headlights on, facing into the moonless night and bleak, sagebrush filled, desert. Nick watched Claudio maneuver himself out of the car. He moved slowly as he shuffled away from the car. Maybe he was still drunk. Tony was already out of the car and stretching his one good arm over his head. After his stretch, he pulled a flask from his jacket pocket and took a quick swig.

Joey pushed his door open, grabbed Nick by the shoulder and yanked him out, tossing him in the dirt. Angelo suddenly appeared standing over him, his menacing figure outlined against the sparkling, star-filled, sky. Why were the stars so beautiful? Maybe he'd be joining them soon.

"*You fuck.*" Angelo kicked him hard in the ribs.

Nick coughed and Angelo kicked him again, this time in his head. Nick winced and bit down on the gag in his mouth. His hands were still tied behind his back so he closed his eyes tightly, trying, instinctively, to protect them. He knew only a miracle could save him now. *Just make it quick*—he said to himself.

"Take it easy," he heard Joey say. "Don't you want him to dig the hole?"

Nick opened one eye and looked up to see Angelo glaring at Joey.

"You dig the hole," Angelo said.

"My back is bad," Joey said. "And the bumpy ride didn't help it any."

"What?"

"It's because of that fuck. He fucked it up when I was chasing him from Rosalie's room. Bastard, let him fucking do it."

"Ah shit." Angelo spit on the ground.

He looked at Tony, who had just grabbed the pickaxe from the trunk and was standing there holding it with his one good hand, the other in the sling.

"Shit," Angelo said.

"Guess Nick's the only one who can do it," Tony said. "Let him dig his own goddamn grave."

Angelo stared in seeming disbelief at Tony. Nick tilted his head an inch and glanced around to see Claudio walking back over. He was still in his tux and neck brace. In fact, all the men all had their black tuxes on. What a weird scene. Nick closed his eyes.

"Yeah," Claudio said. "I agree, let him dig his own grave."

Pain shot through Nick's body. Could he even stand up? He half opened an eye.

"Shit." Angelo looked down at him.

Nick watched. The other men watched. All waited for the verdict. Angelo suddenly pulled his gun and pointed it squarely at Nick's face.

"Get up," he said. "I certainly ain't gonna dig your goddamn hole."

Claudio turned to Joey. "Untie his hands. But leave him gagged. I don't want to hear his trap."

Joey squatted down and untied the belt from Nick's wrists.

Nick pressed his hands in the desert sand and struggled to bring himself to his knees. He rested on all fours a moment to catch his breath, then pushed one foot forward and staggered up. He wavered and turned toward the men. Tony held the pickaxe out to Nick.

"Take it," Angelo kept the gun pointed squarely at Nick's chest.

Nick shook his head. No.

"Take the fucking pick and start digging." Joey stepped forward and held his own gun right up to Nick's face.

Nick turned to him and tried to speak but only made mumbling sounds. Joey pressed the barrel of the gun against Nick's forehead. Nick stared at him.

"Are you gonna take the pick and start digging?" Joey said. "Or am I just gonna blow your head off? Shit, I'll dig the fucking hole if I have to."

"Good," Angelo said. "Just blow his fucking brains out now then."

Joey turned to Claudio, then back to Nick.

"Do it!" Angelo shouted.

Nick's knees shook. He began grunting, coughing, and gurgling.

Joey squinted his eyes and was just about to pull the trigger, when Claudio shouted, "Wait!"

He stepped up to Joey.

"You shoot him, then Angelo's the only one that can dig. And I don't want him getting dirty and sweaty. Take off the gag so this fucker can say his piece."

Joey lowered his gun and Claudio pulled out a pocket knife. He handed it to Joey and Joey cut the gag off. Nick eyed him suspiciously as the gag fell to the ground. Nick took a gasping breath, then bent over and coughed, spitting blood in the sand. He took another breath, then slowly straightened up.

"I got nothin' to say," Nick said. "I just couldn't breathe."

Nick stepped forward and grabbed the pickaxe from Tony. Joey and Angelo both kept their guns trained on him. With the pickaxe in hand, Nick stumbled in front of the car's headlights. He glanced down at his tuxedo jacket and pants glowing white and bloody red.

"Get going," Angelo said.

Nick turned and raised his head to the desert wilderness. He began walking. The men followed closely behind.

"Shoot him if he tries to run," Angelo said loudly.

———

NICK STOPPED and turned toward the men.

"Here?" he said.

"Sure," Angelo said. "That's fucking perfect."

Nick looked at the ground and was about to swing the pickaxe, but instead stopped and turned back toward the men.

"I'm just curious," he said. "What are you guys gonna do with the tons of silver you stole from my dad's vaults?"

"Shut the fuck up," Claudio shouted.

But Nick shouted back, "I was just there with Rosalie,

but there ain't nothin' left, except for a few pallets. The vaults used to be full to the brim, what'd you do with it all?"

"Shoot him, goddamn it!" Claudio yelled as he tried to unclip his own gun from its holster. "I'll dig the fucking hole myself!"

Joey stepped forward again, raised his gun and took his aim.

"Wait!" Angelo lunged and slapped Joey's trigger arm away just as the shot rang out, piercing the silence with a sharp crack and startling the men. The bullet whizzed by Nick's head. He stood frozen in the car's bright headlights.

"Just fucking finish him now!" Claudio said as he finally pulled his own gun out.

"I said wait," Angelo shouted at Claudio. "And put that away."

Claudio hesitated, then slid the gun back in its shoulder holster under his jacket.

Angelo calmly said to Claudio, "Now I'm curious. I thought it was a bit sparse in there. Where'd you take the rest of the loot?"

Joey and Tony both shot quick glances at Claudio. Angelo swung his gun and pointed it directly at Claudio's face.

Claudio stepped back and immediately raised his hands.

"Take it easy," he said. "I can explain, it's part of the plan."

Angelo tilted his head.

Joey still kept his gun trained on Nick watching Claudio closely with one eye, and Nick with the other.

"The plan?" Angelo said. "What plan? You didn't tell

me about a plan."

Claudio took a deep breath, sighed and dropped his hands.

"For Christ's sake," he said. "It's the plan. You're gonna thank me for this. I didn't want to tell you until I had everything buttoned up. I had the boys stash the silver for safe keeping. That way nobody could fuck with it—not Nick, not Frances or anybody else. Who knows what might have happened if we left it at the casino, right?"

"When the fuck were you gonna tell me?" Angelo moved his gun closer to Claudio's nose. "And where the fuck is it?"

Nick watched as Claudio began shaking.

"It's in Mesquite," he said. "On a farm, in a hole, in the ground. I swear to you I was going to tell you."

"Bullshit! Buried in the ground?" Angelo said. "You fucking asshole. You stole our loot and buried it for yourself? Is that right, you fat fuck?"

"No, that's not it," Claudio pleaded. "I did it for us, all of us. You, Mr. Crocetti, the boys, all of us, to keep it goddamn safe."

Angelo turned his gaze to Joey and Tony. "And you guys knew about this too? And nobody fucking told me?"

They both kept silent.

"You expect me to believe that?" Angelo shouted at Claudio. "You think I'm a fucking idiot?"

"It's safe now," Claudio said. "Don't you see?"

"Bullshit!" Angelo roared, and took a step back.

Nick shifted on his heal. Maybe he could run. But he'd make an easy target in his white tuxedo. But he could do it and maybe make it. He should run!

Angelo waived his gun at Claudio, and motioned him toward the car.

"Let's go," he said.

"Where?" Claudio asked.

"To Mesquite, to the loot. If it's all there, then we tell Mr. Crocetti that everything is cool. I forget all this ever happened and we each take our cut then give the rest to the big boss."

Joey and Tony looked at Claudio.

"It's all there, trust me," Claudio said. "Let's go."

Joey looked at Nick then back to Angelo. "Can I kill him now? We don't need no hole anyway. The coyotes and bobcats will rip him to shreds."

Angelo glanced at Nick and thought a moment.

Nick's heart raced.

"No, don't shoot him yet," Angelo ordered. "I got a sudden change of heart. I wanna see the loot first. We can bury him after."

"Shit," Claudio wined. "Just whack him now."

"No," Angelo insisted. "For now, I want him alive. Get him back in the car, but tie him up good so he don't try nothin'."

"Sure," Joey said.

Claudio mistakenly tried to shake his head in disagreement.

"Ahhh shit!" he winced.

Joey tied Nick's hands again, this time in front, and the men piled back into the car. Nick kept his mouth shut this time, so as not to get gagged again. Tony made a quick U-turn, and drove back down the dirt road in the direction that they had come.

"How far is Mesquite from here?" Angelo asked.

Tony sighed, "I don't know, another hour or so?"

"Shit," Angelo said. "It'll be 2 AM by the time we get there."

"Yup," Joey said. "It's gonna be a long night."

CHAPTER 40

They drove down the town's main street, West Mesquite Boulevard. A single spotlight lit the sign for Harley's Service station. They passed Winston's Feed Supply and the Star Diner. The windswept town was dead, without a soul around, like something out of the Twilight Zone.

Tony drove slowly, looking for the right cross street. Angelo kept his hand on his gun in his tuxedo pocket. Joey had a difficult time keeping awake and kept nodding off, his head slowly lowering down towards Nick's shoulder, then suddenly snapping back up as he tried to stay awake. Claudio kept his head tilted, unmoving. It was difficult for Nick to tell if Claudio was sleeping or just nursing his sprained neck.

Nick stayed awake as he desperately ran through various escape scenarios. He had to figure something out if he stood any chance of survival. If he tried and failed, that would be the same as not trying at all. Either way, he'd probably still wind up getting shot, dead and buried. He had to try something, he had nothing to lose. But what could he do? He needed an opportunity.

"Is this it?" Tony said to Claudio.

"Huh?" Claudio lifted his head. "Wait," he said. "It's River Road or something, isn't it?"

"Riverside?" Tony stopped the car in the middle of the deserted intersection.

Claudio stiffly turned to the left, then right.

"This is it," he said. "Make a left."

Tony hit the gas for the left turn, but his hand slipped off the wheel and the car fishtailed violently.

"Shit! Take it easy," Claudio yelled. "Come on, man. My neck! It was all right and now you just fucked it up again!"

"Sorry Boss, my hand slipped."

"Ahhh, fuck!" Claudio rubbed his neck.

They drove a few minutes up the dusty road, crossing the river, and leaving the small town behind. They were on dirt roads now, in the sparse open country.

"Tony," Claudio said. "Better go wake up Miguel when we get there, that way he doesn't set the dogs on us, or call the Sheriff."

"Sure, Boss," Tony said.

"Wait," Angelo said. "Who's Miguel?"

"He's the guy whose land it's buried on," Tony said.

"He knows where the silver is?" Angelo was alarmed.

"He don't know nothin'," Claudio said. "He thinks it's diseased medical waste."

"So, this is where you brought all my dad's silver?" Nick heard himself suddenly say as he tried to remember the route Tony was driving, but it was incomprehensible.

"Quiet!" Angelo pulled his fist back ready to strike Nick.

Nick threw his head back to avoid the punch, but Angelo didn't throw it this time.

Tony drove another mile or so and Nick could see some lights appearing ahead in the darkness.

"Is that Miguel's trailer?" Tony said.

"Don't know," Claudio said. "But drive slower."

Tony backed off the accelerator and the car slowed.

"Wait," Angelo said. "Stop. Roll down your window."

Tony stopped in the middle of the desolate road and hit the power switch for his window. Joey lowered his window too. The cool night air drifted in and felt good to Nick. Fresh air with a distinctive organic, earthy smell. So simple but so good.

Nick heard what sounded like heavy banging and rumbling — weird.

"Is that where the shit is buried?" Angelo said, indicating where the lights and noises were coming from.

"Yeah, maybe, I don't know," Claudio shrugged.

"I thought you said he thinks it's medical waste?" Angelo questioned.

"He did," Claudio wiped his forehead. "I mean he does. That's what he thinks."

"Well maybe he don't think that no more? Let's go, hit it. I think we got more work to do tonight."

Tony stepped on the gas and the tires kicked up a cloud of dust.

"Grab your gun, Tony," Claudio said. "Could be trouble."

"No problem," Tony said. "I can still shoot with my left hand."

Tony turned sharply into the ranch, under the *El Rancho De Milagro* sign.

"Shit," Claudio said. "My neck!"

"Sorry Boss, hold on tight."

"Is that it?" Angelo craned his neck to see the approaching lights ahead.

"Yeah," Joey said. "Looks like we got a little problem here."

"Kill your headlights," Angelo ordered.

"No problem," Tony said.

He cut the lights and drove up the dirt road, then cut the wheel sharply left again and blazed right through the field, heading straight for the lights, straight for the hole. The car bounced and bottomed out as it hit the furrows, kicking up clouds of dirt and dust.

"Oh, shit!" Claudio shouted, his head bobbing around like a rag doll. "Goddamn it!"

———

NICK COULD SEE a state patrol car parked out in the middle of the field, its light flashing and headlights directed at a backhoe. The backhoe's own overhead lights shone down at its bucket while it scooped at the earth. Sitting low in the dirt to the right of the backhoe—an eighteen-wheeled belly dump truck. And next to it, partly in the spotlight, a black fastback Buick Riviera with white vinyl roof.

"Shit," Angelo said. "What the fuck is going on here?"

"Is that Roman's car?" Tony said. "And is that Roman, with those kids, Mike and Ralph?"

Tony brought the Lincoln to a jerking, abrupt stop behind the squad car. Nick landed on Angelo's lap.

Claudio screamed "Ahh, fuck!" again.

Angelo pushed Nick to the floor. "Get the fuck off me!"

Tony put the car in park and jumped out, gun in hand. Joey scrambled out too, but tripped and tumbled into the dirt. Nick heard Joey curse and saw him jump back up to his feet, his gun drawn also. Joey slammed the door on Nick, who now lay scrunched across the hump. Tony had left so quickly, he forgot to shut the engine—it was still running!

Angelo had already jumped out himself and Nick could hear him shouting at Claudio to get out. It even sounded like he was trying to yank Claudio out.

"Take it easy," Claudio yelled.

"Get out," Angelo shouted. "You fuck, let's go!"

"I can't fucking move," Claudio objected.

"Shit!" Angelo slammed the door.

Nick pulled himself up onto the back seat and struggled to sit up. He could see Angelo and Joey stepping gingerly, awkwardly, through the dirt and heading for the ditch. A cloud of dust rose up from the pit and glowed in the lights. The backhoe suddenly stopped and a man with a straw hat and overalls climbed down from it and quickly disappeared behind it.

Nick peaked over the front seat saw two other shadowy figures running toward the belly-dump truck. One man went around the back out of view and the other climbed up to the cab on the passenger side. Angelo was right behind the guy and grabbed hold of his leg. He pulled him down to the dirt. Tony had his gun trained on the guy. Nick heard shots but didn't see who shot, or where it came from. He tried to break his wrists free. If he could get free, he could open the car door and run.

A man came running from behind the belly dump truck, twisting his body around and shooting frantically back at his pursuer. It was Joey chasing him, and shooting. POP! POP! Then POP again and the man fell, rolling in the dirt. Joey approached the man quickly, his gun pointing down. But in an instant POP! POP! from the dirt and Joey crumbled down right next to the guy. Both men now lay, practically on top of each other in the field. But Joey struggled and pushed himself up, pointed his gun right at the guy and BAM! He executed the guy right there, just like that! Then he fell back in the dirt himself. Holy shit!

Over by the belly dump truck, Angelo kicked the guy on the ground. Tony stood by, his gun pointed right at the guy.

"Find the cop!" Nick heard Angelo shout to Tony.

"Shit," was Tony's reply.

Tony ran awkwardly toward the hole stumbling with his one arm in the sling and the other holding his gun. Nick kept an eye on the action by the truck. Angelo kept beating the guy in the dirt—the guy holding his hands up, feebly trying to block Angelo's bone-crunching blows. Was that one of Claudio's men? He looked familiar but Nick couldn't tell for sure.

"Shit," Claudio suddenly shouted from the front seat. "What the fuck is Roman doing here, that snake! I'll fucking kill him."

Tony stood by the edge of the pit and yelled over to Angelo. "Deputy's lying at the bottom, dead. They must have killed him."

"Shit," Claudio said, and struggled to get out of the car.

"So, this is where you took my dad's treasure?" Nick said.

"Didn't we tell you to keep your fucking mouth shut?" Claudio couldn't even shift his body around to face Nick, so he tried to aim his gun back at Nick but couldn't get it around either. Nick ducked and waited for the inevitable.

But nothing happened.

Why didn't he just shoot him? Maybe Claudio didn't want to get his car full of blood? Maybe he was going to try to drag him out of the car? At least then he'd have a fighting chance.

"Ahhh fuck!" he heard Claudio cry.

The door slammed and he heard Claudio hobbling away through the dirt. Nick looked over the seat and saw Claudio heading toward the man lying by the truck—the man that Angelo had practically pummeled to death. Was that really Roman?

Nick squinted to see what was happening. This could be his only chance. Tony and Angelo were running past the pit, chasing someone else. They caught up with the guy and shoved him down in the dirt. Angelo's arm rose and struck down repeatedly.

"Shit!" Nick heard him yell, "I'll kill you fucking motherfuckers!"

Holy shit! This was it. With his hands still tied, Nick pushed himself up and over the front seat and crashed down into the steering wheel. His heart felt like it was beating a million times a second. He stayed low across the front seat. The motor was still running and the headlights still on. He grabbed the column shifter with his tied hands and yanked it down, to throw it into reverse. But the shifter flew all the way down and right into first gear. The car lurched forward, right at the pit. Nick scrambled to jam on the brakes with his elbow and all his weight. He didn't know it, but the car stopped right at the edge of the pit.

He popped the column shifter back up, then carefully down one click into reverse. He peeked over the steering wheel and could see Claudio's shocked expression as he stood by the truck looking back at him.

Nick slammed the gas pedal and the car kicked up a cloud of dust as the wheels spun in the dirt. Rocks and pebbles pelted the undercarriage and sides of the car. The car started backwards, moving away from the pit and away from the men and then gaining speed. Nick couldn't easily steer but he figured it would be best to just keep it straight and try to turn around after he got some distance between them.

But Claudio had opened fire and bullets were now slamming the car. Nick took a quick look back and saw Angelo and Tony behind the truck, firing their guns too, all taking aim right at him!

Nick ducked low. The Lincoln bounced wildly backward over the ruts and furrows, the barrage of bullets pelting and pinging the car, its windows exploding, the glass shattering over the seats. The cool country air rushed in. Then a sudden shot of pain in his left shoulder.

Shit, was he hit? It stung like fire. The car kept on backwards and he still heard the cracks of gunfire, but the bullets had stopped hitting the car. He counted to five, then popped his head up and grabbed the steering wheel. He spun it, turning the car sharply in a huge cloud of dust. It came to a stop, rocking and settling into the dirt. He threw it into drive.

He hoped he hadn't overshot the farm road and that he was pointed in the right direction. He glanced back and could see the lights by the pit, about a hundred yards away. He also saw Claudio's silhouette there, raising his gun up to shoot again. And it looked like Tony and Angelo were running past Claudio coming right for him across the field. Claudio started firing again as the two men passed him. Nick hit the gas. He would get away. As long as there was gas in that car, he would get away!

The wheels spun and a cloud of dirt and dust rose up again, but the car only lurched up and down, and didn't seem to budge. It wasn't getting any traction—*it was stuck in dirt!* Nick gassed it again and again. But the tires just kept spinning, kicking up more clouds of dirt and dust. Nick looked back at the men.

Claudio kept firing, the bullets flying past Angelo and Tony as they ran to the car. Nick frantically kept trying to get traction, but the car only kept lurching and sinking further into the dirt. Nick threw it into reverse and was about to hit the gas again when he heard Tony scream in pain.

He looked back and saw that Tony had fallen. But Angelo was still lumbering over, out of breath, but almost upon the car, just a few feet away! Nick hit the gas and the car rocked, but it still wouldn't move. Panic overtook him. He grabbed the door handle to make a run for it.

But Angelo had already caught up to the bullet-ridden car and opened the door himself. He reached in and grabbed Nick's bloody shoulder and yanked him out. Nick slammed to the dirt.

"You stupid fuck!" Angelo kicked him in the head. "Stupid! Stupid, fuck! You stupid fuck!"

Angelo kicked him again and again. Nick groaned and tried to hold up his arms to protect his head.

Suddenly Angelo stopped. He must have been out of breath. Nick opened an eye and watched him turn and walk away holding his gun loosely in his hand. He was headed to Tony. Angelo knelt down next to Tony's prone body and pushed him over. Tony lay, stone dead, facing up to the night sky.

Angelo stood again and looked back at Claudio, who stood in the distance, his robotic neck-braced figure silhouetted against the bright lights. He stood by the truck, over Roman, his arm outstretched with gun in hand, pointing point blank, at Roman in the dirt.

"Shit," Nick heard Angelo say.

Then he heard a single gunshot, then Pop! Pop! Nick held his head down in the dirt. What the fuck was going on? He tried to crawl back into the car, but he was too weak and there was too much pain. Then he heard footsteps, shuffling through the dirt, coming towards him. When he looked up, Angelo stood over him again.

"Get the fuck up."

Nick squinted in agony. His arm burned like it was on fire, and with every breath he took there were gurgling sounds and sharp pains in his chest. Probably broken ribs. And his jaw felt like it was disjointed and crooked. A few teeth were loose and his bloody lips stung with gritty dirt. Was there really anything else Angelo could do to him? Just end it already. Get it over with.

"I said to get the fuck up!"

Nick managed to roll onto his stomach, his face sideways in the dirt. He summoned all his strength and lifted his hips off the ground.

Angelo grabbed the back of his collar.

"Up!" he shouted, and with a great heave pulled Nick to his knees. Nick lifted one leg to stand and Angelo yanked him again. He was almost up all the way, but the pain was excruciating.

"Let's go." Angelo ordered and pulled him to a

standing position.

He grabbed Nick's arm and started dragging him across the field, back towards the pit. Nick moaned and wheezed with every stumbling step forward, blood soaking through his tuxedo sleeve. Blood all over. Why hadn't he just killed him?

"What are you doin'?" Nick heard himself say.

"Shut up!" Angelo barked. Then, after a moment of thought, added, "You're gonna tell me if it's all there, capisce? Then I'll put you out of your misery. You help me, I'll help you."

With his hands still tied, Nick staggered, spitting blood and bits of dirt from his mouth, utterly defeated. They made their way across the furrows and ruts, past Tony's body, toward the pit and toward Claudio, who stood on the edge of the hole, motionless.

"I didn't mean to shoot Tony," Claudio muttered. "He was my friend. He ran across my line of fire."

Angelo held his gun with one hand and Nick with the other. He fixed his eyes on Claudio. Claudio leaned over the hole and surveyed the stacks and piles of silver. He turned to Nick.

"It's your fault, you know that?" Claudio said. "Tony's dead because of you. Marla is dead because of you. And now Joey's dead too."

Claudio lifted his gun and pointed it directly at Nick.

"Everyone is dead," he sneered. "All because of you."

Nick stared defiantly at Claudio. What more was there to do? In a moment, he'd be dead.

"Wait," Angelo said and reached over to push Claudio's gun away. "He needs to tell me something."

"What?" Claudio said.

"Get the fuck out of the way," Angelo pushed Claudio to the side.

Then he grabbed Nick again and tugged him over to the edge. Claudio turned his attention back to the hole.

The three of them, Nick, Angelo, and Claudio, stood by the edge looking down at the piles of 1,000 oz. silver bars haphazardly stacked seven or eight feet high.

"Is that all of it?" Angelo said to Nick.

Nick hesitated, taking in the scene. Heavy green canvas tarps were pulled back over the dirt, exposing the silvery piles of gleaming bars stacked high, and pallet-fulls of bulging coin bags, and cases of chips, all spread out below, in the huge pit. It was a spectacular but meaningless sight. It was almost over.

"All of it?" Nick mumbled. "Is it?"

Nick staggered a half step closer and leaned over the edge, looking right and left, carefully surveying the pit. Angelo still held him by the arm. The Deputy's body lay at the front end of the pit, only his lifeless legs visible behind a stack of silver bars.

"It's all here?" Angelo repeated.

"Guess it must be," Nick said as he noticed the bolo silver dollar pendant swinging from his neck. "Everything my dad worked for! Everything!"

He straightened up and turned to Angelo and Claudio.

"And for what?! For you?" he said.

Angelo smiled and raised his gun, his eyes crazed with excitement. Nick closed his eyes and in a split second a shot rang out splattering needle-sharp pinpoints of pain into

Nick's face.

It was over. So sadly over!

Nick staggered backward, and saw in slow motion, Angelo's shadow of a body come at him, and crumble at his feet. A thud in the dirt! Nick was still standing! He looked down at his shirt, at the bolo. There were splotches of blood and clumps of hair all over him. What?

He turned to Claudio, the smoking gun in his hand and Claudio staring down at Angelo's body. He had shot Angelo in the back of the head.

"You shouldn't have trusted me." Claudio shoved Angelo's body off the edge with his foot. Angelo tumbled to the bottom and landed at the foot of a high pile of silver bars.

Nick could run. He should run. Maybe Claudio was out of bullets? Or he might miss.

But Claudio had already raised the gun, and now pointed it point-blank directly into Nick's face. Nick's legs shook, his eyes and lips twitched. Strangely, all his pain was gone. His singular focus — Claudio and the gun.

Claudio smiled with that same crazed look in his eyes that Angelo had a minute before — giddy and gloating.

"It's just us," he snickered. "Everyone else is gone."

Nick's adrenalin pumped his heart in overdrive but he didn't dare move a muscle. Say something before it's too late, he thought. Quickly!

"You gonna kill my mom too?" Nick blurted.

Claudio's crazed smirk disappeared and his face flushed.

"Don't worry. I'll take care of her. She's my wife after all."

"But you might as well kill her too, huh?" Nick said.

"You'll get everything then, all for yourself!"

Claudio hand shook, the gun wavering and unsteady in his outstretched arm.

"I said I'll take care of her."

"You don't really love her, do you?" Nick said. "If you did, you wouldn't kill me. You think she'll be happy with me dead?"

Could he actually reason with this monster?

Claudio struggled to maintain his composure, his lip quivered and sweat rolled down the side of his jaw. He glanced down at the sparkling silver, then back up at Nick.

A faint sound of a siren rose in the distance. Claudio's eyes shifted for a split second in that direction, then back to the gun and to Nick.

Nick stared at Claudio, the gun barrel wavering between his eyes. Maybe Claudio's arm was getting tired?

The answer came without warning in a blinding flash of light and an earsplitting crack. Nick squeezed his eyes closed and said a prayer asking that Rosalie and his mom and his sister be safe.

But again, *he was somehow still standing.* The bullet had whizzed past his ear.

He jerked open his eyes in disbelief. Claudio seemed as surprised as he was. Nick lunged forward, hitting Claudio so hard he went flying backwards, his head whiplashing. Claudio cried out in pain and Nick landed on top of him in the dirt. Claudio struggled to aim the gun, but couldn't turn his head fast enough to see where to point it. Nick rolled off Claudio.

Claudio fired wildly, but missed. Nick lunged again, scrambling to grab Claudio's wrist. But Claudio pushed him off and heaved himself up onto all fours, like a dog. Claudio raised the gun from the dirt and was about to shoot again. Nick squirmed next to Claudio and from his back, kicked Claudio hard in the hip, sending him backwards, right to the edge of the pit.

This was his only chance. He rolled himself next to Claudio again and kicked as hard as he could. Claudio screamed and fired the gun wildly as he fell over the edge. He hit with a thump at the bottom of the pit. Then Nick heard an avalanche of silver bars and coins crashing down.

With his hands still tied, Nick snaked over on his elbows to the edge of the trench. He lifted his head and shoulders, as high as he could, and gazed over the edge.

Below, Claudio lay face up, his arms outstretched with the gun still in hand, a pile of silver bars and coin bags on his chest, crushing him. His hand twitched as he tried to lift the gun. He stared spookily up at Nick, his face contorted. He seemed to be desperately trying to say something. He mouthed some soundless last words. But it didn't matter. Nick heard only the feeble gasping that emanated from his deflated body.

The bolo swung from his neck, toward the pit, as if his dad was trying to reach the treasure himself. Maybe his dad had been there all along?

Nick pushed away from the edge, lowered his head into the dirt and rolled onto his back. The stars of the Milky Way were as bright and beautiful as they had been earlier. He took shallow, painful breaths, closed his eyes and began to cry. Incredibly, he was still alive. He reached for the bolo pendant and squeezed it tight.

It's over, Dad. It's all over.

Then, behind him, Nick heard someone clear their throat. *Shit!* He opened his eyes wide and gulped a deep breath. A shot of pain ripped through his chest.

A man with overalls and a straw hat stood over him, and looked curiously at him. The man knelt on a knee and put his hand on Nick's shoulder. Nick flinched.

"Estas bien, sir?" the man said.

Nick eyed him suspiciously. Mexican?

"You have terrible friends, sir, you know this?" the man shook his head. "Terrible."

The man's tone was gentle.

"Take it easy," he said. "You don't look so good. You're bleeding. Let me help you."

The Mexican began to undo the belt around Nick's wrists.

"I am Miguel," he said. "This is my ranch."

"Miguel," Nick looked up at him. "Thanks."

Nick flexed his hands, hoping to feel them again.

"They're not my friends either," Nick said. "They killed my father. Help me sit up."

Miguel helped him. Nick pressed his hand in the dirt and looked down in the pit again—at Claudio's crushed body, and at Angelo's twisted and bloodied body. And at the Deputy, across on the other side of the pit, lying on his side, tied and gagged. It was a Shakespearian tragedy, everyone was dead—*except him!*

Miguel shook his head. "Those men forced me to work for them. They're not good people."

"No, they're not," Nick said. "But you're a good man."

A siren approached from the distance. Soon Nick

could see the flashing lights approach from across the open field. As it got closer, he could see it was a state trooper. He came to a stop next to the other trooper's cruiser. Miguel immediately held his hands up. The trooper jumped out with a shotgun in hand, and crouched down behind his opened door.

"Sheriff. Don't move!" he shouted.

Miguel raised his hands higher.

"We're OK," Miguel shouted. "We not the trouble makers."

Nick raised only his right arm, as his left didn't seem to function.

"Both hands up!" the sheriff yelled.

"Sir, he's been shot," Miguel shouted back.

The sheriff hesitated and eyed them suspiciously. He stood and stepped out from behind the cruiser's door, his shotgun held high, pointing directly at Miguel and Nick.

"Where's Deputy Hensley?"

"He's down in the hole sir," Miguel said.

"Don't move." The sheriff stepped sideways over to the edge of the pit. He glanced down.

"Oh *shit*," he said. "What the hell?"

"They tried to kill us, sir," Miguel said. "But they killed each other instead. And this man's been shot, sir, he needs help. They tried to kill him too, but he's a lucky man!"

Nick looked up at the officer but didn't speak.

"Ed! Are you OK?" The sheriff shouted into the pit. Nick gazed down at the carnage. The deputy's leg seemed to suddenly twitch from behind a stack of silver bars, and a low grumbling sound could be heard.

"Are you OK?" The sheriff shouted again. He looked

over at Miguel and Nick. "You men stay right where you are unless you want your head blown clear off, understand."

"Yes, sir," Miguel said. "Very much, we understand."

Nick nodded.

The sheriff scurried down the side of the pit and over to Deputy Hensley. Nick and Miguel watched as he pulled him from behind a stack of silver bars, sat him up and untied the gag from the deputy's mouth.

Deputy Hensley coughed. His face was bloodied and swollen.

"Wade, thank god you're here," he gasped. "They were going to bury me, alive! I thought I was dead."

More sirens came from the distance. The sheriff helped Deputy Hensley up, and Miguel helped pull them both out of the pit.

"This man is bleeding," Miguel said to the sheriff, pointing back toward Nick.

"What happened to him?" Sheriff Wade asked.

"Beat up bad and shot, in the arm, sir. He's a very very lucky man!"

"We're both lucky!" Deputy Hensley looked at Nick. "And I heard everything, he didn't do nothin', he's innocent."

"I'll call the ambulance," Sheriff Wade said.

"Thanks," Nick said in a raspy voice.

He closed his eyes and laid back, in the dirt. He took small, measured breaths, and opened his watery eyes. An endless canopy of stars sparkled white, red, blue, yellow and orange. They shimmered calmly and silently amid the velvety blackness.

"It's all OK," he whispered to the universe. "Everything's OK now Dad."

CHAPTER 41

Nick lay with his eyelids closed, the sunlight illuminating the bright orange underneath. He could still here the gunfire rattling around in his head, voices shouting and the thumping of unmerciful blows. He tried to move, to twitch, duck or run, but his legs wouldn't work. He couldn't even lift an arm. Nothing seemed to work. His heart raced and sweat rolled down his face.

A warm hand gently squeezed his. Soft fingers rubbed back and forth, caressing. He squinted open an eye. It was Rosalie. She sat next to him on a lounge chair. They were by the pool in his back yard. She sipped a Mai Tai through a straw. The icy drink had a little paper umbrella, a cherry and a piece of pineapple wedged onto its rim. She smiled at him, then put the drink down and picked up her book, *A Separate Reality* by Carlos Castaneda. She wore a mod orange and white flowered bikini. Her smooth skin glistened in the sun.

Nick remembered he had gotten out of the hospital the day before. His left arm was in a sling. They had extracted the bullet and sewn him up. His bolo tie hung around his bare neck and its silver dollar pendant rested on top of the wide elastic compress that wrapped around his chest to support his broken ribs.

He closed his eyes again, feeling the warmth of the late morning sun, the tranquility of the day, and Rosalie's touch. It was July 4th, Independence Day, and life was good.

Rosalie closed her book, put it aside, and stood up.

"It's getting too hot, I'm taking a dip," she announced.

Nick watched her stroll to the pool and dive in. She disappeared for a moment, then popped up and smiled. She was dripping wet.

"Come on," she waved for him. "It's really nice."

"My arm." Nick tried to raise his bad arm, but couldn't.

Rosalie swam back to the shallow end of the pool and stood up, waist high.

"Just come and put your feet in, up to here," she indicated up to her waist.

In a moment he was on his feet and stepping carefully down the steps into the pool.

"See," Rosalie said, pulling him deeper. "It's so nice and refreshing."

And it was refreshing. Nick wished he could dive all the way under. Rosalie smiled and pulled closer, wrapping her arms around him and planting a deep, wet kiss on his lips. He slid his hand down her back to her bikini bottom, then slipped it in, under the fabric. Her butt felt so soft and smooth.

"Hey," she whispered in his ear, then giggled and surprisingly slid her own hand down in front, under his suit.

He kissed her deeper and harder.

"Hey!" someone shouted from the distance. "Cut that out."

They broke apart, and Nick nonchalantly turned toward the house, his waist still under the water. It was Mario, Barbara and Anne Marie.

"What's that hanky-panky?" Anne Marie said.

"Nothing," Rosalie said.

"Hey, time to party," Mario said, and held up two six packs of Heinekens.

"We got chips and dogs too," Barbara said.

They were a little early, but that was fine. Frances had arranged this holiday barbeque and soon everyone else would be there too.

Nick stepped out of the pool and Rosalie helped him towel off.

"Still feeling shitty?" Mario asked.

"Yeah," Nick laughed. "But life's good, right?"

"No shit, man." Mario nodded. "How long before you're all recuperated?"

"He'll be fine." Rosalie patted the towel on his face.

"The doc said a few weeks or so," Nick said.

"You better just keep resting up," Anne Marie said. "Take it easy."

"I am," Nick said.

"You're one lucky dude," Barbara said. "You got good karma."

"Yeah," Mario said and pulled a newspaper out of the grocery bag. He held it up. "And you won't believe this. You made the freakin' headlines man!"

"What?" Nick grabbed the paper and glanced at the front page. "Holy shit," he said. "Look at that."

"Wow, you're famous," Rosalie said.

"I gotta sit down."

Nick sat on the edge of the lounge chair and Rosalie sat next to him, peering over his shoulder.

"The Prince of Las Vegas," she said. "They're calling you a Prince! My Prince!"

"Yeah, with my picture and all. I can't believe that."

Rosalie smiled. "Well, you were always *my* Prince!"

"That's out-a-sight," Anne Marie said.

"What's it say?" Barbara said.

"Yeah," Mario said. "Read it to us."

"Ok, ok, I'll read it to you."

They all sat down, and Nick read . . .

Additional details have emerged from the deadly shootings in Mesquite that killed five people. It now appears that the legend of Jack Romano's treasure trove is true. The shootings appear to have been over control and ownership of a hoard of silver buried at an undisclosed location, said an anonymous FBI official. Although the official declined to speculate on the size of the silver hoard, we have confirmed it was substantial, weighing at least seven to nine tons, and possibly one of the largest silver hoards ever accumulated. It has been confirmed that it belonged to the late Jack Romano, the well-regarded and respected founder of the Cornetto Club Casino in downtown Las Vegas. Mr. Romano was sometimes referred to simply as "The King" because his casino was his castle, and as it now appears that it even had its own treasury, consisting of the tons of silver safeguarded deep within the casino's own massive basement vaults.

"Who wrote this?" Nick looked up, "*Its own treasury in massive vaults!* How would they even know that?"

"Ah, they know a lot of things," Mario said. "Informants, employees, snitches. But keep going, what else does it say?"

Nick continued . . .

Details remain sketchy, but upon Mr. Romano's recent death, the silver hoard was apparently stolen by mob-connected and now deceased Claudio DeVito and his henchmen. After Mr. Jack Romano's untimely and now suspicious death, the DeVito's mob faction had apparently infiltrated casino operations and removed the silver, burying it on a ranch somewhere near the sleepy desert town of Mesquite, ninety miles north of Las Vegas.

Deputy Ed Hensley had stumbled upon the bizarre scene of heavy machinery digging at the ranch in the middle of the night. Upon questioning the workers at the scene, he was violently assaulted by the mob of thugs and left to die. Having survived the attack with only minor injuries, Deputy Hensley is crediting Jack Romano's own son, Nick Romano with saving his life. Nick Romano, having been kidnapped and brutally beaten that same evening, single-handedly saved the deputy, recovered his family's silver fortune and was directly involved in helping to apprehend the mobsters. Deputy Hensley called him a true hero and referred to him as "The Prince of Las Vegas".

Nick looked up.

"I didn't do anything," he said. "It was all just dumb luck. Claudio shot right at me and missed!"

"But you wrestled him to the ground, right?" Rosalie said.

"Yeah, well," Nick said. "I was fighting for my life."

"Then you're our fucking hero man!" Mario said and

patted his back. "That's all there is to it." Mario stood and made a grand wave of his hand. "All hail The Prince of Las Vegas, Prince Nicholas Romano!"

"Sit down. I'm no hero, man."

"You're my hero." Rosalie kissed him on the cheek.

Nick smiled and said to Mario, "You tell the story any way you want."

"It's a fucking great story, man, it is!" Mario said. "I'll tell it the only I can—the way it really is. And it'll serve as a warning to all—*don't come messing with the Romano's and The Prince of Las Vegas!*"

Mario smiled and laid his hand on Nick's good shoulder, "Now let's have a beer."

"Alright man," Nick said and turned to Rosalie. "One ice cold Heineken please."

Rosalie stood and curtsied. "Yes sir, my Lord. I mean your Royal Highness, coming right up!"

"And if we may have the Prince's permission, we'd like to get our bathing suits on and partake in a refreshing dip in the cool waters of the pool," Mario waved his arm with great fanfare.

Nick looked at him and turned his chin up.

"Permission granted," he said. Then with a wave his hand added, "Now off with you all."

They laughed, and the three of them headed back to the house to change.

Nick took swig of his beer, and laid back on the chaise lounge.

"Ooowwww," he had forgotten about his broken rib.

"Take it easy," Rosalie said.

"I know." He laid his head back, then took light, easy

breaths and closed his eyes.

———

A slight breeze blew and he thought of his mom visiting him in the hospital the other day. She was so happy he was OK, but somehow he was embarrassed, like he had done something wrong. Like all this chaos was his fault.

"My baby!" his mom pulled him close, pressing her cheek against his forehead, tears in her eyes. She was so happy, so relieved that he was OK.

"I'm sorry," she said. "I trusted that man. I'm so sorry, I thought it would be for the best. I'm so stupid."

"It's OK Mom," Nick said. "It wasn't your fault. He bamboozled and muscled his way in. He was a charlatan, liar and thief. That's all. Don't worry about it, but I'm OK, right? I'm fine, and you're fine too and that's all that matters."

"I know." She closed her eyes and held her cheek pressed against his.

After she calmed down, she told him she had already gotten all the silver back in the vaults and was making big changes at the casino. She had rehired Lawrence, Bill and Alex, and she was going to get him trained on casino operations and management. Lawrence, Bill and Alex would show him the ropes. He'd learn how Jack actually ran things.

"That's great." He smiled.

She also explained that she had promptly rehired most of the old staff that Claudio had let go. And she even fixed the situation with the replacement chips by extending the deadline to switch any remaining old chips—thereby satisfying and making Sy Zeldin whole again. And, she whispered to him, that she had ordered normal payola payments to the police and politicians again, including all missed payments.

"That's great," Nick sighed. "You're undoing everything that Claudio fucked up."

"Yes," she said, then continued to say that Anne Marie had told her about Claudio being behind Marla getting accidentally poisoned to death — and that it was really meant for him. This, she said, made her absolutely livid and she would have killed Claudio herself had she known what a psychopath he was.

Nick told her about how, out in the desert, Claudio had killed Roman and Angelo outright, and accidentally killed Tony, and even tried to kill him a too.

Frances shook her head.

"I have no remorse that he's dead," she said. "He got what he deserved. And," she went on. "Guess what?"

Nick looked up at her, "What?"

"I'm getting his two-million-dollar life insurance payout."

"What?" Nick eyes widened.

"Yeah," she said. "Don't mention it to anyone, but it's double the one-million-dollar policy amount because the medical examiner determined that he actually died accidentally when the silver bars fell on him, crushing his chest and suffocating him."

"You mean being that it was accidental death, it's double?" Nick said.

"Yeah," Frances said. "Isn't that crazy."

"Wow, sweet justice." Nick smiled.

Frances also explained to him that Claudio's will had named only Marla as the sole beneficiary. But now, because Marla was dead and had actually died before he did, everything was slated to go to her by default, his wife—and now his only heir. Francis stood to inherit all of Claudio's wealth.

"Don't mention that to anyone either," she said.

"Whom I gonna tell?" Nick said.

"I don't know but we have to keep this all quiet. It's crazy, believe me I didn't plan it this way!"

"No, it's great," Nick said. "What sweet irony!"

"And . . ." Frances held a finger to her lips and whispered, "As the longtime mobster that he was, he had some major assets. A large house in Chicago's Bridgeport neighborhood, a very successful pool hall, other businesses, and a huge mansion with a swimming pool and tennis courts in Palm Beach. He also still had a penthouse apartment, here in Vegas. And a bunch of bank and brokerage accounts. Bill is piecing it all together for me but he thinks each account has at least six or seven figure balances."

Frances smiled.

"Holy shit." Nick raised his eyebrows. "That's freakin' crazy. And it's all going to you?"

"To us, dear," she said. "To our family. What's mine is yours—you and Anne Marie. You know that."

Nick shook his head, "What about his old beat up Lincoln?"

"That too." Frances nodded.

"Can you take it to the junk yard and have them crush it?"

"Already did, dear." Frances smiled again.

———

"Hey!"

Nick opened his eyes. It was Mario, toweling off after coming from the pool.

"Are you sleeping, man? The party's just getting started."

"Just thinkin'." Nick sat up and rubbed his eyes.

He took a swig of his beer and looked at Rosalie.

"How's that book?" he said.

"Good," she said. "Deep."

"Yeah," Nick said. "Carlos Castaneda, he's pretty far out."

"Yeah."

Soon, Lawrence, Bill and his wife Eleanor, Alex, and Mayor Duane Thompson arrived.

Lawrence volunteered to get the grill going while Frances seasoned a tray of thick T-bone steaks.

"Those look good," Nick said.

"Patience my dear," Frances said.

Nick stood with Rosalie watching Lawrence grill the sizzling steaks. Mario, Barbara and Anne Marie sat nearby on the lawn, drinking and munching on potato chips and peanuts. Alex, Bill and Eleanor, all sat in the shade across from the grill on the patio, Alex with newspaper in hand. Mayor Duane Thompson sat with them too, smoking his cigar.

"Look at that," Alex said. "What a crazy story."

He gazed up at Nick.

"How'd you do it?" Alex said.

Nick shook his head.

"I didn't do anything," he said.

Mayor Thompson took a puff of his cigar, "I ought to give you the key to the city."

"I just want one of those steaks," Nick said.

"Good that you're getting your appetite back, dear," Frances said.

"Well," the Mayor said. "You deserve the key to the city and a hero's parade. If it wasn't for you, well, I don't know."

He shook his head.

"I don't know how those guys could have been stopped. But thanks to you, boy, why it's a whole new ballgame now. Shit, the FBI even got involved and shut down their whole operation—even in Chicago too. All thanks to you, boy!"

"Did they get the boss, too?" Lawrence asked. "What's his name, Crotchetti?"

"Mr. Crotch." Alex laughed.

"Yeah," the Mayor said. "Crocetti, they got him too. We gave them good information, and with your dad," he looked up at Rosalie, "Joey Messina, surviving his gunshot wounds, and alive and singing, they got everything they needed to bring down the whole damn operation. Sorry, Rosalie."

Rosalie shook her head. "Oh no, it's fine. I told my dad to straighten out, but you think he would listen? Of course not. He knew what business he was in. But shit, he loved it. He's just really lucky he didn't get himself killed."

"He still going to prison?" Alex asked.

"Don't know. They may put him in that new witness protection program," the Mayor said. "That's why they have it—to get the mobsters singing against each other. He'll need to disappear for a long time though. Get a new name, live in some far off little town someplace, etc."

"Maybe we can have some peace around here now," Frances said.

"Yeah, for now," Mayor Thompson said. "But there's too much money in Vegas—we all know that! Oh, they'll be back, they'll always be back at it. It's inevitable."

"So?" Bill said. "We'll just get Nick to take care of the next wave of troublemakers."

"Hail to Nick!" Lawrence raised his beer.

They all raised their drinks.

"Salud!"

Nick smiled, "I didn't do anything, I'm just damn lucky myself."

"No," Anne Marie raised her glass. "You're my fearless brother, salud! To *the Prince of Las Vegas!*"

"Salud!" Nick raised his bottle and took a sip.

He looked toward the hills and thought a moment. Then he put his beer down and grabbed the bolo. His lip began to quiver.

"My dad gave me this bolo tie," he held up the silver dollar pendant and took a deep breath. "It gave me strength. *Dad's strength*—when I needed it most, when I thought I was dead and it swung down from my bloody neck . . ."

Anne Marie stood up and put her arm around Nick. Nick took another deep breath.

". . . Pops pushed me though." Nick nodded. "He pushed me through. I let everyone down, but he was there for me. He gave me strength. I did nothing without him, nothing."

Nick held the bolo higher, "Dad is the real hero. Let's have a toast to Dad."

"I second the motion," Anne Marie said. "A toast to dear old Dad!"

They all raised their drinks again.

"To Pops!" Nick said.

"To Jack," the Mayor said. "And to Nick and Rosalie too!"

Rosalie kissed Nick's cheek.

A cheer went out, then the Mayor pulled two tickets from his pocket.

"And," he said. "I've got two VIP, front table tickets for you and Rosalie to see Elvis at the Hilton.

"What? Really?" Rosalie said.

"Yup," the Mayor smiled and handed Nick the tickets.

"That's freakin' awesome!" Nick said.

Rosalie grabbed the tickets and took a quick glance at them.

"I can't believe this. Elvis!" Rosalie said. "Thank you Mayor!"

She gave the mayor a big kiss on the cheek, then turned to Nick and hugged him.

"Thanks man," Nick said over Rosalie's shoulder.

CHAPTER 42

A month later, and dressed to the nines, Nick and Rosalie strode, hand-in-hand through the Hilton to the show. The atmosphere was electric. Elvis was back in Vegas and a long line of people eagerly waited outside the ballroom. They were mostly older folks, but there were a few young people in the crowd too.

Upon showing their VIP tickets to the staff at the front of the line, they were immediately escorted away by an usher. They followed the young man around the ballroom and into a "Staff Only" hallway, then down some stairs into the underground service area of the hotel.

They made their way to the back-entrance service garage and loading area. Nick wondered what the hell was going on as he hustled Rosalie along, her high heels clicking on the concrete walkway. Up ahead, a crowd of people, also dressed to the hilt, stood waiting.

"What's going on?" Nick said.

The usher laughed, "Oh nothing, just Elvis. Your VIP tickets include seeing his arrival."

"Holy shit," Nick said. "You're kidding."

"No," the young man said. "In fact, looks like Elvis is in the building right now."

"Oh my God." Rosalie gulped.

Sirens could be heard echoing through the loading ramp, then cutting out. Everyone turned to look. Two police motorcycles sped in with a convoy of Cadillac Fleetwood Limousines trailing.

The doors from the first limo opened and three tough guys, wearing suits and sunglasses, jumped out with walky-talkies in hand. They rushed over to the limo that happened to have stopped right in front of Nick and Rosalie, and promptly opened the back door open.

The man himself, Elvis Presley, the King of Rock 'n Roll, emerged from the limo, smiled and stood a moment assessing the scene. Slicked back hair, sideburns, sunglasses — it was really him. He wore a white leather jumpsuit with a flared open collar laced loosely in a long V down his chest, exposing his chest hair. Fringes dangled from the sleeves, and interspersed sparkling sequins adorned the front and sides. A long sash of fringes hung off the left side of his colorfully beaded belt and all the way down the side of the suit's white leather bell-bottoms.

One of his handlers assisted him.

"Ah, thank you very much," Elvis said to the small crowd and glanced right at Rosalie and Nick.

A security guard stepped forward with his arm outstretched, and motioned for them to stand aside. Nick and Rosalie stepped back, their eyes fixed on the King.

Elvis walked briskly, turning his head slightly in Rosalie's direction. His eyes locked onto hers for a split second, then he shifted his glance to Nick.

He walked past without a word. Nick was speechless.

"Elvis!" Rosalie shouted after him. "I love you!"

Elvis suddenly stopped and turned. He looked straight back at Rosalie and Nick.

"Elvis!" Rosalie shouted again.

"Hold on a minute," the King held his hand up.

His entourage stopped and he walked back to Rosalie.

He stepped right up to her and smiled, then reached around his neck and pulled off the white silk scarf he was wearing and looped it around Rosalie's neck. He pulled her in and kissed her squarely on the lips.

"That's for you, Ma'am," he said. "I love you too."

He glanced at Nick and flinched as if doing a double take.

"Hey!" he laughed. "Oh man, are you that Prince of Las Vegas guy? I read all about what you did."

Nick chuckled. "I guess so."

The King put his arm around Nick's shoulder and pulled him to the side. "You're a real hero man, fighting off those mobsters! They're a goddamn tough bunch, man, a real thorn in my side! I wish I could have done what you did."

"Well, thank you, sir." Nick could hardly speak.

Elvis let go of Nick and looked back at Rosalie again.

"And is this your girlfriend?"

"Yes, sir, my fiancé."

"Fiancé? Well . . ." Elvis smiled. "She's a darling. You're a very lucky man."

"We're getting married in a few weeks." Rosalie practically curtsied.

"Well, you just let me know when the wedding is and I'll stop by and sing you a special song, I promise. Just tell 'em it's the Prince of Las Vegas callin'. I'll make sure they know who you are." Elvis winked.

"Wow," Rosalie said. "That'd be great!"

Elvis reached out his hand to Nick. "You take care."

Nick shook Elvis' hand, "Thanks, man."

"No, thank you," Elvis said. "Now, I got a show to do."

Elvis winked and walked away, engulfed by his entourage.

Rosalie beamed at Nick. "That was Elvis! I can't believe it!"

"Unreal," Nick said. "Elvis, the King. *And he recognized me!* Said I was *his* hero. That's crazy, I'm his fucking hero!"

- FINIS -

About the Author

Brian Malanaphy is a native of Brooklyn, New York. He holds a BA in English and Creative Writing from SUNY College at Purchase. He resides in Hawaii and sometimes he does sit, on the beach, under those swaying coconut trees. Other times he's busy writing, contemplating, and squeezing out meaning from the effervescent world.